SHADOWS IN JADE

Tempo book 4

KATE LANCE

SEA BOOKS PRESS
seabooks.net

Print ISBN: 978-1-7638066-1-0
Ebook ISBN: 978-1-7638066-2-7

Published by Seabooks Press
seabooks.net

BY THE SAME AUTHOR

FICTION

Harbour of Secrets
Embers at Midnight
Testing the Limits
Silver Highways
Atomic Sea (As CM Lance)
The Turning Tide (As CM Lance)

NON-FICTION

Alan Villiers: Voyager of the Winds
Redbill: From Pearls to Peace

COVER IMAGES

Front: iStock/alvarez and iStock/tzido.
Rear: Helicopters – Australian War Memorial, EKT/68/0100/VN.
Demo – Mitchell Library, State Library of NSW and SEARCH Foundation.
Vietnamese school – Australian War Memorial, THU/68/0640/VN.
Ammonite – Llez (H. Zell), CC BY-SA 3.0, via Wikimedia Commons.

To the Members of the
1st Australian Civil Affairs Unit

In a time of destruction they did their best
to heal, teach, cultivate and build.

Table of Contents

PART I. APPLE GREEN

1.   JEN: MARY QUANT SHOES (OCT 1966-FEB 1967)

I've loved Tibor Adler since I was six years old.

We met in 1957, at a barbecue my parents' friends were holding to watch a silvery light drift across the night, the amazing new Russian satellite, Sputnik. We kids — the cluster of cousins and friends our hostess Billie always calls the 'horde' — sat together as we ate, balancing plates of smoky meat and tasty nibbles on our laps.

When I confessed I didn't understand how satellites stayed up in the sky, seventeen-year-old Tibor reassured me he was just as ignorant. It was a simple kindness to my small shy self, but his brown eyes left me breathless.

Of course a child of six is supposed to know nothing of love, yet there it was. And now, nine years later, there it still is.

Yet Tibor lives in Sydney, while our home is in Newcastle, one hundred miles to the north. Most of our friends and relatives are in Sydney too and we visit them in the school holidays. But *how* I wish we lived in Sydney and could see the friends and relatives — and Tibor — whenever we wanted.

Newcastle is just a boring industrial city. It's only got one trendy clothes shop, Pumpkins, which hardly compares to Sydney boutiques like the House of Merivale.

But we do have long sandy beaches, and in summer I lie in the sun with my best friend Linda, and swim in the surf, and eat chips from the kiosk, then lie in the sun again. So sometimes Newcastle is okay.

My big brother Leo loves the beach too, and spends every spare moment, summer or winter, bobbing up and down on his surfboard and catching waves. Leo is tanned and tall, and his curls are sunburnt blond. He mostly ignores me. Leo turned twenty recently and had to register for National Service.

A lottery is held every six months to pick boys to go into the Army for two years, and perhaps get sent off to Vietnam. But Leo always says only a few guys ever go and he isn't worried.

Our parents are.

I tell Mum, 'Don't worry, they wouldn't take Leo, he's too lazy,' which makes her laugh, then sigh. 'If only he'd done medicine, or something with a longer course, he could have postponed for a few years ...'

'Oh, Mum, you didn't really think *Leo*'d ever do medicine?'

That brings another sigh. Leo has never had the slightest interest in anything that might demand hard work. He barely scraped into uni in the first place and his finals last year were a close call, mainly because all he ever does is surf and hang around with Bazza and Shazza.

Now he's grudgingly doing a year of teacher training at the Technical College, but still spends most of his time drinking beer with Bazza (Barry, who's also in the ballot) and trying to get Bazza's sister Sharon to go out with him. I think Shazza's still resisting, but that doesn't dent Leo's confidence for a moment.

∽

In September we gathered around the TV to watch the National Service lottery draw. They displayed the barrel and the marbles engraved with birth-dates, and introduced someone supposedly famous to extract the marbles one by one. They don't tell you the drawn dates on the night itself, so Leo has to wait for the letter that might change everything.

But a month later he *still* hasn't heard. I'd much rather be looking forward to Christmas in Sydney (and Tibor), but everyone else is only interested in whether Leo has been balloted in or out. He just grins and says it could be fun to learn to shoot, but doesn't sound quite as smug as he used to.

My family has a strange connection to Vietnam. Mum's brother Pete and his wife have lived there for ages, ever since the old days when it was the French fighting the North Vietnamese.

Now it's the Americans arguing over who owns the rice paddies, which sounds pretty stupid to me. Must sound stupid to other people too, because lately there have been lots of marches against the war. President Lyndon B. Johnson just visited Australia and protesters tried to stop his parade by lying down in front of the cars.

Then NSW Premier Askin — who Aunt Tina always says is as crooked as a dog's hind leg — told the drivers to 'run over the bastards'. And what if they *had*? Poor old protesters.

The headlines keep saying *All the way with LBJ*, which I think is silly too. But Leo says I don't know the first thing about it, and if we don't stop the communists in Vietnam then all of Asia will collapse like dominos under their sway.

When he comes out with things like this, Mum say crossly, 'Don't be *absurd*, Leo. It's a national independence movement, not the communists against the world, and especially not against us.'

And Dad takes off his glasses and sighs (they both do a lot of sighing) and says, 'Leo, you should really be a little more critical of what you read. The papers are simply repeating American propaganda.'

Leo just shrugs and goes surfing.

∽

After school today Linda and I take the bus to David Jones, the department store on Hunter Street, to see if the latest Mary Quant shoes have arrived: and there they are, lit up on a glass stand. Glossy maroon leather, low heels, squarish toes and straps with darling little buttons.

'Oh,' breathes Linda. We gaze in awe, knowing we'll never get to wear them — they cost an impossible eighty dollars, which is about twice a weekly wage. Dad's a doctor and Mum works in an office, but we don't have money like that, not even for the most beautiful shoes in the world.

Linda and I read everything we find about Carnaby Street and Swinging London, and plan to go over there when we're old enough.

We wear our uniform skirts as short as we can, even though the school insists the limit is eight inches above the knees. They make all the girls kneel sometimes and measure with a ruler.

We're in our fourth year at high school and supposed to be studying for the School Certificate exams in a few weeks, so after the Mary Quant shoes we go to Linda's and do some science homework.

But really we just listen to the Beatles on her portable record player. Revolver came out a few months ago and, like the Mary Quant shoes, it's so special and different from anything else here in Newcastle.

The Beatles have long moustaches now and wear bright satin outfits, but I prefer how they were a few years ago: dark-suited and serious, with bouncy songs I'd listen to on my transistor radio. George is my favourite, although Linda likes Paul best.

I walk home happily humming *Good Day Sunshine*, so it's a worry when I go in the kitchen to see Mum's been crying. She takes a breath.

'It's alright, love. I'm just —' She swallows. 'Leo got the letter. He's been balloted in.'

'Oh, *Mum*. Only a few boys get sent overseas.'

'But your Dad and I can never forget the war —'

'That's ancient history. Leo'll be okay. What did he say anyway?'

'He hears they have pretty good surf in Vietnam. Silly boy.'

To Leo's delight Bazza is also balloted in. Bazza's still doing his apprenticeship and Leo has to finish his teacher training, so they'll both go into the army early next year.

Still, I don't have time to think about that because my exams are about to start. I manage to concentrate on studying for a few weeks (although Dad keeps putting his head round the door and asking how can *anyone* work with the radio going).

Then the School Certificate rolls over us.

It's terrifying and boring, and there are hours and *hours* of it. Even when it's over I keep dreaming about having to sit exams for subjects I've never studied.

December comes and I find out I've passed: two As, three Bs and one C. Now there's only Fifth and Sixth Forms ahead of me, then high school will be over forever!

This Christmas, weirdly, Leo says he's not coming to Sydney for the usual get-together. But I'm going, and at last the great day arrives. Dad drives the Holden along the winding Pacific Highway, and we stop for sandwiches outside Gosford, half-way to Sydney. I have cordial and my parents drink tea from a flask, and the amazing chimes of bellbirds echo from tree to tree.

It takes about three hours to cover the hundred miles to Sydney (Australia has just changed over from imperial pounds to decimal dollars, but they say miles will be used for ages yet). It's a nice drive though, and quieter too without Leo, who's always tapping his fingers or whistling or asking how long till we get there.

∽

Dad's sister, Aunt Tina, used to live in a big flat above her nightclub in Kings Cross. But a couple of years ago she bought a two-storey house in a street nearby, with high ceilings and coloured glass in the doors. I usually stay in a little bedroom upstairs at the rear, which was once a maid's, Tina says, and from the window I can see over tin roofs and sooty chimneys to a slice of the blue harbour.

Last time we visited was at Easter, nine months ago, and I asked her son, Róbert, if the old house was spooky with just Tina and him.

'Well, maybe it is a bit spooky, Jenny, but it's still nice.'

My cousin's only eleven, four years younger than me, but he always seems older. He has a round face and thick brown hair, and when he smiles it makes me smile too.

After we get to Tina's today the grown-ups drink tea, while Róbert and I get watermelon and go out to a table in the yard. The garden is only small but it's got a lemon tree and rows of little flowers along the fences.

'I'm going to high school next year, Jenny,' Róbert says, spitting watermelon seeds onto his plate. 'What's it like, really?'

'Well, lots better than primary, that's for sure. You get different teachers for different subjects, and there are laboratories with bunsen burners, and sometimes you heat chemicals in test-tubes so they change colour. It's fun.'

'Our teacher said we'll meet kids from all the other primary schools then,' says Róbert. 'That'll be good. I'm a bit sick of the ones I've known for years.'

'Are they still being horrible about your name?'

He nods in resignation. 'At high school I'm not going to tell anyone my name's Róbert.' (He says it the way Aunt Tina always does, *Rrrow-bairt.*) 'I'm going to be just *Rob* from now on.'

'Rob's okay,' I say. 'Yeah, that's quite mod, really. What does your mum think?'

'Haven't told her yet, but suppose she'll be cranky. Anyway, it's *my* name.'

Aunt Tina is blonde and pretty, even though she's old, almost fifty. But she's also strict and you can see why her staff jump to do everything she says.

'She'll get used to it. *I'll* call you Rob, anyway.'

'Thanks.' He smiles. 'I'll call you Jen too, if you like. That's sort of mod as well.'

I'm surprised. I've never thought of it before, but he's right.

Jen is *very* mod.

I could imagine a Jen in a dazzling Pucci shift, with painted lashes beneath her eyes like Twiggy. A Jen would ride in an Aston Martin — perhaps she'd even drive it herself — with a bright silk scarf around her head. A Jen would wear Mary Quant shoes *all* the time.

'Think I like that, *Rob*.'

'That's okay, *Jen*.' We giggle.

I take another slice of watermelon and say, 'Why does your mum call you Róbert, anyway? Is it Irish, because of your dad?'

Rob shrugs. 'No. I asked her once and she said it was Hungarian, from some promise she'd made to a friend. But it just says ordinary old Robert on my birth certificate. Mum's always been the one who's insisted on this weird version.'

His dad died when Rob was only a baby. For some reason Aunt Tina went back to her maiden name after that, so Bell is Rob's surname too, same as mine. It's all a bit strange, and now I think about it I've never seen any photos round their house of Rob's dad. I wonder if maybe Tina didn't like him very much.

∽

Next afternoon my parents are upstairs dressing for the Christmas party, but I'm already sitting in the lounge-room, impatient to go. I'm in a lovely kaftan from London that Billie gave me. It's made of floaty cotton with wide sleeves, and printed with tiny gold and pink flowers.

I've put strawberry lip-gloss on, and washed my hair and brushed it dry. It almost reaches my shoulders now. A few weeks ago the hairdresser cut me a fringe, so when the rest gets longer it'll look really fashionable.

Rob is being his usual quiet self, sitting across from me in tidy clothes, his hair brushed back with water. His legs are comfortably propped over the arm of the chair (which Tina is always telling him not to do) and he's reading volume 3 of the Encyclopaedia Britannica, *Bolivia to Cervantes*. He expects to finish all thirty books by the time he's fifteen.

At last the grown-ups come downstairs. Mum and Tina both look pretty and smell of perfume, though Dad is the same as ever — glasses, tie, tweedy jacket.

Tina and Rob are going to the party in her smart little Mini, so after the fuss of gathering keys and handbags we finally leave. As Dad drives to the party I gaze at passing glimpses of Sydney Harbour, and think about names.

Whenever anyone says 'Jennifer' I feel as if I'm back at primary school, in trouble and about to be sent to the headmaster (again). Once I got caught reading a book, Biggles, in some boring scripture class. That nearly got me the cane on the hand, the headmaster was so furious. Honestly, you'd think he'd be pleased I was actually *reading* something at school.

And 'Jenny'? It's a lazy, friendly name, like someone who works in a shop or hangs around Leo's surfie friends. Of course I go to the beach, but I'm not a gidget, a soft, agreeable Jenny.

But a 'Jen'? A modern, stylish, *confident* Jen?

I suppose I'm not really that either. Straight brown hair might look good on models but doesn't on me. And I'm thin and flat — so flat that a nasty boy at school christened me 'surfboard,' which is humiliating. Perhaps one day I'll catch up to the other girls in my class, the girls with curvy waists and hips, but I'll never live down being called surfboard.

I can't change that, but I *can* change myself. A bit, anyway.

I take a breath. 'Mum, Dad? I've decided I want to be called Jen from now on, not Jenny.'

Dad says, 'Why, love? Jenny's so pretty.'

'Jen is more *modern*,' I say firmly.

I can hear the smile in Mum's voice. 'If that's what you want, darling. But you'll have to forgive us if we lapse into old habits now and again.'

'That's okay, I don't mind about you two,' I say. 'But for everyone else I want to be a *Jen*.'

Dad parks the car and I get out, my heart thumping. The party is at Nikos and Billie's house in Rose Bay. It's high on the side of a hill and looks out to the harbour, and I love it *so* much. This is where I first met Tibor, nine years ago.

Tina and Rob arrive and park just behind us. We go through the gate and Billie opens the front door, grinning. She's Mum's oldest and best friend, tall and slim and always trendy, even though there's more silver than red in her hair now.

There's lots of hugging and kissing, and Billie has a special hug for me. Tonight she's wearing jeans cut low on her hips and a floaty pale blue shirt with a wide collar. I touch the fabric reverently.

'Crepe, kid,' Billie says. 'House of Merivale.'

'*Oh*,' I say.

'Never know — might be another one under the tree with your name on it.'

'Billie!' I hug her again.

In the lounge-room Nikos kisses the top of my head and says, 'Good God, young lady, you've grown six inches since Easter.'

Nikos isn't Billie's husband but they've been together for years. I don't know why they don't get married, but Billie just laughs if I ask. Even though he's old, Nikos is so handsome. He's got dark eyes and a grey beard and his hands are big and muscular. He and Billie go sailing on his yacht and flying in Billie's little seaplane. I think they're the most glamorous people *ever*.

Their lounge-room is one of my favourite places too, with comfy couches and big windows that look out across the water. You can see the old flying-boat base, and the city and Harbour Bridge, with all the little lights twinkling in the water.

I turn and realise Claire is there, drinking wine and chatting to someone. She's one of our horde of kids as well, but she always makes me feel so ... drab.

She's seven years older than me, with pale blonde hair in a French roll, and blue eyes that Mum calls cornflower. She's famous for her good posture (I'm famous for slouching), *and* she's been to university.

I liked Claire much better when we were younger, when she and Leo would argue and tease each other all the time. Funny though, they don't seem to be friends any more. I think they might have had a fight when we were here last Easter. I asked Leo and he got really grumpy about it.

There's another knock at the door. Nikos goes out and returns with the Adlers and their daughter Devorah and — at last — *Tibor*. My cheeks are warm but I try to smile normally.

Everyone is laughing and hugging and shaking hands, and somehow, in the hubbub, Tibor's eyes meet mine. Understanding flows between us, as it always does when we meet, and I feel something like contentment: if contentment is composed of happiness and hot coals.

Honestly, how could Newcastle ever compare to this?

∞

It's only a party tonight, not actually Christmas, which is in a few days. But it's still fun, with nice food and old jokes that make the grown-ups groan. Tibor's family are Jewish so they don't celebrate Christmas, but something else called Hanukkah. Devorah says it's kind of the same, though different.

Devorah and I didn't like each other when we were little. Our parents were always telling us to go and play together, even though she's younger than me. But we finally became friends because she's sharp and funny, and says things about people I'd never dare. Anyway, how could I not like Devorah? Her brother is Tibor.

And suddenly there he is, two glasses in his hands. 'How's my favourite girl, then?' he says, giving me a quick kiss on my hair and sitting beside me on the sofa. 'Here, have a lemonade.'

'Ah, *hi*, Tibor. Thanks.' (I think my head will float free from my body.) 'Well, we had our School Certificate exams and I passed everything. I even got As in Science and English.'

'Science and English? Planning to be a very literate physicist, then?' says Tibor, sipping his beer.

'Not likely! I only got a C in Maths. Anyway, lady scientists are plain and boring. But what have you been doing?'

'No exams, I'm glad to report. Some office politics though. Worse than exams.'

'Tibor, *nothing's* worse than exams.'

He smiles. 'Well, I'm going crazy. We're setting up an office in London next year and I'm supposed to organise it.'

'You're going to *London*?'

'No, just helping set it up. Why? Should I go?'

'Go to London if you have the chance? Of course you should!'

'But Mary Quant doesn't make shoes for men,' he says, his dark eyes teasing. 'And you're always telling me she's London's only attraction.'

I laugh. 'Silly. There's Carnaby Street and the Beatles and Buckingham Palace too, and *everything's* so clever and cool!'

'So you'll be off there like a rocket then as soon as you can?' he says reproachfully. 'While the rest of us stay behind in drab old Australia?'

'Only for a while,' I say. (I couldn't imagine living anywhere Tibor wasn't.) 'I wouldn't leave forever. But ... I *do* want to travel a bit first.'

'Come on, tell the truth — you really want to marry a Beatle.'

'No I don't!' I laugh. 'Anyway, they're all taken now.'

'A Rolling Stone then?'

'Never. Tibor, I think they take *drugs*.'

He smiles. 'Probably. Most people do nowadays, Jenny. See my beer? That cigarette Dad's smoking? All drugs.'

'I suppose. But listen, there's something I need to tell you. I'm changing my name to *Jen*. I don't want to be Jenny any more.'

He gazes at me. 'Why? Jenny's pretty.'

'It's *too* pretty. Too boring. I want to be crisp and smart and modern.'

'You're certainly smart and modern. Crisp?'

'Oh, I don't know. Sort of like Claire, all cool and sharp.'

'Ah. She is, isn't she?'

'You know,' I say quietly, 'I think she and Leo had a big fight last Easter. Leo's been really strange about her ever since.'

'They're both at complicated stages of their lives, Jenny ... Jen. And Leo — well, he's always going to be Leo. Only interested in the next wave.'

We smile at each other. 'True,' I say. 'But I'd still like to be more like Claire.'

'You'll always be yourself, Jenny-wren, and nothing wrong with that. But did you hear about Claire's new job with the society pages?'

'Society?' says Claire. 'Do I hear the siren-song of my calling? Hello, Jenny.'

'She's Jen, not Jenny now,' says Tibor. 'Way more modern.'

Claire nods and sits down with us. She tilts her head, considering. 'Yes, Jen suits you. You *are* modern, certainly more than me or Tibor, who's practically middle-aged.'

'Thanks, Claire,' I say, pleased. (Of course I don't *really* dislike her. Yes, she is clever and elegant, but she's part of our horde and she's always been nice to me. Oh dear. I suppose I'm not only thin and boring, but mean and envious too.)

Tibor says, 'Twenty-six is middle-aged?' in an injured voice.

'Well, *I'd* define middle-aged as the sort of guy who doesn't turn up for drinks when he says he will,' says Claire coolly.

'Will you ever forgive me for that?' says Tibor. 'I honestly couldn't leave the office that night, the brief had to be ready next morning. Anyway, you and Leo still had fun.'

'And Asher came too,' says Claire.

'What, my little brother actually stopped demonstrating in favour of a night out?'

'He left fairly soon to meet a pretty hippie, I think,' says Claire.

Tibor laughs. 'See? You didn't need me there at all.'

'Probably not. But now, look at us in our middle-aged outfits and Jen in that gorgeous kaftan — is it from Carnaby Street?'

I flush with pleasure. 'Yes, Billie gave it to me last birthday.'

Claire nods. 'You put Tibor and me to shame.'

'But aren't you wearing a *Chanel* suit?' (Billie told me that and even she was impressed.)

She nods ruefully. 'Practising for my new job.'

'I didn't even know you wanted to work at a newspaper, Claire.'

'I've never spoken about it much, but somehow it seems to have happened.' She laughs in a flustered sort of way.

'What will you be doing?' I ask.

'I'll just be a secretary in the Social Department at the Daily Mirror, covering fashion and parties. I fear I may have to wear a hat and gloves at all times. Still, it might lead to better things.'

'But what would be better than *parties*?' I say.

'Real reporting. Politics, war, current affairs.'

I'm puzzled. 'But ladies don't usually do those sorts of stories.'

Claire nods. 'Not many, but there's a few.' She smiles suddenly. 'And I thought you were such a modern girl, Jen! You can do anything you want nowadays, you know.'

'Gosh, that's true. I *will* have to become more adventurous if I'm going to go to London.'

'London,' says Tibor. 'Always comes back to London for you, Jen. But now, what's the latest on old Leo? And why isn't he here for Christmas?'

'Well, he got through his teacher training finals, which amazed *everyone*. Still, I haven't the foggiest why he's not here. Said he wanted to stay in Newcastle for the holidays. Suppose he wants to make the most of the surf before going into the army.'

'And when will that be?' says Claire, gazing at her glass.

'Late January, I think.'

Claire nods and tilts her head back to swallow the last of her wine.

∽

1967 arrives. This year, Fifth Form, I'm going to do English, Science, Maths, Art and French. Linda's doing Economics instead of Art, because she wants to be an accountant. (Sometimes I wonder if she'll *really* come to Carnaby Street with me when we're grown up.)

Just before the school holidays are over, Leo and Bazza take their national service medicals and pass easily, both of them lean and fit from surfing. Early one morning they board a bus with twenty other shuffling boys and disappear, grinning, to the Third Recruit Training Battalion at Singleton, forty miles up the Hunter Valley.

Poor old Mum and Dad! Their usual mild exasperation with my brother changes to a sort of mild anxiety.

We don't hear from Leo for a fortnight, then he phones us and says he's been chosen to do officer training, and he's going away to do a six-month course at some place near Sydney.

My parents' mild anxiety turns to mild perplexity.

Leo? *Officer* training?

2.   CLAIRE: THE SOCIAL DEPARTMENT (APR 1966-FEB 1967)

I was four when we emigrated from London and settled in an old
house in Balmain. It's not far from Elkington Park, where I spent
hours swimming in the harbour pool or playing on the swings, while
my mothers sat beneath the gnarled Moreton Bay Fig trees and
talked about poetry and books and life.

Yes, I have two mothers. Klara became pregnant with the help of
friend Toby Fenn and — so the family joke goes — a clean glass jar.
Toby married Klara to protect me and give me his name, but he died
in the war before I ever knew him. The love of Klara's life is Yvonne,
my other mum. Klara is a poet and teacher, and Yvonne runs her
own publishing house, the Watters Press.

When I was eight, light-hearted Vivy McKee, Jenny and Leo's
cousin, came to live with us as my babysitter: she was just
embarking on her singing career then but she made my home life
even happier. School was a different case, as I was an eccentric
child, precise and reserved. Still, I went my own quiet way, ignored
the bullies and found a refuge for myself in the library.

In any case, my closest friends were — and are — from the horde,
the children of my parents' friends and relatives, although we're
widely scattered in ages: Vivy is older than me by eight years and
Jenny is seven years younger.

Really, I don't even know why I'm thinking about Vivy now. She
isn't here in Sydney any more. Hard to believe it's been so long, but
she went away to sing jazz in Europe nine years ago, soon after that
night we gathered to watch the mysterious Sputnik satellite.

Such a strange evening.

Only four of the horde were there: twelve-year-old me; Tibor,
magnetic at seventeen; Leo, supremely confident at eleven, and shy
six-year-old Jenny. I remember Tibor murmured something kind to
Jenny, who gazed into his eyes and began to worship him. (As a
teenager Jen still does, and it worries me a little that even now Tibor
still so carelessly turns on the charm.)

As usual, self-assured Leo and I were sparring. The first time we'd met as small children, I'd said crossly his eyes were *slippery*, and he'd retorted mine were *sharp*. By now it was one of those old jokes, and somehow it came up again.

Lulled by magical Sputnik, I asked Leo what he'd meant in the first place by 'sharp'. He said it was because I always looked at things as if I could see right through them.

Coming from him that astonished me, because it was so perceptive: I was always trying to see *beneath*, to the hidden scaffolding of the world.

Leo then asked casually what I'd meant by slippery, and I said (more truthfully than kind) it was because he only ever saw what was on the surface of things.

Typically, he took this as a compliment and whispered to Billie, 'I'm going to *marry* her one day.'

Wise Billie murmured, 'Well good luck with that, kid.' It was probably as clear to her, as to me and everyone else, that Leo and I were utterly incompatible.

Even today it's more obvious than ever. Lazy Leo barely got off his surfboard long enough to attend college, while I studied hard all through uni: and did well too. But I've never wanted to be a teacher like Leo. In my heart I've always yearned to write, to make a living as a journalist.

I rarely speak of it though, it matters too much. Perhaps it stems from knowing of the wartime hardships my parents endured, or perhaps I simply want to *witness* history, to illuminate the happenings of the world for myself.

Still, that's all just a silly dream. The few female journalists who report on anything other than society doings are known only for their scarcity and curiosity value. So, pragmatically, after graduating from uni I start at the Watters Press.

My mother Yvonne is easy to work with, and I'm learning lots of interesting things about papers, inks and printing. But secretly I still yearn to do something that demands more of me.

∽

Last year, during the Easter week in April 1966, the phone rang at
the printery and it was Tibor.

'Hey there, Claire — Leo's around. His family's here for a holiday.
Want to catch up for drinks this evening?'

'Great. Where?'

'Tempo? They've just redecorated.'

'Okay, meet you there.'

'About eight o'clock'd be good,' Tibor said. 'Got to finish a brief at
the office first. I'll find out if Asher's free as well.'

I was pleased. I had a new summer dress I'd been hoping to have a
reason to wear, and the evening was warm and just right. We older
members of the horde often had drinks together, especially when
Leo came to Sydney, and it was always easy fun.

We used to bring dates. Tibor's were gorgeous lawyers with
French twists, Leo's wore pale pink lipstick and teased hair, Asher's
were earnest hippies, and mine were Political Science postgrads
with glasses.

We stopped doing that, though, after the evening Tibor's girl fell
for Leo, Asher's snuggled up to Tibor, and Leo's took a shine to my
post-grad. Now we usually just stick to horde kids — at least we
don't have to explain the rapid-fire family jokes.

In the evening I ate with Yvonne and Klara, then got ready. My
new shift was a halter-neck in fine blue cotton, the hem well above
my knees. I combed out my hair — wavy and fair, I usually pull it
back into a roll, but that night I let it brush against my bare
shoulders.

It took two buses to get to Kings Cross, but they were quick and I
was at Tempo just before eight. I met Tina as she greeted guests in
the foyer and we hugged. Her dress was a shift too, short-sleeved,
expensive red Thai silk, and she looked amazing.

We chatted for a few moments. Klara and Yvonne sent their love.
Young Róbert was well, in his last year of Primary school. Tina
thought Tempo's heartblood, jazz, was becoming less mainstream,
and she was worried she'd have to start a discotheque.

'Don't fret,' I said, 'it'll take years for *anything* that trendy to be
acceptable in Sydney,' and she laughed. She called a waiter over, told
him to find me a nice table, then we parted.

After seating me the waiter took my order, and I looked around. The recent redecorations were good. Modern furniture, the stage larger, the bar more comfortable. Tempo was a famous jazz club during the fifties but Tina was right. Jazz was now less mainstream. As I've got older I've come to quite like it — but still, a discotheque? That could be fun.

Tempo was different from its heyday in other ways too. The clientele now flaunted fewer furs and jewels, and there were fewer obvious criminals. Probably a good thing. Tina has always had to skate a fine line between business and the darker side of Kings Cross.

Still, she's had a couple of lucky breaks. One was when liquor was legalised in the fifties, so the criminals turned away from nightclubs to the illegal gambling dens. The other break? Her friendship with Moshe Adler — Tibor, Asher and Devorah's father.

It's an open secret the Adlers were once a powerful underworld family. They may have turned respectable now but the name still matters: and the Adlers have always protected Tina's club.

The waiter arrived with my white wine and I checked my watch. Twenty past eight. Leo and Asher weren't very good at turning up on time, but Tibor was usually reliable. After a mouthful or two I noticed Leo approaching, and waved.

'Hey, sharp eyes,' he said, grinning. 'How're you going?'

Most of the horde kids hug, as easy with each other as a litter of puppies, but with wisecracking Leo I usually kept my distance. I just said, 'Fine. Any sign of the others in the foyer?'

He shook his head, signalled the waiter, and ordered beer.

'Your parents and Jenny settled in at Tina's?' I asked.

'Yeah. Mum and Dad are seeing Billie and Nikos this evening, and Jenny's minding Róbert.' He gazed around. 'Who's playing?'

'I saw the poster, Bernie McGann Quartet. Should be good. Oh, *there* you are.'

'Greetings, comrades,' said Asher, rubbing Leo's hair and hugging my shoulder as he sat down. 'Ordered me a beer?'

'Under no circumstances,' I said. 'You know what you're like.'

'It was only that one time I slithered under the table.'

'Yeah, but after a *single* middy?' said Leo. 'Pathetic.'

The waiter brought over a jug of beer and two glasses. Leo poured Asher a drink and said, 'There you are, Che. Vive la révolution.'

'Mmm,' I said. 'Think that's France and about two hundred years out of date, Leo.'

Asher smiled. 'It'll do. Speaking of Vietnam —'

'*Were* we?' said Leo.

'Come July, are you going to register for national service?'

'Why not? If I don't I'll be balloted in anyway. Better to register and hope not to get drawn.'

'And what if you are drawn?' said Asher.

'Jeez, Asher, don't be such an awkward bastard.' Leo laughed. 'I'll go if I have to, no big deal. Suppose you're planning to fight every inch of the way.'

'Yeah. My draw isn't till next year, but I'll try for a conscientious objector exemption.'

'And if that doesn't work you could drink coffee for days and fail the medical. Hey, I reckon you're half-way there already, mate,' said Leo helpfully.

Asher laughed. His fringe was falling over his eyes, his glasses held together with tape, and his shirt, heavy with anti-war badges, hung on his slim frame. It's almost impossible to annoy him, and despite all his anti-war activities he's brilliant at uni, studying subjects in mathematics most of us can't even spell.

'What about doing a postgraduate course next year instead of tackling the might of the law?' I said. 'You could postpone things for a while then.'

'Nah. Time to stand up for my beliefs, Claire.'

The lights went down, the band began, and the boys turned their seats side-on to watch. I sipped my drink and glanced at them in the dimness. Leo couldn't be more of a contrast to Asher: high-cheeked, long fringe, curls bleached by the sun. Tanned, broad shoulders, muscular body. Attractive enough, I suppose, but I always say I prefer brains to brawn.

The music was excellent and the break came quickly. Asher half-stood. 'My shout, you two, but I've got to go.'

'Mine's a schooner, and Claire's drinking white,' Leo said. 'Why've you got to go?'

'Met a nice girl, going to paint some placards for the demo next week.'

'You and your nice girls,' I said. 'Aren't there any horrible ones in the anti-war movement?'

Asher smiled. 'Not a one. You should join us, Claire, you'd fit in perfectly. And hey, forgot to say before, but your frock looks fantastic too.'

'It's a shift, not a *frock*,' I scolded, pleased. At least someone had noticed. 'Not sure I'd make a good hippie, though.'

'Not only hippies in the movement, plenty of others too. Anyway, comrades, I'll order your drinks at the bar. See you.'

When Asher had gone I said, 'Wonder where Tibor is. Not like him to miss a night out.'

'What was he doing?' Leo said.

'Busy on a brief, something legal. Don't really know.'

'Ah well, might turn up yet. How are things at the printery?'

'Good. I really like working with Yvonne, but —'

'But?'

I shrugged. 'Not sure I want to do it forever.'

'What would you prefer? Not much call round here for French-speaking political scientists.'

'Amazed you even remember what I studied. So how's teacher training going?'

Leo groaned. 'Awful. English and French haven't quite equipped me for the modern world either. I'd be better off in Vietnam.'

'Don't even joke about that. My parents never got over the last war, and I bet yours didn't either.'

'Yeah.' He sighed. 'Thing is, I don't know what to do, Claire. I'm so bloody *bored*.'

'Ha! I thought as long as there were waves to catch you couldn't be bored.'

Leo grinned. 'Guess there's that.'

Our drinks arrived, and we sipped and watched the crowd.

'You didn't answer my question,' Leo said. 'What would you rather do, if not the printery?'

By now the wine must have gone straight to my head, because for some reason I stupidly let down my guard.

'Actually ... I'd quite like to become a journalist and work on politics and current affairs.'

As Leo opened his mouth I said, 'Yes, I *know*, Leo. Women can't do that.'

'That wasn't what I was going to say.'

'All right, what?'

'Why don't you start as a cadet at a newspaper?'

'Because *women can't do that*.'

'No, I read about one who did. Once you got a toe in the door, who knows?' Leo gazed at me, smiling a little. 'I'm certain you'd do it, Claire, one way or the other.'

I scoffed. 'And why are you so bloody sure?'

'Because it's what you've wanted all your life.'

I stared at him, puzzled, then drank more wine. 'Why would you say that? I never talk about it, and certainly haven't to *you*.'

Leo stared back.'Yes, you have. Don't you remember, about seven years ago?'

I shook my head.

'*Really*?'

The lights dimmed. 'No. But shh, they're starting again.'

After a moment Leo turned his chair to the musicians. What on earth did he mean? I've never told him about my dreams.

I pondered, and towards the end of the set, half-way through a slow sax solo, I remembered: and a wave of embarrassment flooded every cell of my body.

People applauded, the lights came on, the band left the stage. And still my face burnt. Leo got up, ordered more drinks at the bar and went to the bathroom. I thought wildly, can I climb out a window in the Ladies loo? (No. The windows are too small.)

The waiter brought our drinks over and I gulped half of mine before stopping, telling myself, look, it's not that bad. Leo returned, sipped his beer, and gazed at me over his glass.

It *was* that bad.

'I see you've remembered,' he said.

'How?'

'I didn't know shoulders could blush. Or arms. Legs too, I reckon. Will I check under the table?'

'*No!*'

'But why are you so embarrassed, Claire?'

'You know why.' How could the idiot not know *why*?

'All right,' said Leo patiently. 'When you were fifteen you told me you desperately wanted to become a reporter. That time in front of the fire at my place. I never forgot. Why did you?'

I gazed at my drink. 'Probably didn't want to recall anything about that night.'

'Come on, Claire. It was nothing, we were just kids. Practically an accident. Bet you've kissed a few other guys since then.'

'Of course I have. Look, it was ages ago and just a stupid, childish moment. But I'd still prefer it forgotten. *Okay?*'

'Okay.'

I took another drink. I certainly have kissed other guys since then, Leo, and more. A year ago I decided the time had come, and enticed one of my post-grad dates into my bed. A nice man, attractive, thoughtful. It was interesting. I tried another. Pleasant but no fireworks, so I'm *still* not sure what all the fuss is about.

I drained my glass, but the music was over, the evening clearly winding down.

'Maybe we'd better —' said Leo.

'Yeah.' I stood up, wobbling. 'Okay. Might visit the Ladies.'

Staring in the mirror, I wiped a smear of mascara from under one eye, applied a new layer of lip gloss and ran my fingers through my hair.

Tina met us as we were leaving. 'Leo, here's my car keys. The Mini's parked outside my house, so take Claire home to Balmain.'

'I can get the bus,' I said unsteadily.

Tina smiled. 'Off you go, love.'

Leo and I walked the two streets from the club to Tina's house in silence. I had a bit of trouble with my heels. The footpath seemed ... unreliable. I sat down in the passenger seat of the Mini with a sigh of relief, glad someone else was at the wheel. Some woozy time later we were driving through Balmain.

'Ah, this way, down here, Leo.'

'I know.'

'Wait,' I said. 'Don't.'

'Don't?'

'Turn left instead. Along here, beside the park. And down there.'

We drove until the street ended and the harbour lay beyond. In Elkington Park the leaves of the Moreton Bay figs whispered in the summer air.

'Claire? Maybe you should go home. You're a bit pissed.'

It was hard to focus, but I blinked and shook my head. 'But how would I do it, Leo?'

'Do what?'

'I really, *really* want to be a reporter.'

'Suppose you go and find a low-level job, pass the cadet exams, then work your heart out.'

'Come on. How do I even get a low-level job?'

'Guess you need a connection in the business.'

'But I don't know *anyone*.'

'You sure?' He smiled. 'Claire, you know one of the most powerful people in Sydney.'

'I do?'

'Talk to Tibor's dad. The crims and the newspapers have always been good mates.'

'Mr *Adler*?'

'He's pretty fond of your family, after all. Remember when Yvonne published Mrs Adler's cookbook and made her a fortune?'

'But I thought he'd gone all respectable.'

'I reckon a few proprietors still owe him favours. Give it a go.'

Lights rippled on the water, leaves rustled overhead, and suddenly my mind was swimming with possibilities, amazing, stunning possibilities.

'Leo, oh fuck, that's *incredible*!'

He laughed aloud. 'Is that the judgement of restrained, sensible Claire?'

'Who?' I reached out and took his head and kissed his mouth as if I've never kissed anyone since that moment in front of a fire when I was fifteen.

∽

Afterwards I didn't see or hear a word from him. The Christmas party came and went, but he stayed behind in Newcastle. Jen said he was going into the army in January: this month. Now.

Stop it, Claire. You *cannot* let yourself think about Leo! Today is far too important: it's the start of my new job at the Daily Mirror and I'm sitting dry-mouthed and neatly-dressed on the 433 bus from Balmain to Central Station.

The air is warm, thankfully not too muggy. I get off at Central, walk to Elizabeth Street, a couple of blocks further to the corner of Kippax and Hay, and there's Mirror Newspapers Limited, a plain brick building of five or six storeys. They say everything rumbles when the massive presses start up in the basement.

A woman at the reception desk phones the Social Department, and a friendly girl comes to get me and takes me up in the lift. I sign some papers and get shown to a desk with a pile of scruffy folders on top. Reassuringly, there's a fairly modern typewriter there too.

Another woman (says she's Mary something) dashes over. 'I've got to go out this *minute* to do an interview. Here are my notes from the big weekend wedding. Type them up for me, will you?'

At my dazed look, she says, 'You *can* read shorthand, can't you?'

'Yes. Okay, that's—'

But Mary is pulling on gloves and settling her hat as she dashed out the door and away.

I don't actually want to be a secretary but it's the only way into a newspaper job for a woman, so I've done a shorthand and typing course at Mrs Moggs' Secretarial College. The shorthand in Mary's notebook is more idiosyncratic than anything Mrs Moggs ever taught us, but eventually I get the notes transcribed and try to make a story out of them.

By then it's mid-morning and the tea-lady brings around her trolley. I take a welcome cup of tea and an arrowroot biscuit. There are seven other desks in the room, with women typing busily, or carrying papers here and there. I get a few sympathetic *hellos* but no one seems to be in charge of telling me what to do.

Just after midday Mary dashes back. I hand her my transcript and most recent attempt at an article. She reads quickly, then winces slightly. 'Oh. Maybe we need to —'

She looks up. 'Want some lunch, Claire?'

I follow her down in the lift and she takes me to a small Greek cafe nearby. We get ham and salad sandwiches and sit in a booth.

After a few mouthfuls, Mary says, 'You're looking a bit less stunned. Good.'

'I'm not sure what I'm supposed to be doing, Mary. Are you my boss? Do I get any training?'

'No, it's sink or swim,' she says. 'I'm not your boss, and in fact we don't see him very often, he's always at the pub or playing golf. But we girls know what's needed for copy each week. So just have a go at whatever anyone throws at you. You'll learn the ropes soon enough.'

'Okay. What were you busy with earlier?'

'Society morning tea. Took one of the photographers, got a few snaps and stories about an offspring's wedding, a charity do coming up, and someone else's travels. The usual.'

'Oh.'

Mary smiles. 'Not your idea of fun?'

'Actually — I'm hoping to sit the cadetship exams.'

'*Really*?' she says. 'Usually only the boys do that and anyway, the job's just carrying copy from desk to desk and picking up whatever you can from the reporters. They're pretty uncivilised too, so I doubt they'll temper their foul mouths just because a girl's come into their territory.'

'I know it'll be rough — but come on, it's the nineteen-sixties.'

Mary shrugs. 'They'll send you out to do their legwork so they can get more pub-time. Police reports, murders, road accidents, gambling raids, scandals. Pretty gruesome stuff.'

'But I'm interested in politics and current affairs too. Perhaps ...?'

'Politics is a very cushy beat and they won't let a girl in easily.' Mary appraises me. 'And you're probably too young and pretty to survive. What, twenty-one?'

'Twenty-two. And I've done uni. Women aren't very welcome there either.'

'True. What subjects?'

'History, French, Political Science.'

Mary nods. 'Not bad. But I'm puzzled. How *did* you get a job here anyway? There are queues around the block for anything we've got.'

'Oh, a family friend suggested me to the proprietor.'

One eyebrow lifts. 'Ah. That'd be the way.'

'But I'm serious, Mary. I'll work as hard as possible.'

'Guess we'll find out. Anyway, let's go and write up this morning's stuff. *And* sort out that article you did. You won't get a cadetship if you can't string a proper story together.' She smiles. 'But the Social Department will smooth off your rough edges. We're smarter than we look.'

3. LEO: SCHEYVILLE (FEB-NOV 1967)

Basic training is hard, and different from anything I'd expected. Officers worry more about how we roll up our socks than how good we are with guns. The yelling is unbelievable — the sergeant-major won't have vocal chords left in a few years. And the food is disgusting.

Two weeks into this hell they show us a cheery propaganda film and ask us to apply for officer training school at Scheyville. I don't hesitate. Officers have food we can only dream of, and people don't yell at them all the time.

Bazza is pissed off with me, but this is survival, mate.

So I do the interviews and sit a few tests. Another medical and some 'outdoor leadership exercises' involving ropes and logs. No sweat. I'm nervous the day the sergeant reads out the names, but when I hear mine I wonder how I could ever have doubted it. Bazza always said I was a smug shit and he's probably right.

When I ring and break the news to the family, my parents are pretty happy my moment of reckoning has been postponed for six months. I doubt my sister cares, probably because it doesn't involve Mary Quant shoes, whatever they are.

Dad says, 'Skyville? Where's that?'

'Near Windsor, outside Sydney. It was a migrant camp after the war.'

'Oh, *there*,' said Dad. 'Scheyville. Now I'm with you.'

'Yeah, so they decided they needed more officers for training the conscripts.'

'And commanding platoons in Vietnam,' Mum says flatly.

Sometimes I wish my mother didn't have such a good grasp of politics. She was in British intelligence during the war, though she never speaks of it. But it gives her an unfair advantage. I can't bullshit her very easily.

'Yeah, but who knows, Mum? Maybe it'll all be over by then. Anyway, better food, better pay — I'm not complaining.'

I can almost hear a certain look I know well passing between my parents, so I quit while I'm ahead. 'Anyway, gotta go, there's half a dozen blokes waiting to use the phone.'

∞

Scheyville? Fuck me dead, it never stops. A marching pace that's basically running. Lessons and exercises all day, every day: fieldcraft, tactics, military law, navigation, physical training. Just minutes allowed between classes to change from boots and greens to training kit and back again, and woe betide anyone who's late to a lesson or meal or whose room isn't immaculate. At least we do have our own rooms, small and basic, with a little blessed privacy.

We're allocated a 'father,' an officer candidate who's done the first three months of the course so is in the senior class. If we screw up he gets punished too. My guy is nice enough but reserved, probably worried about what disasters I'm going to draw down upon our heads. With good reason.

The punishment for screwing up is 'extra drills', or just *extras*, which means up at 5.30 am, in full gear and on the parade ground by 6.00 am. Full gear is boots, greens, field equipment, pack, bedding, rifle, sewing kit (yes), boot polish and water bottle.

Some crisp drilling, then the gear has to be broken down and displayed in inspection order on our beds. After that (oh Jesus), a mad dash for breakfast, then a race back to make sure the room itself is ready for inspection.

Our greatest sin is being separated from our weapon, the 7.62 mm self-loading rifle. Once I leant mine against the mail-room door as I entered for ten bloody *seconds* and got three extras for leaving the rifle unattended. My 'father' was not very happy.

While hard to believe, some are worse than me at training and gradually our ranks thin. I thought I was fit before, but now I'm fitter than I ever imagined possible, and it's good to feel that sense of controlled power, that reserve of strength to call upon.

If we survive the course we'll be commissioned as second lieutenants, supposedly capable of commanding the lives of an infantry platoon, thirty-five men or so.

Most of our trainers have combat experience from Borneo, Malaya and Vietnam, and they talk about '*when* you go' rather than '*if* you go,' but we're kept so busy there's no time, or desire, for reflection. Most of my mates take the approach that (a) it's their job, (b) they're pretty good at it, and (c) if some bastard's shooting at them then they'll get what they deserve.

We do field exercises at night, at dawn, at the end of long, exhausting days. We learn how to attack and defend, to take cover, to manoeuvre, to slip in and out of essential positions during patrols.

We calculate distances to targets, we move in ten-man sections, we give silent field signals, respond to contact, ambush, and counter-ambush situations. We study military history and do weapons drills over and over till we have blisters on top of our calluses.

During battle inoculation exercises we're hit with the overwhelming rackets of gun, mortar and artillery explosions, and somehow still have to prevent it affecting our concentration.

Even when we're not training we're playing viciously brutal sports. We have a little leave, usually one night and the following day and evening. Just long enough to get to Sydney, enjoy spending our minuscule pay, then return. On time or else.

∽

One weekend I borrow a mate's car and race off to Newcastle. I check in with my parents, then go to see Shazza: though she likes me to call her Sharon when we're in bed. Hey, I'd call her anything she wants when she's there, all soft and warm and perfect.

After an enthusiastic welcome, she says, 'Will you get lots of leave, Leo?'

I'm still catching my breath, but manage to say, 'Not much.'

There's another guy Sharon likes, a plumbing apprentice whose marble didn't get drawn. 'Seen Thommo lately?' I ask.

She shakes her head vigorously. 'Um, no.'

Ah, Shazza. I kiss her, and after a little teasing we go for it again. It's as great as the first time, but when we say goodbye I feel a bit low. Shazza said that Bazza's already been deployed to Vietnam with the Seventh Battalion, 7RAR. Hope he'll be okay.

At breakfast next morning my parents still seem stunned at the sight of me.

Dad says cautiously, 'You're looking very smart, Leo.' I run my hand over my head. Can't get used to the short back and sides.

Jenny — now apparently calling herself Jen — says, 'Did you cry when they cut off your hair?'

'No, pipsqueak, I didn't cry.'

'What will you be when you finish officer training? A *general*?'

'A second lieutenant, if I make it. But there's a thirty percent drop-out rate. It's not easy.'

Surprisingly my sister says, 'You'll make it, Leo, I'm certain of it.'

I laugh. 'You'd better tell our sergeant-major that. Anyway, the sun's shining and I haven't been to the beach for ages, so I'll see you lot later.'

I go for a nice surf at Nobby's then lie on the sand in the April sunshine. Not many others around. The water is slowly crashing, wave after wave. It's hypnotically soothing and, for what feels like the first time in months, I relax.

And, of course, my mind blank, I think of Claire.

Claire.

Last Easter — a year ago now — I was in a strange state of semi-suspense. The draw for my intake of nashos was still a few months away and I was doing teacher training, mainly because there wasn't much else possible with my crappy degree.

On a quick trip to Sydney I arranged a night out at Tempo with the older members of the horde, Tibor, Asher and Claire. Claire was already there. I ordered drinks, carefully trying not to notice her bare shoulders, her soft fair hair, her spectacular new dress.

Then Tibor, who'd organised the evening, didn't even bother turning up, the drongo. At least Asher came. He's only a year younger than me, but somehow he's a different generation. Still, he's great to be around, messy, hopeful, enthusiastic, and how he yearns for peace, the fool.

Has no idea what he's up against. Doesn't he know if the military doesn't have someone to fight it won't get any funding? There's *always* got to be an enemy. Doesn't matter who, anyone will do. Now it's those poor buggers in Vietnam.

Asher, mate, no matter how many marches, sit-ins, lectures you do: no one will listen. No one will care. I think about the badges that weigh down his shirt. *Draft beer, not boys. End national servitude. Smash U.S. Imperialism. Bread not bombs. Vote with your feet, vote in the street. Withdraw all troops now.*

And the glorious perennial: *Make love, not war.*

I wish.

Still, what a way to meet girls. Asher's always got a new one, and he left half-way through the evening to go and paint placards with some cutie. Bastard. Still, it was a good night, the music great, and Claire was looking ... amazing, all blue eyes and pale-gold hair.

I kept telling myself, think about Shazza, pretty hazel-eyed Sharon, her nipples hard and brown. Our first time had happened just the previous *weekend*, for fuck's sake! Why would I even notice another woman?

But then somehow Claire and I were talking about the past, when we were barely more than kids. That night beside the fire. Her sweet mouth. Her amazing scent. Her fury with me, too — at her own vulnerability, I suppose. She's certainly kept me at arm's length ever since.

Just memories, that's all, I told myself. Be sensible. Anyway, she was totally pissed. Tina told me to drive Claire home. Okay. She was *so* drunk, she could hardly get herself to the car. Off to Balmain we went. Then she wanted to go to her beloved park. Down the street to look at the water. Ignition off. Silence.

She was unhappy, thinking a life as a reporter would free her. How to make it happen?

I mentioned Moshe Adler, the man with a finger in every Sydney pie, the man whose reputation alone was as good as a bunch of goons to guard Tina's club. Mr Adler? She'd never even considered what he meant to her family, or what he might do to help her.

But when she did — and I can't suppress my smile — that kiss. Oh, *Claire.*

Followed by my long, stupid silence. Christ knows why. Maybe my own confusion — how could I tell her about me and Shazza? Claire's not that sort of girl, she's always got a sort of untouched air. (Still, I wonder how many other guys she *has* kissed?)

And when my marble was drawn, life suddenly became so confusing and shadowy. How could I figure out anything then?

I go for a few more surfs, get a burger from the kiosk, lie down and have a snooze. All too soon it's evening and the sliver of daytime moon is turning silver.

Will it look like that in the sky over Vietnam? Closer to the equator, might be different. And doesn't it rain a lot there? I think of fog, and dripping jungles, and clouds of smoke from artillery shells. Despite the warm air, cold seeps through the sand beneath me.

Time to get going. A quick shower at home and goodbyes to my family, who still keep staring at me in puzzlement. I didn't think I'd changed *that* much.

ᕲᕲ

At Scheyville we're watched constantly, marked on everything. Our scores are even fed into a computer, with punched cards collating every screw-up. Or occasional success.

After three months and the winnowing of more candidates, we become the fathers to a new batch of cadets. Now it's platoon-level work, coordinating thirty or forty men during live-fire exercises, with real bullets zipping over our heads. We call for artillery onto coordinates be only metres from our own positions, but luckily it's an exercise or in one horrifying incident I'd have got us all killed.

We're taught about Vietnam and the Australian forces headquartered at Nui Dat, fifty-odd miles south-east of Saigon. We even get a smattering on the politics of the whole situation, although the wisdom of ever having got involved in the first place isn't much examined.

This six months has been such a grind of learning new, and undeniably interesting skills, that I haven't had time to think about what the ending might mean.

It's expected we'll soon be allocated to the Infantry corps, go to Queensland for jungle training, then be shipped off to Vietnam. But conscripts nowadays have broader skills than the volunteers of the past, so we're given the chance to apply for other corps, like Artillery, Signals, Engineers or Intelligence.

We're handed a form and told to specify three preferences, keeping in mind, as always, the outcome depends upon administrative whim.

Surprisingly, some of Asher's anti-war diatribes seem to have stuck, and I realise I've got slightly different views of what's going on than most of the guys. My parents' weary replies when I was spouting all that crap about dominos are also a counter-balance to the general attitude it's only about Commies (them) versus Goodies (us).

In fact, lately I've had the growing feeling I don't really want to have to kill anyone. Our training has made it perfectly clear our job is not simply a matter of firing back at bastards who shoot at us first, but in some situations we're expected to be aggressors too.

And my error in coordinates that could have wiped out a platoon? I still wake up sweating about that. I don't *want* to be responsible for other lives. I'm barely responsible for my own.

I've tried talking it over with a few mates, but they don't seem to make any distinction between the semi-enjoyable demands of training and what lies ahead. Some are from pretty grim backgrounds or boring jobs, and say this is the best time they've ever known. Of course they feel apprehensive, but none feel — or admit to feeling — the way I do.

So all up, I've got reservations about staying in Infantry. The other corps? I'm a bit claustrophobic, so Armour doesn't appeal. Artillery? No, not after my excruciating mistake. Aviation? I like my feet on the ground. Engineers? I'd be a danger to myself and everyone else: I still carry the scars from Industrial Arts classes.

Specialist corps like Medical, Dentistry or Legal are obviously out, but then I start thinking about the Educational Corps, which trains soldiers wherever they're stationed. I never much wanted to be a teacher in the first place, but somehow survived it — so maybe the Educational Corps would be okay. I put it first, then Intelligence. Mum'd like that. Then Signals. Ah well, let's see.

∽

In August, towards the end of the course, we're helicoptered to

Gospers training area deep in the bushland. The flight is exhilarating, the work exhausting. We dig trenches and establish secure bases, practise search and clear operations, patrol through the thick bush, day and night.

The final exercise is the walk-out from the training area back to Windsor, twenty miles carrying fully-laden packs. It's not easy and I'm left with massive blisters on both feet.

But then it's over.

Our graduation parade in the winter sunshine is surprisingly moving, as we slow-march off between the ranks of our 'sons', soon themselves to be fathers to a new lot of bewildered recruits.

That night my parents and Sharon arrive for the graduation ball. I wear my formal patrol blues, with trouser stripes and high collar, my new second lieutenant's gold pips on my shoulders. And on my collar the badge of my posting: the flambeau, crown and boomerang of the Royal Australian Army Educational Corps.

Shazza looks amazing. Her hair is up with flowers in it, her eyes are shining and her cheeks pink. Her dress is some miracle of engineering that covers the essentials but somehow doesn't, and as we dance I get quite a few envious glances. (Though I dance pretty slowly, my feet still hurt.)

My parents have always got on well with Sharon, and all three are staying at a motel in Windsor. When we say goodnight I watch their car leaving the base, aching with lust. A motel with Shazza? If only.

∞

Next day, our belongings packed, we say our goodbyes and leave Scheyville behind. It turns out my Educational Corps posting is to the Third Recruit Training Battalion at Singleton, exactly where I began army life. Ho-hum. If nothing else, it's familiar.

There's one other education lieutenant at Singleton. He shows me the ropes, then I'm thrown in the deep end.

There are a lot of classes, ranging from basic literacy to courses for staff promotions, and after a time I start to enjoy them. The basic literacy guys, some with pretty difficult backgrounds, are defensive at first but slowly let down their guards.

Most try hard to catch up with what everyone else, including me, just takes for granted. I've always been a reluctant student but now I see how lucky I was to grow up in a house full of books, with parents to encourage me along the way.

At least now I'm not too far from said parents, and we're allowed a little more leave. One weekend I take the train to Newcastle, say hullo, borrow Dad's Holden and race off to Sydney.

I arrange drinks with the horde — I haven't seen them for a whole year and a half, not since that Easter: that amazing evening Claire kissed me.

Our official civvy outfit is black shoes and socks, grey trousers, white shirt, narrow tie and a dark blue blazer. I sigh. I look like someone selling Bibles. Still, who cares? Tempo awaits.

But even Tempo seems to have changed while I've been away. For a start the miniskirts are up to *here*, and the jazz is more like pop. Still, it's bloody good to see the others.

Smooth bastard Tibor is in a suit, his haircut carelessly styled to pretend he isn't. Asher is his usual scruffy self, though Mum told me he's under a lot of pressure: balloted in and he's refusing to go.

And Claire is wearing something green that makes her blue eyes a sort of turquoise. I don't know. I can hardly look at her.

We have a few drinks and I get a lot of jokes about my hair, then Asher says, 'Hey, Leo — I'm up before the magistrate next week. Probably heading for prison time.'

'What?' I say. '*Prison*? Surely ...'

Asher shakes his head. 'Got to set an example.'

'Ah, mate,' I say. 'Sorry. Hope it's not too bad.'

'Don't you need him in Vietnam supporting you?' says Tibor.

'Nah. Anyway, who needs support? I'm stuck in Singleton, might never even leave the country.'

'Dream on,' says Claire.

'So, how's life at the newspaper?' I say as smoothly as I can, given how mesmerising she is.

'Well,' she says, 'it was something of a wrench to leave the joys of the secretarial department behind — gloves, hats and demure demeanour — but I got through the cadet exams and was finally permitted to join the holy sanctuary of the newsroom.'

'Congratulations!' I say. 'Didn't I always say you'd do it?'

Claire's eyes narrow with an unspoken *Don't you dare*, so I shut my mouth.

'Being simultaneously ignored and loathed is quite the experience,' she says. 'But I'm sure I'm all the stronger for it.'

'Frying pan into fire?' says Asher, grinning.

'Absolutely. Now I run around with copy, learn curses I didn't even know existed, and cover for reporters when the lure of the front bar outweighs gruesome autopsies on road-accident victims.'

'But you'll eventually be promoted, won't you?' I ask.

Clair laughs. Her hair is loose on her shoulders and I can almost feel the scent and rippled weight of it against my face.

'*Promoted*? Not bloody likely.' She leans forward. 'Our stories come in from the wire agencies, so one day I asked my boss why we don't have our own reporter in Vietnam. Nah, no need, he said. So I offered to go myself.' She takes a drink. 'The newsroom's hardly been able to stop snickering about it since.'

I'm horror-struck. '*You*? Are you out of your *mind*?'

Her face is cool. 'I'll go wherever I like, Leo.'

'For God's sake, Claire, I've just spent the last six months learning exactly why no one sane would go anywhere near that place.' I can't stop myself. 'Don't even *think* —'

She stares at me as if we're total strangers and shrugs. 'Shh. Music's about to begin.'

∞

Life's pretty busy at Singleton, but a few weeks later I find time to have dinner with my long-suffering parents in Newcastle. They don't hide their relief I'm still in the country, and I'm pretty glad to see they're doing well. Mum's content. She works at the State Dockyard — she's always been mad about ships, and Dad too, that's how they met, about a million years ago.

Dad says he's still enjoying his practice, but he turned sixty-five this year and I suppose he'll retire soon. My sister Jenny — Jen — is bright-eyed and chatty, and doesn't seem at all worried about school.

Shoes still matter, but now the entire focus of her life is a record by the Beatles about some sergeant's club band. I nod and pretend enthusiasm. The sergeants I know swear like souls in Hell and would never wear satin.

When Jen goes upstairs to play records, we have coffee, then Mum says suddenly, 'Oh, meant to tell you, love. Yvonne rang yesterday to say Claire's gone to Vietnam.'

'What? To *Vietnam*?'

'Just upped and left,' says Dad. 'Took her typewriter and bought a one-way ticket to Saigon.'

'But I told her not to go anywhere near the place. Jesus, why didn't someone stop her?'

'Not sure anyone's been able to tell Claire what to do since she was about six,' says Mum. 'But it's all right, love. Journalists usually stay in Saigon and Charlotte says that's been peaceful for a long time. And don't forget, she and Pete have been there since the mid-fifties. They'll help her.'

'Uncle Pete's too fond of a drink, and Aunt Charlotte? Mad as a cut snake. How can *they* help?'

Dad gazes at me over his glasses. 'Never let it be said I'd defend Charlotte, but she *has* kept that orphanage going since —' He thinks. 'When was it, love? When she and Pete ran off and got married the second time round? Dear Lord, you'd think once was enough.'

'Fifty-four,' says Mum. 'After her Général helpfully met his fate at Dien Bien Phu.'

'Wait on,' I say. 'Charlotte's previous husband died at Dien Bien Phu? We studied that. Encirclement, brilliant tactics by the Viet Minh, insane assumptions by the French. Wow.'

'No need to be quite so enthusiastic, darling,' says Mum drily.

I grin. 'Okay. But seriously, how the *hell* do we get Claire to come home again?'

∾

A few days later, all my concerns for Claire have to be put aside. I'm informed that the Army, in all its wisdom, is assigning me away from Singleton.

In December I'm to go to Canungra in Queensland for advanced jungle training, then join the fairly new, small First Australian Civil Affairs Unit. There's a certain logic to it.

1ACAU has a detachment in education, as well as detachments in engineering, medicine and agriculture. It's part of a pacification program designed to bolster support for the allies and the government in South Vietnam: for winning hearts and minds.

And there it is. Sorry, Mum, looks like I'm off to war.

4.   VIVY: AMSTERDAM (JUN-DEC 1967)

How grudgingly men fall in love, I think, wiping off my eye-liner at the dressing-room mirror. My charming husband Henk sometimes seems almost resentful he fell so hard for me and threw away his easy bachelor life. Or at least fell so hard for the woman on stage, microphone at her crimson mouth.

I liked Henk and still do, so when I made it clear I expected little more of him than his name he became much nicer to live with. Now I don't really care about the pretty young friends he takes for 'drives to the country,' although I can't help but envy their silken skin and careless beauty.

Lately my face responds poorly to makeup and — I peer — oh, those bloody creases beside my eyes, although I'm only thirty. Surely my mother Charlotte looked younger at this age? She always seemed angelically beautiful to me, flitting between our Southampton farm and her war work in London.

'But I must help, Vivy,' she'd say. 'All those poor kiddies we're saving from the Nazis. You'll be much happier here with Daddy and Taffy. A *pony* couldn't come and live in London, after all.'

Quite true.

I think even her friends feel that Charlie's best moments were during the war. The rest of her life was something of a mess: affairs, divorce (from Dad) and remarriage to Louis, the French General. It seemed at last she'd found stability, but after years together Louis died in some stupid battle.

Then, soon after Louis' death, my mother visited Sydney, to hear me sing she told everyone. I was eighteen and believed her. It mattered after a lifetime of distance — the closest I'd ever had to a mother was easy-going Billie (who, to my delight, had just become engaged to Dad).

I sigh. That night, that extraordinary night at Tempo.

I was immersed in a slow Ellington number when Billie, a streak of green sequins, dashed out of the nightclub.

During the interval I noticed Charlie sitting surprisingly close to Dad, but really, I had no idea of what had happened.

Later, in the foyer, Dad gave me a sheepish kiss, got into a taxi with Charlie and drove away. Tina, watching, shook her head. 'I'd heard the bitch was ruthless, but she's something else. These things happen, Vivy. Billie'll be fine. Just a bump in the road.'

But it wasn't.

Charlie had to have a husband, even one she'd already discarded, so she stole Dad from Billie, took him away to bloody Vietnam, and left me behind without a thought.

But even if I'd realised at the time, would I have much cared? I laugh quietly. Probably not. After all, that was the evening I first slept with Steve: first slept with any man.

∽

There's a tap at the door. 'Vivy,' says my manager Lucien. 'Here is Nina, remember?'

He ushers in a thin girl with dark hair, a heavy fringe over her eyes. She sits down quickly, glancing around the room. She's a new singer he's taken on — German he'd said — so I was expecting someone solid and blonde, not this semi-child.

'Nina has not much français, yes, darling? Only anglais. Vivy, please assist.'

'Hello Nina,' I say. 'Suppose I can help you find a place. Have you been in Amsterdam long?'

She shakes her head.

'Nina comes today on the train,' Lucien says in his husky voice. 'Peut-elle rester chez toi, Vivy?'

'A *ma* maison? Lucien, non!'

He shrugs. 'Henk n'est pas là. S'il te plaît, chérie. Two, three days, that's all. The last favour for me before I retire, I promise.' Not fair: he knows how much I'll miss him. I glance at Nina's slumped shoulders. Poor mouse, must have been a long trip.

'All right. You can stay with me for a few days to settle in.'

She looks up and I'm slightly taken aback. Her eyes aren't mouse-like at all, they're angry, suspicious. Oh, God.

We go back to our flat and I show Nina the spare room and make food, which she resentfully devours, then we have coffee.

After a time Nina says, 'This is not for long. My boyfriend is coming.'

'That's nice,' I say. 'What will you do then?'

'We will have our *own* place.' She gazes with dislike around my rather nice kitchen.

'Okay. Look, there are towels in the hall cupboard, and the bathroom's down there. I'm a bit tired, so why don't you sort yourself out as you please. I'm off to bed.'

Next morning my guest is a little less unpleasant. Maybe she needed a good sleep. In the kitchen she says hesitantly, 'I have made coffee. And omelettes. If that is okay ...'

'Perfect. Thanks, Nina.'

We eat, but she doesn't look at me.

Finally I say, 'So what are your plans for today?'

She smiles and it's a transformation. 'My boyfriend is arriving by train.' She meets my eyes. 'Tonight, he can stay here too?'

The spare room is a fair way down the hall so hopefully the noise will be contained.

I nod. 'Fine. For how long?'

'Only tonight and tomorrow,' she says. 'He has a friend who —'

'Great. Look, I have to do some shopping now. Here's a key. You'll be all right?'

She nods and says stiffly, 'Thank you.'

Steve Loukas played the piano in my backing quartet and the attraction had been building between us for a long time.

Three years older than me, he was handsome, dark-eyed and passionate. That extraordinary night at Tempo, Steve emerged from the dressing-room and I told him what had happened with Dad and Charlie, feeling confused.

The rest of the band appeared and Jeff the drummer said, 'Coming back to the flat, guys? Got some good grass. You might even try it this time, Vivy.'

I'd always resisted their light-hearted attempts to draw me into what they fondly imagined was the jazz lifestyle, but this time I cleared my throat and agreed.

We crammed into Jeff's old Morris and went back to their flat near the Conservatorium, where they were all studying. They were very serious about their musical training and Steve the most serious of all.

The boys smoked a few joints though I didn't (and almost never have in my life, my voice is too important). But I drank some wine and we played records and chatted. I was simply content to watch Steve's face—darkness, light, concentration, pleasure.

When the others drifted out to the kitchen for food he came to sit beside me on the couch, to show me a new record, he said. It was a Thelonious Monk album, but all I remember is his hands holding the cover as he read some of the liner notes to me.

The others were making a lot of noise and arguing about butter, cheese and random condiments, and Steve murmured, 'Let's go somewhere quieter.'

Then, in his room, the long-awaited moment: kissing, discarding of clothes, touching of mouths, chests, thighs. The comfort of bed, the sweet, strange pressure of a body on mine in the semi-dark, a faint landscape of veins across Steve's hands as he caressed me.

Our breathing a rhythm as easy as music, then a pang, a driving towards an expanse of possibilities, and afterwards, the shy reality. Tissues. Soft laughter. Blankets drawn up. And arms, shoulders, feet, finding their first tentative accommodation with each other.

∽

Steve and I were together for three years. I was singing at most of Sydney's jazz venues, then Steve graduated and wanted to study classical music in Greece, his grandparents' homeland. He came in for a lot of teasing from the band because he'd spent most of his life trying to escape from his background.

(Billie, who got over Dad's betrayal and ended up happily with Steve's father Nikos, would say she always thought his real name wasn't Stavros, but Call-Me-Steve.)

At the time I lived in a flat at Klara and Yvonne's, where I'd moved at sixteen to become wise young Claire's babysitter. The family joke, mostly true, was that it was really the other way around.

After Steve and I got together, Yvonne says there were a lot of slammed doors in the basement, as we fought more and more. I didn't want him to go. I wasn't sure enough of myself to think I had a chance in the European jazz scene, and we fought.

The break came one sad evening at Nikos and Billie's place, where we'd assembled to watch some stupid satellite. Steve held me close in the dark, away from the others at the barbecue. He was leaving in a fortnight. He didn't ask me to come with him. I'd already refused.

It was a big night. I noticed Tina in the garden, weeping, comforted by Billie. I think she'd been a widow for a year by then, ever since small-time crook Jimmy Kelso had driven his car off a cliff. No one much missed him, but I expect it still upset her.

Poor Billie had to comfort me later in the kitchen as well, while Steve and Nikos talked over his plans in the living-room, their voices rumbling, and at home Steve made promises in the dark. We'd always stay friends. He'd be back, only a few years apart. And, especially, he'd write to me every week.

But when we waved goodbye, streamers parting as the ship eased away from the wharf, with Nikos trying to hold back his tears and me not even trying, I knew it was the end.

Steve wrote to me once or twice, then never again. It hurt terribly.

∽

We found a new pianist, but for the first time singing gave me little pleasure. Tina was good to me — we'd have late-night brandies or tea in her flat above Tempo. Róbert was three then, and would sometimes wake up for a cuddle, his round brown eyes as adorable as a puppy's.

'Is it the band?' Tina said one night. 'Perhaps you need to find another.'

'Not them really, though I don't much like the new pianist. He thinks I'm a perk of the job. And he's crap in the slow parts, has no idea about leaving me a bit of space to open up.'

'There aren't many players around who are that versatile, Vivy.'

'No. I've only ever had two — Steve and László.'

'László,' said Tina slowly. 'Yes, he was good. Sometimes I almost imagine he's still here, you know. You remember this used to be his flat?' She sipped her brandy.

'Oh, yes! He'd let the band crash here after gigs, and I'd snuggle up on the couch in your office. László always made sure I felt safe, especially in the club. Such a lovely man, taught me so much about music. Did you ever find out what happened to him?'

'Jimmy said he'd gone travelling, implying he'd disposed of him somehow.'

'Disposed? *Not* —?'

'Not for lack of trying,' says Tina. 'Luckily László got away to Europe, but even after Jimmy died he didn't want to come back. He wrote to me once — too many difficult memories, he said. I've heard nothing since and Moshe can't find him either.'

László, barrel-chested, brown-eyed and cynical, was always smoking his favourite cigarillos. He'd been a music teacher in pre-war Hungary, a prisoner in the terrible Auschwitz camp, then he and Moshe Adler had arrived in Australia on the same refugee ship.

László helped Tina set up and run her nightclub. He also played piano like an angel and encouraged and accompanied me when I was just starting out.

I felt a twinge of guilt that I'd almost let him slip from my mind when he'd done so much for me. But Steve ... *bloody* Steve. He was all I'd thought about for so long. Still, he'd been gone for months now and I really needed to forget him.

One morning I was noodling away on the piano at Tempo, working on a new song. The club was closed and I didn't notice Moshe Adler arrive.

Some mornings he'd come by to see Tina in her office, as he was involved in some way in the club's operation. (Steve used to joke that's why Tempo was never bothered by the Kings Cross criminals. Or the Kings Cross police.)

'Most pleasing, Miss McKee,' he said politely. 'Are you settled in with the new band?'

'No,' I said, unable to pretend any more. 'It's not the same.'

He nodded. 'I believe you are wasted in this country. It is a suitable place to raise a family, but for culture and sophistication?' He shrugged. 'The kind of jazz you sing, the music you appreciate, it is wasted here. In my opinion, of course.'

'Thank you, Mr Adler,' I said. I hardly knew him except as Tibor's rather intimidating father, but he always had a similar look to László. Reserved, watchful, sceptical.

'Have you considered a career in Europe?'

I laughed sadly. 'It's been suggested. But here I've got family and friends. There, where I don't know *anyone*, don't have a *manager*, don't have the *money* —' I stopped, blinking. 'Sorry. Fact is I'm pretty lost. No idea what to do.'

I was surprised at my outburst — and my honesty — because since Steve left I'd been cultivating a facade of indifference. But Mr Adler simply nodded, sat down and lit a cigarette.

'Tina has mentioned your situation. I have contacts in Europe and if you wished to go I might be able to help. You would be safe under my protection, and I would make certain you had an honest manager. Are your parents, perhaps, in a position to assist you?'

I laughed shortly. 'We're not close. My mother runs an orphanage in Vietnam dedicated to her second husband, the late Général Louis de Ferrier. I'm not sure what my father, her first and third husband, thinks about that, but she's always been good with children. Impartially and in the collective, of course.'

'Ah. And not very good with her own?'

I gazed at the piano keys, suddenly blurred, and wondered why I was telling him so much.

'No matter, Miss McKee,' Mr Adler said. 'I would find the expense bearable and of course, you could repay me in time. You have excellent prospects.'

'But why?'

'I owe Tina a great deal. We both believe you have a fine career ahead.' He looked at his hands. 'And your music reminds me of my friend, László. It would please him.'

I left Australia in early 1958 and spent time in the London and Paris jazz scenes, building up a following and releasing a few albums that did reasonably well.

Eventually I repaid Mr Adler, and the manager he found for me, Lucien, became a good friend. A few years ago Lucien wanted to build a presence in Amsterdam, so I came here, met charming, urbane Henk, married him and stayed. He runs a small music business, Straat Records. That's been good for me too, of course.

Amsterdam isn't as well-known for jazz as Paris, but the giants of music still perform: lately I've seen Miles Davis, Charles Mingus, Ben Webster, Nina Simone, Ella Fitzgerald, and Art Blakey and the Jazz Messengers.

I like Amsterdam. I was raised in the English countryside, and Amsterdam's misty canals and old buildings feel welcoming. It's a small town where everyone knows everyone else, without Paris's intensity or London's war-damaged grimness.

And after all, I only lived in Sydney for seven years — from fourteen to twenty-one — and in some ways I feel more at home here than I ever did in that beautiful harbour city. I don't regret Amsterdam.

∽

Henk has returned from his weekend away, so we kiss and chat. I go to lie down for a rest before tonight's performance, and Henk follows me into the bedroom. I'm tired, but my shoulders are sore and he's a wonderful masseur. And lover.

Afterwards he takes a shower, and I fall asleep, relaxed. Our relationship is a puzzle, not only to our friends, but often to me. I enjoy his company and don't care what he does or who he does it with when we're apart. Is it that odd, really?

It's dark when I awake. I dress for the nightclub, and find Henk in the kitchen, making us both supper.

At the table I say, 'Ah, just remembered. We've got a house-guest, a bad-tempered little sparrow that Lucien's foisted upon us for a few days.'

Henk groans. 'Again? Vivy, you *must* say no next time.'

'She's only staying one or two nights, but she's collecting her boyfriend from the station today, so he's staying too. I'm sorry, darling.'

'Early to bed for me, I think,' Henk says gloomily. 'She will demand I produce a record for her.'

I get up, kiss him and put on my coat. 'I'd better go.'

'Do you wish me to drive?'

'No, it's only a couple of blocks, and it's not raining. I'll be fine. See you later.'

It's a fairly quiet night at Het Tuin, The Garden. I do my best but the crowd is small. The owner, Geert, shrugs his shoulders as I leave. It's a chilly spring and I walk briskly home.

When I'm taking off my coat I hear laughter from the lounge room. Henk, Nina and the newly arrived boyfriend I suppose. Henk must have found them pleasant enough as he hasn't retreated to bed. I make myself some tea in the kitchen then go to greet everyone.

'Ah, darling!' says Henk as I open the door to a fog of cigarette smoke and alcohol fumes. 'Join us. Will you have a whiskey?'

'No thanks, love, tea's fine. Hello, Nina — and this is?'

The man is on the couch beside her, and as he turns I'm struck dizzy with realisation, my heart pounding. The voice I'd been hearing was familiar, the form in the dimness is familiar, and the face gazing at me is shockingly familiar.

Nina says proudly, 'Meet Stav, my boyfriend.'

He stands and there's no mistake. He holds out his hand and I shake it quickly, then sit in an armchair before my knees betray me.

'Hello Vivy,' Steve says evenly. 'Thanks for having us here. It's good to see you again.'

'Isn't it wonderful, darling?' says Henk. 'Fancy your old friend from Australia turning up like this with his pretty girlfriend!' He goes to the drinks cabinet. 'I think this is certainly cause for a celebration. Nina, Stav — let me refill.'

Nina tells us in excruciating detail how they met in Germany last year. Then, such *amazing* good luck, just as Nina signed a contract for Amsterdam, Steve (Stav now, apparently) was offered a contract teaching music theory at the Amsterdamsch Conservatorium.

'Amazing,' I murmur. I clear my throat. 'Look I'm a bit worn out, think I'll —' I stand. 'Lovely to see you again, ah, Stav. Must catch up on all the gossip. Goodnight, everyone.' I make it out of there without falling over.

Bathroom, teeth, face cream, nightdress, bed, lights off. But oblivion doesn't come, and I lie on my back staring at the ceiling. The murmur of voices and laughter drifts down the hall to my bedroom.

For God's sake, focus on something else, anything else.

Oh, right, I think bitterly. That'd be Charlie's latest demand. Over time, via letters and phone calls, we've rebuilt a sort of relationship, although I haven't seen her for years. Why on earth would I go to hot, ugly, dangerous Vietnam?

But now my mother wants me to check on a château in Normandy left to her by Louis de Ferrier. She's fond of it, and understandably so — I have wonderful memories myself of the place from childhood vacations. In recent years my parents would holiday there, but I refused to go to see them as I was still too angry at their casual abandonment of me.

About four years ago the place was rented out. I was living in Paris then, so finally agreed to go on my parents' behalf to sign papers and check the tenant was suitable. He was: some bland Englishman with the funds and the will to take on a long lease.

It's not even a château either, that's just Charlie's usual pretentiousness, it's just a neglected old villa. The Englishman said he'd fix things, but I have no idea if he has. Now he needs money for more maintenance, so my mother is nagging me to check whether the proposed repairs are necessary.

Of course I can't go right now: the summertime tourists will soon be flocking to the jazz clubs. But perhaps when it's cooler? If Nina and her boyfriend are going to be hanging around I might want get away for a while. That thought at last is soothing and I slowly fade into sleep.

∽

I wake early. Henk is snoring quietly and I get up and quickly wash and dress. I'll go for a walk, clear my head. This isn't such a disaster. The European music scene is closely connected and I'm just surprised Steve and I haven't run into each other before over these last ten years.

In the kitchen, Steve — *Stav* — is at the sink. He turns. 'Want an apple? I was just stealing one.'

'Please, help yourself to anything,' I say. 'Just off for a stroll. See you later.'

I flee. I don't want to talk to him. What could I possibly say? I don't want to know what he's been doing. Who he's been doing it with. I'm content, my life is settled. I don't *want* to talk to him.

Around another corner and ahead is a small green park. I find my favourite bench. A few rays of morning sun emerge and glimmer on the small pond. An elegant *blauwe reiger*, a blue heron, stalks thoughtfully among the reeds.

I take a deep breath, close my eyes and relax. Footsteps crunch as someone walks on the gravel in front of me. I look up. Oh God.

Stav says awkwardly, 'Sorry. I wasn't following you. Just came down that lane there and across the grass.'

'Of course,' I say. 'Lovely morning for a walk.'

'Yes.' He gazes into the sky. 'Might rain later, though.'

'Suppose it might. Usually does. Here in *Amsterdam*.' My teeth are suddenly clenched.

'Look, Vivy, I'm sorry we ambushed you last night. I had no idea it was your place.'

'Oh? Nina didn't mention any of Lucien's more prominent clients when he signed her?'

He shrugs a little. 'She's not much interested in other singers.'

There's a silence, then he sits gingerly on the end of the bench. More silence.

'Are you well?' he says.

'Yes, I love Amsterdam. My career is fine. Henk and I are very happy.'

Stav clears his throat. 'Good. I'm looking forward to living here. I've spent most of the last ten years in Athens, Vienna, Rome. Suppose that's why we haven't crossed paths before.'

'Suppose so.'

'Sorry I didn't write much.'

'Wasn't really expecting it.' (He'd *promised* and oh, how his silence had hurt.) 'Starting off on a new life in Athens, you must have been busy.'

'Overwhelmed, really. Confronting all the years I'd spent as an Aussie pretending I wasn't half-Greek.'

'Must have been quite a homecoming.'

'No. My few relatives are on an island in the Mediterranean, my Greek was atrocious, and the coursework was almost beyond me. I nearly went back to Sydney several times.'

'But you managed.'

'Eventually. But after that it's why ... in the end, I chose to be Stav, not Steve.'

I laugh lightly. 'Well, I've stuck with the same name all my life, but I'm glad you've finally figured out what you want.' I stand. 'Now, I'm going *that* way. And I'd quite prefer it if you didn't.'

∞

A foolish moment of defiance. Nina quickly recognises Henk's potential, perhaps as lover but certainly as owner of Straat Records, and becomes a fixture around the place.

Over the second half of 1967 Stav and I are forced into a certain proximity, so we develop a bland social relationship, chatting lightly about music and concerts, and of course the news from Sydney.

My mother keeps annoying me about the villa in Normandy: now it seems the rents aren't coming through. My parents are prosperous enough, so I have no idea why this is such a concern. But in any case, I'm certainly not running off to France right now, my work is my priority.

Oddly, to the world I'm simply pretty Vivy, the sultry chanteuse; amusing and sophisticated. Most people have no idea how single-minded I am.

Do they imagine I get by without practising every day? That a repertoire of hundreds of songs simply bloomed complete in my mind? That my emotional interpretations are some sort of *accident*?

I have worked, dear God, how I've worked!

Unlike Nina, the sulky sparrow. She's already the toast of Amsterdam, all tight jeans and gamine charm. She sings of lost love with a dewy pout and not the slightest edge of experience to convey the truth of it.

Christ, I'm getting old and cynical. I was so satisfied with my career before, but suddenly I'm tired and a little anxious. Am I afraid of losing Henk? Nina has become one of his 'little friends,' and suddenly she seems to matter, when none of them have mattered before.

It's absurd, but I'm even flirting with the idea of having a baby. I'll be thirty-one this year so I'm probably well overdue. When we married I stopped taking the pill, but didn't become pregnant.

Henk was tested and came home joking, 'My swimmers are all fine,' so it was clearly me who had some sort of problem. At the time I wasn't interested in the exploratory operation the doctors suggested, but now … perhaps?

And Stav? The passionate boy has become hard. He's fond of Nina, but it's clear music is still the only thing he loves. Perhaps all that kept us together so long ago was the single-mindedness we must have recognised in each other.

We quarrelled constantly. I don't remember why. All I remember is my yearning: the frustrated yearning no sex could ever satisfy.

∽

Henk says, packing a shirt into his suitcase, 'Will I need my grey suit?'

'Unlikely, darling,' I say. 'Countess Frederika's weekends are always fairly casual.'

'Good. I doubt Nina has anything formal to wear in any case.'

'You could always get her something. Business expense, naturally.'

He smiles. 'Vivy, darling, you're not jealous are you?'

'Just a touch. A bit bored, really.'

'It is only two weeks before we launch her first single. This exposure is important.'

'Of course.'

'My blue sweater, do you think?'

'Yes, that suits you.'

He puts it in the case then sits on the bed beside me.

'Vivy, you know you don't have to be bored. You know what we agreed.'

'Yes, darling, but I'm not in the mood for an adventure.'

He runs his fingers through his blond hair, now fashionably long (Nina approves). 'What about your old boyfriend, Stav?' He shrugs. 'He and Nina are pretty well done, I think.'

'Oh? I thought it was the love of the ages. According to her.'

'Everything changes, Vivy,' says Henk, smiling with his quite extraordinary charm. 'Except us, we know each other so well. I never want us to change.'

'Well, better make certain Nina understands that,' I say lightly.

'She is very young. She will find out soon enough how the world works.' It's a relief to hear his words, and we embrace for a long time in the evening light.

Then he kisses me. 'I love you, Vivy, never forget that. And I love our life together just as it is.'

'Off you go, darling, and have a wonderful weekend. Give my best to Frederika.'

∽

Tonight I've got a gig at Het Tuin, and Geert is cheerful. Even this late in the year we're getting plenty of tourists visiting the club (relatively famous in Amsterdam terms), before they make their way to ogle the girls in the nearby red-light district.

Het Tuin runs over several floors in one of Amsterdam's old, narrow buildings. I'm singing in the top room tonight, and when I come on stage I notice Stav at one of the side tables.

He raises his glass to me and I nod. Suppose he's at a loose end with Nina away for the weekend. Still, what does it matter? The place is packed!

I launch into my first number and everything works, song after song. It's satisfying: oh, more than that. I'd forgotten how pleasing applause from a large audience can be, and they call me back for three encores.

Later, I wipe off my makeup at the dressing-room mirror, and smile. What a night! Who cares about Nina or any of those hungry young chanteuses? They could never do the songs I do, with the expression, the mood, the sheer *depth* I bring to them.

A knock at the door, and Stav enters with a bunch of spicy-scented carnations, my favourite. I know he didn't have to go far to find them — Amsterdam has flower-sellers on most corners — but it's a nice gesture.

I accept his peck on the cheek and fill an old vase with water.

'Sensational, Vivy, the best performance of yours I've ever seen.'

'Well, you've missed rather a lot of my singing over the years, so that may not be the compliment you intend,' I say, arranging the flowers. 'But I'll accept it anyway.'

I sit down again at the mirror, to remove the last of the makeup. 'Nothing to do? You could have gone to Countess Frederika's manor if you wanted.'

Stav shrugs. 'Not sure I could stand hearing, yet again, about Nina's single being launched —'

'— in two bloody weeks?' I say. 'Nor me. Still, it must be a novelty for her.' (I may be permitted a little smugness. My sixth album, *Vivy After Midnight*, is selling very well.)

'Don't much care. Actually, Nina and I are finished.' He pauses. 'But don't you mind Henk spending so much time with her?'

'It's his business.'

'Not quite what I meant.'

'But it's what I meant. We're adults and our marriage has a very strong foundation. Little friends with a lot more substance than Nina have come and gone over the years.'

'And — little friends of yours?'

'Oh? One or two.' I smile drily. 'I have a lot less free time on my hands than Henk.'

'You work harder, you mean.'

'Of course. If nothing else you should know that about me.'

'I do now. I'm not sure I understood it back then.'

I glance at him. Stav and I rarely mention our relationship, ended ten years ago. But I'm on a high from the night and suddenly that seems a long and forgettable time in the past.

'Look,' I say. 'Do you want to get some food? I'm starving, and if you've got any gossip from Sydney I'd love to hear it.'

Of course, in staid Amsterdam most restaurants are closed by now, so we end up at a street vendor's cart near Centraal.

We buy cones of patajes, the delicious hot chips with light mayonnaise sauce. Then we get coffee and sit by a narrow canal.

The Amsterdam autumn sky is typically overcast, but the night air is mild. I gaze at the rippled reflections of golden-lit bars along cobbled roadways, while Stav reads out a letter from his dad, Nikos. He and Billie are planning to sail their yacht to Tasmania, and I shudder at the prospect.

'Weeks of discomfort and they'll imagine they're having a *wonderful* time.'

Stav laughs. 'I couldn't bear it either. They're mad, both of them, all that sailing and flying. They'll never understand the pleasure of just sitting down and enjoying music.'

'I had a letter from Tina a few weeks ago,' I say. 'Apparently Americans on R&R are swamping Kings Cross, but they only like pop or psychedelic bands. She's trying out some new programs at Tempo, but isn't sure how it will go.'

'Poor Tina,' Stav says. 'Her first love was jazz — must be hard to have to change.'

I nod. 'At least here it'll always find appreciative audiences.'

'You hope. But what about *my* uncertain life? Experimental music only attracts the truly committed and if it wasn't for teaching I'd never play a thing. And my contract at the Conservatorium is up in the middle of next year.'

'What will you do then?'

'Don't know. London perhaps? Or maybe home to Sydney.'

I scoff. 'If jazz has a hard time in Sydney, experimental music won't have a chance.'

'Unkind, but probably true.'

I can't stifle a large yawn. 'Think I need to go now. I'm exhausted.'

Stav walks me to the flat, a kiss on the cheek, then he's gone. Good, that was a pleasant, civilised evening.

⤜⤐

A fortnight later it's Nina's record launch. I don't go because I've got a gig, but in any case she wouldn't want anyone there who might steal some of the limelight.

Stav isn't invited because they've definitely parted. Nina's got her own flat now, paid for by Henk, I suspect.

So I have another good evening at Het Tuin, and Stav takes me out afterwards. But winter is almost here and the patajes cart shut, so Stav offers to cook me something at his place.

'What?' I say. 'You mean you've got a saucepan left after the sparrow moved out?'

'You're joking. She's got no idea what saucepans are for.'

'And you do? Don't remember skills like that in Sydney. Seem to recall you and the band eating nothing but junk food.'

'I learnt to cook in Greece, student necessity,' he says. 'I'm not as good as Dad, but you probably won't get food poisoning.'

'That's a relief. Okay, let's.'

His flat is on the second floor of an old house overlooking a canal. The living room has a piano, guitar, flute, saxophone, music stands and stacks of notation books scattered everywhere.

'Ah,' says Stav, grabbing piles of music and moving them on top of other piles. 'Hadn't expected a visitor. Sorry it's a slum.'

'Musical slums are the best sort.'

He laughs. 'True. All right, here's a glass of red. And —' he puts a record on a turntable and carefully lowers the needle. 'Thelonious Monk's latest. See what you think.'

I sip the wine and watch the rain falling on the canal. Does he remember our first night together, when he read me the liner notes from a Monk album? I doubt it. Chopping sounds and metallic clanks come from the kitchen, soon followed by rather nice smells. After a time Stav brings in crockery and cutlery for the small dining table, then several steaming plates.

'Just ordinary stuff,' he says. 'Dolmades, spanakopita, salad.'

'Ordinary? I'm impressed. Smells great.'

The food is fantastic, and finally I say, putting down my fork, 'Well, if I get food poisoning it'll have been worth it.'

'You won't, I swear. So what did you think of the new Monk?'

'Great. The Ellington track is perfect.'

'You always did prefer the standards. I reckon he's going to get weirder and weirder and end up in my experimental music world.'

I smile. 'That I'd like to see.'

'Ah, who knows. Maybe I'll make my way back to jazz instead.'

'That I'd like to see, too.'

'Actually,' he hesitates. 'In the kitchen I realised something. Two months ago it was exactly ten years since that night at Dad and Billie's. Remember, Vivy? When everyone came along to watch the satellite?'

'Ah yes. The night we split up, you mean. Heavens, how time flies,' I say drily.

He smiles. 'After the other evening I wrote something. The canal, the patajes, the peace. I'll play it for you later.'

'The peace?'

'Yeah. Didn't you feel it?'

I nod slowly. 'Yes. I liked the quietness, the simplicity of it.'

We clear up the remnants of the meal, then go to the living room with brandies.

Stav clears his throat. 'Will I —?' He waves at the piano.

It's a short composition, perhaps five minutes. I watch him, focused on the music, his well-defined hands moving confidently, his black brows drawn in concentration.

He's not as classically handsome as his father Nikos, there's a certain dissatisfaction, even sadness, to his face. Who knows, perhaps his break with Nina hurt him more than he lets on.

Ten whole years since we parted? God. His ambition was always greater than mine — I wonder if he feared how much he felt for me, in case it held him back? Oh, *Steve*.

I try to see him objectively, as a stranger, but suddenly I'm swamped with the memory-sensation of the warm corner of his neck and shoulder, the place my head once fitted so well.

The music, Vivy, *concentrate*.

It's exquisite. I hear golden ripples, soft air, the ease of friendship, of connection. Of old connection. Deliberately-suppressed connection. My eyes sting. Don't be a fool. He's not Steve, he's Stav. And someone you hardly know any more.

The music flows like the canals, ending with shimmering droplets. A long silence. A breath. Of course I know him. I *know* this man. I get up and wrap my arms around him from behind, and the scent of his hair is heartbreakingly familiar.

'You liked it, then?' he says, a smile in his voice.

'I liked it. Turn around.'

He does so. I sit on his lap and we embrace for a long time. I rest my head in the sweet angle of his neck and shoulder, and sigh.

'Actually, Henk wants me to have an *adventure* with you, so he doesn't feel guilty about Nina.'

'And what do you want, Vivy?'

I raise my head. This is the first time I've seen his eyes so undefended, so vulnerable.

I stroke his cheek. 'I think, Stav, perhaps ... I do want to have an adventure.'

5.   Claire: Child of Dust (Sep 1967-Dec 1967)

That night last September was the final straw, the night I met Tibor, Asher and Leo at Tempo, as so often before. By then Leo and I hadn't seen each other for a year and a half, not since that foolish kiss, now obviously forgotten.

He was fresh out of officer training and looked like a stranger. He was always tanned and broad-shouldered, but now? Short-haired, fair eyebrows, a hardness I'd never before seen in him.

He was nice enough about my having finally made it into the newsroom (which was a hell of a lot more difficult and depressing than I made out), but I couldn't believe his response when I mentioned *possibly* reporting from Vietnam: condescending, dismissive, appalled.

So I turned away and played nice Claire for the rest of the evening, then went home and started calculating my finances. I told Yvonne what I was planning, and swore her to secrecy. I didn't tell Klara: even the thought of war causes her anguish. How could I explain I needed to be *there*, to be where history itself was being made?

Even telling gentle Yvonne was hard. But she's always been the backbone of the family, and with her eyes glinting with tears she proved it once again. There was some money — not a lot as the printery has had a bad year — but with my savings, enough.

I bought a ticket, packed my portable typewriter and a few clothes, got on an aeroplane and left poor Yvie behind to tell everyone.

∽

My first time on a plane? As if an armchair in my lounge room suddenly tilted back and left the earth like a flying carpet. Terrifying and exhilarating at first, but after hours and hours of it almost boring.

We stop in Darwin, then Singapore for a few hours, then there's another leg to Saigon, four thousand miles from Sydney.

Coming in to land at Tan Son Nhut Airport, there are so many planes and helicopters, rank after rank, set out on the airfield below. It's late morning and I follow a stream of Asian people and men in khaki down the plane steps. The heat feels like a solid thing and it's hard to breathe.

Yvonne had telegraphed Vivy's parents to meet me. It's probably pretty easy for them to pick me out, and in the waiting crowd I have little trouble identifying them.

'My God,' says Charlotte. 'Little Claire. Last time we met, you were a babe in Klara's arms. Oh, *sweetie*.'

She hugs me. She's wearing a linen top and slacks, her blonde hair in a pony-tail. Pete has thick charcoal hair, his face tanned. They're both in their late fifties, though Charlotte looks younger.

Pete says, 'Welcome to Saigon, Claire. You can stay with us as long as you like. Plenty of room. Car's out this way.'

I exchange some traveller's cheques into local cash, then we go out to the car, where a Vietnamese man is waiting behind the wheel. 'Claire, this is André,' says Charlotte, and we nod, then she sits in the back beside me. We set off, soon slowed by traffic.

'Airport used to be twenty minutes from the city,' says Pete. 'Takes an hour now with all the bloody military traffic.'

'Let me see you, darling,' says Charlotte. 'My God, you've got Toby's eyes. *So* blue.'

We chat a little about Klara and Yvonne, but it's hard to hear. Bicycles, motorcycles, cars and army trucks stream around us, roaring, honking and clattering, while sunlight flashes off the moving glass and chrome. The car windows are open in the heat. Unfamiliar and sometimes horrible smells assault me: drains, rotting fruit, dung.

I breathe through my mouth as broad avenues, roadside markets, handsome old buildings and occasional bombsites pass by in a blur. The car stops at last outside a handsome old building with vivid pink bougainvillea swaying against the walls.

'Let's get inside, sweetie,' says Charlotte. 'André will bring your luggage.'

Up a broad flight of stairs to a white salon, high-walled and blessedly cool. Two fans on the ceiling are moving the air about, and it feels wonderful.

'*Vinh*,' calls Charlotte. 'Drinks, please. Sit down, Claire.'

I fall into an armchair. An old Vietnamese man brings in a tray of drinks.

'Coca-cola, soda, tonic, gin?' says Pete.

'Just some cold water would be wonderful.'

'Oh no, Claire,' says Charlotte. 'Never, *never* drink the water here or you'll have dysentery forever. Only whatever comes out of a bottle.'

'Soda then, please.'

It may be the best thing I've ever had in my life. I'm drenched with sweat and ineffectually wipe my forehead.

'Here you are,' says Charlotte, handing me a handkerchief.

'Do you ever get used to it?' I ask.

'Partly,' says Pete. 'But look, you've had a long flight. We'll show you upstairs and you can have a rest. There's a fan in your room and you'll cool down a bit. Evening is a little more civilised.'

∞

When I awake it's still hot, but now the dim sky is raining heavily. I rub my eyes and stand at the window, looking out to the street from the second floor. Water pours down in silvery sheets, clattering onto roofs and overflowing spouts and gutters. The motorcycles below are dodging and honking as before, but their riders are now wearing plastic ponchos.

My watch says it's nearly five. I take a tepid shower in the small ensuite and put on my lightest cotton dress. In the salon downstairs, Pete is in an armchair reading the paper. 'Ah, you're up,' he says. 'Sleep well?'

'Yes,' I say. 'But it's so humid. Does it often rain like this?'

'We're at the tail end of the wet now. January and February are nicer, especially around Tet — the Lunar New Year — all flowers and parties and family gatherings.'

'Even in wartime?'

'Tet pays no attention to such petty disruptions. Now, Claire, a pre-dinner snifter?'

'Gin and tonic, please.'

Pete goes to the drinks trolley and pours the gin. I sit in another armchair and sip it gratefully and gaze around.

The salon is larger than I'd realised. It must run the full width of the house, as a dining table set with flowers sits at the far end. Palm trees in pots soften every corner, the ceiling is intricate with plaster bouquets, the marble fireplace is touched with gilt, and Chinese rugs soften the smooth, dark timber floors.

Outside, the pelting rain slows and almost stops. Pete opens two lots of tall French doors that lead onto small balconies, and a slightly cooler breeze flows in.

He settles himself again. 'Apart from Yvonne's telegram we don't actually know much about your plans, Claire, so what comes next?'

Beyond him the sky is charcoal, and the long pale muslin curtains roll slowly in the soft air. They mesmerise me but I try to be sensible. 'First, I have to get press accreditation from the Americans. I've heard it can be hard.'

'True, but at least they allow female reporters into their war zones — the Australians won't. As you say, you need credentials, but even so that may not happen unless you're on assignment for a big bureau like AP or UPI. And the few girls who've managed to gain a foothold are still seen as high-risk. Disparaged too — ugly stuff.'

'Yes, I've heard all the arguments.'

Pete smiles. 'And not put off in the slightest.'

Pete is Jen and Leo's uncle, and his smile reminds me of Leo. He must have been very good-looking when young and the stories about flings with Billie and his two marriages to Charlotte make a certain sense. There's a cleverness about him too: Vivy once mentioned he managed Spitfire factories during the war.

I suddenly realise I'd been expecting to meet the father who had so disappointed Vivy — a drunkard in thrall to ruthless Charlotte, wasting his life in a tropical hellhole — but luckily I don't have his daughter's weight of expectations. Pete's tanned cheeks may be a little alcohol-flushed, but his eyes are kind and shrewd.

'Do you help out here with Charlotte's orphanage?' I ask.

'That's her well-oiled machine, but I do what I can. A bunch of stern nuns actually run the place, but we try to apply pressure to keep it going in the local swamp of corruption.'

Charlotte comes in. 'Hello, darling. Hope you had a good rest.' She gets a drink from the trolley and sits down with us.

'I did, thank you,' I say. 'What a beautiful house this is.'

'French, of course. Some wealthy plantation owner wanted to pretend he was on the Place des Vosges, not Tu Do Street.'

Through the veranda doors the dim evening horizon is lit up with quick flashes, followed by a thudding roll of thunder.

'Oh, the storm's coming back,' I say.

'No,' says Pete. 'That's bombing out in the countryside. You'll get to know the difference.'

The old servant, Vinh, is laying the dining table at the other end of the room. I glance at the glinting cutlery, crystal glassware and gold-embossed plates, and Charlotte smiles. 'It came with the house, so we may as well use it.'

'I suppose it just looks incongruous,' I say. 'I mean — here, in the middle of a war.'

A man enters, but I can't see him clearly in the dim light. 'Does the war make the tableware incongruous, or vice versa?' he says.

He gets himself a drink and sits down. Charlotte reaches to a side-table and clicks on a lamp, and I realise the man is the Vietnamese chauffeur, André.

'Hello, sweetie,' she says. 'It'd be wonderful if my tableware could outshine anything, but I suppose war will always win. Now Claire, you met André briefly earlier. He's offered to help show you around till you find your feet.'

I'm not sure if I want anyone to show me around. I like to discover things for myself, but still, I'll need an interpreter, at least for a while. 'Thank you,' I say, and André nods.

In the lamplight his face has a European cast. Is he only half-Vietnamese? From his name perhaps the other half is French.

'André is our right-hand man,' says Charlotte.

Pete smiles. 'Originally our right-hand kid, in fact. When I got here in fifty-four the first friend I ever made was this little street urchin. How old were you then, André?'

'Thirteen I believe,' he says quietly. 'When my father fled to France in 1942 he took our *livret de famille*, our family documents. But before she died my mother told me I was born in 1940.'

'When I was setting up the orphanage I couldn't have done it without André,' says Charlotte. 'He knew everything.'

'Only from experience,' André says, shrugging. 'The authorities had sent me to so many by then.'

'*And* you'd run away from so many by then as well,' says Pete.

André smiles a little. 'I only stayed with you because you didn't try to stop me leaving. And your battles with bureaucracy made me feel almost sorry for you.'

Pete laughs, then a small gong sounds.

'Let's eat,' says Charlotte. We rise and move to the other end of the room. Pete sits at the head of the table, André opposite me. As Vinh pours the wine, Charlotte says, 'Heavens, when we first met André I'd been living in Vietnam for four years. I thought I had *some* sort of grasp on how things worked.'

'As a socialite, of course, tante Charlotte,' says André. 'As someone confronting the legal, medical, military and political ramifications of helping half-breed orphans — ah, you had no idea.'

Charlotte laughs and holds up her glass. 'Well, let us thank André for his patience, and welcome Claire to my incongruous table.'

We clink our glasses, and Vinh serves the food. I wasn't sure what to expect, but it's delicious. Meats, rice, unusual greens, with every flavour bright, crisp, savoury. No one says much except for the occasional murmur of appreciation.

As Vinh clears the plates Pete says, 'Was the meal as exotic as you'd feared, Claire?'

'I was a little worried it might be fiery, but it tasted wonderful.'

'We use chilli and powerful spices of course, in some dishes,' says André. 'But that would be unkind to a newcomer.'

'And to me,' says Pete ruefully. 'Don't have quite the iron constitution of years gone by.'

'Let's get comfortable,' says Charlotte. 'Brandy, everyone?'

We go to sit in the lounge area again. The armchair is soft and the muslin at the French doors rolls dreamily in the humid breeze. I sip the brandy and realise I'm still tired despite my nap.

'Do you hear much from Vivy?' says Charlotte, almost too casually.

'Now and again,' I say. 'She seems content in Amsterdam. Wonder if she'll stay there for good?'

'Mmm.' Charlotte sips her drink.

'Has she ever visited you here?'

Pete shakes his head. 'Took her a while to forgive us, and by the time we were on civil terms again she was well settled in Europe.'

'Think she'd be happy her divorced parents remarried,' I say. Damn, was that too tactless?

'The only thing Vivy really cares about is music,' says Pete wryly. 'And she was young then and expected different things of us.'

'God knows, we've both disappointed her,' says Charlotte, her eyes distant.

André is silent, his gaze on the pale moving curtains. I wonder how much he knows about the family? Probably everything, from the way Pete and Charlotte speak so casually.

And he called her *tante*, too, aunt Charlotte. Has André become the child who's not disappointed in them?

Through the French doors the night sky is edged with washes of light from the street below, the traffic noise an overwhelming rush like waves at the beach.

I yawn extravagantly and can't stop. 'Sorry, I'm just so ...'

'Off to bed, sweetie,' says Charlotte. 'Plenty of time to catch up tomorrow.'

∽

I'm amazed at how well I feel next morning. At breakfast Pete tells me André is waiting to chauffeur me to my bureaucratic appointments.

I need a visa from Immigration, to be renewed every three months, an accreditation card from Military Assistance Command Vietnam, MACV (which everyone calls mac-vee), and an accreditation card from SVG, the South Vietnamese Government. These are just the first of a ludicrous number of acronyms to become part of my everyday life.

André, in black trousers and white shirt, is waiting beside the car, apparently oblivious to the morning heat. He nods and we get in. As he starts the car he says, 'First, we had better get some passport photos for the cards. There is a studio not far away.'

As we drive through the bright, noisy streets I glance at him but he doesn't say anything. We stop outside a row of garish small shops covered in Vietnamese writing, and André takes me into one.

He speaks to the smiling middle-aged man, who poses me in front of a wall and takes photos, then goes into another room to develop them. I walk around the studio looking at the displays, glamour shots of Vietnamese women, young men in uniform, looking proud or stunned.

André says, 'After this we will go to JUSPAO and try for a MACV card.'

'JUSPAO?'

'Joint United States *something something* Office. They run the information service, psych operations, briefings, everything to do with the press. Ah, yes, the *something something* is Public Affairs. They are based in the Rex Hotel, just a block from Tu Do Street.'

The photographer comes back with my photos. I pay him then we go to the car. André says, 'The places we must visit are not too far apart, but you would find walking in the heat difficult.'

We park outside the Rex Hotel. I gather my handbag and briefcase (with copies of stories I've done for the Mirror) and we go inside. It doesn't look much like a normal hotel, because everyone is in uniform and there are guards at the doors.

'Is this MACV?' I say.

'No, just one office of it. It is actually based in a massive compound over near the airport. They call it Disneyland Far East. It is supposed to have twelve acres of office space.'

'Wow, that's big.'

'It is a big war.'

A man behind the front desk points us to a room down a corridor, with a sign stating Office of Information. Inside there are seats and a counter with a uniformed man behind it. He looks up at us.

'Ah. Mr Girard?'

'Sergeant Carter,' says André, a little surprised.

'And?'

'Miss Claire Fenn. An Australian journalist.'

'How do you do?' I say.

'And I suppose Miss Fenn here is seeking accreditation?' Sergeant Carter says.

'Yes,' I say. 'I'm an experienced journalist, and I'd like ...'

He smiles gently. 'Of course you would. So you're a stringer for AP? Or would that be UPI? Reuters, maybe?'

'Well, no. But ...'

Sergeant Carter sighs. 'André, you know I can't. Gotta be working with the big boys or no *way*. You know the drill. No cuties who just want to play intrepid journo.'

'But I'm not ...'

I'm stupidly flustered. I've never met a Black man before. Actually, a golden-brown and very handsome man who talks like someone in an American movie. (Of course he does! Get your wits together, Claire.)

'How did that happen?' says André, nodding at Carter's left arm, which I realise has a cast on it.

'Shrapnel. Why I'm grounded and going nuts in this place.'

'Come on, Larry,' says André. 'There must be some way.'

The sergeant shrugs, and after a moment says, 'Maybe try Ann Bryan, Nguyen Van Thinh street. Took on the Pentagon when they blocked *Overseas Weekly*, and won too. She's kind to strays.'

'I'm not —'

'Thank you, Larry. I owe you a drink.'

'Yeah? I'd probably wake up in the Hanoi Hilton.'

André laughs. 'True. But not if you paid for the drinks.'

'Then what's the point, man? Get outta here. Nice to meet you, Miss Fenn.'

'Thanks very much,' I say, though I'm not sure if he's been helpful or not.

∽

In the car, André says, 'That did not go very well. Let us try Immigration next and your three-month visa. It may be easier.'

We drive off and I say, 'Is Sergeant Carter a friend of yours?'

'Not close, but we get along. Usually Americans do not become friends with Vietnamese.'

'Why not?'

He glances at me. 'It could get them killed.'

'But what about the locals? The women in bars?'

'They are probably supporting half-a-dozen family members. They are not making friends.'

'But why would being friends with locals get soldiers killed? Don't the South Vietnamese support the fight against the North?'

We stop at traffic lights and André turns to me.

'Claire, you *do* understand that until thirteen years ago there was no such thing as *two* Vietnams? There was only one, and most people wanted their leader to be the man who'd fought the Japanese and freed them from the French. Only the corrupt — and the Americans — disliked that prospect, so they cancelled the elections.'

'Well yes, I heard they didn't go ahead, not sure why. I know people fled from the north —'

'The US spread the story they were going to drop nuclear bombs on Hanoi.' André says, half-smiling. 'Wouldn't *you* flee?'

We drive through the intersection. After a moment he says, 'Of course it is more complex than that. Most of those who left were Catholics. The Americans claimed they would be persecuted, and ferried thousands south on the US Seventh Fleet.'

'Really? Why?'

'To bolster their puppet, Ngo Dinh Diem, a very conservative Catholic. Diem held a referendum which he won decisively, with more than one hundred percent of the Saigon vote.'

'*What*?' I laugh.

'A touching display of the people's confidence, I agree.' André smiles. 'So Diem declared himself head of an independent republic, deposed the playboy Emperor whose loyalty lay with whoever paid him, and started persecuting anyone he deemed a communist — basically non-Catholics.'

'Buddhists?'

'And Confucians and Cao Dai. Eighty percent of the country.'

'But Diem's gone now, killed in a coup four years ago.'

'He was soon replaced by Thieu. I believe Ho Chi Minh said at the time, *I can scarcely believe the Americans would be so stupid.* It was certainly for the worst.'

As André parks the car, he says, 'Never forget, in Vietnam all families have their connections, north *and* south. And other than those who profit from the American war, everyone else simply wants to live in peace in their own united country.'

'Are you saying most people *sympathise* with the communists?'

'I am saying most people are Vietnamese, Claire.'

∞

At Immigration no one apparently speaks English, so I'm grateful André is with me. Two clerks flip though my brand new passport and ask André a lot of questions in a very unfriendly manner.

He turns and says, 'Claire, do you have your old press card from the newspaper in Sydney?'

I find it in my wallet and André hands it over. The clerks look at me, look at the card, and are finally convinced it's me. The visa is issued and suddenly everyone smiles and shakes my hand.

As we return to the car I say, 'What on earth did you tell them?'

'That you were not a communist and you are a real journalist.'

'Should we show my press card to Sergeant Carter then?'

'Sadly, Sergeant Carter has a much stricter definition of 'press,' and I am not sure the Mirror makes the grade. But I have suddenly had a thought — your old card might work for South Vietnamese Government accreditation. Let us try that.'

So off we go in the muggy heat to another large building. I try to look nothing like a communist, while André speaks to officials who stare at me curiously, then glue my photo to a card and laminate it. Again, once finished, there's happiness and handshakes all round.

After we leave, André says, 'They were pleased because much of the foreign press do not respect local accreditation requirements. But in fact this card may have its uses. Usually a MACV card is required to get into the US press briefings. But with this one you can get into the ARVN briefings, which take place just before the US ones — so you may be able to attend both.'

'Ar-ven?'

'The South Vietnamese army.' We get into the car and André gazes at me. 'I know you probably want to experience action, Claire, to jump into helicopters and report all the drama, but you are up against many other senior journalists. Yet here in Saigon, with an ARVN card, you may actually find some very good stories. A lot is decided here and much is overlooked.'

'I'm already getting a sense of that. Thank you, André.'

'Now,' he says. 'Remember Larry's suggestion? Nguyen Van Thinh is just off To Do Street. Let us see if Ann Bryan can help.'

He asks at a cafe in a cramped alleyway, then we climb to the second floor of a small apartment building. We knock and someone yells, 'Come in.'

Ann Bryan is typing quickly at a table stacked with books and papers. She's in her thirties, a clever-looking redhead with a generous smile. She says, 'Just gotta finish this off. Make yourselves comfortable and check out our last edition.'

She nods at a couch with a stack of newspapers beside it. It turns out *Overseas Weekly* is a tabloid with a lot of comic pages and bosomy girls not wearing much, but from the stories it's clear there's some serious investigative reporting going on as well.

Ann pulls a page from the typewriter and adds it to a pile.

'Okay, done. Now, who are you?'

'This is André Girard, and I'm Claire Fenn. I'm a reporter, but can't get accreditation.'

'Of course. MACV unhelpful?'

'Yes, though a man there suggested I talk to you.'

'You sound Australian,' Ann says. 'You know Kate Webb?'

'Yes, I am. I read her articles, she's great.'

'One of my stringers. But I can't pay much and MACV hates what we write. War profiteering, racial abuse, drugs, corrupt officers, whatever. The soldier's point of view, not the establishment's, so you won't get any brownie points working for me. But you might get some good stories.'

'That sounds great. I've got copies of my work here.'

She scans them, then looks up. 'Okay, Claire, not bad. Even if you can't get to war zones, a lot around here is worth reporting too.'

'Yes, and I've got an ARVN press card, so that might help.'

'Good. So there's something I've been thinking about —'

'I'll do it,' I say.

'Those half-American kids ending up in orphanages because their mothers can't support them and no one wants them. What's MACV planning to do about them?' Ann says. 'Write me a good article on that and we'll see.'

'All right,' I say, feeling breathless. 'Thanks, Ann. I think I can manage that.'

∽

'Of course I'll help,' says Charlotte over dinner. 'You can come and meet the nuns who run the orphanage, Maison Lien.'

'What does Lien mean?' I say.

'Lotus,' says Pete. 'Very pretty name.'

Charlotte smiles at him. 'Pete is being diplomatic. It's actually named after my late husband's illegitimate daughter.'

'Oh. Does she live here too?'

Charlotte shakes her head. 'She's dead. Louis was in Vietnam in 1945, long before we met. When we were posted here in 1951 he discovered Lien existed. The child was in an orphanage, neglected. She was a darling.' Charlotte sighs. 'But she died of tuberculosis. Louis was devastated and told me if he didn't return from the war I was to set up an orphanage in her memory. So I did.'

'But I haven't heard *anything* about this before! Do your friends, or Vivy, know about Lien?'

Charlotte shakes her head. 'Not really. Man-eating Charlotte makes a far more amusing tale.'

'And all quite true, of course,' says Pete affectionately. 'No, Claire, Vivy clings to her own black-and-white view of the world. And it was a long time ago anyway.'

'But it's a beautiful story,' I say.

'The reality is a little harsher,' says André quietly. 'Since the Americans came, corruption and inflation has destroyed much wealth, and even Maison Lien is struggling. As a prosperous Australian you may be shocked at the conditions there.'

'But what about government assistance? Or grandparents or relatives?'

'There is little kindness here for what they call bui doi — *children of dust*,' says André. I glance at him, a child of dust, but his face is still.

'Mixed-race babies are despised by most locals, you see,' Charlotte says. 'Ancestral Vietnamese lineage is all that matters.'

'And now, with thousands of foreigners here, rural life destroyed and few jobs for women, there are so many unwanted babies,' says Pete. 'It's a disaster. And we're running out of money.'

'The only asset I have left is Louis' *château* in France,' says Charlotte. 'And it's hardly a *château*, just a villa. It's rented out, but I have no idea of its state and Vivy's too busy to check. It'll have to be sold soon, though.'

'Oh,' I say, my face reddening. 'And here I am enjoying your lavish hospitality —'

Pete laughs. 'Dear Claire. The costs of this house and our life here are *nothing* compared to what's needed to support the orphanage, pay off the church hierarchy and keep the corrupt bureaucracy happy. Don't even let it cross your mind.'

'It's true, sweetie,' says Charlotte. 'Our life might look lavish, but the house is falling apart, the food is simple Vietnamese fare, and I suspect the servants only stay with us out of pity.'

'You are underselling this place, tante Charlotte,' says André. 'I certainly find it a calming refuge from the rigours of my job.'

'So you don't actually work here?' I say.

'Oh, no,' says Pete. 'André is employed by the South Vietnamese government.'

'Really? What do you do?'

'I am an interpreter for the Ministry of Culture and Education, although we assist other departments when needed.'

'But you're so *scathing* about the government.'

'I know them very well,' says André. 'Of course I am scathing.'

I laugh, and think what good company he's been today. He holds out his wineglass to mine, his hand fine-boned and brown, and we clink glasses.

I say, 'Well, thank you very much for all the inside information.'

'I barely touched the surface,' he says. 'I thought you would be horrified. Don't all Australians follow the US anti-communist line?'

'The government certainly does, but not everyone,' I say. 'A friend of mine jokes about his mother always saying, "Don't be *absurd*, Leo, Vietnam's a local independence movement, not the bloody communists against the world".'

'Good God,' says Pete, 'that's a pitch-perfect imitation of my sister,' and Charlotte laughs. 'Eliza hasn't changed a bit.'

'Your friend — Leo — is he an anti-communist, then?' says André.

'He's a conscript,' I say. 'I suppose he's fairly conservative. Soldiers usually are.'

∽

André is correct. I'm shocked at the state of the orphanage and the children. The building is old, peeling, dark and rundown, while the sight of the children is simply overwhelmingly sad. Although the nuns and a few young aides are doing their best, there aren't enough staff, and some toddlers are crying unattended, their faces grubby and forlorn.

Lined up on wooden benches, they eat a small lunch of rice and vegetables in tin bowls. Later they're seated en masse on potties, then briskly cleaned and sent out to play in a cement courtyard.

André murmurs, 'Look beyond the dirty faces, Claire.'

Just then, several children start laughing as they play, and I see a young helper hugging a boy who's fallen over.

'I'm hopelessly unfamiliar with kids,' I say. 'Are they truly all right?'

'Of course they should have more, but I promise you, this place is much kinder than some I have known. Those little girls with rag dolls? Their fathers were clearly black Americans. Without this they would probably be dead.'

'But what sort of future can they have?'

'Charlotte works closely with agencies to find them adoptive homes, in the US, in Europe. There are more lonely families than you could imagine, and some surprising success stories.'

The orphanage is on a busy street about three miles away from Tu

Do, in a ramshackle, two-storied building centred on the courtyard where the children play. When he's not at work André drives me over there to talk to the nuns, meet the children and read their sad histories of unwed mothers, foreign fathers and departed parents.

Now, in the evenings, Charlotte, Pete and André talk over what I'm writing and help make it stronger. But despite the often painful histories we discuss, André rarely reveals his own feelings.

I've never really known any Asian people before (Australia has worked shamefully hard to keep itself white), and at first André's looks, and the way they change in different lights, disconcert me.

He's taller than the local men, with greenish eyes and a mahogany glint to his black hair. One moment he appears remote and Vietnamese, then in an instant his laugh or expression is that of his French father.

I find I'm growing to like him. He drives me around, describes local customs, tells me amusing stories about scandals, Vietnamese and American. He also explains some of the history that helps make this country more understandable. I may have studied history at uni, but Asia's past was certainly not on our curriculum.

What I find most astonishing is how long the Vietnamese have been fighting for their independence. The Chinese invaded two millennia ago, and over one thousand years the Vietnamese fought them off. Then the French arrived in the eighteen-hundreds: it took a century to kick them out. The Japanese lasted barely five years. The Americans? In the face of such resolve, their swaggering confidence seems a little premature.

Over weeks I write and rewrite my orphanage story, and finally offer it to Ann Bryan, dry-mouthed with anxiety. But she likes it and publishes it and, to my joy, it's even picked up by the Australian newspapers. The tales of several children who'd found good homes were so touching, Ann asks me to do another article on that aspect alone.

'But not *just* the success stories,' she says. 'The whole picture, even the adoptions that don't work out. And the bottom bloody line: why don't the Americans do something about these kids? Why are private charities and Catholic nuns and Buddhist priests left to pick up the pieces?'

∞

To cope with the heat I wear mostly loose shirts, jeans and sandals, while Charlotte's hairdresser cuts my long wavy hair into a short urchin style, back off my face. The lady-like demands of my life at the Mirror — hats and gloves, for God's sake! — are now a world away and I couldn't be happier.

A couple of months of working and learning about this strange country pass by and suddenly Christmas arrives. We go to morning Mass at handsome old Notre Dame Cathedral, not far from Pete and Charlotte's place.

Pete grumbles, saying, 'It's absurd. Charlotte and I are lapsed C-of-Es. They'll probably throw us out. What about you, Claire?'

'Technically Jewish through my mother. André?'

'Sort of a Buddhist,' he says. 'So they won't have to throw us out, we'll just be struck down by divine lightning.'

But the day is peaceful. People smile and greet each other, the women elegant in long silk ao dai dresses, the men solemn in suits. I don't follow what's going on, but I stand with the others and hum along with the hymns.

Candles flicker in the warm air and the stained glass windows glow like scattered gems. They were made in France nearly ninety years ago and show a very European holy family, but I'm probably the only one who finds them incongruous.

I think about the many Christmases before this: the parties at Nikos and Billie's house, the old friends coming together every year. And of course I think about Leo, and kisses, and partings.

But seated now with André, Pete and Charlotte, in an Asian cathedral four thousand miles from Sydney, I feel myself surprisingly at home.

6.   JEN: SWEET SIXTEEN (DEC 1967-FEB 1968)

I can't believe another year has passed. Fifth form was okay. I'm still trying hard in Art and French, though my Science is slipping and Maths is a disaster. English? I used to be good at it, mainly because I read books *all* the time, but our new teacher dislikes me.

I suddenly grew quite tall, and the English teacher is short. It's unkind to think that's perhaps the reason, but it's hard not to. He looked so irritated the day he realised I overtopped him, and muttered something about giraffes.

Are grown-ups really *that* petty? He's pompous and smug too, or *I* think he is. But perhaps he realises that's what I think. I don't know! He just hates my essays and marks them down, but never explains what he doesn't like, or tries to help me do better.

My grammar and spelling are fine, but he says coldly that my essays are lazy and *immature*. He spends a fair bit of time with his favourites in the class — and he makes it obvious they are his favourites.

Perhaps I *am* immature. I turned sixteen last March, and there's that awful old song, *Sweet Sixteen and Never Been Kissed*. Just the thought of it makes me go red, because it's true.

Anyway, I'm learning everything I possibly can to prepare myself for the future. Dad got me a subscription to Petticoat magazine for my birthday, and now it arrives from London every week with useful articles like: *How to be a beauty in bed, How to throw a fondue party, How to get over a broken romance.*

It has pictures of amazing people too, like Twiggy, Michael Caine, Vanessa Redgrave, Jean Shrimpton, John Lennon, and Jimi Hendrix. And the *clothes*: silver lamé shirt dresses, velvet kaftans, Pucci prints, sequinned sleeves, soft ruffles, textured tights, and paisley — *pink* paisley!

So really, why should I care about horrible old school? The summer holidays are here, I'm free for six weeks, and best of all, we're in the Holden on the way to Sydney!

I flip through my latest Petticoat. *Is this the winter you'll wear red lipstick?* Red lip gloss? Yes, please. But curls seem to be in, which is a worry, though at least I'm blonde now.

Mum lets me bleach my hair, like most of the other girls at school, and it's grown long, with a heavy fringe. But I'm as thin as ever. Not trendy-thin like Twiggy, just embarrassingly thin.

Still, it's Christmas at last and soon I'll see Tibor again. As I go to sleep every night I imagine situations that might bring us together. Snowstorms. Cyclones. Unspecified disasters that encourage — that *demand* — human proximity.

I imagine how it would feel to have his arms around me. To have him kiss me. I wouldn't be so immature then.

∽

After dinner at Tina's tonight she says, 'What's the news from Leo? Still teaching soldiers at Singleton?'

'Not any more,' says Dad. 'A few weeks ago they transferred him to a small unit called Civil Affairs. They teach, do medical clinics, agricultural training, that sort of thing.'

'In Australia?' says Tina.

'No,' says Mum. 'Vietnam. He's on a jungle training course in Queensland at the moment. All the soldiers do that before going overseas, even the support services.' She sighs.

'The unit's quite small and Vietnam postings depend on someone being rotated out,' says Dad. 'That must happen fairly often. He'll find out his movements in a couple of weeks.'

We all move into the lounge-room, while the grown-ups chat over drinks and Rob and I watch *Bonanza* on TV, though we have to keep it turned down. I like Little Joe best, but Rob's favourite is the father, Ben Cartwright. I wonder if that's because Rob's never had a real dad?

At least he seems happier now he's at high school. He's getting taller and has longer hair, which suits him. Then the ads come on, so Rob and I get ourselves some orange juice from the kitchen.

When we come back to the lounge Tina says to Mum, 'How's Claire going in Vietnam? I haven't seen Klara and Yvonne lately.'

'She's well,' says Mum. 'We got a card from Charlotte and Pete. Claire's with them and getting a little work, though things are fairly quiet. They're all looking forward to the Lunar New Year holiday.'

Bonanza starts again, then after some wise advice from Ben Cartwright the episode comes to a satisfying conclusion, and we turn off the TV.

Tina and Mum are chatting about something that happened years ago at Tina's jazz club, and Tina opens a photo album on the coffee table and flips through the pages.

Mum says, 'Oh my goodness! Weren't we elegant then — remember Billie's emerald sequin dress? And there's Charlotte, the merry widow, dropped in to see Vivy sing.'

'Wasn't a widow for very long,' says Dad dryly. (Aunt Charlotte got married a lot of times.)

'Let *me* see,' I say, and wriggle beside Mum on the couch. The black-and-white photo shows a table at the club, people smiling at the camera. My parents are there, with Vivy, Uncle Pete and another man. Aunt Charlotte is in a dark lacy dress, and Mum, Tina and Billie are in sparkly gowns. Everyone looks glamorous in an old-fashioned sort of way.

'When was that taken?' I say.

Tina nods. 'Mmm, fifty-four. Not long before I became pregnant with Róbert.'

'But Vivy was so *young*,' I say. 'And already singing at your club?'

'Eighteen,' says Tina. 'But yes, that was early in her career.'

'Who's the man beside you?' I ask.

'Oh.' Tina's face changes but I don't understand her expression. 'That's Jimmy. Jimmy Kelso. My late husband.'

He's standing with his hand on Tina's shoulder, grinning and raising his glass to the camera. He's got light eyes, curly hair and a confident, cunning face.

'Wow,' I say. 'He's nothing at all like Rob!'

Tina shuts the album. 'Not much. Suppose Róbert takes after me.'

'But —' I say, puzzled.

Mum says, 'Time you kids were asleep,' and that's that.

In my bedroom I wriggle under the blankets and turn towards the narrow window, a half-moon in the sky, and ponder.

Rob's hair is thick and dark brown, as brown as his eyes. I thought Irish people were reddish or pale, but Rob looks European like Tibor, or Tibor's dad, Moshe Adler.

Oh! My eyes open. Could that be it? (I'm not ignorant, I'm a doctor's daughter and learnt the facts of life ages ago.) Could Mr Adler be Rob's *real* father, and the story about Rob being named after some mysterious dead friend is just a red herring?

But then I try to picture Aunt Tina and reserved Mr Adler in bed together and giggle. That's just silly. Of course they're old friends, but in love? Impossible.

Still, it's strange: why doesn't Rob look anything like blonde Tina or sly Jimmy Kelso? Why is he so like someone with Tibor's background? Then I'm happily sidetracked by thoughts of Tibor and soon fall asleep.

∞

Last night's photo album is still lying on the coffee-table. I pick it up for another look at the nightclub pictures. Fifty-four, Tina said, so that's thirteen years ago, when I was only three. Somehow it seems such a far-away, different world.

The clothes are dated but Mum's pretty, just the same as now, though Dad looks younger. Billie's like a model in her sequinned dress, Charlotte reminds me of Marilyn Monroe, and Jimmy Kelso is sort of handsome, but there's something about him —

Rob sits down beside me with a thump. 'Show me,' he says, and takes the album. He stares at the picture for a time, then turns the page.

'There's Vivy,' I say. 'Doesn't she look amazing?' My cousin, dramatic in the spotlight, is simply dressed in a black top, narrow trousers and flat shoes, her wavy chestnut hair cascading over her shoulders.

Rob turns the page. Another picture of Vivy at Tempo, but this time she's applauding the man who's playing the piano beside her, his eyes closed, lost in the music. Solid and middle-aged, he's got dark hair and deep lines bracketing his mouth. Funny, he reminds me ...

I glance in surprise at Rob, who gazes solemnly back, and slowly nods.

'Who's *he*?'

'My dead father, I think. My real father, László Richter. He was Hungarian, like Mr Adler. He's why I look the way I do and have my stupid name.'

'Wow.' After an awed silence I say, 'Do you mind that he and your mum weren't married?'

'I mind more that he's dead.'

'Jimmy Kelso's dead too.'

'I don't care about him,' says Rob. 'He had mean eyes.'

'That's just what I was thinking. But how do you *know* about this László?' Rob is an excellent sleuth, but this is still a pretty amazing discovery.

'One night I saw Mum looking at these pictures and she seemed really sad. A few weeks later a friend of hers was here and when Mum was out of the room I asked her about the man in the picture. She told me his name and said he'd died.'

'I'm so sorry, Rob. That must have been a shock.'

'It's okay. I'm glad I know. Parents always think they have to shield kids from everything but I expect she'll tell me about it when I'm older.'

∽

But now it's the Christmas party! As usual it's at Billie and Nikos's place and I'm in the trendiest dress *ever*. It has a layer of floaty voile in red, blue and white stripes over a white layer, and looks like a pastel Union Jack.

The sleeves are slightly flared, and the skirt is short. My shoes are white T-bars with little square heels. (Not from Mary Quant of course, but still pretty.)

Underneath I'm wearing a special bra, a slightly padded one. That's embarrassing, but my body is taking its own sweet time to change the way all the other girls have changed. The bra makes the dress fit perfectly and I suddenly don't look like a kid any more.

We cram into Dad's station wagon and head off.

My heart is thumping so much I can hardly breathe. The grown-ups chat about various things, then at last we're here. The sky is almost dark, the horizon pale gold, the stars just appearing. We haven't been to Sydney for a whole year, and I'm sixteen, and soon I'll see Tibor.

Hugs and kisses at the door, and Billie is wearing the most amazing long, drifty green silk kaftan. Nikos is laughing and saying something about Steve and Amsterdam, but I'm not listening. Inside, I quickly check the lounge but the Adlers haven't arrived yet.

In the kitchen I meet Claire's parents, Klara and Yvonne. I adore Yvonne, who's kindly and sort of untidy. Klara is small and white-haired. She only seems to think about literature so I'm never quite sure what to say to her.

I recall the conversation from the other night, and ask, 'How's Claire going in Saigon?'

'I worry she's not eating well,' says Yvonne. 'We send her money but she says she has enough.'

'I do not believe her,' says Klara, who has a faint accent because she's from Finland. 'She is so stupidly determined to be independent.' Klara sighs, turns away and pours herself a drink.

'I'm sure she'll be fine,' I say, listening as the doorbell rings.

Then come the voices I've waited to hear for so long: Mr Adler's deep, measured rumble. Mrs Adler's warm murmur. Devorah's light laughter. And there. There. It's as if I can hear the vibrations through the very soles of my feet. I smile. Oh, *Tibor*.

∽

Everyone gathers in the lounge room. Devorah lifts locks of my long blonde hair in surprise, and we laugh. I nod politely to the Adler parents, who are more interested in something Billie is saying, then let myself look at Tibor.

Suddenly the world settles into harmony. He gives me a hug and says 'Wow,' glancing at me in approval, and my neck goes hot.

'Hi, Jen,' says someone else: Asher, Tibor's scruffy little brother. He's part of the horde of course, a bit younger than Leo, but for some reason we don't usually talk much.

'Asher's just been sprung from gaol,' says Tibor.

'Really?' I say. 'I didn't even know you were in gaol.'

Tibor laughs. 'He decided to challenge the might of the National Service Act, so he's just spent three weeks in the brig at Holsworthy Barracks for not attending a medical. They didn't know what to do with him in the end, so kicked him out to consider his options.'

Asher has none of his brother's charm. 'Yeah,' he says, smiling briefly. 'The court wouldn't accept I was a conscientious objector. I'm going to appeal next year.'

'But what happens if the appeal fails?'

'Join the army or spend two years in jail. Hey Jen, where do they keep the drinks?'

'In the kitchen, of course. Come on,' I say, leading them next door. 'There's beer in the fridge. And red wine over there.'

Tibor pours himself wine while Asher takes out a bottle of beer, opens it and fills two glasses.

He hands me one. 'Here you are.'

'But I'm only sixteen. Well, nearly seventeen.'

'So?'

I glance at Tibor and he shrugs. 'You'll probably hate it.'

I take a sip. It tastes a bit like leather at first, but the second sip is nicer. 'Okay. Thanks, Asher. Anyway, my parents give me wine sometimes with meals. Mum says that's how the French teach their kids about drinking.'

Asher nods. 'See you later,' and ambles away. Some newly-arrived guests crowd into the kitchen talking loudly, putting plates of food on the table and pouring drinks. Mum sees the glass of beer in my hand and gives me a stern look.

'Jen, you go carefully with that, understand? And only the one, no more.'

'I will, Mum, just seeing what it tastes like, really.'

There's further hubbub as someone else arrives, but eventually the kitchen quietens down, as people return to the lounge room to chat and enjoy the view over the harbour. The kitchen has the same outlook as the lounge, and I go to the sink, sip my beer and gaze through the window. As the last few people leave the room I'm intensely aware Tibor is still here with me.

Reflections twinkle on the rhythmic bow-waves of a ferry as it leaves Rose Bay jetty and slides past Shark Island towards Watsons Bay. The distant Harbour Bridge is outlined with golden lights and the city glitters like a fairyland.

I sigh contentedly.

'What?' says Tibor, coming to stand beside me.

'It's just so beautiful. I *love* coming to Sydney and I love this house too. The nicest things that have ever happened in my life have happened here.'

I glance at Tibor and wonder if he knows what I mean.

He says, smiling, 'Same for me, Jenny-wren,' and lightly kisses the top of my head. I feel a shock all over my body, and deep inside a sort of tingling, like something both wicked and wonderful at the same time. I glance up at him, amazed.

His face is so close, and I can't stop myself from reaching out and holding his cheek. It's warm and smooth and hard.

'Jen?' he says.

Without thinking I press my lips against his smiling mouth. It feels even more wicked and wonderful: until Tibor steps back.

He clears his throat. 'Think that beer's gone to your head, Jen. You're not old enough to —'

'I *am* sixteen, Tibor,' I say, trying to control my voice.

'And I'm twenty-seven. You're a child. Come on, let's go and enjoy the party with the others.'

There's a silence. I look down. 'I'll be along in a minute.'

'Fine.' He pats my shoulder, as he would a child's, and leaves.

My legs almost give way with embarrassment. He knows. He *knows* I'm just a kid wearing a shameful padded bra, pretending to be mature enough to kiss an older man. I put down my glass and stare desperately around the room for escape. *There*, the door to the garden stairs.

I quietly slip outside and stumble down a few steps, then sit down suddenly and try not to think. No, Tibor, it wasn't the beer that went to my head, it was you. I groan.

'Are you okay?' Asher comes down the steps and sits beside me, and I shift away. He puts his glasses in his pocket and rubs his eyes.

'It's okay. I don't have designs on your body, padded bra or not.'

'*What*?' I gasp.

'Look, Jen, I understand the pressures on girls to fit in.'

I'm mortified beyond all human endurance, and hide my face in the crook of my arm and hiss, 'Go *away*, Asher.'

'You should say, fuck off, Asher.'

'Why?'

'It's more emphatic.'

'That's swearing.'

'Yeah. So say it.'

'Fuck off, Asher.'

'Come on. A bit stronger.'

'Fuck *off*, Asher.'

'Better.'

'Fuck *off,* you annoying *bastard*.'

'Now that's good.'

Suddenly I'm trying to swallow my sobs. Finally I manage to halt, sniffling. Asher offers me the tail of his baggy shirt to wipe my eyes.

I do so, then hide my face in my hands. 'Sorry,' I whisper.

'Sorry, too. I shouldn't have made that crack about your bra. You look really nice, you know?'

'But it's not *me*,' I say bitterly. 'I'm a child. It's just pretend.'

'Well unless you're a genetic weirdo, it's only for a short time.'

'I probably am. A genetic weirdo.'

Asher laughs and I lift my head. His eyes are as brown as Tibor's, but I'm glad to see they're not the slightest bit engaging or delightful. In fact, they're kind of sad.

'What was it like … when you were in the army gaol?' I say.

He hesitates. 'Not much food. Or sleep. They'd wake me every half-hour, supposedly to make sure I wasn't a suicide risk.' He laughs shortly. 'A few nights of that and I just about was. Anyway, I'm out now.'

'But what about next year?'

'I'll worry about that then. Come on, Jen, let's go back to the party.'

Asher stands up and returns to the kitchen, and with a sigh I follow him. I'm sixteen and *still* never been kissed. But at least I've given someone a kiss. Does that count?

∽

In early 1968 the Beatles release a record called *Magical Mystery Tour*. It's fine, but not as good as their others. Some of it's almost like vaudeville and *I am the Walrus* is just silly, but Linda loves it and plays it over and over on her record player.

We talk about what's going to happen this year in sixth form. Neither of us can believe high school will soon be over forever.

Poor Leo missed out on Christmas because he was in Queensland on some training course, but in late January he comes to Newcastle for a week's leave — pre-embarcation leave, which apparently means he's going to Vietnam soon.

When he arrives it's a bit of a shock. He has even more muscles than before, his hair is so short there's only a hint of curls on top, and he has new frown lines between his sun-bleached eyebrows.

He looks like a stranger, but then he grins and he's almost as he used to be, though not quite. He's calmer, for a start. And very serious. How serious I only realise next morning when I open the Herald and see Claire's name, with a story about orphans in Vietnam.

It's amazing to see 'By Claire Fenn, our Reporter in Saigon', but I don't have time to read it as Leo comes in, glances at the headline and grabs the paper from me.

He turns to our parents at the breakfast table and says, 'Is she *still* over there? It's been four bloody months. Why hasn't she come home yet?'

Mum says, 'Perhaps she's having a holiday of sorts.'

'No one in their right minds would have a holiday in Vietnam,' says Leo, and leaves the kitchen. Later I go to his bedroom, where he's lying on his bed, looking at the ceiling.

I ask, 'Are you okay, Leo?'

'Fine.'

'Will Claire be okay?'

'No idea.'

'What will you be doing in Vietnam?'

'No idea again.' He laughs in a tired sort of way. 'I'm in a unit called Civil Affairs.'

'Will you be teaching?'

'Didn't you pay the *slightest* attention last night when I was telling Mum and Dad?'

I smile and sit down. 'Maybe not. Tell me again.'

'Civil Affairs helps the locals out with clinics, farms, schools. So yeah, I'll probably be teaching English to Vietnamese kids.'

'You won't be on patrols and getting shot at?'

'No patrols, but ...' He shrugs. 'Australian forces are based at Nui Dat, fifty miles from Saigon, and it's quiet compared to some places. But you never know.'

'Will you see Claire?'

'Unlikely. Australian soldiers don't get leave in Saigon.'

'Oh, *Leo*.'

'What?'

'I'm sorry it's all such a mess. I wish we could go back to a few years ago when you only had to worry about surfing. And Shazza. Did you see her this time?'

'No. She's too busy with some plumber whose marble didn't get drawn.' He sighs. 'Yeah, sometimes I wish I was back then too. But everyone has to grow up, even little miss *blondie* here.' He reaches over and ruffles my hair.

'Leo!' I throw a pillow at him and for a moment he's his old self as he grabs it, laughing, and throws it back at me. But next day, when he's saying goodbye at Newcastle station, uniformed and efficient, there's no trace of the brother I used to know.

He rings us from Sydney just before they fly overseas. 'Look, it'll just be a teaching job in the countryside, I'll be fine,' he says. 'Don't *worry*. I'll write.'

Mum and Dad are pretty quiet for a few days after that. Still, if Leo says he'll be fine, then he should know.

∞

In amongst all this I start to wonder if sheer embarrassment is a trigger of puberty as yet unknown to science, because not long after that excruciating Christmas party my flat chest suddenly starts to blossom.

I'm able to wear my first real bra, soft hairs appear here and there, and I have a light, achy period. At long last I've become a woman!

Someone in my class holds a party and invites kids from another school. And in the dark I kiss, *properly* kiss, a boy who doesn't know me as 'surfboard' but as someone who has every right to wear a bra (even if it's only a 28AA).

The kiss is nice too, sort of warm and wet, with tongues involved, which is a bit of a surprise. It has a hint of that lovely wicked feeling, though nothing like the time with Tibor.

But best of all I've been kissed *before* I'm seventeen!

So perhaps Tibor was being wiser and kinder than I realised by holding back. Of course he shouldn't kiss a mere girl, that wouldn't be right.

But a woman, a real woman? Be patient, Jen.

7.   LEO: TU DO STREET (JAN-FEB 1968)

I've got one night free before the flight to Vietnam, so I meet Tibor and Asher at Tempo, but the mood is nothing like it used to be. Tibor's almost pompous, not his usual light-hearted self, and he's got some sleek lady lawyer, Ursula something, with him.

I ask how everyone was at the Christmas party and there's a bit of a strange pause.

Asher gazes at his glass and says, 'Jen was great, looked really modern and grown-up.'

'Jen?' says Ursula.

'Leo's little sister,' says Tibor, and finishes his whiskey.

'Hear anything about Claire?' I say as casually as I can.

'Not much, doing well in Saigon,' says Asher. 'Saw her story about orphans in the paper.'

'Yeah. So did I.' I take another mouthful. 'What about you?'

Asher glances at me. 'Had three weeks in Holsworthy brig for refusing to attend the medical.'

'Ah. Can't have been much fun,' I say, knowing full well the kind of bastardry he'd have attracted. 'You okay now you're out?'

'Strange how well you can sleep when no one wakes you every half hour.'

'I bet. So what's going to happen?'

'Applied for conscientious exemption, but the court appearance is months away.'

'And hanging over your head all the time,' I say.

'Yeah. So I'm just doing casual jobs now.'

'*Jesus*, Ash, you were the only one of us to get a decent degree,' I say. 'You should be in a post-grad course, not stuck in limbo.'

Asher shrugs.

'But you're in the army,' Ursula says to me, frowning. 'Why are you being so sympathetic to a draft-dodger?'

I say carefully, 'Because I know a fair bit about Vietnam, and it's not *that* great an idea for us to be over there. Besides, he's my mate.'

Asher grins. 'You just want me to buy the next round.'

'Sprung.'

The lady lawyer persists. 'Most Australians think conscription develops fine young men.' Her eyes flicker over Asher, with his scruffy hair and anti-war badges.

'Perhaps,' I say calmly. 'But getting killed won't develop much for anyone.'

'If Vietnam falls to communism, then all of Asia, *including* us, will fall too,' she says coldly. 'Surely that's obvious.'

'That point's been made once or twice. But I reckon Asia's a bit more complicated than a kid's game of dominos.'

'And how are your parents going, Leo?' says Tibor with a touch of desperation.

'Fine.' I hand my glass to Ash. 'Just a middy, thanks. Got a joy-flight tomorrow.'

He goes to the bar and Ursula says, '*Joy-flight*? Why aren't you out fighting for your country?'

'Just unlucky, I guess.' I stand up. 'See you next time, Tibor.'

I catch up to Ash. 'Forget that drink. Need sleep more.'

'Okay.' He thumps my shoulder gently. 'Hey Leo? As a certified military thug are you okay with me taking a stance against hegemonic fascist imperialism?'

'When you put it like that, mate, sure I am.'

He laughs. 'You know, sometimes I reckon you've got it harder than me.'

'Why?'

'I *know* what I believe in, so just grit my teeth and keep going. But you — I dunno — you see too many sides at once, and feel for them all.'

'Bloody lunatic, no one's ever said that about me. Of course I know what I believe.'

Asher's dark eyebrows go up. 'Yeah?'

'Don't raise those expressive brows at me, young man. Yeah.'

'Anyway, I'm just glad you're in Civil Affairs and not the infantry. Reckon at heart you're more of a peacenik than me.'

'Pretty-well disguised for a hippie,' I say, laughing.

'So when do you think you're going over there?'

'Ah.' I pause. 'Didn't want to spoil the mood, but actually I'm flying out tomorrow.'

Asher hugs me fiercely. 'Take care of yourself, you silly bastard.'

'Course I will. Just *please* don't ask me if I'm going to see Claire.'

'Absolutely my next question. So are you?'

'Dunno. Not a vacation, won't have time to socialise. Ash, dunno. Really.'

He nods. 'If you do, give her my love.' He grins. 'You could give her yours too.'

I shake my head. 'Bastard. Claire's not ...' I clear my throat. 'Well, got to get back. Good luck with the exemption. Hey, do you want me as a character witness?'

'No way. Don't need to land myself in even deeper shit.' He sighs. 'Come home soon, Leo.'

'It's just for a year. Won't be long.'

∾

Thankfully I don't have to suffer the gruesome farewells a lot of my travelling companions endure at the airport. Instead I have a good natter with my family on the phone before I go. Admittedly, when I hang up I have to blink away a few tears.

And then? After so long I just want to get *going*: and when the plane leaves the ground I feel as light as air. There's a brief stop at Darwin at about three in the morning, then Singapore comes next. We have to change our army shirts for plain white ones while we're there, some political thing.

We eat breakfast at Singapore airport, and watch the manicured air hostesses milling around. I didn't realise mini-skirts had got that short, but I'm not complaining. I haven't had sex since Shazza dumped me for the plumber.

Back on board it's still a long flight ahead.

There's about twenty of us and I'm seated with two other Civil Affairs men, Glen and Davo. They're both engineers and fascinated by drains, so a fair bit of chit-chat occurs about water-pumps, which I have no trouble tuning out.

In the afternoon we approach Saigon's airport, Tan Son Nhut.

The three of us stare out at the square miles of huts, hangars, vehicles and planes below: jets, transports, gunships, bombers, and row and rows of helicopters. What a display of power.

Our plane banks steeply as we approach for landing, apparently so we'll be less of a target to any watching Viet Cong. That whole idea seems pretty unreal until I notice glinting off water-filled mortar holes all around the airport.

Down the steps and into the heat. We're met by a movement control officer who takes us into the terminal and shepherds us through customs and immigration. Once that's done he checks his clipboard, and turns to us.

'Men, we had you down to catch Wallaby Two this afternoon, the RAAF Caribou to Nui Dat. But an engine blew out on the runway and they can't get spare parts for a day because of Tet. So it'll have to be Wallaby One tomorrow morning. You'll stay overnight at the airport, at the US transit facility Camp Alpha, and be brought back here tomorrow at 1000 hours. Any questions?'

Davo says, 'Ah, when do we get issued our weapons?'

'When you get to Nui Dat.'

'But is it safe without them?'

The officer shrugs. 'Things are quiet. Tet, the Lunar New Year holiday, has just started and everyone's busy visiting families and celebrating. Though they let off a lot of fireworks too, so don't let the racket make you jumpy. Anything else?'

'How far is it to —' I quickly unfold a piece of paper my mother had insisted I take '— Tu Do Street, District 1?'

The officer laughs. 'Jeez, five minutes in Saigon and already you want a bar girl?'

'I've got relatives living there, near the Caravelle Hotel.'

'Ah, where the journos hang out. About five miles from here, but you're not allowed to take leave tonight anyway, you're too new in country.'

'But isn't it safe?' says Davo.

'Not that fucking safe. Now, gentlemen, your truck's just outside to take you to Camp Alpha. See you tomorrow.'

⁓

The truck trundles from the terminal building along streets full of jeeps and transports, then into the Camp Alpha section, near the heliport.

We line up and are admitted, then a bored American corporal sends the enlisted men to large dormitories, and points us 'loo-tenants' to a row of small buildings. Mine has half-a-dozen double rooms. The man I'm sharing with nods, lies down and promptly goes to sleep.

I crash out for an hour as well, then wake up, not sure what to do. Mum had insisted, several times, I ring my aunt and uncle as soon as I get to Saigon.

We'd passed an officers' mess on the way to our billet so I get up and go back to see about using the phone. Aunt Charlotte answers, her voice throaty and low. We've never met but she's a legend among my parents' friends.

Seductive, determined, a force of nature itself, Mum once said, laughing. She's in her late fifties I think, but sounds younger. And sexier. She's the relative who was widowed at Dien Bien Phu, and famously seduced Uncle Pete and whisked him away to Vietnam.

(But maybe it was *re*-seduced, they'd been married before in the thirties. Or was it the forties? Keeping track of that generation's liaisons is bloody hard going.)

'Hello, Aunt Charlotte. It's Leo Bell. I'm in Saigon tonight —'

'Leo, how *marvellous*! Where are you, sweetie?'

'I'm at the airport, the transit camp. Mum said I should ring —'

'Leo, you just get in a taxi and come here. We're having a family feast. It's Tet, you know!'

'Yes, I know. But we're not allowed out on leave tonight.'

'Are you at Camp Alpha? Hut number?'

I tell her. 'Right, I'll talk to someone,' she says. 'Of course you'll get leave if you're coming to see *us*. Now, do you have the address?'

'Yes, I have it. But are you sure? Security might be —'

'Leo, it's *Tet*, the most beloved, sacred event in the Vietnamese calendar. No need to worry. Have you just arrived?'

'Yes, but I'm a bit tired —'

'Well, sweetie, tonight you certainly *won't* be,' she says. 'Now, don your gladrags, and wait a little while I sort things out.'

She hangs up and I'm left staring at the receiver, laughing in disbelief. Oh Mum, force of nature hardly comes near it.

I go back to the hut and have a shower and put on a light shirt and trousers. About twenty minutes later a US corporal knocks on my door. 'Sir, here's your leave chit. Curfew is at midnight. I'll take you to the main gate and you can get a taxi from there.'

'Ah, I only have Australian cash on me,' I say.

He hands me an envelope. 'You're authorised for a small amount of MPC, should be enough.'

At my puzzled look, he says, 'Military payment certificates. Monopoly money. Locals accept it for currency.'

He drives me in a jeep to the main gate, where small blue and white taxis are lined up. Off we go, and I sit back and shake my head in amazement. I didn't even have time to find out if Claire was around. Perhaps she's away taking notes in some hellhole.

Christ, I hope not. My heart thuds, although that's probably because we nearly collide with a ten-ton truck and then a rickshaw, as we career along leafy boulevards and through narrow streets with bright shops spilling onto the footpaths.

Thankfully we arrive in one piece, and when I get out of the taxi I can only gawp at Charlotte and Pete's house. It's three stories high, like a small palace with columns and decorations, with great pink arches of some tropical flowers. I knock at the carved timber doors and an old Vietnamese man opens it, and ushers me in.

'Leo darling, *welcome!*' Charlotte says, fluttering down the marble stairs in a red Vietnamese-style dress. Her skin is smooth and her blonde hair flows back off her face and down to her shoulders, rather like a mane.

When she hugs me, all warm breasts and musky scent, I have to remind myself she's my mother's age, for God's sake. Luckily Uncle Pete isn't far behind, so some handshaking and back-slapping gets me out of Charlotte's worryingly pleasant embrace.

I knew Pete when I was a kid. He's Mum's brother, though taller than her of course, and now greyer and heavier. Old photos show they were alike when young: slim, dark-haired and olive-skinned (I vaguely recall some Asian great-grandmother back in the family tree, but I always zone out when Mum talks about the old days).

All the time my senses are on high alert for a third person: and there she is.

'Hello Leo,' she says.

'Hi Claire. Good to see you.'

Good? Fucking idiot. Her pale blonde hair is now short, back off her face, almost boyish, but she's still a vision in a silky blue dress. I bound up a couple of steps to meet her, and she coolly offers her cheek for a kiss.

I oblige of course, my head spinning, then somehow we're upstairs and in a long, cool, colonnaded room facing the street. It's evening and candles are flickering around the room onto mirrors and potted trees, while lights glow from the street below.

'This is amazing!' I say.

'Yes, it is,' says Claire. 'I love it.'

I turn. 'But Aunt Charlotte, how on earth did you get me leave for tonight?'

'Just Charlotte, sweetie.' She shrugs lightly. 'Well, I know so many people here, and the US command can be *wonderfully* helpful at times.'

Suddenly there's a crackling rat-tat-tat and I go to grab my rifle, which of course is not over my shoulder. It's back in Australia and a new one, hopefully, is waiting for me at Nui Dat.

'Don't worry, it's only fireworks, Leo,' says Pete. 'They'll be going all night.'

'Ah. Letting off crackers in a war zone could cause the odd misunderstanding,' I say, my breathing returning to normal.

Charlotte laughs. 'Saigon's hardly a war zone, though of course there have been a few ugly moments. But the war itself is a long way from here. And thank God for that.'

'Absolutely,' says Pete. 'Now what can I get you all to drink?'

As we're settling into comfortable armchairs, Charlotte says, 'By the way, I've organised for André to take you back to the airport later. He's borrowed our car to visit some friends. We're all under midnight curfew at the moment, so he swears he'll be here by eleven.'

'Thanks very much,' I say, and have a swig of beer. 'André's your chauffeur?'

Pete says, 'He does drive us around sometimes, my eyesight's not what it used to be. But no, he's a good friend, an interpreter with the government. He's smoothed our paths over the years, and now he's assisting Claire.'

She nods. 'I couldn't have got my stories without his help. I've got a series coming out soon on ARVN, the South Vietnamese army.' (She calls them 'ar-ven' like a seasoned professional.)

'In combat?' I say, willing myself to stay calm.

She smiles wryly. 'No, Leo, not in combat, I'm still not accredited. A lot of them are based here — the US turned the defence of Saigon over to ARVN Rangers some weeks ago. They're mostly conscripts, poor kids from the country. Desertion is a big problem and corruption among the officers is breathtaking. And as for the way the Americans treat them —'

'How?'

'With their usual sensitivity towards other cultures. Accusations of laziness, cowardice. Somehow, in the US view, that's not connected with the lack of the training they'd promised.'

The old Vietnamese man and a young woman carry in platters of food and set them on the table. Pete goes over and hands them red envelopes. He says something and they smile and reply, then leave.

'New Year's money,' he says. 'Vinh and Thu are going home to their families now, so we're having a self-serve picnic on the roof terrace tonight. Everyone grab a platter.'

The food smells delicious — I'm starving, haven't eaten properly since this morning — and we carry it up one flight of stairs to a less ornate level.

'This was the children's floor,' says Charlotte. 'Quarters for the governess, school and play rooms. We've furnished a couple for guests, but it's a bit of a battle with the mildew. The roof leaks like a sieve in the rainy season.'

We climb one last flight of stairs, then step out onto the flat roof. It looks magical, like something from a story-book. Dozens of silk lanterns dangle above us, glowing red, pink and orange.

Waist-high walls surround the roof, topped with ornate urns and stonework and long creepers of jasmine. Pots of small yellow blooms sit here and there — 'Tet flowers, very special,' says Pete.

The table is set with shiny glasses and plates, and bottles of wine sit in silvery buckets of melting ice. We set the platters on the table and sit down to eat and drink, and it's probably the best meal I've ever had.

Around us fireworks crackle almost constantly but I start getting used to it. After eating we relax in wicker armchairs and sip brandy, gazing over the lights of the city.

The sky is dark as it's a new moon tonight (which is why it's Tet — I know that much at least). We talk about family and friends, while voices and laughter rise from the street below against a hum of traffic and the occasional honks of horns.

'So orient me,' I say lazily. 'Where's the airport, the river? Haven't the faintest idea where I am.'

'Metaphorically or literally?' says Claire.

'Both. You know me so well.'

She laughs. 'Well, we're facing south-west. If you go about four miles straight ahead you hit Cholon, the Chinese market district. Great for shopping.'

'And if you go left along To Do street,' says Pete, 'there are the big hotels where most of the journalists live and work. The Continental–'

'From *The Ugly American*?'

'Right. And the Caravelle. Between them, in an old opera house, is the National Assembly, the rubber-stamp for President Thieu.'

Claire says, 'The Rex Hotel's a block over, in that direction too. It's where they hold the daily US press briefings, the five o'clock follies — famous for the credibility gap between what they say and the truth.'

Pete says, 'Along Tu Do are the notorious bars as well, all the way to the wharves on the river. What else? Oh, about half a mile north there's the shiny new American embassy — most well-defended spot in Saigon we're told. See those lights? They're having a big party tonight.'

'And which way's the airport?'

'North-west from here, maybe five miles. And the Presidential Palace is about half a mile west too. So this is a great place to live. Central, lovely old buildings, busy city life.'

Charlotte stands, refills our glasses from the decanter, then turns and goes to the low wall overlooking the street. After a time she comes back.

'Speaking of busy city life, darling,' she says. 'Notice how quiet it's become?'

It doesn't sound very quiet to me, but both Claire and Pete listen intently. Pete goes to look at the street as well, and when he sits down he's puzzled.

'Odd. This is nothing like Tet in previous years,' he says. 'A lot less noise and traffic.'

'And fewer people around too,' says Charlotte slowly.

'Do you think it means trouble?' I say. 'I thought there was a cease-fire.'

'There was, but this morning the Viet Cong attacked in the central region, so it was called off,' says Claire. 'All US units are on alert, though not many are based around Saigon. Most are up north, protecting the marines at Khe Sanh.'

Charlotte says drily, 'General Westmoreland is utterly convinced that'll be the next Dien Bien Phu. Someone should tell him he's not fighting the last war.'

'Claire, didn't you say Saigon's being protected by ARVN Rangers?' I ask.

She nods. 'But it's Tet, so a good half of them are on leave.'

'Come on, this is a sacred holiday,' says Pete. 'Just as much for the North as here. They'd have to be crazy to break such a tradition.'

'Or clever,' says Charlotte, ashing her cigarette.

Claire says thoughtfully, 'Yesterday at Cho An Dong market I noticed something odd. Quite a lot of young men. Healthy young men in everyday black pyjamas.'

'Why is that odd?' I say.

'With conscription, young men are almost always in uniform, police or military. Most civilian males in Saigon are older or disabled.'

'What — you think they're Viet Cong, planning to attack?' I say.

Claire shrugs. 'How could they possibly do that without tanks and artillery? No, perhaps they *are* insurgents, but they've come home to celebrate Tet like everyone else.'

'*Really*?' I say.

'They have family and friends here, this is their home. They might want a different government and a reunited country, but then so do most Vietnamese.'

She smiles at my expression. 'You look how I used to look when André first explained this to me.'

Charlotte glances at her watch. 'Speaking of André, it's eleven-twenty already and he said he'd be here by eleven. Unlike him to be tardy.' She looks at me. 'Leo, I think we'd better put you in a taxi, or you won't get back to the airport before curfew.'

'That late already?' I say. 'Wow. What a great night.'

'Come down to the street with me,' says Claire. 'Should be able to pick up a taxi.'

I thank my aunt and uncle, and promise to see them again when I'm next in Saigon, then Claire and I hurry down three flights of stairs to the street.

The traffic is surprisingly sparse, and no taxis go past. We walk towards the big hotels and there are none waiting there either.

'I suppose everyone's grabbed them in a rush to get home before curfew,' Claire says. 'Let's go the other way, we might find one.'

But no taxis. Claire checks her watch, and says, 'We'd better get back to the house now, it's ten to twelve. The white mice, the police, are pretty much shoot-now, ask-questions-later kind of guys.'

After a few steps I say, 'Claire? Have you forgiven me yet?'

'What for?'

'Trying to tell you what you should and shouldn't do.'

'Oh *that*. Yes, all is forgiven.' She smiles. 'It was the best incentive I ever had to push me into coming here. Thanks, Leo.'

I laugh. 'Don't mention it. And are you happy here?'

'Ecstatic. I'm learning so much, and writing good stories too.' She gazes at me. 'You?'

'Happy's not quite the word. Look, I'm well-trained and going to a fairly quiet part of the country. Hopefully I can do something useful there as well. I guess we'll see.'

We reach Charlotte's house as tolling bells mark midnight. 'That's Notre Dame Cathedral, just up the road,' says Claire, closing the tall carved doors behind us.

Pete and Charlotte are in the salon on the first floor. 'No luck with a taxi?' says Charlotte. 'Strange. And André hasn't rung, either.'

'Want some coffee?' says Pete.

'No thanks. I'm not sure what to do. Should I phone Camp Alpha?'

'No need,' says Charlotte. 'I'll give them a quick call. Sleep here and just turn up in the morning.'

I'm surprised. 'That's pretty relaxed of them.'

Charlotte shakes her head, laughing. 'Sweetie, you have no idea. Now, you can stay in the guest bedroom upstairs. It's got towels and razors and whatever. Claire will show you. Our suite's downstairs, so tell me if there's anything else you need. Otherwise we plan to sleep like the dead after all that lovely wine.'

∽

I follow Claire upstairs, unsure of what to say. Or think. This evening Pete and Charlotte were a buffer between us so I could pretend everything was easy and normal.

But all the time I'd been aware of her. How could hair cut as short and wild as an urchin's be so pretty? How could a dress covering her body to the neck be so seductive? How could anyone's *eyes* —

'I've got the governess's room,' says Claire. 'It has its own bathroom, all 1920s plumbing, but it works. Here's the guest room, and there's a fancy Art Deco bathroom just down the corridor.'

She opens the door and turns on the light. 'Ah,' she says. 'Pete mended that leak, but apparently not well enough.'

The bed, bed-covers and rug are dark with mould and the place smells like a swamp. Claire switches off the light and we leave, closing the door on the mess behind us.

'Look, I'll sleep on a couch in the salon downstairs,' I say.

'There isn't a couch in the salon, it's all armchairs,' says Claire. 'May as well stay here and crash with me.'

'Are you sure? I don't want ...' I'm perfectly aware she likes to keep her distance from me.

'Let's consider it my contribution to Australia's war effort.' She smiles wryly. 'Couldn't be any worse than that time we went camping with Asher and Jenny, all squished together in the tent.'

'Not sure I'm up for telling ghost stories at midnight,' I say. When we went camping we were only kids, and even then I found Claire's presence disturbing.

She shakes her head. 'Honestly, Leo, no need to look like a maiden aunt. I'm hardly going to ravish you.' I smile as she opens her door. Luckily the bed in question is a double and looks welcoming and incredibly comfortable. I try to stifle a yawn.

Claire says, 'You use the other bathroom and I'll get ready here.'

When I return she's changed into a long silk wrap that covers her from feet to neck and still makes her look desirable beyond human endurance.

She gets in the bed and pulls a sheet over her. I sit on the other side, remove my shoes, and lie back, fully dressed.

'Good-night, Leo,' she says and turns on her side, away from me.

'Good-night, Claire.'

Soon her breathing is soft and regular. I stare at the faint outlines of the ornate ceiling above us, and think, just twenty-four hours ago I was in Singapore, and twelve hours ago I was on a plane approaching Vietnam, and six hours ago I was on a magical Saigon roof-top, and right now I'm in a bed with Claire asleep beside me, and I've never been happier in my life.

A couple of hours later I come slowly awake. Claire is facing me now, asleep. Faint light through the curtains shows the curve of her cheek, her fair brows, her soft lips. I gaze desperately, trying to memorise every line of her face, knowing it's impossible.

Perhaps my breathing changes, perhaps it's just the intensity of my stare, but her lids flicker and she slowly opens her eyes. A beam of light shows the sea-blue of her irises, calm and reserved.

'Claire,' I whisper. 'I'm *really* sorry I didn't keep in touch. I'm a fool. You mean so much —'

I feel rather than hear the explosion, like a shudder through the room. Then two more, louder. Far away a crackling begins, and continues. I try to hear it as fireworks, but know perfectly well it's not.

We sit up. 'What, *where*?' says Claire.

Another run of gunfire and explosions. Shoving my shoes on I say, 'I'm going to the roof.'

She grabs some slippers and follows me up the stairs and outside. We try to see where the noises, and now flashes of light, are coming from. 'North, not far away,' says Claire. She gasps. 'The American embassy! Or the British perhaps.'

'Not sure anyone gives a damn about the Brits,' I say. 'So …'

'So.' We stare at each other.

Suddenly flares light up the sky, then slowly turn and fall. To the north-west, where the airport is, vivid flashes are followed by rolling explosions.

Gunfire rattles through the night between more bright lights — mortars, artillery? Here and there all over the city gunfire starts and stops, with an occasional whoomp of explosives.

'Holy shit!' My heart is thudding. 'I need to get back to the airport.'

'You can't,' says Claire. 'No transport till morning.'

'Do you have any weapons here? Even a pistol?'

She shakes her head. I put my arm around her shoulders and hold her, her heart beating as quickly as mine. We stand, stunned at the mayhem.

Pete and Charlotte come on to the roof beside us and watch in silence. Helicopters are thudding near the embassy now, and streams of bright tracery are flowing upwards to attack them from the ground.

Charlotte whispers, 'Dear God.'

A loud batch of gunfire and explosions starts in the direction of the airfield, but a lot closer.

'Presidential Palace? Maybe ARVN headquarters?' Claire says breathlessly.

Pete clears his throat. 'We shouldn't be here, out in the open. Come downstairs, safer there.'

We follow him to the salon, and Charlotte goes to make tea. We sit down but I can't relax. Christ, I need to get to the airfield.

We drink tea, as the gunfire and explosions become more intermittent, then only occasional.

Charlotte says, 'Right, let's go back to bed. You too, Leo, there's nothing to be done till sunrise. You were travelling all day yesterday and you must rest.'

Claire and I return to her bedroom. We lie together easily now, her head on my shoulder, our arms around each other.

'Don't you think you should, perhaps, go *home* soon?' I say, without much hope.

She laughs softly. 'No.' She looks up at me and again I'm struck by her calm blue gaze. 'Oh, Leo, I'm just getting started. And I love this place, I love Saigon.'

'Well, right now it's a bit too exciting for my taste.'

'You don't know how things will be where you're going, either.'

I sigh. 'Guess not.'

'Come on, slippery eyes,' she says. 'Get an hour or two of sleep. You'll need it.'

She hardly needs to prompt me. Breathing the scent of her hair, I slide again into sleep.

∽

Claire wakes me, holding a cup of coffee and a plate of bacon and eggs on a tray. She's unfortunately already dressed, in sensible war-correspondent-type shirt and jeans.

'It's seven,' she says. 'André will drive you to the airport. Things are quieter now.'

'He's arrived, then?'

'Yes. Flat tyre last night and his friends' phone wasn't working, so ...' She shrugs and leaves.

I eat, grateful for the food, wondering what lies ahead today. Soon I'm washed and ready, and meet Pete and Charlotte at the bottom of the staircase.

'*Darling* Leo,' says Charlotte. 'It was lovely to see you, despite the fireworks. Now *promise* —'

'I promise. Next time I'm here. But haven't the foggiest when that'll be.'

'Take care of yourself, boy,' says Pete. 'Only nephew I've got after all.'

They hug me, and Claire comes down the stairs behind them, smiling brilliantly as one of the tall carved doors opens and light floods the hallway.

I turn and Pete says, 'Ah, André, meet our lad, Leo. Leo, André.'

The man holds out his hand and I shake it, distantly registering that he's part-Vietnamese, well-built, and darkly good-looking.

André says, 'Welcome, Leo, to the Year of the Monkey.'

'What are Monkey years like?' I say.

'Erratic, changeable. They suit gamblers and risk-takers.'

'Sounds about right,' I say. 'Look, we'd better go.'

André nods. 'Some civilian traffic is around now, so we should be fine.'

Claire gives me a quick hug. 'Good luck, Leo.'

I glance at her, understanding at last the reserve in her eyes. Her smile on the stairs had not been for me.

∽

André drives well, skirting quickly around damaged cars, piles of fresh rubble and roads blocked with hard-faced ARVN soldiers. I don't even have to ask myself what she sees in him, it's pretty obvious.

Me? I'm just the guy she keeps at arm's length. Don't know why, really. I'm fairly ordinary, but maybe that's it. Claire is anything but, and she deserves a man to match her. This one? Christ, for all we know he could be Viet Cong.

That 'flat tyre' last night sounds pretty suss, for a start. Maybe he was out helping his VC mates instead. Lately some high-level South Vietnamese officials have turned out to be Northern agents, so what are the odds for a good-looking smooth-talker who can move easily between the allies and the locals? Perfect for the job. I'd hire him myself.

The sounds of shelling and gunfire are louder as we approach the gates of the airport. The car stops and I say curtly, 'Thanks for the lift,' and get out. André looks as if he wants to say something then nods and drives away. *Look after her, you bastard*, I think.

I show my ID at the gate and jog to the Camp Alpha entrance, show my ID again, then find yesterday's billet. It's only eight, so I have an hour's snooze, change into my uniform, pack, and try to find transport back to the RAAF muster point.

I hitch a lift with an American jeep and the driver says excitedly, 'VC attacked the airfield last night but they're being beaten back.' There's a series of rumbling explosions, and the driver says, 'Hear that, Aussie? We're getting 'em! Okay, entry's just over there.'

I thank him and carry my pack through the massive, busy terminal to the meeting point. Other men from yesterday's flight assemble near me. Just before ten o'clock a movement control officer checks our names and sends us out to the loading area and a waiting RAAF Caribou.

We file up the wide rear ramp and buckle ourselves into canvas and webbing seats along the sides. It's a snug fit, because stacks of boxes and mailbags are already tied down along the centre line of the plane. A few quick words between the loadmaster and the pilots, crackling instructions over the radio, and we're backing away between rows of other planes.

The explosions in the distance barely match the racket of roaring propellers, whining jet engines and thwacking helicopters. So *many* transports, gunships, choppers, bombers and jets are loading, unloading, landing or leaving the airfield.

The place is as busy as a hornet's nest and feels just about as hospitable too. Metal patches cover bullet holes in the Caribou's fuselage and there's armour plating around the cockpit seats. No armour plating around us, though.

Suddenly we're out on the strip, accelerating and taking off steeply in a ridiculously short time, the Caribou speciality. The gaping rear entry ramp of the plane is left open (I find out later for a fast exit), so takeoff is pretty anxiety-inducing and I'm not the only one clutching my seat.

We level out and I stare at the river below curling through Saigon; curling past the wharves at the end of Tu Do Street.

Then we're over a gold and green patchwork of fields and roads and trees, and only about twenty minutes after takeoff we're descending in a tight spiral towards Luscombe Field at Nui Dat. With a thump we're down and being told to get out, fast, and over to the terminal shed. Holy shit. I'm here.

∽

I'm met by Mick, the Education Officer I'm replacing. He takes me to our quarters near the centre of the Nui Dat base, not far from the airstrip. For now we're sharing a tent.

We eat at the mess then go to a briefing from some pretty serious-looking officers. It turns out the fighting I saw in Saigon last night was just the start of something big.

The CO says, 'We're getting reports of Viet Cong and North Vietnamese Army attacks on hundreds of place all over the country. They're calling for the people to join them. Fortunately most of the people have gone to ground instead, and ARVN and US forces seem to be beating them back almost everywhere.'

He nods to his deputy, who says, 'They also attacked Baria early this morning. HQ sent in two platoons, but we're getting reports that forces are larger than estimated. Until the situation is clearer, for the time being Civil Affairs activity will cease and personnel remain here. We'll update you tomorrow morning.'

Back in our tent I ask Mick about Baria. 'It's actually Ba Ria, but lazy bastards don't even try for the Vietnamese name. It's the nearest largish town, about five miles south-east of here. Pretty peaceful, good for food, souvenirs and getting your laundry done.'

'Is that where I'll be teaching?'

Mick nods. 'One of the high schools there. Lovely kids, hardworking, shy, earnest. But very much the French style of education — silence, rote word-lists, old textbooks, so I've tried to make it a bit more interesting. Got the kids singing along to my records, mainly folk songs, Bob Dylan and Peter, Paul and Mary. The Doors and Jimi Hendrix aren't exactly hummable.'

I smile. 'Okay. And the Viet Cong?'

'They're here, of course, especially in the Long Hai hills near the coast, about ten miles away. But they don't bother Civil Affairs. The word is that they think we're harmless and a bit stupid.'

Over the next few days about twenty Australian soldiers are wounded. They defeat the guerillas in Ba Ria, but during further skirmishes three of our men are killed. It's a pretty sobering introduction to the place. There's a lot of noise too from planes and choppers at the airfield, distant artillery and mortar fire, and the rumbles of B52s bombing the Long Hais.

Poor old Mick is champing at the bit to return home but has to show me the ropes first, so two weeks after I arrive things are quiet enough for us to go to the main high school, Chau Van Tiep.

I'm amazed when we drive in an open jeep with only our rifles for protection, but Mick just shrugs and says, 'If they wanted to get us they would have by now.'

On the outskirts of Ba Ria I'm appalled to see enemy bodies lying out in the open, rotting and covered in blowflies, and stinking worse than I ever imagined was possible. Rats scuttle as we pass and thin, mad-eyed dogs lurk in the grass. Apparently it's ARVN practice to leave the bodies exposed as a horrifying object lesson.

It's a massive relief when we get to the school in the centre of town. I will myself to stay in focus. Mick introduces me to the staff (my barely-adequate French helps here) and I finally meet some of the kids I'll be teaching. As promised he gets his choir to perform, eight shy teenaged girls in white dresses who look, and sing, like angels.

Still, I'm quite unprepared when they start the old folk song *Five Hundred Miles*. My throat contracts, my eyes blur, and I swallow fiercely and gaze at the ground, and hope no one notices. That night I deliberately down a few extra beers to forget, but lie awake, haunted.

If you miss the train I'm on, you will know that I am gone
You can hear the whistle blow a hundred miles
A hundred miles, a hundred miles, a hundred miles, a hundred miles
You can hear the whistle blow a hundred miles
Lord, I'm one, Lord, I'm two, Lord, I'm three, Lord, I'm four
Lord, I'm five hundred miles from my home

Oh, Christ. Claire's only fifty miles away, not five hundred, you maudlin fool, but even if she were lying here beside me she'd still be unreachable: mind, body and soul.

And after today — and those dreadful, unforgettable corpses — I can hardly remember what home feels like.

8.   Vivy: Paris in Bloom (Apr-May 1968)

The winter and early spring of 1968 is glorious: for me. The rest of the world is apparently in upheaval. Stav loves politics, so I get to hear about the sleazy presidential candidates, the endless student protests, the horrible murder of Martin Luther King, and of course, Vietnam (*always* Vietnam).

Stav watches TV from his rumpled bed sometimes, annoyingly, over my shoulder. And yes, King's death was in April, so what began as an autumn adventure has continued until spring. Not what I'd expected, and it's affecting me more than any fling should.

To my further annoyance, that dissatisfied yearning from our first relationship is slowly returning. But the Vivy of today is far more reserved and cynical than young, starry-eyed Vivy, and I manage to keep my cool.

Oddly, at the same time Henk and I are getting on wonderfully. In fact, after months of disengagement, we've just resumed our love-life. Luckily I don't yearn for Henk, I simply enjoy his easy charm and good-natured support. Perhaps in some primitive way I'm reasserting my rights as a wife — or perhaps I'm simply steeling myself against Stav's departure?

From Henk's side, I'm glad to hear Nina is starting to bore him.

'I have done *everything*, Vivy,' he says from our bed, as I get up to wash. 'I made her a record and it does okay. What more can I do? She is lazy. She wants me to be her *manager* now. No. I cannot.'

He leans against the pillows and lights a cigarette. I return from our tiny en-suite, pulling on a silk kimono that's cool against my skin, and sit on the side of the bed.

'Of course, being a manager's a totally different thing from your record business,' I say. 'Look how hard poor Lucien had to work over the years.'

'Is he enjoying his retirement?'

I nod. 'But I still desperately need a new manager. Another thing to worry about.'

'Do not concern yourself, lieveling. We will find you someone, and I will keep looking after your affairs until then. I promise, you are the *only* one I would do that for.'

'Thank you, darling.'

Henk taps his cigarette in the ashtray. 'And you, Vivy? Your little adventure has gone on for quite a while. Should I be worried?'

'Stav will be gone soon. No.'

'Ah. Let me hold you, darling.'

After a time I say, 'Perhaps ... when things get back to normal, we could think about — you know — finding out why I can't have a baby and getting it fixed. And then? It could be a whole new chapter in our lives, Henk.'

He chuckles. 'Dear Vivy, what a mother you would be. But it is not the right time.'

I sit up and he pushes back the blankets and gets out of bed. His fleeting expression, before resuming his usual geniality, tells me he'd prefer no new chapters in our lives at all.

'Oh?' I say. 'Not the right time because of ... the business?'

'Such a worry to me. Let us talk about it next year. Not so far away!' He goes into the en-suite and closes the door. I recall him saying, *I love our life together, just as it is.*

He wants nothing to change between us, including a child. But would I really want one in the first place? I'm not sure. I'm not sure about Stav, either. How will I feel when he leaves? And that foolish, elusive sense of yearning catches in my throat again.

∽

A week later I realise my period has not occurred on schedule — and suddenly recall it didn't appear a month ago either, when my only bed-partner was Stav. I'd put the missing period down to life's turmoil and too many late nights, but twice in a row?

Oh dear. I *feel* perfectly normal. I haven't had much of an appetite but I'm not a big eater, it interferes with singing. Now I notice my breasts are tender too. I sit down slowly on my bed. If I am, what on earth will I do? It's one thing to have adventures, it's another to bring a little cuckoo home to my marriage nest.

If Henk doesn't want his own child, he's hardly going to want another man's. Although technically illegal here, medical abortions are available, and they've recently become legal in Britain: I have options at least.

Yet that leaves another possibility.

Would Stav welcome a child? We've never discussed it, apart from my lofty declaration at eighteen that I'd never let mere pregnancy interfere with my career.

And if Stav wanted a child — wanted *this* child — would I go with him then to London, or Berlin, or wherever? I'm thirty-one, at the peak of my talents. What about *my* career?

I dress and go out to the kitchen. I'll have some breakfast I think, then feel suddenly ill. *No*, I tell myself, no, no, you're talking yourself into it. Look, maybe just a cup of tea. My gut relaxes. I vaguely recall 'dry biscuits and a cup of tea' as the remedy for nausea. What a prospect.

I cautiously sip the tea, and it stays down. All right. Just carry on as usual. Practise vocal exercises. Go for a walk. Buy the newspaper. Read letters.

Coming back from my walk I gather the mail, then put the kettle on. This is fine. I'll be able to figure out something. I check the letters. A couple of bills, something from my father.

Darling Vivy,

I hope you're well and happy. Things here are rather difficult as the orphanage is in difficulties and we've exhausted most of our funds. The church and government agencies are indifferent, surprisingly so, given the bribes we've paid them over the years.

I know you've always assumed we're well off. Sadly, no longer. The only asset we have now is Mi-Côte, the villa in Normandy, but we've received no rents from the agent for six months.

He's not replying to our letters or telegrams either. Darling girl, I know your life is full and busy, but I can only beg you to take a few days off, go to France and find out what's happening there: and see what needs to be done to prepare the place for sale as soon as possible. We have no other option. If you can help us, my dear, please do so.

All our love, Dad and Mum

I rub my face with both hands. Not *now*, Dad! Then after a time I sigh and think, Don't be a selfish cow, Vivy. It sounds as if they're desperate, and I've put off doing this for ages.

Actually, the timing isn't too bad right now. Geert is closing Het Tuin this weekend for some repairs, so I suppose that would free me to go to France. And the trip itself might be a nice change. What to take? Spring is still cold. My green coat?

I groan. Stop mentally packing your suitcase. And stop avoiding the real problem.

∽

That afternoon I visit Stav's flat. He's playing a short phrase on the piano with variations.

'I think I like it better in the minor key,' he says. 'What about you?'

I sit on the lounge and listen as he plays it again. Lately I could hardly avoid learning a lot about Stav's music, but I've enjoyed it. It's a long way from jazz but it adds to my own understanding.

'Yes,' I say. 'That's more open. Unfinished.'

'Exactly.' He smiles. 'The final section of something I'm working on. Called *Winter 1968*.'

'Unfinished, eh?' I say drily.

'Between us? I can't see an ending now, Vivy. Ever, to be honest.' He comes to sit beside me. 'I've decided to take the Berlin job. More opportunities for me — and if you wanted to come, it could be a career boost for us both.'

'I thought we'd agreed this was simply an adventure.'

He nods. 'But it's too hard to imagine ending it now. Let's not. Come with me.'

'Heavens, that's ...' My heart is thumping. 'Stav, there's something I wanted to ask you.' I take a breath. 'How would you feel, perhaps ... about us having a baby?'

'Wow. That's a bolt from the blue.' He shakes his head. 'Impossible. We're still young. How on earth could we deal with a child? And what about your career?'

'Thirty-one and thirty-four. We're not that young, Stav.'

'You've never said anything like this before. Why now?' He stares at me. 'You're not … you *couldn't* be. You're on the pill. What the hell's going on?'

I shrug. 'I think I am. Probably six, seven weeks by now. And no, I'm not on the pill, I'm supposed to be infertile. That's what the doctors said, anyway.'

'Pretty stupid doctors, then,' he says shortly, and gets up and sits again at the piano, now a barrier between us. 'I just want you to stay the same, not lob a bombshell into our lives. A *baby*? Christ.'

'Funny, you sound just like Henk. Maybe I only attract men incapable of new directions.'

There's a long silence, then Stav says carefully, 'Look, maybe we could think about it. When we're more settled? But not *now*, Vivy.' He leans forward. 'The sensible thing is to have a quick, safe medical procedure, and perhaps later, when …'

He's as ruthless as ever, but it's basically what I've decided to do anyway.

'Okay. Makes sense,' I say. 'Now you've decided on Berlin, what's the timetable?'

He's surprised. 'Well — ah, leaving in about a fortnight.' He gazes at me. 'I hope this doesn't change — I hope you'll still think about coming with me, Vivy. I do love you.'

'Of course, darling. But listen, my parents *desperately* need me to dash off to France for a couple of days to sort out their house. I thought I'd do it this weekend.'

I hug him. My throat aches with the emotion I'm starting to understand will never be satisfied.

'Got to go, love, pack for the trip,' I say. 'Let's talk when I'm back.'

∽

I've always liked Amsterdam Centraal, an optimistic Victorian mini-palace, all turrets and arches and sensible Dutch clocks: a big, handsome, busy station. At ten a.m. I settle in my seat, handbag on my lap, holdall up in the luggage rack. I'm wearing a light sweater, my thigh-length green coat, and grey trousers tucked into a pair of new (and charmingly impractical) boots.

I'm ready to face the world with my supply of dry biscuits and a thermos of tea. I'll arrive at Gare du Nord in Paris at three o'clock, and need to get myself across the city to Gare Saint-Lazare, where the Normandy train leaves at four-thirty. Then two and a half hours to Trouville-Deauville, a change to the Villers-sur-Mer line, another half an hour's travel, and I arrive at seven-thirty this evening. Suddenly I don't feel very energetic at all.

A whistle blows, a jolt and the train slowly starts. It gathers speed, passing west through the Amsterdam suburbs, then south via Haarlem and Leiden. First stop is Den Haag, where it starts to rain, and by Rotterdam it's pouring.

I open my handbag and check my purse for the key to the flat. Of course it's there, don't be silly. The villa, Mi-Côte (so-named because it's half-way up a hill), has a small flat for the owners to use, locked off from the main part of the house. It's where I stayed during my flying visit four years ago to sign the lease with the Englishman. I try to recall his face, but can't — very forgettable, glasses, bland. Oh well, I'll see him tomorrow.

I hope the flat's been kept aired, though I'll have to make up the bed and get in some provisions. But I'll only be there a couple of nights, should be fine. I close my eyes and suddenly fall into one of the deep slumbers that have afflicted me these last two months. I wake again as we're approaching Belgium, when the inspector comes through to check our identity cards. A genial older Dutch woman is seated beside me now.

She nods as I rub my eyes and says confidingly, 'It always used to hit me like that too.'

I smile politely. God, is it so obvious? The lady leaves at Antwerp and a businessman takes her seat. He rattles his newspaper importantly and reads. Good.

After a long time, with stops at Brussels and Mons, two visits to the loo (another side effect of my present state), and another ID check, we arrive at Gare du Nord. It's been raining heavily for hours but seems to have stopped at last.

Right, I tell myself briskly. The Normandy train doesn't leave Gare Saint-Lazare for ninety minutes and Saint-Lazare is only two kilometres away, so I'll just stroll over and get some fresh air.

I haven't been to Paris for a few years so that should be rather nice. I gather my holdall, recalling soft days of russet leaves scattered on the pavements, and hum, *The falling leaves/Drift by the window/The autumn leaves/All red and gold*. But it's spring now, and the magnolias and wisterias and cherry blossoms will be magnificent. Ah, Paris in bloom!

Smiling, I walk out of the noisy station concourse. And stop. The fleeting spring flowers have come and gone, and all that's left are slimy heaps lying in puddles everywhere. And worse, I seem to have landed in the middle of some stupid demonstration.

Students are yelling, placards hoisted (Oh God, bloody Vietnam *again*), police on horseback are flailing their truncheons and bricks are flying through the air. I dodge into an alley and try to get away, but others have the same idea. Down that laneway? I emerge to an even noisier crowd.

I try to figure out where I am, and where I've got to go, but it's unbelievably slow progress. An hour passes as I try to find a path that's not blocked by furious demonstrators. Or police. Or ankle-deep puddles. My feet *hurt*, and I'm still streets away.

Anxiously, I feel in my pocket for my train ticket. Good, it's safe. I bought a through ticket for the whole trip so I didn't have to queue at Gare Saint-Lazare — a wise move, I reassure myself. But will I get there in time? I'm just going to have to push my way through this horrible crowd, I can't go around it any more.

For some silly reason I keep yelling apologies as I shove and wriggle and drag my holdall past people, trying not to think of bricks falling on unprotected heads, especially the heads of innocent jazz singers who don't give a stuff about Vietnam and just need to get to Gare Saint-Lazare.

And ahead, there it is at last! How beautiful it is, with its elegant arches and warm brickwork and large clock: its large clock showing the time as twenty-five past three. I gasp and start to run as best I can in my new boots, and hit a patch of rotting, slimy blossoms. My left ankle wrenches and for a moment I seem to fly, then come down hard on my knees and hands.

Rain starts falling again.

∽

Two kind young people, a boy and a girl, drop their placards and help me to my feet. I say I'm fine, though I almost moan when I put weight on my left leg.

My holdall lies half submerged in a puddle, and the contents of my handbag are scattered beneath the feet of the crowd. The young people find and return my biscuits and flask of tea (thank God), and my cosmetics and all the other things that went flying from my bag as I hit the ground.

I thank them as they help me across the square and into the station. The clock strikes four-thirty. I've missed the train.

There's a small cafe just inside the long, skylit concourse, and my helpers guide me to a table. 'I am so sorry, we must return to the demonstration,' says the girl. 'It is *essential* to show our resistance to the war!'

'Of course, such an important cause. Thank you *so* much.'

They pat me kindly on the shoulder and leave. I open my supposedly waterproof holdall, stare at the tideline of mud transferred to its contents, and quickly zip it up again. A waiter comes over and suggests coffee, and my stomach lurches.

'Is the salle d'attente still at the end of the concourse?' I say. He nods and points, and I get gingerly to my feet. Luckily my holdall has a shoulder-strap, so my hands are free to help me make my way gingerly to the waiting room.

When I lived in Paris I'd take the train from this station to jazz festivals in the coastal towns not far from Villers-sur-Mer. The waiting room often had a very pleasant fire going in winter, but when I push the door open today the fireplace is sadly dark.

I find a seat and take stock. First, some tea. I brush slime off my flask (my handbag is so squalid I can hardly bear to reach inside). But the tea is still warm, so that's a comfort.

I nibble on a salted biscuit and think, I'm cold but at least I'm not in a draft. And my coat kept most of the rain out. Some of it, anyway. It's just that my legs feel ... awful.

I look down. My knees are muddy and there's blood on the left one, which is already swollen.

Below it my ankle throbs but I dare not take the boot off in case I can't get it on again. I look with hatred at the treacherous heels of my new boots. And I didn't bring any other shoes. *Christ.*

Keep calm. There's another train at six-thirty, only an hour and a half to go. I'll be all right. At any other time I'd have had a warm meal, a glass of wine. *Ugh.* A biscuit will do. I doze for a bit, hobble to the loo, then doze again.

At long last it's six-fifteen. I make my way slowly to the platform, show my soggy ticket and board the train. It's still raining and getting very windy. My wrists ache now too. I hold back my tears — they're just self-pity, I tell myself fiercely — and think about music, new songs, some variations I could try. And very carefully avoid any thought of Stav.

Somehow I endure the infinity of the journey to Trouville-Deauville. I must transfer then, to la Ligne de la Côte Fleurie (of course there are no flowers in sight), but at least the train is waiting, and the conductor carries my holdall over for me. Another cold half-hour passes as the lights of farmhouses and small towns flicker through the droplets on the window.

Finally, *finally*, the conductor calls out, 'Villers-sur-Mer, Villers-sur-Mer.'

I'm the only one getting off. The conductor puts my holdall on the platform, and the train leaves. It's nine-thirty, the station is quiet, and suddenly some of the lights go out. I see the attendant and ask, 'Fermez-vous la gare? Il y a un téléphone? Taxi?'

'Oui, fermée. Pas de téléphone. Taxi dehors,' and gestures with his head. I stumble outside to a taxi sign. No taxi. The station goes dark and the only light is from the street-lamps glinting on the puddles. The rain gets heavier and, shivering, I discover my coat is even less waterproof than my holdall. At last I see lights and a taxi pulls up. I almost sob with relief.

'Mi-Côte, Rue de Verdun, s'il vous plaît,' I say, falling into the back seat. The driver grunts and puts the car into gear. We travel about two kilometres and pull up at last outside a familiar two-storied house. It must be almost ten o'clock. Twelve hours ago I was settling into the train at Amsterdam Centraal, foolishly ready to face the world.

'Vingt francs,' says the driver. I reach into my handbag, trying to ignore the slime, and feel for my purse at the bottom. And feel again. And again. My hair lifts in horror. It's not there. My purse must still be lying somewhere near Gare Saint-Lazare.

My purse with my cash. My ID card. My key to the flat at Mi-Côte.

'I've lost — j'ai perdu —' I say hopelessly.

The driver sighs and presses the horn for about ten seconds.

I say wildly, 'I can get some money telegraphed to me *tomorrow*, I promise ...'

A light comes on over the front door of the house. The rain is still pelting down, and a man emerges, opening an umbrella. He comes to the driver's window and says, 'Marcel? What is it?'

'You have a visitor, Professeur. Penniless one. Twenty francs, please.'

'Ah, indeed.' The man fumbles in his pocket for his wallet and pays the driver, who pockets the money and says, 'Okay, lady.'

I open the car door and step out with my bags, managing to shut the door behind me. But my knee has frozen and as I try to move forward I tumble into a large, muddy puddle.

Marcel says, 'Drunk one too,' and drives away.

I burst into tears.

∽

The man says, 'Oh, dear,' and somehow helps me into the house and seats me on an old leather couch in front of a fire in the salon.

I stop crying. 'I'm not drunk, truly. I lost my *purse*, probably when I slipped over in Paris. Outside the Gare Saint-Lazare. On the wet blossoms.'

The Englishman nods calmly, as if that explains everything, then says, 'And you would be —?'

Clearly that doesn't explain everything.

'I'm Vivy McKee. The daughter of the people who own this house.'

'Oh?' He stares at me. 'Ah, now I remember. A few years ago. You don't look —' He stops. 'Can I get you coffee? Fruit cake?'

'No, no, thank you. Tea would be good. I've got biscuits here.'

He goes out to the kitchen, while I chew a biscuit and stare mindlessly at the flames and think, dear God, thank you for the sheer existence of warmth.

Similarly, I bless the cup of tea when it appears in front of me. The man sits in an armchair and sips his own tea, and asks politely, 'And you're here, Miss McKee, because ...?'

'Oh. Haven't you heard from the agent at all?' I say. 'No rent has been paid for months now and my parents have asked me to visit and find out what's happening.'

'Ah, yes, the agent. I'd quite like to have a chat with him myself. Monsieur Baudet appears to have done a runner — with the rent too, by the sound of it. He's gone. Office closed down and no one knows where he is. Or is willing to tell me.'

I'm suddenly struck by a bout of shivering, and have to put down my tea before I spill it. The initial warmth of the fire has faded and the cold from my wet clothes is seeping into my bones.

'Ah, I need to get changed,' I say, through chattering teeth. 'My bag, my clothes?'

The man puts the bag in front of me, and I unzip it. No, no miracles have occurred. 'Everything's *wet*,' I say hopelessly.

I expect the man doesn't want any more tears, so he says hurriedly, 'Look, I've got spare pyjamas and a warm dressing-gown. Why don't you go and have a hot bath before you get pneumonia?'

'But I *can't*. I lost the key to the flat along with my purse.' I try, unsuccessfully, not to wail.

'Well, naturally, I don't have a copy of that key. The agent has it.'

'The *agent*,' I whisper in despair.

'But look, use the bathroom here, the downstairs one near the kitchen.' The man smiles. 'Your parents' house after all.'

'Thank you, that's very kind.' I swallow the threatening tears. 'I'm terribly sorry, in all the fuss I think I've forgotten your name.'

'Brian. Brian Appleby.'

Of course. How English. 'I'm so sorry, Mr Appleby, for descending upon you like this. I certainly hadn't planned —' I start shivering again.

'You'll find fresh towels in the airing cupboard. Please, go and make yourself comfortable.'

I take my toiletries bag from my sodden holdall and limp to the bathroom. It's pleasantly warm from the pipes circulating water heated by the fire. I start running a bath, then catch sight of myself in the mirror. Ah, no wonder he didn't recognise me. My dank coils of hair and streaks of mascara would make even my parents dubious.

I sit on a chair, wincing, and remove my boots and torn trousers. My left knee is swollen and bloody, the ankle blue.

The bath is full now so I gingerly step in, and settle into the hot water. Agonising. Wonderful.

There's a tap on the door. 'Clothes are just outside,' the man — Brian — says.

Slowly I wash my hair and aching body, trying to absorb every iota of warmth. Then I clumsily get out, dry myself, and retrieve the garments. Thank God, warm socks, flannelette pyjamas, a dressing-gown, slippers: they're all too large but feel wonderfully cosy.

I towel my hair dry. It's longish and wavy but my hairbrush tames it a bit. Cosmetics? No, who cares? I still look better than before. I rinse out my undies, hang them to dry in the airing cupboard, and pile my disgusting clothes and loathsome boots in the corner — deal with them tomorrow. For now I'm warm.

I limp back to the fireplace, where Brian is reading a book, with bandages and a first aid kit beside him. 'I noticed the blood,' he says politely.

I'm not arguing. I roll up my left pyjama leg, apply a dressing Brian hands me, and manage to wrap the bandage firmly around my skinned knee. But I can't reach my swollen ankle, so Brian briskly wraps it and pulls the sock and slipper over it again.

'I can't thank you enough, Mr Appleby. I've never ... this is such a *disaster*.' I sneeze.

'You're welcome to have my bed upstairs,' he says. 'I'll sleep down here on the couch.'

'What about the other bedrooms?'

'Unusable. Why I needed funds six months ago for repairs.'

'But my parents sent the money for that. Didn't you ...?'

'The agent said it never arrived, so I wrote to your parents again.'

'Care of the agent too? They haven't heard from you for over a year.'

I sneeze again. 'But look, I can't possibly get up the stairs with this leg. Please — just give me a pillow and duvet and I'll be very, *very* happy here on the couch. I could sleep on railway tracks right now.'

At last reassured, he finds me some bedclothes and disappears upstairs. I hobble to the loo once more (dear God, how does *any* woman put up with nine months of this?), lie down on the couch, curl up beneath the duvet and try to forget this ghastly day.

Next morning I feel even worse than last night and my head seems stuffed with cotton wool. I cautiously stand, able to put a little weight on the bandaged leg, and head for the bathroom. Brian is reading the paper at the dining-table on the other side of the salon.

He looks up and says, 'Bacon and eggs?'

That thought makes me groan and start to retch, and I hurry out the door to the bathroom. I drink some lukewarm water and slowly the wave of nausea passes. This is horrible.

Back in the salon, Brian says tentatively, 'Perhaps some dry toast and a boiled egg?'

I murmur agreement, and totter to the couch and wrap myself in the duvet. While I was gone Brian has built up the fire, and grateful tears sting my eyes. What is *wrong* with me?

Silly cow. You're pregnant, you ache in every muscle and bone of your body, and ... (I sneeze) you've got a cold. Oh no, that might damage my voice! Brian has kindly put a box of tissues within reach, and I sadly blow my nose.

Outside the sun shines brightly on the garden. I mutter bitterly to myself, Would have been bloody nice *yesterday*, but no sounds actually emerge from my throat. I curl up, hands over my face.

'Um,' says Brian, and puts a tray down. It holds a plate of dry toast, a boiled egg (its top neatly cut off) and a steaming cup of tea.

I carefully eat, and afterwards whisper hoarsely, 'Thank you. Sorry, losing my voice.'

'So it seems.'

'But I've got to —' My voice squeaks and fails completely.

Brian hands me a notepad and a pen.

I scribble, *Must ring husband, tell him to telegraph me money.*

Brian nods. 'But you can't speak, Miss McKee — sorry, Mrs McKee. Would you like me to explain the situation to him?'

Miss McKee. Mrs van Leyden. Call me Vivy. Yes, please. I scribble down our phone number and we go to the phone in the hall. Brian dials the long-distance operator. No one answers the phone in our flat. Brian tries again. No response.

Just remembered he's away for the weekend. Don't have the number, was in my purse.

Brian nods. 'It's Saturday, so he can't send you money till Monday in any case. Perhaps just rest. I've rung the locksmith and he'll come over later and make a new key to the flat.'

I go back to the lounge and stare at the fire, then pull the duvet over my head.

Some time later Brian clears his throat. 'Ah, Vivy? The locksmith will be here soon.'

I sit up, swallowing painfully. There's a fresh cup of tea in front of me. Is this man a mind-reader? I sip, realising I'm still in the dressing-gown and pyjamas.

'I found you some old jeans, t-shirt, sweater, moccasins. They'll more-or-less fit.'

You _are_ a mind-reader. Thank you.

Brian smiles a little. 'I have two sisters. I'm well-trained.'

Back to the bathroom. I painfully dress, rolling up sweater sleeves and jeans legs. I brush my hair and try to tie it back into some semblance of its usual waves, powder my red nose and add a little eye makeup and some lipstick. I sigh. I look like a madwoman coming in from a snowstorm.

At the far end of the salon, Brian and the locksmith are at the door of the flat. 'Monsieur Guillot!' I croak, then grab my notepad. *Bonjour, M. Guillot.*

The locksmith turns, stooped and mustachioed. 'Mademoiselle Vivy? C'est toi, la petite fille!'

Moins petite maintenant. Il y a longtemps.

He nods. 'Près de vingt ans, je pense.'

Over the few wonderful years I came here for holidays I was best friends with M. Guillot's daughter.

I write, *Et Marie-Ginette? Elle va bien?*

'Ah, oui. Elle est mariée et vit en Bretagne. Trois enfants maintenant!'

Trois? Merveilleux! (Three kids? Poor Marie-Ginette.)

M. Guillot finishes and hands me two keys. 'Vivy, content de te revoir,' then turns to Brian, who hands him some notes from his wallet. 'Merci, Professeur.'

After the locksmith leaves, I say — I write — *How much was it? I must owe you thousands.*

'Not at all. We'll work it out when you get funds. Do you want to see the flat now?'

I'd rather just sit by the fire, but I can't impose on this nice man much longer. I haul myself to my feet and write, *Would you have some painkillers? Anything will do. An elephant gun, perhaps?*

Brian smiles a little. 'Only paracetamol.' He goes to the kitchen and returns with tablets and a glass of water. I take the tablets, then we open the door to the flat. A wave of cold, dank air flows out. I try to say, 'Oh dear,' but can't.

Brian says, 'Hmm. Doesn't smell right.' He pushes back the curtains. There are puddles on the floor and water stains on walls and curtains.

'Burst pipe, I expect,' he says. 'Last winter in the freeze, probably, so it'll take a few weeks to dry out. You can't stay in here, Vivy.'

I scribble, *My favourite place in the world is the couch, anyway.* My knees buckle a little but I get safely back to the fire.

'Would a few pieces of apple be welcome?'

I nod. He brings me slices of fruit, which taste wonderful and sit easily on my stomach, then I hide under the duvet again. That evening and the next day pass in a haze. I lie gazing at the fire, and occasionally consume apple, toast or tea, go to the bathroom, blow my nose or sleep.

∽

When I wake up on Monday I still feel like hell, but I *must* ring Henk and get him to send me money, then tackle why I'm here in the first place.

The mystery of the missing rent is solved, but what's to be done about the agent who stole it? And I haven't even mentioned to Brian that my parents want to sell this place when his lease is up. Will he be upset to be tossed out?

A rusty version of my voice has returned, and I grate, 'I'll ring Henk and see about a money transfer. Do you do that through the post office?'

'I imagine so but I haven't myself. You'd need some kind of identification, I expect.'

I stare. 'My ID card was in my purse. I don't *have* any other identification.'

He nods thoughtfully. 'It seems that purse was rather fundamental to your entire life.'

'But what if someone's got my card and is, oh, robbing *banks* or something?'

'Waving your ID gleefully at the teller as they do so?'

For the first time in days I laugh. 'Perhaps not. Oh dear. I'll ring Henk now.'

Thankfully he's back from his weekend away. 'Vivy!' he says. 'You sound terrible.'

'I have a cold, I was caught in the rain on the way here. And I lost my purse. Darling, I have no money, no identification! What can I do?'

'A money order perhaps — but that would not work if you have no identification. Perhaps I could post you a cash cheque instead. What do you think, lieveling?'

'The mail could take days and I wanted to be back before next weekend. I have a gig.' I don't mention it's also the weekend Stav said he'd be leaving Amsterdam.

'Ah, but you will need your passport to travel home if you have lost your ID card. So I think you will have to wait for the post, Vivy.'

He's correct. I sigh. 'Yes, darling, please send me both cheque and passport. And would you mind ringing Geert to cancel my gig?'

'Of course, and I will send everything to you today. Tell me the address again?'

I do so and we part affectionately, although I think I hear Nina's rather unpleasant giggle in the background. Ah, well.

Brian is reading the paper at the table, sunlight on the garden behind him.

'The best we could sort out is that Henk will post me my passport and a cash cheque. But they won't get here till the end of the week. I'm terribly sorry, but I may have to stay longer.'

'Please, it's not a problem,' he says, folding up the paper. 'I actually spend most of the time upstairs in my study, or down at the Black Cow cliffs anyway.'

'The Vaches-Noires? Surely the beach is better for swimming.'

'Not for recreation. Or perhaps in an odd way it is. I'm a scientist you see, a palaeontologist.'

'A ...?'

'I study fossils, and the cliffs here are extraordinarily rich — pliosaurs, ichthyosaurs, early marine carnivores, incredible range of ammonites, sea urchins, sponges. *Ammonoidea* are my speciality.'

'Oh?'

'Abundant, widespread index fossils, ideal for identifying epochs of stratification. You'd have seen pictures of them, of course?' he says, smiling.

'I'm not entirely certain ...'

'Let me —' He dashes out to the hall and up the stairs, and returns with something the size of his palm, like a circular coiled tube made of stone.

'*There*,' he says, grinning proudly. 'A rather good find.'

'It's ... very nice,' I say. I'm astonished at Brian's transformation from someone so colourless and diffident to this passionate, happy man.

'That's why I love this place, perfect for my research. Once we sort out the agent and the missing money. I'll be delighted to sign a lease for another four years.'

'Let's sit by the fire.' Settled again, I say, 'It's not just the missing money. My parents have hit a rough patch and desperately need extra cash to keep running their orphanage in Saigon.'

'Ah. Look, if they have to raise the rent I can pay some more.'

'They need rather a lot, Brian. They actually want to sell this house when your lease ends.'

'Oh. But that's in just a few months.'

'Yes. Isn't there somewhere else in the village you can rent?'

'No, it's very popular with visitors. I haven't noticed anything suitable for ages.'

'I'm really sorry to spring this on you when you've been so kind.'

He gazes at the fossil. 'I do understand.' He looks up. 'If we could find the agent and some of the money he's purloined might that at least delay my departure?'

I nod. 'Of course.'

'As an outsider, enquiries are difficult. People are friendly enough, but in their minds I'm still a tourist. But you? They might be more willing to open up to you about the agent.'

'It's possible. My stepfather, the Général, was popular in the town. We could certainly try, but —' I sneeze. 'Sorry. I was planning to return to Amsterdam as soon as the money arrives and I'm well enough to travel, so there may not be much time.'

'Ah.'

'But, let's see. I might make a miraculous recovery by tomorrow.'

'Certainly, but in your condition you mustn't exert yourself.'

I stare at him. 'My condition?'

Brian gazes calmly back. 'Oh. I'd assumed your nausea and sleepiness was from something more than a sprained leg and a bad cold. I *do* apologise.'

'No, it's true. I am,' I say slowly. 'How did you get to be such an expert on pregnancy, anyway?'

'My sisters are overly and indiscreetly communicative. I know all sorts of things men aren't supposed to know.'

'Handy, if nothing else. At least your dietary suggestions have been perfect.'

'Felicity had dreadful morning sickness, so finding anything to stop her rabbiting on about it was a great incentive.'

I smile. 'Look, perhaps if I feel better tomorrow we could try talking to some of the locals.'

'Excellent. By the way, I'm doing a load of washing while the sun's out. If you like I could include your muddy clothes. I promise to avert my eyes from anything too lacy or transparent.'

'I'd appreciate that. Both the washing and the averting.'

∽

Next morning, Tuesday, I feel a lot better. My knee has gone down enough so I can wear a now-clean pair of jeans I'd packed, and Brian finds me an old pair of sandshoes at the back of a cupboard that fit (probably once Charlie's).

We're in Brian's car, an old Hillman Minx. He changes gear and says, 'Would you mind if we take a quick visit to the Black Cow cliffs first, before we go interrogating the locals?'

'Haven't your fossils been waiting patiently for you for a million years?'

He looks pained. 'Try one hundred and sixty million, but no. The cliffs erode constantly and the storm that thrust you so unexpectedly into my life may have released something of interest.'

'Good luck then. But perhaps I'll stay in the car.'

He turns towards Rue Alfred Feine, the street that runs along the seafront, and a few minutes later we reach the cliffs. Brian heads off with a rucksack and some mysterious tools, while I sit and watch lines of low waves rolling onto the beach. Seagulls wheel across the blue water in the golden light.

I open the car door and take a breath of air, which hits me like champagne. Rounded dark boulders dot the beach, the black 'cows' that give the cliffs their name. I hobble over to sit on one in the sunshine and for the first time in days — weeks — *months* — I feel free of all my worries.

In a peaceful haze I look back to the town's seafront, lined with eccentric old houses, all half-timbered walls, hooded windows, curved eaves and tall spindly turrets. To twelve-year-old me they were like fairy-tale buildings, and even now they still enchant.

Mi-Côte itself is not nearly as grand as these mansions. My stepfather Louis said the house was once a Victorian villa, built for the head gardener of a long-gone estate. Still, it has its own exuberant eaves and eccentric layout and dovecote tower, and I've always loved it.

Time passes, and I think, how different this sun and sky and blue water is from grey Amsterdam: a beautiful city, but, oh, the rain, the clouds, the fog, the icy winter. I take another deep breath of air.

Good, no congestion. If I take care my voice should recover unharmed.

Strangely, that doesn't make me feel happy: it almost feels as if a cloud has come over the sun. I try to recall the delight of those nights at Het Tuin, singing for a welcoming audience, but all I remember is smoke and beer, and the intense, overwhelming presence of Stav.

What did he say about the Berlin job? *More opportunities for me — and if you wanted to come, it could be a career boost for us both.*

Suddenly my mind is crystal-clear. Of course I'm not going to Berlin to support Stav's career. I love him and always will, but he only wants, he only ever wanted, an undemanding version of Vivy, a Vivy who brings no changes into his life. And isn't that exactly what Henk wants of me too?

My throat aches, and it's not from my cold.

A little while later there's a happy shout and Brian is walking back along the beach towards me. He's cradling something in his arms and grinning.

'Ye gods,' he says, as he reaches me. 'I think it's a complete *Peltoceras schroederi*! Would you mind opening the boot?'

I do and he places the large rock inside and packs it with a pile of dirty towels that have clearly done the same job before.

He eases his rucksack beside it. 'A few nice *Kosmoceratinae* as well,' he says. 'Thanks for bringing that storm with you. It washed out some good finds.'

'Glad to be of service. Now, let's go into town — I want to see if Madame Cloutier, the boulangère, is around. She used to know everything that was going on. Let's talk to her.'

Madame Cloutier is as warm, plump and shrewd as I remembered, and she hasn't forgotten me either. She comes from behind the counter and kisses me.

'Little Vivy. How wonderful!'

'Madame Cloutier, it's so good to see you.'

She nods. 'You are here for holidays, chérie?'

'Just a quick visit. Do you know Brian Appleby? He's living at Mi-Côte.'

'Of course. Bonjour, Professeur.'

I nod. 'I need to talk to you about something.'

She gazes at my reddish eyes and says, 'Tell me.' (I said she was shrewd.) She closes the shop door, turns the sign to Fermé, and we sit at a cafe table.

'Did you know Monsieur Baudet, l'agent immobilier?' I say.

'His office is — was — on Rue Boulard,' says Brian.

'Indeed, I do,' Mme Cloutier says grimly. 'He stole the rent from my little cottage. You too?'

'Yes, thousands. Does anyone know where he is? Why won't people talk to Brian about it?'

She pats my hand. 'Baudet stole from many people but they are afraid to talk. He has very bad friends, criminals in le Milieu. He is now in Paris, the Pigalle district they say, but no one is brave enough to report him. Ce salaud. At least he will never dare to come back here.'

'Ah. Thank you, Mme Cloutier. It all makes sense now.'

'It is painful to lose money, but life is still good. And now you have come for a visit you must return to us more often. Eh bien, Professeur, would you care for some croissants? He is very fond of them,' she says confidingly to me.

∽

We sit in the afternoon sun at Mi-Côte and to my surprise Mme Cloutier's croissants, light and flaky, go down easily with a smear of strawberry jam.

'What did Mme Cloutier mean — ah, le Milieu?' asks Brian.

'Organised crime. Like the Mob in America, vicious gangsters, so it's understandable no one has pursued Baudet. The only people who could get to him would be ... *oh.*'

'Vivy? You've gone rather quiet.'

'My God, *other* gangsters! Brian, we might be able to find Baudet.'

'You know some gangsters?'

'Not precisely. An ex-gangster.'

'Just the one?'

'Lucien, my old manager, was hired by a family friend, Mr Adler — and *he's* the ex-gangster.'

'Vivy, I'm having to reconsider my opinion of you as we speak.'

'It could work. As soon as I'm home again I'll contact Lucien.'

I take a nap on the lounge, content. In the evening I wake to a freshly built fire. Brian is sitting in the armchair reading what looks like a scientific journal, and in the background a soft, dreamy, jazz number is playing.

I come properly awake and sit up. That's *my* jazz number, a song from my second album.

'How did you get hold of that record?' I ask Brian, who puts down his journal and takes off his glasses. 'It's almost impossible to find now.'

'It was here, along with three others of yours. Your parents must have left them. They're well-used, the sleeves are worn.'

'Yes, they'd stay here sometimes before you rented the place. But I didn't know ...'

I didn't know they ever listened to my music, Charlie especially. Dad had heard me sing now and then before he ran off to Vietnam, but not Charlie. She always said she disliked jazz.

I swallow. They never *told* me. But here in Mi-Côte, while I was stewing resentfully in Paris or London, they were listening to my songs.

I swallow again, but it's no good. I can't stop the tears. Brian hands me the box of tissues.

'Sorry,' I whisper.

'Par for the course. My other sister Susan sobbed from the moments of conception to delivery.'

I laugh weakly. 'Damn it, Brian. Stop being so understanding. I'm not used to it.'

'I wondered about that.'

I'm silent. He's correct. I'm not used to being understood. I spend my life as light-hearted Vivy, bending to the unspoken demands of others. Accepting Henk's little friends, accepting Stav's ruthlessness, and never, ever changing.

But I *am* changing. My body is suddenly alien, I can't eat normally, the thought of nightclubs stifles me and I'm so sick of grey, grey Amsterdam. And most particularly I do *not* want to be Henk's acquiescent wife or an accessory to Stav's career.

'Think I'll make some tea,' I say, and by the time I return with the cups I'm feeling calmer. We sip tea and gaze at the fire.

After a time Brian leans forward. 'See this, Vivy?' He holds out a glinting disk, a tiny version of the thing he'd shown me yesterday. 'A pyritised ammonite I found years ago.'

'Heavens, is it gold?'

'Just iron sulphide, fool's gold. A baby cephalopod once lived inside it, a sort-of octopus.'

'A baby?' I ask. My throat aches.

'Yes. Then it died, fell to the sea floor, got buried under mud, and minerals replaced the shell. Then the earth shifted, the sea floor moved up and I was lucky enough to discover it. Here.'

He puts the golden disk in my palm. It's only two centimetres across, the ridges of its coiled shell rounded and perfect. There's a silence as I stroke the small, beautiful thing.

Eventually I say what's been on my mind for days.

'When I get back to Amsterdam I must end my pregnancy.'

Brian says carefully, 'Does your husband not want the child?'

'Not any child, ever. But as it happens it's my lover's and he also doesn't want a child. So.'

'And what do you want?'

'I have no idea.'

Brian hesitates. 'That must be ... difficult.'

'Oh?' I say shortly. 'Felicity and Susan haven't equipped you for this awkward moment?'

'In fact, at rather difficult times in their lives they've both had to have terminations,' Brian says. 'Sometimes it's necessary.'

'I'm sorry,' I say. 'I was being horrid.'

'You have every right. Why is neither man supporting you?' He shrugs. 'My turn to apologise. It's none of my business.'

'No, it's a good question. Just unanswerable.'

⁓

Next day I slowly climb the staircase to the first floor to see what repairs are needed. Brian has turned the central bedroom, the large one beneath the dovecote, into his study.

There are papers and chunks of rock everywhere.

'You may find it difficult to believe,' he says, 'but there's a system to all of this.'

'I find it impossible to believe. Are you sure the weight of all these stones isn't going to bring this floor crashing down?'

'*Stones*? Fossils of great significance to modern science, if you please. And no, probably not. But don't bounce around, just in case.'

'And how *could* you? This room has the best views out to sea.'

'Indeed, and it's a constant inspiration to me. Daily.'

'I doubt you've ever opened the doors to daylight.'

'Of course I have,' he says. 'How else would I examine phragmocones?'

'I'm not even going to ask —'

'Probably a good idea. See, I *can* push back the curtains and open the doors. Come on.'

We stand on the small balcony outside and gaze companionably at the blue sea in the distance. After a time I say, 'Enough of the sightseeing. What about the other rooms?'

'Well, my bedroom's in the east wing, above the flat. It's fine, but the other three rooms are the problem, leaking roofs and rotting floors. Come and see.'

We stand at one door. 'Wow. Disaster,' I say.

'This is the worst, but once we fix the roof and replace the boards it'll probably be fine.'

'*If* we can get back the money to fix things from the criminal M. Baudet.' We both sigh.

That evening passes peacefully in front of the fire — light food, reading, records — and on Thursday the postman delivers a small package with my passport and a substantial cheque.

'Thank heavens,' I say. 'I can repay you at last. Let's go to the bank, then look up timetables at the station. And can I take you out to dinner tonight?'

'You supping on dry biscuits and me devouring a feast?'

I nod. 'Sounds perfect.'

I cash the cheque and force a wad of money into Brian's jacket pocket as he protests. 'Put it towards the roof or whatever if you don't want it,' I scold.

At the station we work out the trains I need to catch, the first at 9.30 tomorrow morning, then I buy a ticket through to Amsterdam.

In the evening I get ready to go out. I wash my hair, tame it into pleasing waves, apply flattering makeup, but unfortunately only have the same jeans and sweater I've been wearing for days.

'Sorry I haven't got a sparkly gown for tonight,' I say.

'There are some very attractive high-heeled boots in the rubbish bin,' Brian says. 'What about them?'

'They can stay *exactly* where they are. I'm wearing my sandshoes all the way to Amsterdam. In fact I'm never taking them off again.'

The restaurant is in one of the old, tall houses on the waterfront. Our table overlooks the beach and the sea, with scattered lights on the water and the lamps of fishing-boats far away. I eat sparingly, though the food is delicious.

I tell Brian about my life as a singer and he tells me about his life as an academic, and we discover that devious, implacable, back-stabbing feuds are common to both. We can hardly stop laughing.

In a pause he says, 'By the way, I've actually been to Vietnam, to where your parents live.'

'Oh?' I'm taken aback. 'Hope you weren't shooting at anyone.'

'No, the Indochinese War — well the first one — was over, and things were quiet for about thirty seconds. I was a naive post-doc student, and my supervisor a French academic with a passion for Vietnamese ammonites.'

'*Are* there Vietnamese ammonites?'

'Indeed. I found that small golden fossil in the mountains of central Vietnam. There are ammonites *everywhere*, Vivy, that's what makes them so marvellous.'

'So you say.'

'My supervisor had connections and we got flown to different sites around the country.' He shakes his head. 'Seriously, it's almost too beautiful for words.'

'Isn't it just all jungle and rice paddies?'

He smiles. 'Yes. But jungle like blue-green velvet, paddies with lacework dikes, grassy bamboo, golden plains, soaring cliffs. But most of all, what's so stunning is the layers upon layers of *green*, everywhere. Emerald, obviously —'

'Obviously,' I say.

'But peridot too, tsavorite, tourmaline, chrysoprase, prasiolite, aventurine. And jade in every shade from apple to kingfisher to imperial.'

'Is that a foreign language? I hear *emerald* and *jade*. The rest?'

'Sadly my references do tend to be geologic in nature. Just accept that those minerals, and the country itself, exhibit the most astonishing hues of green.'

I shrug dismissively. 'I've never imagined Vietnam anything like that. I think of heat and dust and conflict, if I think of it at all.'

'It's not your favourite place?'

'God, no. Long, tedious story.' There's a pause, then I say, 'Funny, it's just occurred to me — a week ago I was packing for my flying visit here and didn't even know you.'

'No,' Brian says thoughtfully. 'Nor I you.'

'This visit's certainly been a combination of fun and physical agony, but I'm glad I came.'

'You do realise the tale about the penniless drunk visiting me late at night is already folklore? Rather than call me Professeur, the shopkeepers now wink and say *eh*, Professeur.'

I smile. Fancy ever thinking this man was ordinary. Yes, he's undramatic — no blond glamour or dark smouldering charm — but his kind grey eyes, high-bridged nose and amused mouth make for a presence that's far from ordinary.

I realise with a pang I'll miss him. I'll miss this airy seaside life too. Ah well, back to reality.

∽

Next morning Brian drives me to the station. I check and double-check my ticket, my money, my passport and, tied to an unmissable pink tassel I found in a drawer, the new key to the flat.

Reading my mind again, Brian says, 'I'll start drying out the flat.'

I nod. 'After I contact my old manager, I'll ring you. I'll write to my parents too and explain. Perhaps we can avoid selling the house — I've even got some savings I could dip into, for purely selfish reasons, of course. I'd quite like a holiday here some time.'

'Excellent. Another poor soul falls victim to the allure of fossil-hunting.'

'Possibly more the allure of sea and sunlight.'

After a moment Brian clears his throat and says, 'Thought you might like this, even if it is from Vietnam.' He puts the golden ammonite in my hand, the baby shellfish that died in the dark so long ago. I feel stupidly touched, and he hands me a tissue.

'Now, now, no weeping for science's loss, Vivy. Plenty more where that came from.'

I laugh and quickly kiss his cheek, then the train chuffs to a halt beside us. Brian helps me aboard, and in a few moments Villers-sur-Mer is slipping away behind me.

Part II. Kingfisher Green

9.   CLAIRE: BUTCHERS OF EDEN (FEB-APR 1968)

After André comes back from dropping Leo at the airport on the morning of the Tet offensive, he drives me to the American embassy. A low hole has been blasted through the embassy's eight-foot wall, and helicopters are circling and thwacking above.

Australian reporter Kate Webb is squatting on a footpath, scribbling in her notebook. By now we've become acquaintances, though we're not close. It's hard to move beyond her reserve, her quiet voice, her air of concentration.

She gives me a quick smile as I crouch beside her.

'What's happened, Kate?'

'They got through the wall but not into the Embassy building.' She swallows, and beneath her dark fringe her eyes are distant. 'They're all dead, the VC. Lying on the gardens and grass. It's a slaughterhouse ...' she shakes her head.

I nod. 'I saw choppers above here last night.'

Kate grimaces. 'I went to a party here earlier in the evening. Got up early this morning for a flight but something felt wrong. Heard gunfire and guys in a jeep yelled out, *US embassy*. Ran all the way here. Got shot at a few times.' She stops and clears her throat. 'Sorry Claire, must keep going, get the story out.'

'We'll give you a lift back to your office,' I say. 'Come on.'

'Don't you want to do your own story?'

'Hey, I reckon you've got the scoop here,' I say, and she smiles shyly in thanks. Kate Webb's report of the attack on the brash new American Embassy is indeed a scoop, and one haunting line of it becomes legendary: *It looked like a butcher's shop in Eden, beautiful but ghastly.* The story brings her prominence, a job with UPI, and MACV accreditation.

Of course I write what I can, but the agencies are flooding the wires with their own reports so mine is swamped. I gain no prominence, no accreditation, and only occasional articles for *Overseas Weekly* to keep me going.

∽

When André arrived that morning of the Tet offensive, Leo saw only the end of his hopes and had no idea how anxious I'd been. It's all part of the *ambivalence* of Saigon. Yes, of course there's a percentage of people here whose prosperity ties them to the corrupt South, and another percentage who are willing to risk everything for the hardheaded North.

But the majority are stuck in the middle, the ordinary Vietnamese who just want to live ordinary lives, as well as the conscripts on all sides: the unhappy proxies for global berserkers drunk on cold-war cash and pitiless ambition.

André works for the government of South Vietnam, and who wouldn't be cynical about that cesspit of self-interest and larceny? Of course I worry when he's out beyond curfew, or visits people who never visit us, or doesn't ring when he should. He may indeed support the North, quietly or actively, but it's impossible to tell where his — or *anyone's* — true allegiance lies.

And it's much safer all round not to dig. Hence, ambivalence.

By now I've grown accustomed to the fine-boned beauty and good humour of the quick, clever Vietnamese, and it's obvious how attractive a man André is. Yet we're not lovers, despite Leo's misgivings. I'm not even sure we're friends. Our oddly pleasing intimacy is only of the mind.

In fact, that applies to most of my relationships with men and I'm not sure if I should be worried. With the pill, women are supposed to have entered a new world of pleasure and sexual freedom, yet at twenty-three, I certainly haven't.

My brief experiments at uni didn't help and, annoyingly, the only times I've felt the kind of joy everyone else seems to experience were those few kisses I had with Leo.

I went out with a couple of reporters in Saigon, but after a skirmish or two felt no desire to go any further. One called me a bitch and both called me frigid.

That's par for the course for female journalists. We're either sluts or cold-hearted machines, say the male reporters. And the work of those females who dare behave with the easy latitude of the men?

It's mocked with a petty spite I've never heard from any woman.

At least André accepts my passion for my career, and every day helps me navigate the maze of personal and political minefields of Saigon. He may or may not have some devious long-term plan to make me a pawn of Uncle Ho, but thank God he doesn't keep telling me to go home.

Still, it was good to see Leo at Tet, to spend that happy evening together and the unsettling night. I think I surprised both of us with my offer of bed-sharing but, despite life in this high-tension city, some anxiety within me has slowly eased.

Is it because I'm doing what I've always wanted to do? Or is it because it was Leo himself who helped me become a reporter? I was oddly moved to see him here, so far from home. The glib surfie has gone, and in his place is a short-haired stranger with high cheekbones and alert eyes. But still with that infectious smile. Oh, Leo.

It's clear there's an attraction between us, but I also know he doesn't understand (or care) what lies ahead for those women who settle down for love. That's what they all *really* want, men like to say, nodding smugly. Perhaps some do. But not me.

And not the other female journalists either, who've fought their families, their employers, even their governments, to work here in Vietnam. We all want to bear witness to the significance of this conflict, to comprehend and interpret it in our own words and images. Yet everyone demands, Why here? Why now? Why take the risk?

But no one ever asks that of a male reporter.

∽

'Dear God, I need a gin this *moment*,' says Charlotte coming into the salon in the evening. She sits down with an extravagant sigh as Pete makes her a drink. She's wearing a cropped cream jacket over a navy linen shift, and I say, 'You're looking very elegant.'

'Thank you, darling.' Charlotte kicks off her high heels. 'Afternoon tea with senior MACV wives. And that simpering bitch, Madame Thieu.'

'What, the President's wife? Rarefied circles,' I say.

Charlotte smiles. 'Sometimes. Sadly, the wives I like will be going home soon, rotating out with their be-medalled husbands, and I doubt the next lot will be nearly as much fun.'

'Of course they will, tante Charlotte,' says André. 'And they will appreciate you too.'

Charlotte shrugs. 'Well, they should. Anyway, I heard something rather interesting — Madame Thieu was congratulating herself for being so amazingly kind to her daughter's classmate at their posh school. Turns out the girl's father has just been exchanged in a prisoner swap of some very high-level NLF officials for captured Americans.'

'I thought Thieu was utterly opposed to that,' says Pete.

'Indeed, but the Americans insisted,' says Charlotte, sipping her drink. 'And this only a few weeks after Tet, too.'

'Why is that so interesting?' I ask.

'The girl's father just happens to have been a famous Saigon social butterfly, a rich, utterly devoted capitalist with friends at the most exalted levels of business and government. And yet he's been an NLF agent for years.'

'Strange background for a communist,' I say.

'Probably because he isn't,' says Pete. 'It's the *National* Liberation Front, and lot of people here don't want communism *or* Thieu's dictatorship. These are educated, conservative people, Buddhists, Confucians, Catholics, nationalists, but whenever they propose even the mildest of reforms, Thieu jails, tortures and often kills them. So a secret body like the NLF is the only way to survive.'

'But they've still got to work alongside the communists,' I say. 'How can they be comfortable with that?'

André says, 'For decades, Claire, Vietnam has *begged* the world for help to throw off its colonial rule. But even after fighting the Japanese it was immediately handed back to the French. Apart from the communists, no one has ever helped this country.'

Charlotte laughs, waving a cigarette. 'Sweetie, they're bedfellows, not a married couple.'

'The Americans are blinded by their bizarre need of extremes,' says Pete. 'Scary Uncle Ho or tinpot dictator Thieu, no other option.

To accept that most people want to live peacefully with the north, to have a working economy, a sane government?' He shakes his head. 'Quite beyond them.'

∽

The Tet offensive isn't just Saigon's problem. Across South Vietnam, seventy thousand men have attacked every city and large town. It's not restricted to a few days either.

Fierce battles break out for weeks afterwards, especially in the Chinese market district, Cholon, which is left in ruins. The resilient traders slowly rebuild, but it's a bitter reminder of what could happen anywhere.

Yet despite this, the NLF don't inspire the popular uprising they'd hoped for: they are defeated everywhere. Even allowing for the ghoulish inflation of body-counts, the insurgents die in the tens of thousands for far fewer allied losses.

Tet is actually a rare military victory for the US and South Vietnam, but the many lies of the credibility gap mean it's transformed into defeat. The much-touted end is not in sight and the enemy is not a spent force, especially when entire battalions can emerge like ghosts out of everyday life and strike at will.

It isn't only the battles that demoralise, either. The attack on the new embassy, proud symbol of American might, is militarily trivial but emotionally shocking: Two of the dead guerillas were trusted, accredited staff drivers.

Sadly, General Westmoreland remains obsessed with defending Khe Sanh. He refuses to accept the plight of the imperial city of Hue, where ten thousand guerillas, including two hardened battalions of North Vietnamese soldiers, hold out for much of February.

The civilian casualties are appalling and the famous old royal citadel is almost completely destroyed. Two French journalists are captured in Hue by enemy soldiers, then later freed.

One, Catherine Leroy, takes intimate portraits of desperate marines, devastated refugees, and the first pictures ever seen of the Northern soldiers.

It turns out that the faceless enemy have young, shy, resolute faces. *This* is the dastardly foe for which America is squandering its wealth and reputation?

Tet's display of commitment by a people determined to reunify their own country slashes through years of deceit and wishful thinking. For the first time many Americans start to wonder if the war is truly winnable, if the cost in lives and money is bearable; even if the despised, long-haired protesters have been right all along.

At the end of March 1968, President Johnson, grimly aware that support for his flagship mission has collapsed, appears on television to say he is partly halting US bombing raids, hoping to initiate peace talks, and will not stand for re-election in November.

It's a breathtaking turnaround, but the war itself grinds on.

∽

In April, Leo is in Saigon for a course and comes to dinner at Tu Do Street. The atmosphere is a little more serious than our light-hearted Tet party three months ago. At least André isn't there, which is probably a good thing.

I gaze at Leo, thinking he seems both relaxed and more wary than at Tet. I say so and he laughs.

'Relaxed yet wary? Probably true. Most of the other soldiers get around armed to the teeth and terrified. They look at us in Civil Affairs and call us crazy CA bastards for going into villages in small groups and lightly armed.'

'*Are* you crazy?' says Pete.

'Not really. Our intelligence officers spend a lot of time talking to villagers, watching the comings and goings. Paying attention to the atmosphere. Noticing when people stay home, when they avoid a gaze or return it openly. We're cautious, not crazy.'

'And what do your enemies think of that?' Charlotte says drily.

'They're not crazy either. It's no skin off their noses if we offer the villagers clean water, clinics and schools, especially when it costs us real money. Everyone knows it's just a propaganda exercise — the government never does anything purely for the benefit of ordinary people.'

'And yet you are,' I say.

'A drop in the ocean, Claire. Still, teaching is pretty satisfying, we're helping the local schools in lots of ways. And the medical clinics do great work as well. People who need treatment at last have the chance of getting it.'

'Not a drop in the ocean to them,' says Pete. 'It'll change their lives forever.'

Leo nods, unsure.

After dinner he and I go to the rooftop to drink brandy. The Tet bushes have long since dropped their yellow flowers, but pots of jasmine and a small frangipani tree perfume the night air. We settle into the wicker armchairs, the street below busy with cars, conversations, laughter, hawkers' calls.

'How's your old mate André, then?' Leo says.

'Fine. Actually ... he's come to live here now. His flat near Cholon was blown up, mortars from one side or the other, and he had nowhere else —'

'Yeah, guess it's hard to find a place to live in a big, busy city.'

I smile. 'Look, Leo, money's tight for Charlotte and Pete, and André's rent is important. I pay what I can, but I don't have his income. He helps Pete out, too — they fixed the roof at last. And he lives in the old school-room at the back of the house, a long way from me.'

'Still pretty convenient.'

'Come on. I think you're assuming too much.'

'Am I? I saw how you looked at him that morning after Tet. I'm not a fool.'

' André's my *friend*. I was relieved, that's all.'

'Yeah? Perfect double agent material too. Tet might have raised a few problems for him though — hard to know where the old loyalties lie.'

'Yes, it bloody *is*, Leo. The whole situation here is far more nuanced than I ever expected.'

After a time he takes a drink and says, 'You're right, this is a pretty strange place. A war where the front line is everywhere and nowhere.'

'That's unusually poetic of you.'

He grins. 'Sometimes I teach the kids English using folk songs. The clear, repetitive lyrics makes it easy for them. *Wild Mountain Thyme. Five Hundred Miles. Catch the Wind. Farewell Angelina.* Guess it's been something of a sentimental crash course for me.'

After a moment I say, 'Have you had to do any fighting, Leo?'

'No, thank God. Actually, I was lying about feeling relaxed, too. I'm on a hair-trigger. It's the *uncertainty* of every moment — bad for the nerves. Still, I'm glad I'm in Civil Affairs, at least trying to kill people isn't my daily routine. Asher might have been right, after all.'

'About?'

'He said I was more of a peacenik than him, which I thought hilarious. But when I see the engineers building schoolrooms, or the pregnant women having checkups, or the clinics relieving years of misery, I'm glad at least I'm not contributing to this bloody mess.'

I nod. 'Something to be proud of, then.'

'Not sure about proud, but you're right about nuances. Did you know my unit delivers mail between NVA prisoners and their families, or takes bereavement payments to families who've lost breadwinners, even if they're Viet Cong? Weird.'

'Only seems weird because you don't understand who you're fighting.'

'*Yeah*?' He laughs.

'Yeah. You're using lazy Americanisms and they're wrong. Most fighters are locals, not North Vietnamese Army, and they're nationalists, not communist Cong. Their real name — National Liberation Front — says a lot more.'

'Come on, Claire. That's just semantics.'

'Not if semantics means you don't know who you're up against and why they're fighting. Your province, Phuoc Tuy, used to be a Viet Minh stronghold against the French. The NLF are just the next generation of those independence fighters, and they have widespread local support.'

He's puzzled. 'But Phuoc Tuy's relatively calm.'

'God, Leo. It's *calm* because most of the locals agree upon one thing: they're going to resist colonisers in any way possible — whether a thousand years of the Chinese, a century of the French, or a decade plus of the Americans.'

'A *thousand* years of the Chinese?'

I lean forward. 'The Americans are deliberately and criminally ignorant about this country. They're the ones using semantics. Try *resettlement* for obliterating ancestral homes, *collateral damage* for slaughtering innocents, or *kill ratios* for complete fucking *lies*.'

'Lies?' he says, startled.

'Someone checked those numbers. They're statistical nonsense.'

He laughs, flustered. 'Jesus, Claire, sure you're not Asher in disguise? You've never had such strong views before.'

'Hey, I wasn't here then and I didn't know what I know now.' I sigh. 'Sorry for the vehemence, Leo. This country is amazing, but it breaks my heart.'

There's a silence, then he nods. 'Okay, let's forget politics for now.'

We gaze silently at the horizon, where flashes of light show that something routine and probably very ugly is happening out there.

After a time Leo clears his throat. 'I actually wanted to ask you ...' He takes a breath. 'Look — is there any chance at all for me, Claire? I know we squabble like kids and it doesn't make any sense, but I really care for you. I think about you all the time.'

I'm silent.

After a few moments he says, 'Sorry. Forget it. Bit drunk.'

'No, don't be sorry. Leo —' I hesitate. 'Look, I don't *want* a boyfriend. I've never understood why everyone makes such a fuss about sex, it's not important to me.'

'Not important?'

'No. I've never felt those famous fireworks. Of course I like cuddling, but —'

'Maybe you haven't met the right guy,' he says with a touch of smugness.

'Well, I'm pretty sure you're not him,' I say, annoyed. 'Your attitudes are so old-fashioned for a start. I mean, *look* at the women you grew up with! Your mum, Tina, Billie, my mothers — all talented and accomplished, yet you still don't appreciate what women are capable of.'

'But I've got modern attitudes. I know some girls want careers before they settle down.'

'What about those who don't *ever* want to settle down?'

He laughs at the idea, which is a mistake.

'You think in stereotypes, Leo. Good girls and bad girls. Madonnas and whores. Madonnas marry and have babies. Whores just get used and forgotten.'

He's horrified. 'I'd never do that to you, Claire!'

'What if I don't *want* marriage and babies? What am I then, Leo?'

He's confused. 'Of course men take some girls seriously, others are just for fun. That's how it *is*. But you? I take you very seriously, Claire, believe me.'

'And Shazza? What about her?'

He says slowly, 'How do you know about Shazza?'

'Jen's very chatty. She wasn't to know you'd never mentioned her to me, not even once.'

'Casual thing, that's all.'

'So Shazza was good enough to screw but not to love?'

'Well — she liked other guys, too.'

'Oh. She was a *bad* girl, then.'

'That's not fair. It was what we both wanted.'

'Then why not talk about her? You didn't want to sully my good girl's ears with the truth? Christ, Leo, it's the twentieth century!'

'I just ... dunno. Maybe there wasn't enough time.'

'Enough time for me to pour my heart out to *you* and ...'

'And —?' he says pointedly. 'Yeah. So you're allowed to pash me whenever you want, Claire, but I have to back off while you play footsie with a good-looking interpreter-cum-double agent?'

'He *isn't*!'

'Guess we'll find out if the North wins, won't we?'

We stare at each other, at loggerheads once again, and the evening shudders to a halt.

∽

I set up an office in the smallest room on the third floor, probably once a maid's, but it has space for a desk and chairs, a filing-cabinet and my typewriter. Today I'm staring out the window, pondering my strange relationship with Leo.

After that disastrous evening he wrote me a letter in stilted High Victorian prose arguing he wasn't in the slightest bit old-fashioned, and it made me laugh.

I can never stay annoyed at him for long, and now we write fairly often to each other. I think his letters to his parents are light-hearted, but with me he knows he can be more honest, especially since he's already had to confront a few ugly scenes.

I know he still wants me to get out of here and go home, but at least he bites his tongue on that topic, and even more wisely, doesn't mention André.

There's a quick knock at the door and I come back to reality.

André says, 'Might have a story for you, Claire.' He moves some folders from a chair to the top of the filing-cabinet and sits. 'Perhaps not a story yet, just something to keep an eye on. No attributions, of course.'

'Of course.'

My desk-lamp highlights his face, the arc of his cheekbone and line of his jaw. As usual, I detach myself from any sense of attraction by wondering why some human forms are so sculpturally fascinating. It helps.

André leans forward. 'Last year I was called in to interpret between Australian and Regional Force commanders in Phuoc Tuy province. I got to know Minh, one of the RF soldiers.'

'RF are the local militia, aren't they?'

'Indeed. It seems the head of the Australian forces decided he wanted a minefield laid from Dat Do to the sea, eleven kilometres long. His experts advised against it, because minefields must be patrolled and they did not have the soldiers. So the brigadier simply insisted that the RF would do it. The RF said they too did not have enough men, and in any case it could not work.'

'Why not?'

'The brigadier was deliberately ignorant. In his imagination the NLF were streaming *down* from the north towards his province, and a minefield would protect the locals. He did not know, and did not want to know, that most of the locals around Dat Do *were* the NLF. What was worse, he did not accept that they are masters at turning munitions back against their owners.'

'But I read about that minefield last year,' I say. 'Setting it up caused some casualties, but it was declared a success, enemy supplies stopped moving, and so on. Didn't the brigadier go back to Australia and get a promotion?'

'Indeed he did. But last night I happened to meet Minh again. Over drinks he said *no one* was ever tasked with guarding the minefield. He told me that more than twenty thousand landmines were laid, but before the work was even finished the NLF had lifted twelve thousand of them.'

'What?'

'The NLF lifted *twelve thousand* mines, Claire, the latest M16 jumping jacks. Some of their people died in the process of course, but most are now extremely skilled mine-handlers with a large and lethal arsenal.'

'Christ.'

'This year a new brigadier, equally ambitious, equally ignorant, equally careless, decided to attack the NLF entrenched in the Long Hai Hills — fifty square miles of jungle and caves. Not only did he send too few troops for the job, but the NLF had planted those stolen mines everywhere. So they have been causing many deaths, both military and civilian.'

'Ah,' I say. '*That's* why the casualty rates have been so high lately.'

André nods. 'And now the official line is to blame the RF, because they did not prevent the theft of the mines, even though it was clearly an impossible task.'

I sit back in my chair. 'That's an amazing story, André. But how can I write it based upon a single uncorroborated report?'

'Not at the moment, but I expect more will unfold.' He pauses. 'Also, I am concerned for Minh. The RF in Dat Do are outnumbered by the NLF, so mutual accommodation must take place. Both sides keep a low profile — often brothers must face each other — but unexpected events can upset that balance and ugly things occur. Minh's family are with him and he is afraid.'

'Then why on earth does he stay?'

'He is a conscript, it is his job. Or perhaps he has his own political beliefs.' André shrugs. 'His reasons are probably as complicated as they are for everyone.'

As André leaves I glance after him, and wonder (for the thousandth time) how complicated his own reasons might be.

I open the folder where I keep the official casualty lists and flip back to last year — to the names of the boys whose poor families will never again know a moment's peace.

I start adding up the numbers, then sit, astonished. In 1967, over *half* the Australian deaths and woundings were caused by landmines. Not firefights. Not ambushes. Not mortars. Not any of the multiple perils of war: simply mines.

Our *own* mines.

For a moment — until I can no longer bear it — I think about the people doomed by the brigadier's arrogant minefield. The soldiers maimed while setting it up. The guerillas dying alone in the darkness. And the troops sent out to bring glory to their leader, with only an abattoir ending ahead of them.

10. LEO: HISTORY LESSONS (FEB-MAY 1968)

Over the following months I get to know Nui Dat. The place was once a rubber plantation so there are trees around laid out in neat rows. I hope they make good camouflage, but unfortunately there's a lot of open space as well.

The perimeter is eight miles of barbed wire enclosing a camp of five thousand men. They live in enclaves of tents and tin huts, sharing canteens, cinemas and a chapel. Helipads are dotted around.

At one end of the airstrip, Luscombe Field, is a natural amphitheatre facing a small stage where visiting entertainers put on shows. We don't get the big-name Americans, just young hopefuls in sequinned minis and go-go boots, but I'm told they're a diversion.

After Mick leaves I share the tent with Jim Simpson, known to all as Simmo. He's a Civil Affairs doctor, quiet and dark-haired and blessedly easy to live with. Since Scheyville I've had the obvious nickname Dingdong, but Simmo actually calls me Leo now and then, which feels pretty civilised.

Our tent has a canvas roof, sandbag walls, wooden pallet floors, two beds with mosquito nets, a couple of steel lockers, a small table and chairs and, at the rear, a protected hole in the ground, a weapons pit. If the stand-to signal says we're under attack, we have to grab our rifles, ammo and water canteens and, quickly checking for (the absence of) snakes, jump in. And wait.

The First Australian Civil Affairs Unit is small, only about fifty men, and the Education detachment even smaller. Currently there's me, one private and my boss, a captain who handles the external liaison. There should also be at least two more members, but we're short-staffed.

February 1968 disappears in trying to deal with the fallout from the Tet offensive, but in March things start to settle down. As well as teaching again we're busy sorting out repairs for the schools damaged in the fighting, and working on a new library and science block for Chau Van Tiep high school.

We're kept busy also distributing books, clothes and educational toys, and trying to get vocational training under way for all the new refugees created by Tet, now living in temporary camps.

The US has its own Civil Affairs units too, but we run separate operations, which is probably a good thing. Before we start any project we always talk to the villagers to find out what they want, but (says my boss) the Yanks just turn up, walk all over everyone, build some bit of crap that looks good in reports, and don't even look back when it's blown up next day.

Life settles into a routine of rising at dawn, malaria tablets, godawful breakfasts, inspections, meetings and work. Then at dusk more malaria tablets, drinking (though I don't go as hard as some) barbecues, watching movies, writing letters, and sleep.

The officers' mess is a long way away and a bit snooty towards us bottom-of-the-ladder second lieutenants, so Simmo and I sometimes buy cans of beer from the diggers' watering-hole, the Goldfinger Club, and drink in our tent when we want some peace and quiet.

A big surprise is that despite all our 'jungle' training there's barely a vine in sight. Simmo tells me that the vast Mekong Delta, south of here, is full of the rice paddies that produce most of the country's food, and that's where a lot of conflict takes place. Real jungle? Central, west and northern regions, not here. So much for all my efforts at Canungra.

Instead, the trees here have an almost outback feel, smallish, gnarled, and khaki-coloured. Among the bushes are stands of feathery bamboo, tall thin palms, and clumps of plants like mad feather-dusters which turn out to be banana trees.

The grass is bright green, the earth red-orange, and wherever there's a lagoon or dam it's covered in pink lotus flowers with big leaves. They're not grown to look pretty, though: every part is edible to the Vietnamese.

Nui Dat itself is based around a hill, but most of the land is flattish, with fields or plantations, apart from the Long Hais, like a row of ominous pyramids on the south-east horizon.

They're thick with vegetation, deep caves, impenetrable ravines, and lots and lots of Viet Cong, who've apparently lived there contentedly for years.

∽

It's stiflingly hot every day, and in April some of the other Civil Affairs men organise a swimming day at a Vung Tau beach for the kids of Regional Force soldiers. The RF are the local militia of the South Vietnamese army, not as well equipped as ARVN yet they do a lot more of the fighting. Most are older men living in villages with their families.

The outing is apparently a big hit with the kids, but I'm not there because I'm in Saigon for a few days to attend a course from USAID, the United States Agency for International Development. USAID is part of CORDS, the Civil Operations and Revolutionary Development Support agency, and it's mostly *rah, rah, how good are we* stuff. (Turns out that CORDS is also knee-deep in some very murky clandestine ops, but luckily our command keeps us away from all that.)

In Saigon I get the chance to go to dinner at Tu Do street. I'm not too sad to find out André isn't there — he's probably out reading Marx with his Red comrades. Still, it's good to chat, and after dinner Claire and I go to the roof-top.

It's a beautiful night, but somehow we argue about André. And then we argue about the war. Look, I can understand why places with the Yanks dropping bombs and napalm everywhere might be pretty unhappy with their visitors — but *us*? Our forces are so civilised to the locals the Americans call us fucking pussies.

So I'm pretty stunned at some of the things Claire says, but suddenly a lot of little things make sense.

Even in supposedly 'friendly' Ba Ria it's hard to miss the cool sidelong glances at our loud armoured troops. Hoa Long, a village south of our base, is very, very unfriendly: no one ever goes there alone or after dusk. And Dat Do, nine miles away and not far from the Long Hais, is apparently chockas with NLF sympathisers.

We leave politics aside and I make the fatal step of asking Claire if there's any hope for me. Big mistake. Shazza comes into the equation and the evening crashes and burns. Back at the Bachelor Officer Quarters I can't sleep, even though the bed's pretty comfortable after months in a tent.

Problem is, Claire's right and we both know it. Of course I've never mentioned Shazza, all beehive hairdo and kitten heels, I'm not stupid. Even though Bazza used to say, 'Go for it, mate,' we both knew my involvement with his sister was pretty half-hearted. I was a bastard to her and she's a lot better off now with Thommo.

But Claire was right about more than Shazza. *Your attitudes are so old-fashioned ... Your mum, Tina, Billie, my mothers — all talented and accomplished, yet you still don't appreciate what women are capable of.*

True. Mum's the cleverest, kindest person I know. My aunt Tina handles Kings Cross thugs without turning a hair. Billie? A transport pilot in the war who flew bloody *Spitfires*. Klara? A famous poetess. Yvonne? A pilot *and* a successful publisher!

Then there's me. A surfie with a crap degree, a conscript in a bastard of a war, coping (badly) with sweat-rash, sunburn, heat, centipedes and scorpions.

I sigh. But then, maybe it's not my attitudes are old-fashioned but, like most guys, I play along with the others. Us diggers aren't so much bronzed ANZACs as blokes terrified of not being one of the boys.

Last week, for instance, some blowhard was sounding off in the mess, saying women reporters in Saigon don't work, they just spend their time on their backs in the Caravelle: and I didn't punch the bastard. Some other prick said they're only here to find husbands, and I just nodded: a sheep like all the others pretending we actually understand women.

Yet I *know* how passionate Claire is, and how talented. Her articles draw stunning, vivid pictures, she sums up situations perfectly and, in the mildest of words, cuts like a scalpel through all the official bullshit. She's exactly the sort of reporter this war needs, but *Christ* how I wish she wasn't. I hate the thought of her being touched by the random violence of this place.

Anyway, I send her a letter, half-joking, half-apologising for my stupidity, and she forgives me, as she does so often. We start writing more regularly, which is good for my state of mind. I don't beg her to get away from here as fast as possible (much as I'd like to), but at least I can tell her the things I can't tell my parents, and she understands the rest.

Look, I'm only a teacher in Civil Affairs, doing hearts and minds stuff, and with luck I'll never have to shoot my rifle in anger. But even after just a couple of months I've seen a lot I want to forget.

Like the haunted troops back from patrols who drag on cigarettes and drink and stare for hours at the ground, or the scarred locals with lost limbs and spiderweb burns, or the refugees in the barbedwire compounds they have to call home after our smug allies have atomised their villages, or the wailing of people in such grief I never want to know anything like it for as long as I live.

Most of all, I'd love to forget the bodies I've seen, with their shattered bones and shocked faces, and rotting, ripped-open bellies. But try as I may I can't get the blowflies, the rats, the feral dogs, and the fucking *smell* out of my head.

Our school textbooks are supplied by the government, and their version of history is same as the half-baked assumptions I brought from Australia. But now I'm starting to see something far more unsettling.

I came here thinking of our base as a bulwark to protect the locals from the sly, infiltrating communists, but it's really an island — grimly tolerated, exploited and despised — in an ocean of people who've been fighting off invaders for two thousand years.

And we're next on the list.

⌘

I was lucky to get to Saigon for that course, as otherwise we don't normally go there. We usually take short leaves in the port town of Vung Tau, about fifteen miles south of Nui Dat, and for our five-day 'out of country' leave go to Hong Kong, Bangkok, Australia or Taiwan.

I've got a couple of days off in Vung Tau and travel there in a jeep with two other Civil Affairs men — my doctor tentmate Simmo and an interpreter, Lofty, a lanky redhead, one of our small group of Liaison Officers.

Simmo's heard of a child in Vung Tau with a cleft lip and palate, and hopes to arrange surgery for her. But she's not at school she's at home, and home is one of Vung Tau's famous sleazy bars.

We turn up on a Tuesday morning, so the place is empty apart from some women in short, glittery dresses and lots of makeup, who come over giggling and ask us to buy them drinks.

The interpreter apparently tries to say we're there on serious business and Simmo is a doctor, and everyone laughs. A woman says, 'Oh, doctors and nurses, yes, we can play doctors and nurses,' to many more giggles.

Somehow the message gets through that we're indeed serious and everything just stops. One woman goes to find the mother of the little girl who needs surgery. Another asks if we want tea, others go back to reading, or staring into space, or playing chess on a small board. One sad-faced woman breastfeeds a baby.

The mother and little girl come downstairs. The girl has shy brown eyes and a bow in her hair, and a twisted gap in her upper lip she hides with her hand. With Lofty interpreting, Jim arranges for them to go to Vung Tau hospital for assessment, then to Saigon for an operation to correct the deformity.

Tears slide down the girl's cheeks as her mother sobs, and I find myself swallowing a lump in my throat as well. For some stupid reason the kid reminds me of my sister.

Simmo and Lofty drop me at the billet. Away from the ramshackle bars and military buildings, I'm surprised to see Vung Tau is quite a pretty little town, and not too badly damaged.

I go for lunch at the Peter Badcoe Club, the Rest and Convalescence Centre on Back Beach. There are a fair few other Australian soldiers there, sunburnt, beefy and very loud, but I keep to myself, nurse a beer and wonder about the morning.

The bar girls of Vung Tau are a running joke, desired and despised. At first glance they live up to all the usual clichés, but then this morning I saw only tired women, trying to survive with their kids in such surroundings. What crap lives.

Later I go down to the beach and have a swim. The waves aren't great but I borrow a board from the Club and have a reasonable surf, though the water is dirtier and warmer than my favourite beach, Nobbys, with its fresh air and blue sea. Last time I was there, Jesus, was nearly a year ago and I was wondering what Vietnam would be like. Well now I bloody know.

So by the afternoon I'm feeling a bit bleak. I go back to the billet and have a snooze, then later meet up with some blokes for drinks at the Club.

Then they insist we go to a bar and hire a couple of rickshaws and pour me into one. I don't much care by now. We end up at a bar and I'm sitting down with a fresh drink when I suddenly realise it's the place I was in this morning.

The boys disappear one by one — got to admit the women look okay at night — then one snuggles up to me, says her name is Trinh, and asks me to buy her a drink, the non-alcoholic 'tea' the women make money on.

I do so, then she says, 'You here this morning,' and I realise she's the mother of the child with a cleft palate.

We stare at each other for a moment and I sigh. 'Where's your little girl?'

'Sleep. Upstairs. I never think she get fix, you know? Very happy now.' Her eyes are sad.

'Must have been difficult.'

'My husband die in army —' she stops and laughs mockingly. 'That what all girls say, make soldier sorry for them. Not true. I just get pregnant, work, you know.'

'Isn't there anything else you can do?'

'Wash laundry, clean US base? Not enough money, Aussie. I work *hard* here, for daughter, mother, grandmother, little brother. At least little brother go to ARVN soon.'

'Does he support the government, then?'

Trinh looks at me incredulously. 'He *conscript*. He hate government, hate America, hate Uncle Ho. But no choice.' Her face is hard. 'No choice for anyone.' She drinks her tea then looks up and smiles brilliantly. 'Lot of questions. We go have fun now?'

'Ah, probably not. Too drunk.'

She strokes my thigh. 'Oh, but you so big, strong man, Aussie, you come on.'

Earlier the boys had gone into detail about the going rate for various erotic exertions, so I get out some money in the middle range and hand it to her. 'Buy your kid something, or your brother. Or whatever. I gotta go.'

'Okay.' Trinh shrugs and moves to another table.

Well, that was a bundle of laughs. Could I screw one of these women? Technically yes, a couple are very sexy. Do I want to screw one of these women? Not much. Ah, fuck it.

I stagger out and get a rickshaw back to the billet, go to my room and pass out. Next day I do a fair bit of drinking, surfing and lying on the sand, then the following morning get a lift with a convoy back to Nui Dat.

∞

One night Simmo and I are buying cans of green at the side window of the Goldfinger Club when I see a familiar face about to enter the canteen.

'*Bazza*, what the hell are you doing here?'

'*Leo*, man! Same as you, but having farewell drinkies with a few of your mates.'

'Great to see you. How are things going?'

'Perfect. I'm out of here next week, and if you hadn't been such a wanker doing an officer's course, you'd be going home with me. Sorry now?'

'Fuckin' oath. I didn't even have the foggiest you were around.'

'Wasn't here much, up near Bien Hoa lately, and spent last year laying some minefield over at Dat Do. But the VC lifted most of the mines and now they're going pop all over the Long Hais. Glad to be getting out of here.'

'You're looking pretty fit, Bazza, better than the old days.'

'You too. Hey, did you hear? Shazza and Thommo got married. She's running his plumbing shop now, always was a smart cookie.'

'Smart enough to give me the boot. Good on her.'

We joke around a little longer, then Simmo and I walk back to our tent. 'That was Bazza,' I say. 'Old surfing mate from before we enlisted. Going home next week, lucky bastard.'

Simmo nods, but after we're comfortable and he's had a surprisingly long drink he says, 'Did I hear mines at Dat Do being mentioned?'

'Yeah,' I say. 'Sounds like a bit of a screw-up.'

'Could say that. When I'm not doing clinics I keep the Vung Tau hospital records up to date. They scare the shit out of me.'

'What?' I laugh. 'Yeah, landmines are a bastard, but —'

'When they were laying that minefield early last year, Leo, seven of our guys died and nine were wounded. When I say wounded, I mean one bloke said his dick was now longer than his legs and he wasn't boasting.'

Simmo takes another drink. 'Then the VC simply lifted most of the mines, and late last year used them to kill ten guys and maim thirty others. Ever tried to take a boot away from someone clutching it because their foot's still inside?'

'Christ, Simmo, that's —'

'Come this March and April, and our latest glorious leader's Operation Pinaroo. Some gung-ho bullshit in the Long Hais, playing hide'n'seek with NLF battalions who've been holed up there forever.'

'Yeah, heard it wasn't going great.'

Simmo laughs bitterly. 'Another ten guys blown up in six weeks. And *forty-four* mutilated.' He shakes his head. 'In a just world they'd still be walking around on their living, flesh-covered legs. Forty-four people! Hey, count 'em.' He points around the tent getting louder and louder. 'One, two, three, *four, FIVE —*'

'Come on, mate.'

Simmo is silent for a time, then shakes his head. 'You know, in everything I learnt at Scheyville I cannot conceive of — what would those pricks call it, the ones who think war is a game? Oh yeah. An *own goal* like this.'

I put my hand on his shoulder. 'Jim, it's okay.'

'I treat guys at Vung Tau straight out of the dustoff choppers. Poor bastards are only terrified of what's happened to their balls, but they've lost arms, legs, and have no *idea* what's ahead of them. Know what a spine looks like, Leo, ripped open the length of a back? Or a stump of bone in a thigh like a cooked steak?'

He downs the rest of his drink without stopping, then opens another can. 'You don't want to know. That piece of shit who insisted on his fucking minefield when everyone warned him it'd be a disaster? Rotting in hell'd be too good for him.'

∽

At a meeting a few days later the CO says, with all the joy of someone facing execution, 'HQ were very impressed with the initiative of those men who took a number of children on an excursion to the beach at Vung Tau some weeks ago. They propose another such event, with a photographer and reporter from the Sydney Mirror newspaper to immortalise the occasion.'

He glances around the room and chooses a couple of people, then says, 'Lieutenant Bell. I expect some of your students would also care to be involved.'

It's not a question, so I get roped in to help organise the outing. We have to hurry too, the Wet will begin in May. Finally everything is sorted out. The buses are organised, escort troops are ready, my class of fourteen-year-olds are beside themselves with excitement, and we hear the Mirror journalist and photographer have just landed in Saigon.

Then disaster. The journalist buys a deliciously cool shaved-ice drink from a street stall, and within hours has to be hospitalised with dysentery.

The CO says, 'No journalist. Unbelievable. And of course the Mirror doesn't have any staff here.' He looks around the table. 'Now, HQ says we must offer a substitute. Who would be good with words? Ah, the Education detachment. Lieutenant Bell — I'm sure you're up to the task.'

I start sweating, then a marvellous idea suddenly blossoms.

'Sir, I actually know an ex-Mirror journalist living in Saigon. A freelancer who could probably get here tomorrow with the photographer. Will I organise it?'

'Good man,' says the CO. 'Go ahead.'

So I ring Claire. She says dubiously, 'I thought the Australian command wouldn't let female journalists anywhere near their military operations.'

'This isn't an operation. Female singers entertain at the amphitheatre, and last month we had someone from Women's Weekly doing a tear-jerker on Our Boys. No reason why you can't come for a feel-good story like this.'

'Wow,' she says. 'Will it pay well?'

'Yeah, HQ are getting pretty desperate.'

'That's fantastic, Leo! Okay, what next?'

'Get yourself to Tan Son Nhut by nine tomorrow and fly down here with the photographer. He'll have the travel documents, amended for one C. Fenn, Journalist.'

'Wait a minute. Do they know I'm a woman?'

'Nah. Should be fun.'

∽

That evening I'm feeling good and shout Simmo to some drinks in our tent. He's been reserved since the night he went ballistic about the Dat Do mines, and just sips politely at his can.

'It's *okay*, mate,' I finally say. 'You're not the first one to rip me a new arsehole for displaying my ignorance. Seems the longer I'm here the less I understand. Did you know the Chinese were here for a *thousand* years, but the locals still threw them out?'

Simmo nods. 'Guess they really know how to fight. They got rid of the Chinese, then the French decided they wanted the joint. But the Vietnamese never gave up, just went overseas and studied politics and revolution so they could keep going.'

'Wow. Fought the Japanese too, didn't they?'

'Yeah. Vichy France tossed the Japs the keys to the place, but the locals were promised their postwar independence, and brilliant Uncle Ho was leading them. But as soon as the shooting stopped, the place got handed back to the French.'

'Got rid of them though in '54, wasn't it?'

Simmo nods. 'Free elections and Ho was clearly on track to win. So the Yanks threw a tantrum, drew a random line across the country, and handed the south to Ngo Dinh Diem, a Catholic bigot who liked locking up anyone who wasn't. *Gotta* be communists if they're not Catholics — obvious.'

I laugh and hand Simmo a fresh can. Glad to see he's much more relaxed now. 'What happened to that prick anyway?'

'Finally went too far even for Yanks, so they let a bloody coup in 1963 sort him out, hoping someone at least capable would get in.'

Simmo laughs dryly. 'Kennedy got killed a few weeks later, and new-kid President Johnson decided he had a winner: escalating some bog-standard Cold War meddling into a campaign to bomb North Vietnam *back to the Stone Age.*'

I stare at him. 'Wait a minute. Seriously? They didn't actually *say* that, did they?'

'Did you see 'Doctor Strangelove'?

'Yeah, pretty funny.'

'General Curtis LeMay, originator of that charming phrase, was the inspiration for General Jack D. Ripper, busy launching nukes at the Soviets to defend *our precious bodily fluids.*'

'My mad anti-war friend Asher told me something like that but I didn't believe him.'

'Well LeMay said it and now he's fucking doing it.'

'So what then, Simmo?'

I have a reasonable idea, I'm not as oblivious to world affairs as everyone seems to think — but it's great to see Simmo coming out of his shell.

'Half-a-dozen coups later, Thieu gets to be top dog and the plan is for South Vietnam to get off its arse and fight the North. But suddenly the Yanks decide, hey man, gotta have our *own* boots on the ground, and come in all guns blazing.'

Simmo grins ruefully. 'And that, Leo mate, is why you and me are sitting in a tent right now, sweating and drinking warm beer.'

∽

Early next morning I race off to a jewellery shop in the Ba Ria market and buy a gift for Claire, something I've been thinking about for a while. Then I wait with two other excursion organisers at Luscombe Field for Wallaby One to land.

I notice a platoon from 7RAR not far away, all their gear packed, plus twine-wrapped cartons of souvenirs, probably the popular tape decks from the American PX store. Rotating out, lucky shits.

I realise Bazza is standing with them, and go over to say goodbye. We joke around for a while then everyone turns at the sound of a plane, a dot in the distance.

'Hey Bazza, do me a favour?' I say.

'Depends. What?'

'Go for a surf at Nobbys when you get home.'

'Think I'm a fuckwit? First thing I'll be doing.'

I laugh. 'And ... maybe send me a postcard of the beach, yeah? I really miss it.'

'Okay, but you'll be home soon enough. Well, gotta go. Good luck, mate.'

We pound each other's backs, then he lines up with the other soldiers.

There's a roar as the Caribou lands and the pilot hits reverse. The plane slows to a halt, people start exiting the rear, and I forget Bazza, forget Nui Dat, forget everything at the sight of Claire's cap of fair hair.

'*She's* the journo? CO's not going to be very happy,' says one of the other organisers. 'Hey, Dingdong, how come you forgot to tell us your journo mate is a girl?'

'Oh, didn't I mention that?'

11. VIVY: THE TINY AMMONITE (MAY 1968)

As if to mock the drama of last week's trip, the return to Amsterdam is smooth and fast. At Centraal I take a taxi to our flat, which is dark and cold. It's Friday, so I suppose Henk has gone away somewhere.

I make some dry toast for dinner. Yum yum. Afterwards I think, well, no use postponing the inevitable, and ring Stav.

'Vivy. You're back. I thought it was going to be days ago.'

'So did I, but I wasn't able to travel until now.'

'I had to ring Henk to find out what was going on,' he says, his voice a little injured. 'He gave me your phone number in France but when I rang this morning a *man* answered.'

'Yes, the tenant. I'd already left.'

'I see.' There's a pause. 'And have you decided what you're doing? I've delayed leaving for Berlin for a few days to give you time —'

'Then don't, Stav. I'm not coming.'

A longer pause. 'Ah. Very well. Your choice, Vivy. Have you sorted out the ... problem?'

'Not yet.'

'Well don't leave it too late.'

'As you say, my choice.'

'I hope you don't imagine you can pass it off as Henk's,' he says coolly. 'Nina tells me everyone knows he's had the snip.'

My heart thuds. 'What Nina says and what's actually the truth aren't necessarily the same thing,' I say as calmly as I can. 'In any case, it *is* my problem. Enjoy Berlin, Stav.'

I put down the phone, and sit for a time, staring.

I remember chatting to Frederika once at a party and the subject of kids arose. I said something like, 'Well perhaps in a year or two we'll try again. Henk's business is still so demanding.' Frederika's fleeting expression left me puzzled at the time. Now it makes humiliating sense.

On his return that afternoon, Henk is as welcoming as ever. He kisses me and strokes my breasts, his usual overture to bed, but I pull away. I seem to smell Nina's perfume on his clothes.

'You are tired, my darling?' he says. 'Such a long trip. Now let us have a drink, and tell me all about your adventures in France.'

'Not a drink, thank you.'

'Ah, I see you are still unwell. Here, lieveling.' He pulls out a kitchen chair for me and puts the kettle on the stove. He turns and gazes at me as I sit down wearily, and frowns in puzzlement.

'Vivy? You look strange.'

'I've had a cold.'

'No, not that. You feel different, your breasts.' He stares at me, then takes a breath. 'Ah. That is why you were raising the question of children before you went away. You are pregnant, I think?'

'Yes.' I decide to call his bluff. 'But aren't you delighted at the prospect of fatherhood, Henk?'

He turns off the stove and stands back, his arms crossed.

'No, I am not. That baby must be your lover's.'

'How can you be so certain? We've been sharing a bed too.'

He's silent.

'Henk? How are you so sure?'

He smiles confidingly. 'Ah, my darling, you have found me out. A few years ago I decided you should never be forced to put family before your career, so I made a sacrifice.' He mimes snipping something with his fingers.

'You had a vasectomy and didn't *tell* me?'

'Why should I burden you with my concerns? It was painful, but I did it for us. For *you*.'

I can't say anything.

'Now,' Henk says briskly. 'Will your lover accept his responsibility? He must pay for the abortion, of course. And be *very* discreet. I cannot have my private business the subject of gossip.'

'Then perhaps don't talk to Nina. Ever.'

'Vivy, this is not a time for jokes. I know a doctor here who may help, but of course, London may be the better option. However you must decide on an abortion for yourself. You are a modern woman, I cannot insist.'

I take a deep breath, my heart thudding at his betrayal. But, as usual, I keep the peace. 'Yes, of course. Obviously the best thing. Just give me a little time to clear my head after that ghastly trip and I'll sort everything out.'

∽

Passing a bookshop a few days later I notice a display in the window and stop suddenly. I go in and pick up *A Child is Born*, by Lennart Nilsson. It caused a sensation a few years ago with its other-worldly photographs of embryos at different stages of development.

My first missed period was early April. I must have conceived a couple of weeks beforehand, so now I'm eight or nine weeks pregnant. I flip through the pages. There: eight weeks, three centimetres across, curled up in 'the primeval sea'. Such a small untidy blob, yet it's already had such a devastating impact on my life.

I quickly put the book back. I don't feel sentimental, more ... confused. Stunned. Aghast. How could I have imagined for a moment I could have a baby? That even with the support of Henk (or Stav) I'd have been capable of coping with such a cataclysm! It's as ludicrous as if I'd set out to climb the Matterhorn in my high-heeled boots.

Of course I must face reality. I'm sure Henk's 'doctor who can help' will be most efficient once I make an appointment.

Still, it won't be necessary this minute, and I'm still so *foggy*. I can't sing and simply want to doze all the time, so I ask Henk to postpone my appearances at Het Tuin for another few weeks.

After a time I decide that resuming my normal routine might clear my head, so every day, whether I feel like it or not, I do vocal exercises and practice my songs. Slowly I start to feel better, and about three weeks later I ring Geert at Het Tuin.

'Hoe gaat het, Vivy?' he says. 'Hope you have good rest.'

'Bedankt, Geert. I'm ready to come back to work now. Did the band sort out a new saxophonist?'

'Ja. Nina find someone.'

'Oh. Well, I'm fine now, so I'll come on Thursday as usual.'

'But Henk says you are still sick, need time off work. So I end our contract, as he ask.'

'What? He *asked* you? No, no, I *want* to work.'

'I am sorry, Vivy. I sign new contract for Nina already. I hope you feel better soon.'

He puts down the phone, and I'm left staring in horror. Henk, unbelievably, has installed Nina not only in my bed but in my job as well.

∽

I'm overwhelmed and start yearning for the security of the couch in front of the fire at Mi-Côte. Since I returned to Amsterdam, I've often recalled Brian's kindness and easy company, but — I realise with shame — I've hardly given a thought to the theft of my parents' money. So to avoid thinking about Het Tuin I stir myself and at last ring Lucien in Paris.

'Chérie!' he says in his husky voice. 'Good to hear from you.'

'You too, Lucien. I still don't have anyone to replace you yet. How I wish I did.'

'Oh? That is odd. It was months ago I gave Henk the names of three good managers to contact. You need someone qualified to find you work and handle your money, Vivy.'

'He's been busy. You know.'

'Ah.' I sense a note of pity in hard-boiled Lucien's voice. Is Henk's focus on his little friends so obvious to everyone? And I certainly can't bring myself to say that Henk has done the complete opposite of finding work for me, so I clear my throat and explain the situation with my parents' rent, agent Baudet and his Mob links.

'Le Milieu, Pigalle?' he says slowly. 'A tough territory. But yes, Monsieur Adler may have useful connections. He will know what to do. I will ring him.'

'Ring? An international call? Lucien, that'll cost the earth. I'll reimburse you, I promise.'

Lucien says with a gravelly laugh, 'Reverse charges to Monsieur Adler, naturellement. He will want to know. He is very fond of you, Vivy, and says you help him remember his old friend.'

'László? Has he still not turned up?'

'It seems not. Now and then Monsieur Adler asks me to check on all the jazz pianists I can find in Europe, but no László Richter is among them.'

'Ah. Anyway, thank you, dear Lucien. I'll wait to hear from you.'

Just the sound of his voice has left me feeling better, so I sit down and write my parents a letter about the theft of the Mi-Côte funds.

I tell them Brian will deposit his rent directly into their account from now on, and also that I'm contacting Moshe Adler for help. Dad knows him from the old days so will understand he may have useful (if lawless) connections.

I seal the letter and drop it in the postbox on the corner, then relax in an armchair, pleased. I remember saying lightly to Brian I could dip into my savings to help with repairs to Mi-Côte, and start pondering.

Then I suddenly recall Lucien's words: *It was months ago I gave Henk the names of three good managers to contact.*

That *is* odd.

Despite complaining about the workload, Henk has chosen to remain as my manager: someone with the right to deposit my earnings, access my savings and charge me fees for services rendered. And Henk's business, Straat Records, is always short of funds.

I spend the afternoon searching fruitlessly for my bank-book. Next morning I go to the bank and speak to the manager, and he kindly helps me understand the stream of transactions through my account since my husband took over my finances.

The manager cancels my old bank-book and issues me with another, although it probably won't have quite so many transactions in future.

Despite the mortgage payments, I had still scrimped and saved and built up the sum (amazing to me) of 15,000 Dutch guilders, perhaps 4,000 US dollars. But now a mere tenth of that — $400! — remains of my nestegg.

This is far worse than losing my job at Het Tuin. Forget my half-baked plan of helping out with Mi-Côte, I could barely survive on my own for more than a month or two with that.

Survive on my own? I gasp at the thought, then think, Well, you can't stay here, can you? Not with someone who's sabotaged your job and so casually ripped you off.

A colder part of me whispers, But Vivy, you *knew* he was a liar. It's your own fault, of course it is. You were too single-minded about singing and neglected everything else. What did you expect?

I rest my aching forehead on my hands.

Not this. Not *this*.

∽

'Vivy? Surely you have not forgotten to defrost the joint of lamb?' Henk says. 'I was particularly looking forward to it tonight.'

'Sorry. I'm tired,' I say. 'But perhaps that's because I spent this morning at the bank.'

'Oh?'

'The manager had to issue me with another bank-book, as mine appears to have gone missing. Along with most of my savings.'

Henk smiles. 'Ah, my darling. As it happens, I was planning to restore some of those funds tomorrow. I am sorry. It must have come as a shock.'

'It certainly did. What have you done with my money, Henk?'

'*Our* money, lieveling. Kept Straat Records going, of course. Earlier this year I had a cash-flow problem. You, of course, were absorbed in your little adventure with Stav, so I thought it best to simply cope. And now better times have returned! A new contract for Nina, an excellent advance. Tomorrow, Vivy, I can fix things up.'

'Tomorrow?'

'I promise.'

He turns and looks at me, his arms folded. 'But you have also promised me something, have you not? You are being very slow in dealing with your little problem.'

'Funny,' I say. 'Stav called it a problem too.'

'There is nothing funny about it, Vivy,' he says coldly. 'Will I ring my doctor friend and make you an appointment?'

'If you like.' Suddenly I laugh wildly and shrug. 'And suppose I simply decide I *won't* do what you want — what then, Henk?'

Gazing into my eyes with an expression I've never seen before on his charming face, he punches me, hard, in the belly.

I fold over, gasping, and he says calmly, 'Well, *that* then. Darling.'

∞

I sit on the side of the bed, shaking. He's never hit me before, there's never been a hint he was capable of it. But there's never been a hint I was capable of defying him either. My belly aches and I wonder if the tiny creature that's brought so many complications into my life is safe.

I laugh bitterly. Why should I bloody *care* if it's safe? It might have been better if Henk's blow had dislodged it and removed the complications.

God, I'm exhausted.

My husband left after delivering his crude judgement on my small mutiny, saying he was going to Nina's flat for the night. Is bloody Nina's rent coming out of *my* money?

Will I ever get any of it back, despite Henk's promise? At least we've both paid into the mortgage on our place, so if we divorce, I'll still have some assets to my name.

If we *divorce*? This fracture in my civilised marriage is beyond comprehension. Should I seek a divorce? I don't even know what the grounds would be in the Netherlands — perhaps wife-beating is perfectly acceptable behaviour?

I sleep fitfully and wake as tired as I was last night. After breakfast I force myself to take a walk. I drop into the bank to check my account, and see at least some money has returned to me: 4,000 guilders, about $1,100. That's a relief, but I wonder if I'll ever see the rest of it.

When I return, Henk isn't at home, thank God. I sit at the kitchen table and try to think what I'm going to say or do when he returns, this stranger I thought I knew.

My head spins. I don't have a job. I only have a fraction of my savings. Stav is gone and Henk has betrayed me in every area of our lives together.

And I'm *still* pregnant.

Henk arrives home, his arms full of flowers. 'My darling, I am so *sorry*,' he says. 'I cannot believe what I did last night — have I *ever* done such a thing before? Oh God, please believe me, it will never happen again. I was so shocked, you see.'

He puts the flowers on the table and automatically I rise to get vases. As I'm filling them with water Henk sits and rubs his face. 'I have *wept*, Vivy, I have wept for my stupidity, my cruelty. You have been the finest possible wife.'

'Yes, I have,' I say, unwrapping a bunch of rather beautiful oriental lilies and arranging them.

'I will do anything for you to forgive me. I have already organised for you to have a real break, so I can treat you like a *queen*! You have been working so hard and I did not see it.'

I arrange a second bundle of flowers (perfumed, long-stemmed roses), and say, 'Yes, about that. Something we didn't have time to discuss last night. Geert said you've cancelled my contract at Het Tuin and installed Nina in my place.'

'Not precisely, Vivy. You need a rest, and she will fill your spot for now. A *place-holder*, if you will.' He beams.

'I don't need a place-holder, Henk. I need a job. How will we pay the mortgage if I don't work?'

He glances away, and after a moment says, 'Not to worry. My parents' financial trust now owns this place and we get it for a minimal rent.'

I stop unwrapping the third lot of flowers and stare at him. 'But … what, *where* have my mortgage payments been going every month?'

'Into my business, of course, Vivy.'

I sit down slowly. 'Sorry, how does your parents' trust *own* this place?'

'I sold it to them, of course. For a good price.'

I shake my head. 'But Henk, *I* own half the flat.'

Henk licks his lips. 'Surely you remember, oh, six months ago? We were filing some business documents and I gave you the transfer authority to read and sign. You were quite happy to do so.'

'But I don't have the slightest recollection of that.'

He smiles. 'We had drunk a great deal that evening so perhaps you forgot. And you were *busy* with Stav at the time, as I recall.'

'Do you have copies of the papers?'

'At the lawyers, of course.'

I'm still holding the flowers and my hand crushes a spray of petals: a sour scent rises. After a moment I say, 'And where is the money from this sale of our property?'

'In the business.'

'But half of it is *mine*.'

'We are married, Vivy. What's mine is yours, and so on, as they say.'

I stand up. 'I want it. I want *my* half of the money.'

Henk shakes his head pityingly. 'Ah, you are sometimes very stupid, Vivy. You will get it back eventually. For now, Straat Records would fail without it.'

He stands and I'm aware of the size of his fists. He smiles. 'Now, let me make you some supper, darling. Remember, you must rest.'

∽

In the growing dawn I stare blankly at the ceiling. Thankfully, last night Henk took himself to Nina's again, blathering again about my need to rest. I don't need to bloody rest! I need my job and my savings and my share of this flat, or how will I even survive? I have nothing.

Especially, I have no marriage. Most people I know in Amsterdam are Henk's friends or business buddies. There isn't a soul here I could trust to take my part in this bizarre explosion — implosion? — of what I thought was the foundation of my life.

After a small breakfast I put on a coat to go for a walk, but the door won't open. I try to unlock it but my key won't even enter the lock. I peer through the glass beside the door, but can't see anything.

Feeling panicky I go to my handbag, empty the contents onto the kitchen table and find my powder compact. By turning the mirror this way and that I can finally see why I'm trapped.

It's an absurdly easy trick: a key is sitting in the outside of the old-fashioned lock. I hear footsteps coming up the stairs and feel a moment of terror, then realise it's my upstairs neighbour.

My heart thudding I yell, 'Mevrouw! Mevrouw Hoekstra!'

She stops and stares at me shortsightedly through the watery old glass. 'Mevrouw van Leyden?' she says.

'Ja, ja. De sleutel zit vast!' The key is stuck.

'Ah. De sleutel?'

'Open het, alstublieft! Mijn man is — um — vergeten dat ik hier ben.' It seems absurdly unlikely my husband forgot I was here and left a key stuck in the door, but who knows?

She puts down a bag of shopping and turns the big key, and I open the door. '*Bedankt*, Mevrouw Hoekstra.'

'Je man is vergeetachtig,' she says, nodding sagely. Your husband is forgetful.

'Oh, *ja,*' I say, as if I deal with his poor memory every day. 'Goededag, Mevrouw.'

She nods and takes her bag and plods up the steps.

I take the key and go back inside and sit down with a thump at the kitchen table. What will I do? My God, I've got to get out of here! Henk *locked* me inside my own home? Is he insane? I stare at the old key with horror and drop it on the table. *Ugh*! it rolls and clinks.

I gaze hopelessly at my belongings scattered across the table, scattered as they once were at Gare Saint-Lazare. My familiar cosmetics, a new purse, some crumpled tissues, a bag of biscuit crumbs, the little golden ammonite, and among them the thing that clinked: the pink-tasselled key to the flat at Mi-Côte.

I push everything back in my handbag. In the bedroom I open a large suitcase, throw my still-unpacked holdall into it, plus more underwear, sweaters, trousers, socks, shoes.

The most expensive gems from my jewellery box go into a velvet bag. Anything else? Yes. I find my swimsuit and beach towel, and stuff them in the suitcase.

Right. Get out of here.

∽

I lock the flat behind me. It was foolish of Henk to use his key to imprison me: we only have two copies, his and mine. I keep mine and take pleasure dropping his into a rubbish bin at Amsterdam Centraal before I board the 10.30 train to Paris.

The trip is smooth and, not leaving anything to chance, I take a taxi from Gare du Nord to Gare Saint-Lazare. It's a beautiful day, the streets are blessedly empty of protesters, and the waiting room at Saint-Lazare even has a cosy fire.

I have plenty of time to spare so find a public phone and ring Lucien, who says he'll come over to see me at the station. 'Chérie,' he says gruffly when we meet on the concourse and hug.

'Lucien, it's so good to see you.'

'Let me get you coffee, Vivy. We must talk.'

'Tea, please, but yes, we must.'

When we're settled in a corner of the cafe, he says, 'I spoke to Monsieur Adler. He sends you his salutations. Il est très mécontent, very unhappy, that a criminal stole money from your family. He will do whatever is possible to help.'

'That's good news,' I say.

Lucien gazes at me. 'But Vivy, you are unwell?'

I laugh in disbelief at my situation. 'Lucien ... je suis enceinte.' It sounds less frightening in French, but suddenly I'm hit with the wave of despair I've been holding back for days.

'Mais, c'est *merveilleux*, Vivy. But why do you cry? Your husband is not happy?' Lucien frowns. He's never liked Henk.

'No, not at all. But worse than that, he has taken all my money and put it in his business.'

Lucien's frown deepens. 'He did not find you a good manager?'

'No, I trusted him. And he cancelled my contract at Het Tuin and gave the job to his petite amie.' I take a shaky breath.

'Ce *salaud*. What now, Vivy?'

'I'm going back to Normandy. I've got a roof over my head there and I'll have time to think. I'm just in shock at the moment.'

'Naturellement. I will help you with anything, chérie, just tell me.'

I reach out and touch his stubbled old face, furious on my behalf. 'Cher Lucien. I'll be all right. It's good to be able to tell somebody.'

He shakes his head in disbelief. 'Ce connard. I never trust him, never.' He sighs, then smiles. 'Ah, but you will make très bonne maman, Vivy. I know it. I am so happy for you.'

I smile and nod. Lucien is a devout Catholic so I don't want to raise the thorny issue of abortion right now.

Today I'm feeling almost normal, and there's still plenty of time to take action. We talk longer about Lucien's life in retirement, and Manon, the wife who's tolerantly born him five children, but then I have to catch my four-thirty train.

When we part I watch him stumping away along the concourse, grey-haired and determined in his dark overcoat. At least I have one friend in this world.

∽

My escape to Villers-sur-Mer continues easily. The countryside between the outskirts of Paris and Trouville-Deauville is beautiful in the evening sunset. When I transfer to la Ligne de la Côte Fleurie there are flowers everywhere.

The steam train is warm and the twinkling lights of the passing villages are charming. At Villers-sur-Mer station, a familiar taxi is waiting. 'Ah. Bonsoir, Monsieur ... *Marcel*, n'est-ce pas?' I say to the driver.

'Bonsoir, Madame,' he says sternly. 'Today, you have your purse?'

'*Certainement*. Mi-Côte, Rue de Verdun, s'il vous plaît.'

He sighs, puts my bag in the boot, then we head off. As we pull up at the house I realise the only light is from the street-lamp. The house is dark, and Marcel nods his head towards it. 'Le Professeur has gone yesterday to London.'

'Oh. That's fine. I have a key.'

I pay the fare, then Marcel gets my bag from the boot and carries it towards the house. 'Over here,' I say, when he stops at the main entrance. 'I'm staying in the flat.'

Marcel looks dubious, but brings my bag across to the door of the far wing. 'Bonne nuit, Madame,' he says, and leaves.

For a moment I panic. What if I've lost the key? What if it doesn't *work*? But I haven't, and it does. I yank the bag up two steps and go inside, find the switch, and the light comes on.

To my left is the bedroom, with its tiny ensuite at the rear. I leave my suitcase beside the bed and return to the living area. Gazing around, I'm surprised I'd forgotten how oddly shaped it is, almost like a triangle.

Kitchen benches run along the left-hand wall, the base of the triangle holds the window, sink, table and fridge, while the third side (which backs onto the salon) has the fireplace. A sofa sits in the middle, and the door to Brian's part of the house leads from the narrow tip of the triangle.

The flat doesn't smell as musty as it did last week, the water on the floor is gone and the air mild. Brian must have had a fire going ever since I left, and has even left a stack of wood and newspapers beside the grate. I crumple paper, add kindling, set it alight and soon it's burning merrily. What a delight!

I go back to the bedroom to unpack. Heavens, the bed is already made up with fresh sheets as well. Oh, you kind man! But that's odd. I'd joked about returning next year. Why would he think I'd need the bed so soon?

I put my things away in the wardrobe and chest of drawers, then check the larder cupboard — probably some dusty old teabags somewhere. But the teabags sitting there are fresh, and beside them are several tins of nice soup. That's my supper sorted out: thank you, Brian.

Perhaps I have *two* friends in this world.

∽

Next day I walk down the hill from Mi-Côte to Rue des Belges. It's only about four or five hundred metres to the town shops, but by the time I've hauled myself back up the hill with a couple of bags it seems a lot further. Still, I've got croissants and fresh bread from Madame Cloutier, plus jam, milk, eggs, apples and bananas.

And two packets of dry biscuits just in case, although I'm feeling unusually well. The day has turned cool so I build up the fire again and eat a croissant and an apple. I watch the hypnotic flames for a time then mentally shake myself.

There's a fist-sized bruise near my navel that aches but it hasn't apparently affected the viability of my 'problem', so the time has come to face reality. An abortion here in Catholic France will be almost impossible, especially as I don't have a medical history with any local doctors, so London it has to be.

I lived there for a few years in the late fifties, so know it reasonably well. I had a tiny flat in an old building not far from Covent Garden underground, and could walk to Soho jazz clubs and the National Gallery and the wonderful shops, although I didn't have the money to buy much.

Lucien and I were getting to know each other then — he'd come over from Paris and organise gigs and small tours for me — and apart from the pangs of separation from my Sydney life I loved London.

Not far from my flat was a medical practice with a nice female doctor I'd occasionally visit, so she'd be able to refer me to a clinic. After this time of confusion in Amsterdam it's now mid-June, so I'm twelve weeks pregnant. I *must* get moving.

Villers-sur-Mer is half-way between Caen and Le Havre, both of which have ferry services to Portsmouth, so once I'm there I can take the train to London.

Luckily I don't have to worry about a visa. I was born in England so have a British passport, and my marriage to a Dutch man makes travel easy within Europe as well.

All perfectly doable but, oh God, the tedium. I'll go to the small travel agency in town tomorrow to book. I'm too tired today.

∽

Fermé jusqu'à juillet says the unhelpful sign on the travel agency. Closed until July. But I need to see travel timetables *now*, not July. The library perhaps?

As a child I'd sometimes go there with my stepfather Louis. He'd flirt gallantly with the elderly librarian and read the newspapers, frowning over reports of atomic bombs and the refusal of Indochina to quietly submit to French rule, while I'd read picture books and dream about being a famous singer.

The place hasn't changed much: an old stone building, cosy and glue-smelling. I have a feeling the rather nice-looking librarian is the same one: perhaps she wasn't so elderly after all.

'Madame Desvignes?' I say tentatively. 'Je suis — j'étais — Vivy de Ferrier.'

In my rusty French we establish that yes, it's been almost twenty years, and how I've grown, that I'm on holiday in Villers-sur-Mer, and how sorry Madame was that the Général died, mon Dieu, was it thirteen years ago?

That out of the way, I ask about timetables for buses and ferries, and indeed, the efficient Madame Desvignes has them at her fingertips.

I sit at a table by the window and jot down schedules. Looks like the best plan is two hours on the evening bus to Caen and its port at Ouistreham, then the night ferry at midnight, arriving at dawn in Portsmouth.

I'll get a cabin — expensive but I'll need the sleep. I return the timetables with thanks to Madame Desvignes, and trudge back up the hill to Mi-Côte.

This evening, then. I pack my holdall for an English interlude, then tidy the small flat, have some afternoon tea, and open one of the dusty old books stacked on a shelf for wet-weather reading. But I keep thinking of the evening to come and barely a word makes sense.

Finally night falls and I get ready. Silk shirt and sweater, tweed trousers, scarf, coat and flat-heeled boots: appropriate for the Matterhorn of a trip to London.

I pack my usual flask of tea and some biscuits, enclose the hearth with the fireguard, turn out the lights and lock the door. Down the hill with my handbag and holdall to the bus stop.

The seven o'clock bus arrives and about ten people climb on board. I'm glad I don't recognise any of them. I'm not sure I could bear another round of 'Twenty years? How you've grown'.

The bus stops and starts, people get on and off, and eventually we reach Caen. Another bus, a shorter trip now to Ouistreham port, and finally the terminal. (And thankfully a loo. Go through this horror for another six months? I don't think so.)

We have to wait for the ferry to arrive from Portsmouth before entering customs. I buy my ticket for a sleeping cabin and get a magazine from a newspaper stand. It's all party clothes, latest makeup, cookery tips.

I skim it, throw it away and reach into my handbag for a biscuit.

My fingers brush something smooth and cool, and I take out the golden ammonite, the shellfish once floating in *the primeval sea.*

Funny, where did those words come from —? Of course, the book about embryos. I gaze at the fossil. I suppose its little occupant once drifted serenely in the ocean too, before it met its fate millions of years ago. It wouldn't have known … just as the interloper in my belly won't know.

God, don't even think about that. But suddenly I'm overcome with a haunting half-sensation, half-emotion, as if a tiny sea-creature is curled deep within me, a creature dreaming it's found a safe refuge in a warm, ancient sea. The fossil in my hand becomes a golden blur.

Stop it, Vivy!

I swallow, and there's a murmur around me, and a thudding noise as the ferry from Portsmouth, brilliant with lights, slowly draws along the wharf outside, and men run back and forth with cables to secure it. I wipe my eyes firmly, and people disembark into the customs hall.

Time to stop ruminating. In a while we'll enter customs ourselves then finally board the ship. I close my eyes, my thumb caressing the smooth fossil in my hand. Getting sentimental won't help, Vivy. Just keep focused and do what you have to do.

I hear a few people trailing out of customs, past our waiting area. Still ages to go. There must be dozens to be processed before we can even begin.

More people shuffle by.

Someone sits down on the bench beside me. I shift a little to make room, and smell fresh sea air and the pleasant scent of a man. He clears his throat.

'Vivy?'

My eyes suddenly open wide. '*Brian*?'

'Are you going to Portsmouth?'

'Well, yes. Have you just returned? Silly me, of course you have.'

'How *are* you?'

'I'm … okay.'

'You've still got my ammonite, I see.'

I nod. 'I'm going to London. To … to end the pregnancy.' I try to hold them back, but tears slowly trickle down my cheeks.

Brian gives me a tissue and I wipe my face.

'Thank God you're here,' I say. 'No one's handed me a tissue for *ages* now.'

'I have my uses.'

'You certainly did a fine job of the flat. But how did you know I'd be back so soon?'

'I was emulating those Pacific people who build runways to entice aeroplanes to land. A kind of seaside cargo cult.'

I laugh weakly. 'It worked.'

'But now you're off to London.'

'Not for very long.'

Brian says gently, 'Vivy, are you quite certain you want to go?'

I take a shuddering breath. 'I must, there's no alternative. My marriage has ended and I'm alone. I have to rebuild my career. I can't *possibly* have a baby by myself. How would I cope?'

'I expect every woman wonders that. More importantly, what do *you* want?'

I picture the sea-voyage in front of me, the train trip, the hotel, the doctors, the anxiety, the operation, the pain. And then the long, lonely trip home again.

'What I want is to be curled up in front of the fire at Mi-Côte. But I have to ...'

'No, you don't. You don't have to do anything.'

'But if I don't, I'll have a *baby*. And then what?'

'Would you like to have a baby?'

'Yes. No. I don't *know*! Sometimes it seems almost plausible. Other times, madness.'

'While I hate to raise the thorny issue of my sisters, in fact I've had a similar conversation with both of them upon the occasions of their first pregnancies.'

'But they're married, they had husbands to help.'

'Felicity did. Susan didn't.'

'Really?'

He nods. 'Of course it was hard for her, but she's very happy now. In any case, you're not alone. People in the town are fond of you, and your ex-manager Lucien clearly adores you.'

'Why do you say that?'

'He rang and interrogated me, wondering how I fitted into the situation. I hope I reassured him. He's the one with the gangster friends, isn't he?'

'Absolutely. Be warned.'

After a silence, he says, 'And I'd help you too. You wouldn't have to be alone.'

'Don't be silly, Brian! I'm a complete *idiot*. My husband had a secret vasectomy and told me I was infertile so I became pregnant to my now ex-lover. Which means I'm a fallen woman as well.'

Brian shrugs with worldly regret, and I laugh at my own absurdity. 'But really — why would you complicate your life with me?'

'I'm a palaeontologist, Vivy. I like complicated things. As you know, I particularly like ammonites, precious, mysterious creatures, with long hidden histories. Why wouldn't I'd like you?'

I gaze at the golden disc and after a time say hesitantly, 'You know, I had the strangest sensation a while ago. As if a tiny sea-creature had taken refuge in me, knowing I'd protect it absolutely, without question. It simply trusted me.'

I sigh. 'Honestly, I have no idea if I want a baby or not, but suddenly I feel as if ... I shouldn't, I couldn't, betray that creature's trust.'

I carefully put the fossil away in my handbag, and look up. 'Have we missed the bus back to Villers-sur-Mer?'

'Probably,' Brian says. 'But we can take a taxi.'

'I'll go and get a refund on my ticket to Portsmouth. It'll pay for the taxi.'

'You can get your refund, but I've already arranged the ride home for myself. It's outside.'

'Oh dear. Not Marcel?'

'I'm afraid so.'

'Will he wink and say *eh*, Professeur?'

'Without a doubt.'

12. Jen: A Peaceful Political Discussion (Aug 1968)

A few of the kids in my class have become very serious about Vietnam: the mother of one was even arrested and jailed for two weeks for protesting. It's confusing.

My brother's over there teaching English to Vietnamese kids and *he's* not a murderer! Yet it's obvious something is very wrong with what the Americans — and us — are doing to that tiny country.

Leo left for South Vietnam eight months ago, at the same time as the Tet battles began. I read a horrible report by Kate Webb about an attack on the American embassy, and even now I'm haunted by her vision of a wild, beautiful garden scattered with blood and human flesh.

I hope Leo will be all right. He sends letters but they're pretty upbeat so I don't know if he's hiding anything. Claire wrote that he visited her and Aunt Charlotte and Uncle Pete when he was in Saigon a few months ago. She said it was an interesting evening, which doesn't say much either.

Perhaps we'll find out more this weekend. It's the August school holidays and we're off to Sydney for Tina's fiftieth birthday party!

I pack my suitcase, humming *She's Leaving Home* from Sgt Pepper's, and carefully fold my party dress on top, a new one from David Jones — short, black satin, with long blousey sleeves. Then I add the pair of *real* Mary Quant shoes Mum found for me in a sale. They're a season behind, but still better than anything else in Newcastle.

I'm as pleased as ever on the drive to Sydney, but also strangely distracted about other things. Well, Vietnam is obvious — but Petticoat magazine? Lately, ever since that tedious Bonnie and Clyde movie, Petticoat only shows dull 1930s-style 'midi' skirts. But I can't even *imagine* a time when minis won't be fashionable! Could *Petticoat* be starting to bore me?

No. Come on, Jen. You know what the real problem is.

School.

My maths is awful, and in biology and chemistry I feel as if I'm missing some sort of key everyone else seems to have. French and art are okay, but English is still difficult because of my unpleasant teacher. I have a gloomy feeling I'm not going to do very well in the Higher School Certificate in November.

And everything's so *complicated*, what with boys and kissing and feelings and not being sure about anything. I don't think our sex education lectures (with warnings about hormones turning boys crazy, and always noting our periods on a calendar, and not crossing our legs or we'll get cramps) are going to help untangle those complications, either.

I *should* be happier. I'm more confident now about my looks after all, especially since a few parties with kids from other schools have shown me that being tall, with long blonde hair, makes me attractive. At least to the people who didn't grow up with me. But really, I'm still just *me*.

Of course, thoughts of Tibor still enchant. Most nights I fall asleep imagining hazy, delightful scenarios where we're forced together by circumstances beyond our control, and everything between us is understood and nothing ever needs to be discussed.

Is this why I feel anxious? Will *this* be our time? After last year's silly misunderstanding (oh, that awful bra!) everything's completely different now.

Finally I'm a woman: seventeen, attractive, fashionable.

I take a deep breath. So what comes next?

∽

The birthday party is at Tina's house, where we're staying. I put on my black satin dress and Mary Quant shoes, and mascara, eyeliner, eyeshadow and pink lipstick.

Dad says I look very pretty but do I really need so much makeup? I smile and ignore him.

Mum is wearing a lovely red jersey dress, while Tina is in a glamorous suit, and when Billie arrives she's wearing boots and a *midi-skirt* in flowing navy crepe. Suddenly that silhouette looks absolutely perfect (sorry, Petticoat, you were right after all).

As always, lovely Nikos kisses the top of my head and jokes about how grown-up I am. Klara's blue kaftan suits her eyes, and Yvonne's top has little round mirrors embroidered all over it. Their outfits are amazingly cool, but they have nothing more to tell me about Leo's life in Vietnam. Apparently Claire doesn't say a lot to them either.

Asher arrives: round glasses, scruffy hair and a duffel-coat. We get ourselves beers and chat briefly, then other people start turning up. I don't know them very well — they're from Tina's jazz world or Yvonne's publishing world.

Mr and Mrs Adler and Devorah arrive, and Devorah looks great in a sort-of Pucci print top and flares. She tells me Tibor will be along a bit later.

People move around Tina's stylish lounge and sitting room, laughing, drinking and gossiping, while a jazz trio plays in one corner. Yet I don't feel the dreamy contentment of our usual parties: there's a funny knot in my stomach and my throat feels tight.

Then at last I hear Tibor's voice at the door, and have that strange sensation of feeling the vibrations through the soles of my feet. I move to the hall to meet him, smiling, thinking, *Ah*, everything's all right now.

Suddenly I hear other tones, warm and confident. Tibor is with a woman whose dark hair falls in a pretty tangle onto her shoulders.

Her eyes are sooty and sophisticated, her dress is something I saw in Vogue from the Paris collections, and she's wearing Mary Quant *boots* in a style so new they're not even released here. I feel cold.

The woman smiles and offers her hand. 'You must be Jen. I'm Ursula West. I work with Tibor and he's told me so much about you.'

'Jen!' says Tibor. 'You look great.' He holds back from any hug.

'Hi,' I say. I shake Ursula's hand. 'What sort of law do you do, Ursula?' (I cannot conceive how I actually speak.)

'Probate and estates. Wills and inheritance and the like.'

'Lovely,' I say. 'And how are things going for you, Tibor?'

'Can't complain. We got that office in London sorted out finally. I didn't have to go over there after all. No Mary Quant shoes!' he laughs.

'*Honestly*,' says Ursula. 'He went on so much about Mary Quant I had to get some boots on my latest trip. Do you like them?'

I glance at her exquisite footwear. 'Yes. Although I think Biba is the latest thing now.'

'Oh,' says Ursula uncertainly. 'Perhaps next visit.'

'Of course,' I say. 'Do come in and see everyone.'

They move away to the lounge room and the other guests.

I take a big gulp of my beer, which makes me cough, but at least it's something to do. I stand in the empty hall in my slightly crumpled black satin dress and my shoes from last season, surprised to notice the knot has gone from my stomach but the centre of my chest feels as if someone's taken an apple-corer to it.

Well there we are, I think stupidly. *That's* what comes next.

Asher comes out to the hall. 'Okay, Jen?' he says.

'Okay.'

'He's such a shit, you know.'

I nod and clear my throat. 'Need a refill. Kitchen?'

⁂

From the window I can see Rob and Devorah sitting with bottles of soft drink at the garden table. A bonfire burns in a metal drum nearby and glows on their young faces. I feel a million years old.

We go outside and Devorah says to Asher, 'Hey, I've got a new *name*! And you have too.'

'Yeah?' he says.

'I'm Dev and you're Ash. So we're Jen, Rob, Dev and Ash.'

'Okay,' says Ash. 'But we sound like some tragic old bunch of folk-singers.'

'But *think* about it,' says Devorah. 'Us four are the last of the horde. All the others have grown up, and *you* barely count. Anyone past twenty-one is almost too weird to talk to.'

'I take that as a compliment, Dev,' says Ash. 'But Dad's going to hate the new names.'

'He should be thankful. I could be out protesting otherwise.'

'And why aren't you?'

'Don't know. I should be, shouldn't I?'

'We've got a sit-in at Martin Place tomorrow,' says Ash. 'Wanna come?'

'Hey, can *I*?' says Rob. 'That'd be great.'

'Better ask your mum first,' I say.

Rob sighs. 'Fat chance, then. But I could say I'm going to study at the Mitchell Library, it's just near Martin Place. Then I could be swept up in the glorious wave of historical events.'

'Not quite the Cuban revolution, mate,' says Ash, sounding tired.

'Do you think people are becoming more anti-war nowadays?' I say. I'm proud of myself for carrying on a conversation with what feels like a bleeding cavity in my chest.

'Maybe,' says Ash. 'But the government'll just keep on ignoring them. Nothing will change unless the Yanks change first and tell their little lap-dogs what to do.'

'What if Nixon wins the presidency?' says Rob. 'He says he'll end the war.'

Ash laughs. 'Have you seen those dead, soulless eyes lately? Don't believe it. If he really planned to end the war, by now he'd be as dead as Martin Luther King and Bobby Kennedy.'

Somehow I say, 'Riots, murders — what a time in America. Even the police are so violent now.'

Ash nods. 'On second thoughts, you kids'd better not come tomorrow. The cops now hide their ID numbers before wading into demos, so they're getting away with all sorts of bastardry.'

'I'll still come,' I say. 'I can look after myself.' A truncheon couldn't hurt as much as my heart right now. Might be something of a distraction, really.

'Sure, Jen?' says Ash. 'Never shown much interest before.'

I shrug. 'I've been thinking about the war lately. It's just wrong, all of it.' I'm surprised to hear myself, but it's true.

'Okay,' says Ash. 'Wear sensible clothes though. Jeans, flat shoes. Might have to run.' He smiles a little. 'Not black satin, no matter how mod.'

Dev says, 'Mod isn't the cool word any more, Ash. *Cool* is the cool word.' She stands. 'And if you're going to be *boring* and leave me and Rob behind we're out of here.'

'Wait a min, Dev, want to tell Jen something,' Rob says. 'Hey, remember that stuff about my real dad?'

'Yeah?' I glance at Ash.

'It's okay,' Rob says. 'I already told Dev.'

'Real dad?' says Ash.

Rob nods. 'He wasn't that Irish guy Mum was married to. My dad was your father's friend, the one who died.'

Ash says, 'László Richter? The one in the photo on our mantelpiece?'

'*Look* at me, Ash. Come on.'

Ash stares at Rob's strong features, dark hair, clever eyes.

'Reckon this face is Irish — or Hungarian?' says Rob. 'I look more like you and Dev.'

'Wow,' says Ash. 'I never ... but yeah, you do.'

'So I asked Mum,' says Dev excitedly. 'And guess *what*? She told me the truth. Sort of. She was cagey about the real dad question, but she said that László *isn't* dead. That was a story they put around to protect him from the Irish guy, who was a gangster.'

'This means my father is *alive*,' says Rob. 'Can you believe it?'

'That's *brilliant*, Rob,' I say, briefly forgetting my own sorrow. 'But where is he?'

'In Europe. He didn't want to come back here, not even after the gangster died.'

'Have you asked your mum about him?'

'You *crazy*, Jen? She'd throttle me. But as soon as I can I'm going to Europe.'

'That'll be a while yet, won't it?' Ash says.

'Only five years to go till I'm eighteen.'

'Europe's a pretty big place,' I say. 'Where will you begin looking?'

'László was a jazz pianist,' says Rob. 'And your cousin Vivy's a jazz singer over there. She'll remember me from the horde. I'm sure she'll help me find him.'

'She won't remember you, Rob, you weren't even three when she left,' says Ash.

'But Vivy and Tina were very close,' I say. 'I bet she'd help.'

'Hey, in five years I'll be nineteen,' says Dev. 'Let's *all* go to Europe then!'

'Can't. Mum'll kill me if I don't do uni first,' I laugh shortly. 'Though I probably won't even get in now anyway.'

'No, come on, *let's*!' says Rob.

'Five years is a long time,' says Ash slowly. 'I can't even imagine what or where ...'

'Stick-in-the-mud,' says his sister. 'You'll probably be teaching boring maths somewhere, while we're all out having fun.'

'Probably,' says Ash. 'Anyway, Jen, I'll pick you up at noon. Sensible clothes, remember.'

'You've got a car?' I say.

'An ancient Holden. Don't be too embarrassed.'

'No, I'm impressed. Leo would be amazed to hear you've learnt to drive. He always said you'd be a danger to the world on a tricycle.'

⤙⤚

Leo was wrong. Ash drives calmly and carefully. After last night's party Tina and my parents are sleepy (hung-over, Rob whispers) so there's only a modest resistance to me going to a 'peaceful political discussion'.

I'm wearing jeans, sneakers and a ribbed jumper with blue, purple and black stripes that go nicely with my blonde hair. (Yes, I'm going to a demo, an expression of judgement on an immoral war, but I've still got to look nice. And it takes my mind off my pain.)

We park in a small street near Sydney University. The day was sunny earlier but now clouds have come in. When we get out of the car I start shivering.

'Here you are,' says Ash, taking a black woollen bundle from the back seat. 'I thought the weather would change. My duffel-coat from when I was fifteen. It'll fit you.'

I gaze dubiously. An ugly, baggy duffel-coat? But I'm freezing, so quickly pull it on, wrap it close and push my hands into its deep pockets. The hood feels like a scarf around my cold neck.

'Fantastic. Thanks, Ash.'

'I thought you'd be mortified to wear something so untrendy.'

'I am. But it's cosy, and makes me feel ... safe. No, *brave*, like I can tackle anything.'

'Well put your purse and things in the pockets, don't bring your shoulder-bag.'

'What, too trendy for a sit-in?'

'No, too risky if the strap catches round your neck,' he says. 'Come on.'

We walk up to the Front Lawn of Sydney University, beside what Ash calls the Quadrangle, a long sandstone building with towers and gargoyles and Gothic windows, more like a castle than a university. Crowds of people are milling about on the grass, or sitting in groups, holding posters and signs: *Peace Now*, *Get out of Vietnam*, *Save Our Sons*, *End the Slaughter*, *Resist the Draft*, *Where is our Conscience?*

A couple of other girls are wearing duffel-coats, and look as if they don't care about anything and no one could ever break their hearts. I shake back my hair and feel like that too. For a moment.

One comes over to us, a very pretty redhead, saying 'Asher, *wow!*' They hug, then she moves on, looking back over her shoulder. Another girl waves and smiles, while two others are giggling together, pretending not to stare at him.

What? When did *Ash* become attractive?

We sit on the grass and I glance at him as he leans back on his hands. He's nothing like his brother (my standard of male beauty), but with his shoulder-length dark hair, round John Lennon-style glasses, and olive skin, Ash is now actually … nice-looking. How odd.

I gaze at the crowd. A lot of the men here are nice-looking too. In fact, what a lot of surprisingly attractive people are attending this demonstration. Perhaps my social life will improve at last!

'Hey Jen,' interrupts Ash. 'What were you saying last night about not getting into uni? I thought you were doing okay at school.'

'Something's gone *wrong*, especially in maths,' I say. 'I had a sore throat and was away for a few days. After that, things got sort of foggy. Everyone else seems to know how to fling variables around to solve equations and I just don't understand how or why.'

Ash takes a small notebook and pen from his pocket. 'What, you mean an equation like this?'

'Yeah. You've got Xs and Ys here and there, and people just move them to either side of the equals sign, or top or bottom of the fraction and I don't understand why they *can*.'

'Oh. Look, if you've got a variable down here, if you move it to the other side it's got to go on the top, or vice versa. That's all.'

'Don't be *silly*. That's too easy. How do you know it works?'

'Maybe because it has from about the ninth century onwards. Hasn't failed yet.'

'Really?'

'Really.'

'Show me a hard one, then.'

'Okay.' Ash scribbles. 'What would you do here?'

'Well, going on your simple-minded technique, move that here and that there, and that goes to the other side, then it's obvious X equals ... *oh*. It works! Show me another.'

We go through several more examples, then I sit back amazed. 'How come I didn't understand this before, when it's so easy?'

'You were away, you missed some small insight, and afterwards everything seemed more complicated than it really was. That's all. Whenever I get that foggy feeling I always go back to when it started and there's usually some little thing I haven't quite grasped.'

'*You* get a foggy feeling? But you're a genius.'

Ash laughs. 'Not quite. Everyone gets that feeling. It's a good clue.'

'Wow. I remember now when chemistry became first incomprehensible — Avogadro's silly number. What on earth is *that* all about?'

'How long are you staying in Sydney?' says Ash. 'I could give you a hand there too.'

'A week. I've got my textbooks, supposedly to study.'

'Okay. I'll come over tomorrow if you like.'

'That'd be amazing. Thanks a lot, Ash.'

'Here you are. Have another look later.' He hands me the pages of equations from his notebook and I shove them into my remarkably useful coat pocket.

A loudspeaker crackles and a man starts speaking. A few different people talk about Vietnam and resisting the draft, then a handsome bearded boy stands on the steps and sets fire to a paper, and everyone cheers and claps. Then a woman says through the loudspeaker that they're marching to Martin Place, and assembling for a non-violent protest outside the Parliamentary Offices.

'Let's drive,' says Ash. 'It's about two miles and I've done enough marching lately. We can get a bit of food too.'

∞

We park not far from Martin Place and sit in the car eating sandwiches from a small shop. I'd wondered if I'd feel awkward with Ash today, but feel comfortable.

As we finish our soft drinks, I say, 'Did you set fire to your draft papers like that guy on the Front Lawn?'

'No. That's a whole new thing, actively resisting the draft itself. When I got sucked into this stupid mess the idea was to register, then apply to be classed as a conscientious objector. But I failed because I wasn't morally opposed to *all* war — I'd have fought the Nazis, for instance. Then I wouldn't go for the medical, so they put me in military prison for three weeks.'

'I remember, last Christmas. You'd just got out and looked really sad.'

He smiles briefly. 'I was. Still have nightmares, in fact.'

'Wow, Ash. I'm sorry.'

He shrugs. 'Now I'm appealing the court's decision. Might be more persuasive, have a different magistrate, whatever.'

'And if it fails again?'

'Because I registered I'm now officially under military orders, so probably two years gaol. That's what happened to Simon Townsend — ended up in solitary for months at Holsworthy.'

'That's right, there were all those marches and protests.'

'For once they worked. They finally allowed his exemption and he's out now, though I bet he'll never get over it. Another guy buckled and was shunted off to be a military cook somewhere.' Ash clears his throat. 'But I won't buckle.'

'You'd go to *prison*?'

He nods. 'Nowadays you get your two years in a civilian gaol, like Long Bay, but that's an even worse prospect. Since so many guys are refusing to register, the government's going after a few people to try to scare the rest.'

'Are you one of the few, Ash?'

'Yeah. Not a distinction I'd ever hoped for. I thought by now I'd be an academic, doing research in higher mathematics, not a clown in this bloody circus.'

'But can't you get an exemption to do more study?'

'Too late.'

'When do you have to go back to court?'

He clears his throat. 'Uh, soon. Thursday in fact.'

'Ash, that's *awful*. Will you have lawyers to help?'

'Yeah, and my parents are supporting me, too. But in the end I have to stand up alone and make my case. Bit scary.' He gazes at me. 'Hey, don't look so appalled.'

'But you're so nice, Ash. I wish they'd leave you alone.'

'Jen, you *should* say, I wish they'd fuck off.'

I smile. 'Now you just want me swearing again.'

'Always comes in handy.' He glances at his watch. 'Okay, the march should have reached Martin Place by now. Let's go.'

∽

The crowd isn't only students, there are lots of older people, with trade union signs and Save Our Sons posters. Ash says there must be about three hundred protesters there.

We find a spot in the crowd and sit down on the cold cement. A drift of light rain passes over us and I pull the hood over my hair, glad once again for the cosy duffel-coat.

As everyone gradually sits I see what I hadn't before. Around us are rows of policemen, looking big and angry and impatient.

'Interesting,' says Ash. 'That's a *lot* of muscle. Actually, Jen, maybe you'd better not stay —'

A woman stands up with a loudspeaker. 'Don't forget, everyone, *non-violent* resistance, no matter what the provocation. Remember Mahatma Gandhi and Martin Luther King. Just go limp, don't fight back, they can't arrest all of —'

She grunts as she collapses, tackled by a policeman twice her size, and suddenly they're charging at us from every side, roaring and wildly punching and kicking out.

'Curl up, Jen!' says Ash urgently. He wraps his arms around me, his hand holding the top of my head, and I cower, eyes squeezed shut, hearing noises I can't comprehend: thudding and screaming and incoherent roars.

Suddenly Ash is yanked away from me and everything is bright and terrifying. I'm grabbed and dragged along the ground, then shoved hard against the door of a police wagon, then pushed into it. Others are flung after me and I crawl to a corner as it fills up.

The door slams, the locks clunk closed. I pull myself onto a bench, shaking. People are swearing or groaning as the wagon starts and bumps along the road.

'*Jen*,' someone says and grabs my hand. I hold it for dear life. '*Ash*!'

He pushes closer to me. 'Listen, Jen. Don't be scared. They'll lock us up, parade us in front of some magistrate, give us a fine, and then we'll go home. It's all right.'

'Okay,' I say, trying not to cry. 'Are you hurt?'

'Just a bit bruised. You?'

'The same. Ash, *why*? We weren't doing *anything*!'

'We were defying their authoritarian world-view, so of course they had to kick the living shit out of us. The fascist bastards can't even conceive of people who believe in something enough to stand up to the government.'

A few guys start singing, '*We shall overcome* ...' and I join in. The wagon bounces along for a while then turns and stops. We wait, and after about ten long minutes the door is unlocked.

'Come on, freaks,' says someone large and blue-uniformed, pulling us out of the wagon. 'Line up and shut up.' He pushes me away from Ash. 'And no holding hands, you queers.'

The hood of my coat falls back and he looks at me. 'Oh Christ. Who arrested a *girl*? Twice the fucking paperwork. Stand over there, you silly bitch.'

A few policemen go around writing down everyone's names, phone numbers and addresses on clipboards. When one gets to me he flips to a new page with a put-upon air, and says, 'Your parents should be ashamed of you, girlie.'

My parents? God, what will they say?

He takes my details then another policeman says, '*You*, this way.'

I follow him along cement corridors that smell of disinfectant and urine to a sort of cage. Is that a cell? The policeman unlocks it and says, 'Inside.'

He locks the door then leaves, and I think fiercely at his back, Fuck *off*, you bastard (it does make me feel a bit better). Then I sit alone on a bench against the rear wall, and wait. And wait.

Along the corridor I can hear the boys being herded into their cells. There are lots of them and it seems to take ages. After a while they start chatting and laughing, singing protest songs and arguing happily with each other. Sounds like a bloody party, I think bitterly.

Time passes. At first I'm bored, then I'm screamingly bored. So this is what gaol is like. And if poor Ash doesn't win his appeal next week, this will be his life for *two years*, so I shouldn't complain.

I curl up on the bench and pull my hood over my head, but can't even doze, so sit up again. Paper crackles in my pocket.

Okay, I'll revise those equations Ash and I did when we were out in the soft air, beneath the blue sky — when we were *free*! I sigh in self-pity then think, don't be silly. The air was cold, the sky was grey and you're hardly locked away for thirteen years like the Count of Monte Cristo.

I read through the equations, pleased they still make sense. Maybe I won't fail maths after all. More time passes. Evening must have come by now. I hear footsteps and a different policeman arrives, unlocks the cell and grunts at me to follow him.

We walk along more corridors, thankfully less pee-scented, then arrive at the near-luxury of a room with chairs. I'm told to wait (what else is new?) and after a while dozens of other protesters start arriving, including Ash.

'Hey, Jen,' he says. 'You okay?'

'Yeah, but so *bored*. This is torture.'

'Think that's the idea.'

Someone calls out several names, and those guys leave. A little while later a few more, then Ash has to go along with a couple more. Finally they call my name. The room next door has a high bench with a cranky-looking man behind it.

'Name and address?' I tell him and he stares at me with dislike. 'Miss Bell, you are charged with obstructing access to the men's toilets in Martin Place. How do you plead?'

'Um, no I wasn't blocking anything. I was just sitting ...'

'Fined forty dollars for obstruction. Next.'

Someone ushers me to another door, and outside Ash is waiting with his parents and mine.

'Oh, Mum, Dad!' I wail and they hug me.

'Jenny,' Dad says. 'You could have been *hurt*!'

'I must apologise,' says Mr Adler severely. 'It is Asher's fault, not your daughter's.'

I pull back from Mum's comforting shoulder. 'No it *wasn't*, Mr Adler! I wanted to go. And I'm *glad* I did! I'm glad I stood up — well, sat down, really — to oppose the war and conscription. It was the right thing to do. And I'm going to do it again.'

∾

True to his promise, Ash comes over next day and my father gives him a stern look.

'Dad, he's helping me with *maths*. We're not overthrowing the government. Not today, anyway.'

'Jenny, you do realise you'll be paying off that fine out of your allowance for months?'

'Yes, Dad. Come on, Ash. Avogadro's number is calling us.'

We get Avogadro's number under control, which actually isn't too painful, then go back to maths.

We tackle a few harder equations and even do some calculus, which usually terrifies me. I don't understand why it all never made sense before, but now it does.

'You're an amazing teacher, Ash. Really.'

'It's more your own confidence, Jen. And you're finding this interesting for the first time too.'

'Well it *is* interesting, I never saw that before.' I hesitate. 'And thanks for helping me too, when I know you've probably got a lot to think about before ... Thursday.'

Ash shakes his head. 'I'd rather do maths any day. Tomorrow we can go over a few physics topics. But on Wednesday I probably need to stay home and sort out my things, and talk to Mum. You know.'

'I know. And — remember the party just a few days ago? When I felt so horrible because of ... anyway, I've stopped feeling horrible and almost don't even care now. Isn't that weird?'

'No, it's good.' He smiles a little. 'You're loyal, Jen, always have been. But you can't be blindly loyal or you end up with blinkers. A bit like the people who think the police can do no wrong.'

I feel close to tears. 'Here's your duffel-coat too. Thanks for letting me wear it.'

'It doesn't fit any more, so you keep it. It looked good on you.'

'Thanks, Ash. I really love it.' I swallow. 'And anyway, on Thursday you might get a sympathetic magistrate and then you'll be free to go and do your research, not ...'

'Maybe.'

I have a sudden idea. 'Hey, I know, what about your father? He has lots of contacts, couldn't he *persuade* —'

Ash laughs. 'Sadly, those days are over. Dad had a certain power when the politicians loved illegal gambling dens. But those smug hypocrites profiting from Vietnam's misery? He's got no traction at all.'

∽

Thursday comes and I insist I'm going to court to support Ash. Surprisingly Mum says she'll take me, though Dad says, 'You can go, but do you really have to wear that awful coat? Just behave, Jenny.'

Ash and his parents are waiting outside the courtroom and we all say hello. Ash's hair is tidy and he's wearing a suit and an open-necked shirt.

'Dad insisted on the suit but I couldn't cope with a tie,' he says.

Then an official calls out something like 'Commonwealth versus Asher Adler, please take your seats in the courtroom.'

Ilona, Ash's mum, hugs him fiercely and whispers to him. His dad Moshe hugs him too, and he's got tears in his eyes, something I've never seen in a grown-up man.

Ash turns to me and says, 'If we don't meet for a while, Jen, maybe write and send me some maths problems?'

'Ash, you idiot, don't even *say* that.'

I'm crying now and he hugs me too. He feels strong and warm and brave, but when we enter the courtroom, and he sits down with his lawyer at the front, he looks slight and worried.

A small crowd of supporters are there. I notice the pretty redhead that hugged him at the demo, and the girl that waved. He seems to have a lot of friends. That's *good*, I firmly tell myself.

Then everything goes very fast. The legal history of moral objections to war, laws with long names from various years, other people who've been prosecuted, pronouncements by various prime ministers, and on and on.

Then finally Ash has to stand up and argue why he should have a conscientious exemption from serving in an unjust and immoral war.

Yes, *yes*, I think. Of *course* you should!

But after writing something down the magistrate says irritably, 'Appeal denied. You can't pick and choose what war you object to, Mr Adler. You are fined two hundred dollars and ordered to report for your medical.'

Ash says steadily, 'I refuse to report for my medical and I refuse to serve in the army.'

The magistrate stares at him. 'Well, in that case, Mr Adler, I sentence you to two years of imprisonment. Officers of the court, please take the prisoner to the holding cells.'

Sick with horror, I watch as two men take Ash's arms and lead him to a door on the far side of the courtroom. Then the door closes behind them.

13. Claire: The Art Deco Bathroom (May-Aug 1968)

'Claire, darling, phone for you,' calls Charlotte from the hall downstairs. 'Leo, and he sounds pretty pleased with himself.'

Leo certainly is. He's cooked up some scheme to substitute me for a Mirror journalist who's fallen prey to the notorious pitfall of a shaved-ice drink.

But it all sounds reasonable, and God knows I need the work, so next morning I turn up at Tan Son Nhut airport. I'm delighted to discover I know the photographer waiting there for C. Fenn, Journalist.

'Claire, you bloody beauty,' he says. 'It *is* you! I'll be damned.'

'Greg? Haven't seen you since —'

'Since you left us all behind in your dust. No one could believe you'd actually *done* it, raced off to Vietnam. How're you finding it here? Lots of work?'

'Some,' I say. 'Look, they're calling us. I'll fill you in later.'

I haven't been in a Caribou before but I keep my anxiety to myself during the fast, steep takeoff. It's only a short flight to Nui Dat, but despite the racket I get to hear all about Greg's wife and the new baby and the new house.

It's clear he's a happy man. He was always one of the nicer guys at the Mirror, even though the bar there for civilised behaviour wasn't set terribly high.

We come in steeply and I try not to shriek. Still, we touch down safely and with roaring engines the plane halts, then we're hurried out the rear ramp.

Across the tarmac I see Leo's tawny hair and delighted grin, and for some reason my eyes sting for a moment. (Enough of that.) Greg and I get introduced to Leo's two mates, who seem nice enough but pretty stunned at the sight of me.

'Okay,' says Leo cheerfully. 'Into the jeep, then we're off to Ba Ria and the high school. Claire, Greg, you come in the back seat with me, a bit safer there.'

We quickly pass through Nui Dat — all I see is trees, tents, sheds and bare dirt — and at the gates our documents get checked, then we're onto the road.

During the fifteen-minute trip I'm crammed against Leo, trying not to notice his proximity, as everyone trades chit-chat on people's jobs, time in the country, what's happening today, and the sad fate of the other journalist (the non-female one, the *real* one).

We arrive at Ba Ria, a town of stone and brick buildings, some pockmarked with bullet holes, with trees and bushes dotted here and there. Two yellow buses full of gleeful kids are waiting outside the high school gates, with two jeeps of American troops beside them. One of the jeeps carries a very large machine gun.

'Security detail,' says Leo. 'They want to show us how helpful the US forces can really be.'

Greg and the other two Civil Affairs men go on the boys' bus, while Leo and I get on the girls' bus. The girls call out happily, 'Chao anh Leo,' hello brother Leo, and Leo introduces me as 'Nha bao Claire,' journalist Claire. All sorted out.

We sit together in the only free seat. More distracting proximity but I can deal with it. The bus set off to Vung Tau on what Leo says is a one-hour trip. After five minutes of polite conversation, suddenly there's the deafening clatter of a machine gun.

Leo yells, 'Down, *get down*, allongez-vous, oh *Christ* —'

The girls throw themselves onto the bus floor screaming in terror, then the gunfire stops and the convoy comes to a halt. Leo looks out the back window and swears, then races out the door to the jeep behind us. He yells at the sheepishly grinning American with the machine gun, who shrugs.

The girls stop sobbing and sit down and we start off again.

'He thought the grass on the side of the road looked suspicious, so he decided to do a bit of *clearing by fire*,' Leo says. 'Stupid bloody thug.'

'One way to break the ice.'

Leo smiles. 'Yeah, I was feeling a bit shy earlier. But hey, it's good to see you, Claire.'

'You too. And thanks for the work opportunity. Let's hope the rest of the day is a bit quieter —'

Suddenly there's a shudder, a far-away explosion, and black smoke drifts over the distant hills.

Leo leans across me to get a better look. 'Probably a landmine.'

'Are those the Long Hai Hills?' They rise emerald and abrupt from the plain and stretch a long way away.

He nods. 'The Third Battalion's on a big op there at the moment. It's a wilderness, just jungle, ravines, caves. Poor bastards. They're running into a lot of mines.'

'M16 jumping jacks?' I ask.

'Yeah. How did you know that?'

'I've been hearing about the Dat Do minefield, apparently set up against expert advice and now the source of a whole lot of new NLF munitions.'

Leo nods. 'About right. Funny, just before your plane arrived I saw my old surfing mate Bazza, one of the guys who built the minefield.'

'That'd be Bazza, brother of Shazza?' I say.

'The very same. Apparently Shazza survived her encounter with me and is now happily married. *And* having a career as well.'

'Good for her.'

'But Claire — really, who told you about the minefield?'

'Someone who interpreted at the meeting between the brigadier and the RF commanders, who insisted they had no men to patrol it. And now the RF are being blamed for the whole debacle.'

'Ah. Our old mate André. Gets around, doesn't he?'

'He's being helpful. With proof this'd be a fantastic story.'

'*And* you'd be blacklisted for highlighting the vacuum between the ears at the top. No outings like this, for instance.'

'Are we having a picnic lunch?'

'Too right, with a barbecue.'

'Ah well, I guess journalistic integrity has to go by the board occasionally.'

We drive into Vung Tau, once the French resort Cap Saint Jaques, where horse-drawn carts still trundle along the streets. It's a mix of old villas and low new buildings, with pink and purple bougainvilleas beside creamy frangipani trees in the small gardens.

Unlike Ba Ria, the buildings show little damage. 'Nice, isn't it?' says Leo. 'The NLF doesn't bother attacking this place much.'

At Back Beach the children eat their own bodyweight in lunchtime barbecue, then go swimming. The girls wade into the water, squealing in delight, modestly covered in shirts and shorts, and the barechested boys yell and splash ecstatically. The beach is ocean-facing, wide and shallow, so it's safe for them — most haven't been to the seaside before.

I'm intrigued to notice groups of ordinary Vietnamese enjoying a day at the beach too. It seems almost incongruous, given the state of wariness of our security escorts, but I suppose any chance at an everyday life has to be grasped.

While Greg takes photos of happy kids and the beautiful beach, I take notes and interview some of the people lying on towels around us, and Leo's Civil Affairs mates.

Later I get into my bathers in the womens' changing room, wade into the gentle surf and swim. It's been a long time since I did anything so easy and pleasurable.

I float into deeper water, gazing at the soft white clouds building up in the blue afternoon sky. Leo swims out to me and says, 'I'll be your shark bait if you like. You can escape while I sacrifice myself.'

'*Are* there sharks?'

'It's the South China Sea. What do you reckon?'

'Okay, let's go closer in. No sacrifice required.'

We lie on the sand to dry out. I glance discreetly at Leo's body beside me, his long tanned back, firm muscles, broad shoulders. Once again I'm forced to detach myself by wondering why some human forms are so sculpturally fascinating.

By mid-afternoon it's time to go. We don't want to be on the roads after dusk, that's begging for trouble. The bus is warm and dozy, and everyone is peaceful after the day's exertions.

'I was thinking, Claire,' Leo says. 'If you want to know more about the mine casualties, my doctor tentmate Simmo might help. They're no secret, but he's got the context and the numbers. Just don't point out what stupid bastards are running this war until Simmo and I get safely back home, okay?'

I smile. 'May not be a story in it anyway, but could be useful.'

Leo clears his throat. 'Actually, got something to thank you for saving me from being the poor bunny forced to write up this day.'

'I'd have done it, anyway. Needed the work.'

'Yeah, but.' He hands me a small parcel of dark silk. I unwrap it to find a bangle, a smooth circle of jade. From its deep emerald hues I know it must have been expensive.

'Leo! That's *beautiful*.'

'See if it fits. You're supposed to squeeze your hand through —'

'Ooh, ouch ... *there*, courtesy of my suntan oil,' I say. 'Not sure it'll ever come off again though.'

'Not supposed to. Vietnamese women wear them their whole lives.'

'Do they? Why?'

'They say jade is alive. It protects you and becomes part of you.'

'Those colours are gorgeous,' I say, holding up my wrist and admiring it. 'Look at this blueish bit and the apple-green, and those deep emerald swirls. But you can still see *through* it.'

'Strong as steel, and over time the colours become richer. That's what the jeweller said, anyway.'

'You're an easy sell,' I say. 'But thank you, Leo. I love it.'

We sit together in easy silence, the bus rattling along, then he says quietly, 'Had a thought, Claire. What if we wait till we're both old and grey, and *then* we get together? Mightn't have many other options by that stage, after all.'

'Yeah?' I say. 'Reckon *I* will, mate.'

'True. But I'll definitely be unlovable by then.'

'Is that your idea of selling yourself? It's not very persuasive.'

'I'm starting slowly, a guerilla attack. Is it working?'

I shrug. 'I'll have to see when we're old and grey.'

Leo gently squeezes my hand. 'I'll take that as a yes.'

Our fingers slowly intertwine and I don't let go. I'm relaxed, the bracelet feels wonderful, and his hand is warm and comforting.

'Old and grey,' Leo murmurs. 'Looking forward to it.'

∽

The story I do for the Mirror with Greg's photos is well-received. Still it's pretty superficial, so I freelance a longer, deeper account, *The Peaceful Day*, and it's perhaps the best thing I've ever written.

Somehow (I don't know how) all the threads come together, the children, the soldiers, the ordinary people, the beauty of the beach, the pain of the scarred towns, the sense of this war as something taking place on another plane to everyday life, as if different worlds are only occasionally intersecting.

It may be a slow news week but the story is picked up everywhere, and amazingly, Australian Associated Press, AAP, offers me a part-time job.

I'm suddenly *persona* extremely *grata* with MACV as well (my more critical comments have clearly sailed right over their heads), and within days they've issued me a laminated accreditation card.

André says, his eyes amused, 'I am glad your journalistic credibility has at last been recognised. But do you understand the true reason Vung Tau does not get attacked very often?'

'No, why?'

'Because it is not only a rest and recreation resort for the allies, it is also used for exactly the same purpose by the soldiers of the NLF.'

'But those people on the beach I interviewed were so *nice*. I suppose one or two were a little reserved and *really* didn't want their photos taken, but ...'

We start laughing.

Still, grim reality is never very far away. After eight months of trying, I now have a free pass to jump on any US transport, go anywhere in the country, see whatever I want and write whatever I want. The trouble is, what I really want to write is this: beyond the brute physicality of weapons this is a war of the mind, and the real battlefield is the sheer will of the ordinary Vietnamese.

André has told me something his militia friend Minh said, that's left me stunned. It seems that girl volunteers in the NLF, fifteen-year-olds, have become the best mine-raisers in existence. With *bare feet* they slowly cover every inch of a minefield, until they brush up against the tiny triggering prongs of a mine.

The girls halt their slow dance, gently shift the dirt, and slide in a wire that blocks the trigger. Even more carefully they go deeper, to the live grenade beneath, the supposed 'anti-lift' device, slide in another wire to block it, and safely retrieve the mine. Then it's used against boys who don't want to be here.

Can invaders shadow-boxing whatever they imagine 'communism' to be this week defeat a people so utterly committed to their independence?

Think my money's on the fifteen-year-olds.

∽

As an AAP part-timer, I write stories of special interest to Australians, such as the day at the beach, visits from Australian politicians, or a new article on the Australian forces which, to Leo's disappointment, doesn't get me a return visit to Nui Dat.

Like other reporters from small organisations, I file my copy through the telexes of the Reuters office on Han Thuyen street, opposite a park that's a block away from Tu Do. The office itself is upstairs and not large, barely fitting the chief correspondent, a few staffers, a local reporter and three telex operators.

I'm still fairly isolated as a journalist. I see Ann Bryan now and then, but she's always madly working and not easy to catch up with. Clever Kate Webb might have become a friend, but she's often out in the field, and when she returns she's strung-out and silent.

But then, through the Reuters office, I meet some other Australian reporters: energetic Michael Birch (who works for my agency AAP) and his friends, thoughtful Bruce Piggott and Frank Palmos, a large-eyed recent arrival.

Perhaps it's my new-found credibility as the owner of a MACV card, but they're easy to get on with, and we sometimes eat together. They're a lot of fun and I start to feel more grounded than before.

It's also good to see that after February's Tet offensive the Americans have finally stopped under-estimating their opponents and start paying more notice to intelligence reports. In April they hear another attack is being planned for the end of the month and move troops to Saigon.

Still, apart from some trouble on the northern border nothing much seems to happens here: until a few days later, on 5 May, when it's a Sunday morning and I'm sleeping in.

I wake to a loud knocking on my door, so I jump up, pull on a wrap and find André standing there, pale and sweating.

'My God,' he says. 'You're all *right*.'

Now I hear explosions and gunfire, not very far away.

'What's happening?'

'Can I sit down?' he says, breathing heavily. 'I've just run all the way from the Ministry.'

'Here, the bed. What *is* it?' I've never seen André in such distress.

'We were called into work early today, as the NLF has begun a new attack on Saigon. Reports were that five journalists, four of them Australian, had driven to the Cholon district. They were attacked. One escaped, the rest died. They said one of the dead was from AAP. I just ran. *Christ*, Claire. I thought it was you.'

André suddenly sobs, his hands over his face. I sit beside him and hug his bowed shoulders, my eyes filling with tears of sympathy. After a time he takes a shuddering breath and sits up, rubbing his face. 'My apologies, Claire. I must suppose that more than one Australian works for AAP.'

'Not that many. André, I'm so *terribly* sorry.'

He nods and lifts his hand, and wipes a tear from my cheek. We gaze at each other. Such green lights in those brown eyes, I think, with the strange sense he's doing exactly what I'm doing: trying to remain detached and objective.

And failing. Both of us failing.

Slowly, irresistibly, our faces come together, as if some agreement is at last being formally sealed. He smells of lemongrass and coriander, his mouth is warm, his palm cups my face, my fingers stroke his hair, and I fall into a dark, deep sweetness. Then it ends.

André pulls away and we stare at each other saying foolish things: that was — I didn't mean — please — so beautiful — I'm sorry — we should — we shouldn't — We definitely shouldn't.

I take a breath, painfully aware of my body. His body. I stand and tighten my wrap. 'We'd better go and find out more.'

André nods and gets to his feet. 'I'll meet you at the car.'

I'm left standing there. This is *nothing* like the times I kissed Leo, they were such simple moments of delight. *This*? My heart is thumping, my mouth tingling, my body shockingly alive. I want to fall onto the bed and hug a pillow and groan. Or howl.

Stop. Quickly, wash, dress. Go and do your work.

∞

The surviving journalist is large-eyed Frank Palmos. The dead are Ron Laramy, a Briton, and three Australians: John Cantwell from Time-Life, and my new friends, Michael Birch and Bruce Piggott.

They'd seen smoke and helicopter gunships over Cholon that morning and set off in a small, open Mini-Moke to investigate. Civilians were fleeing and yelling at them to go back, but they didn't, they stupidly didn't.

Around a corner they ran into a roadblock, then guerillas started firing. Frank threw himself out of the car and played dead. He heard Michael yelling 'Bao chi, bao chi' — 'Press, press' — then, Frank says, one guerilla said bao chi 'mockingly' and shot Michael and the others at close range.

Frank leapt up and ran, joining a group of fleeing Vietnamese, and got away among them. He's clearly shattered and the press conference ends quickly. André and I leave in silence, and I feel sick as we drive back to the house.

We park and André sighs. 'An Australian yelling out bao chi? Saigon jargon, meaningless to a peasant guerilla. And even if they had understood, NLF journalists always wear uniforms and carry weapons. Five white men in civilian clothes, driving into a battle? To guerillas they could only be CIA officers.'

'Are you *defending* them?' I say.

'No. But when you arm naive young men, from either side, and fill their heads with tales of enemy inhumanity, subject them to pain and fear, how can you wonder when they run amok?'

'There you go again — ambivalence. I'm so fed up with bloody ambivalence!'

'What?' says André, puzzled.

'Nothing's straightforward here, nothing makes *sense*. The good guys consistently do the wrong thing, the bad guys have right on their side, the so-so guys just feather their own nests. This place is simply *insane*!'

I don't say, I'm confused. For so long I've kept my feelings at bay — for Leo and for you — and now you've shattered my defences and I'm more vulnerable than ever before in my life. I don't *want* this.

Too late I realise I've said it aloud.

'You don't want ...?'

'Earlier, in my room. I *can't*, André. I have to work.'

'It was nothing,' he says quietly. 'We were both in shock. It will not happen again.'

∽

The battle of Saigon continues for a week or more of vicious house-to-house fighting, which leaves most of the houses in ruins. The casualties for American and ARVN forces are the highest they've been for any month of the war, but the NLF casualties are much greater. This time there's no talk of inflated kill ratios when the bodies of the enemy lie broken in such numbers along the streets.

Late May and early June bring even more attacks: these new offensives are being called mini-Tets. Some say they're to give teeth to the North's stance at peace negotiations in Paris, but in any case the talks quickly stall through arguments over the shape of the negotiating table. Round implies equality (North) and rectangular implies opposition (South).

For the next two months things are relatively quiet in Saigon. Leo and I keep writing to each other. A couple of extra men have joined his detachment so they're able to teach more classes, not just schools, but adults and refugees.

His pet project is a new library and science block at Chau Van Tiep high school, and I get to hear about the engineering, the library stock and the science curriculum in great detail.

Leo also gets landed with the job of acting Youth and Sports Adviser, because the real one has disappeared on leave. So I also hear about various sport stadiums, new and planned, old and needing repair: stands, fences, fields and swimming pools. I don't mind. I've never known him so engaged before.

His letters end warmly, but with a touching restraint. Oh, Leo.

At the same time, thankfully, my relationship with André is also back on track: calm, friendly, informative, and helpful beyond anything I have any right to expect. But things have become more difficult for Charlotte and Pete.

Without much luck they've been trying every funding avenue possible to keep the orphanage going. It's outrageous they can't get more support, given the bribes they've paid over the years to the church and the government.

They own the orphanage building (not far from Cholon, yet luckily unaffected by the mini-Tets), but profligacy and corruption are swamping their small resources, and the costs of care, food and maintenance simply keep rising.

Beyond our rent at Tu Do Street, André and I contribute as much as we can, but it's still not enough. The friends Charlotte had in the US hierarchy have now been rotated home, and the new incumbents don't appreciate the influence she has in Saigon: or had.

In July, at last, a hopeful letter arrives from Vivy, who's been to Normandy to find out why the money from Charlotte's villa hasn't arrived since last year — it turns out the agent has simply stolen everything and run away.

Still, Vivy thinks Moshe Adler might be able to help through his European connections. It sounds a fairly slim chance, but if anyone can do it I suppose Moshe can. Pete takes some heart from the news, but Charlotte becomes thinner and smokes too much.

∽

A third phase of mini-Tet offensives begins. It doesn't affect us in Saigon because the NLF have learnt that house-to-house fighting benefits only those with squadrons of helicopter gunships to obliterate the houses.

This time it's mostly attacks on bases near the Cambodian border: until one night in August.

Since the February offensive the NLF have had a new and fearsome weapon, a self-propelled 122-mm rocket. Unlike close-range mortars they can reach more than seven miles. Fired from the outskirts of a city, nowhere is safe.

And in the early hours of 22 August, a stream of these terrible rockets scream overhead and hit dozens of sites in Saigon. We're already half-awake when the phone in the hall rings over and over, and a near-hysterical voice tells us a rocket has hit Maison Lien.

André drives Charlotte, Pete and me there, none of us speaking, all dreading what we will find. The orphans sleep in dormitories, the boys in one wing, the girls in another — and both are on the vulnerable upper floor.

It's a shocking relief to get there and find the rocket has hit only a corner of the building near the kitchen, rather than the dormitories. Lights from an ambulance and two fire engines are flickering on the burning debris as we rush from the car.

'Thank *Christ*,' says Charlotte, as we see that the nuns have gathered the children and taken them to an open area away from the building.

The mother superior, shaking, says to Charlotte and Pete, 'Madame, Monsieur — Soeur Agnès, Soeur Bernadette, they go to prepare breakfast. I fear they are dead!'

They were in the kitchen when the rocket struck? I feel sick. Agnès is merry, Bernadette stern. They'd both helped me enormously with my articles on the orphans.

Charlotte gasps and half-collapses, but Pete holds her.

'Are you *sure*?' I say. The nun points hopelessly at the debris. At the same time a fireman yells, and starts pulling rubble off a pile, thankfully away from the flames. André and I rush over and, together with the fireman, start throwing bricks and cement and plaster from the spot where a foot is protruding. Gradually we uncover a body: a body praying loudly to her God.

'Soeur *Bernadette*!' I say. 'Êtes-vous vivante?'

'Naturellement. Le bon Dieu m'a sauvée.'

We help her slowly sit up, then get to her feet. She dusts off her habit and adjust her veil.

'Et les enfants?' she asks.

'Tout va bien,' is the best I can manage.

My voice is shaking: I've noticed a bloodied, shattered arm protruding from the rubble. Someone from the ambulance leads Sister Bernadette away, as André and I glance in despair at each other. We fall to our knees and start freeing the other body. Please, please, not sweet young Sister Agnès!

But it is: once so alive and now terribly, terribly dead. Her face, all sensitive mouth and wide cheekbones, is mercifully untouched, but her veil is pulled away and her shorn black hair exposed. I know that would mortify her, so I gently pull the veil back into place.

There is no longer any urgency. We carefully remove the cement and bricks holding Sister Agnès down, then the ambulance men bring a stretcher, cover her and take her away.

Breathing heavily, André helps me rise. I hold his arms for a moment, shaking, then he says, 'Tante Charlotte?' I turn to see she's lying on a stretcher, Pete kneeling beside her.

'*No!*' I say.

Pete says, 'She's — her breathing, her heart, she's fainted. I don't know what to —'

'*Go*, for God's sake,' says André. 'Pete, go with her. We will handle things here and meet you at the hospital later. Go!'

Pete leaves with Charlotte in the ambulance, then André and I can only stand and watch as the firemen gradually extinguish the flames. At some stage I grasp his hand and he holds it: I'm grateful. I think it's the only thing keeping me upright.

When the fire is out and the firemen have checked the rest of the building, the nuns, weeping and murmuring prayers, herd the children back to their beds.

In the distance we hear the explosions of more rockets. The firemen look at each other, roll up their hoses and go to their next job.

As André and I drive to the hospital, the dawn sun glows red through a sky of drifting smoke. I feel as if I'm shaking, about to shatter, although my body is oddly still. We park the car and walk through the corridors of the hospital to Charlotte's room. She's asleep, Pete sitting beside her bed. He smiles wanly as we arrive.

'How is she?' I say.

'Not too bad. She gets asthma when she's stressed and her heart doesn't much like it. But she's resting now. How were things when you left the orphanage?'

'Much of the building was saved and everyone is now safely back in bed,' says André. 'Do not worry, Pete. You must simply take care of Charlotte.'

He nods. 'You know the pair of you look like ghosts, covered with dust and blood?'

'Do we?' I say. 'That explains the looks we were getting in the corridors.'

Pete says, 'Go home. I'll stay here and get some rest on a pallet.'

'But we can keep you company,' I say.

'Off you go, kids. I'd rather be alone with Charlotte anyway.'

We hug him and leave.

∞

André and I drive home in silence. I'm still aware of a sense of trembling, of fragility, throughout my body. We park the car and walk up the stairs to the third floor, then stand together in the corridor: the corridor with my room at one end, André's at the other.

The house is silent. We're as grotesquely ghostlike as Pete said, covered in dust and blood. We gaze at each other wordlessly for a long time, then I say, 'My ensuite is too small,' and lead André along the corridor and into the big old Art Deco bathroom, all rounded corners and green and cream tiles.

I start unbuttoning my shirt and say, 'Take off your clothes.'

'Claire, are you sure?'

'Yes.'

I shed everything but my (unremovable) jade bangle. Naked, I turn on the taps and step into the large shower and run water through my hair.

'Come on,' I say.

André removes the last of his clothes. His body is beautiful. Brown, lithe, male.

He steps into the shower and I hand him a bar of soap. He gazes at me, smiling, and uses it to lightly rub my wet shoulders.

I turn away. 'No. Wash everything.'

He runs the soap slowly up and down my back and over my buttocks and down my legs to my feet. Then I turn to face him. '*Everything.*'

He caresses my breasts and belly and thighs, and all of me that was trembling, shivering, fragile, shatters very, very softly, and flows away with the water.

'You, now,' I whisper.

I stroke the sculpture, the fascinating sculpture of his body, his fine smooth skin, his narrow muscles, his dark hair. His vulnerable, mutable masculinity. He gazes at me half-smiling, breathing deeply. I put down the soap and slowly wash the suds off my skin: and then off his.

His face is still, focused upon mine, and I take his head between my hands and kiss him over and over. Then I pull him towards me and into me. And I let his rhythm and urgency show me where I want to go, and where I need to go.

∞

We lie in André's bed, my head on his shoulder. I gaze at the long pale curtains rolling slowly at his window, greenish in the shadows of the afternoon rain.

'On my first night in this country,' I murmur, 'I was hypnotised by the salon curtains, flowing that way. They were like water in the evening breeze.'

André says, 'Even today I watch them for hours.'

I look at him. 'Did you think, that first night, we'd end up here?'

'You dazzled me, Claire, and of course I could dream. But you? I did not dare expect you.'

He leans over and kisses me. I stretch towards the silk of his skin, the scent of his body, and open to him as easily as a flower. Then once again all I care about is my own pleasure.

When I wake again, I contemplate André's sleeping face. His Vietnamese mother's long black lashes, his French father's straight nose, his own sensitive mouth. My lover, now. I lightly stroke his hair and Leo's jade bangle catches the light.

And ... what if?

What if it had been Leo in the Art Deco bathroom last night, Leo who'd looked into my eyes, Leo who'd trembled beneath the flowing water and groaned as we celebrated that small victory over our own fragile lives?

The mere thought fills me with lust again and I gasp.

Does this mean my desire for Leo is as intense as it is for André?

That it wouldn't have mattered *which* man I made love to last night? Oh, God. That's a complicated question, and my mind feels blank and empty. But then, Leo is far away from me — and in truth I don't understand our strange bond — while André's legs are pleasingly, and promisingly, entwined with mine.

He stirs, turns sleepily towards me, and murmurs, 'Are you all right, Claire?'

'Yes. I've felt enjoyment before, but not such ... pleasure,' I say.

He nods. 'For me too, it was extraordinary.'

After a peaceful silence I say, 'And now?'

'Now? Dear Claire, I think we must be wise.' He sighs. 'You are still a white woman and I am still a child of dust. Together we offend almost everyone in this country.'

I laugh quietly. 'Should they become aware we are lovers, yes. But in our usual roles? We could be discreet and go on as before.'

'That might be more dangerous than you imagine.'

'Isn't everything here? What about last night, when death arrived so suddenly?'

André nods. 'And then, after death, you offered me life itself. Claire, you are very brave.'

'No, not brave. I've been hiding myself away from the world for a long time. But it's not enough. I want life, I want *more* life, André. I want it for both of us.'

He gazes at my eyes and silently strokes back my hair. I can't decipher his expression. Is it regret, admiration, pity ... sorrow?

It doesn't matter. I've made my decision. I run my thumb along the sweet curve of his mouth.

'I'll cope with the danger, André.' I shrug. 'Just never tell me to go home.'

14. VIVY: ROMANCE ISN'T EVERYTHING (JUN-SEP 1968)

When we get back to Mi-Côte I'm exhausted — physically and emotionally — and just want to hide away in my flat for a couple of days. Brian brings me food, but I'm too tired to talk.

Then I wake up feeling better. The day is clear and warm, so we drive to the Black Cow cliffs for Brian to chase fossils and me to sit on the sand and be lulled by the waves. He comes back almost empty-handed.

'Slim pickings, I fear. I need a storm. Vivy, you've failed me — you didn't bring even a small whirlwind in your wake.'

I'm lying on my tummy (thickened a little now) and look up. 'I'm sure there'll be storms ahead. Be patient. What happened to your whatever-it-was, the big one you found?'

'The complete *Peltoceras schroederi*, you mean?'

'Of course. On the tip of my tongue.'

Brian spreads a towel and leans back on his elbows. 'One reason I went to London the other day. Took it to a colleague at the British Museum, and when he recovers from his amazement we're going to do a paper on it.'

'Lovely. Did you get to see your family too?' I rest my head on my arms again. The sun warms my back so nicely if I were a cat I'd purr.

'Yes,' he says. 'My nephew Kit, Susan's son, will soon be three. For some reason his mother didn't want him to have a geologist's hammer for his birthday, so we agreed on a train set.'

'How unimaginative. Perhaps you could smuggle a few chisels into the train set?'

'I fear not. As Susan pointed out, she has some very nice porcelain.' He hesitates. 'I had another reason to go. My fiancée, Annabelle, was in something of a state. The wedding's in four months, which seems ages to me, but apparently not anyone else.'

I'm glad my face is hidden. Given that we've barely spent a week in each other's company it's absurd to feel this is something Brian should have mentioned before.

Perhaps when he picked me up out of the mud puddle? *Oh by the way, we don't know each other but I'm engaged to an English rose named Annabelle.*

That's so silly I manage to look up and smile with proper warmth. 'Congratulations! Yes, I expect there's a lot to be done.'

'Not so much the wedding. She's concerned about something else, but says she'll sort it out. Apparently the seating arrangements may need United Nations intervention.'

'Is Annabelle a scientist too?'

'She's actually the singer in Electric Cloud. They had that hit, *Leave Me Tomorrow.*'

'Heavens. That's a *very* good song — I'm impressed.'

'She was just a kindergarten teacher when we met, years ago, so it's been quite a roller-coaster.'

We settle into our usual easy silence in the sunlight, the waves rushing peacefully onto the shoreline. I rest my face on my arms again and scold myself. Of course a man as nice as Brian would have a fiancée. It's surprising he's not already married, he's my age, thirty-one, after all.

I'm ashamed to admit I'd had a faint flickering hope ... well, my future life as a single mother would be much easier with a man by my side, and the more I know Brian the more attractive he is. I can't even imagine how I ever saw him as bland.

I suddenly recall he appeared, *very* memorably, in a sultry dream last night and my neck goes hot. Overactive hormones, Vivy, that's all. Brian has only ever offered me friendship, a gift in itself.

Anyway, I've had enough of expecting men to take care of me: look how well that's ended up! This is a *good* thing. Fewer complications, well-defined boundaries. I've got enough confusion ahead to need any more.

And there are things I should tell Brian, too. I clear my throat. 'You probably wonder why I came back here.'

'To be honest, I didn't really think it was the fossils.'

'Henk, my husband. I'm humiliated to even ...' I rub my face. 'Seems he's stolen my money, given his girlfriend my job and sold our flat behind my back. When I expressed displeasure he hit me and tried to imprison me. But I got away and I'm never going back.'

Brian sits up. 'Dear God, Vivy. Why didn't you call the police?'

'Henk is Dutch and best mates with the Police Commissioner. I'm a foreigner and not. Anyway, I couldn't bear being in Amsterdam itself one moment longer.'

'He *hit* you? I'm hardly the fisticuffs sort, but if we ever meet —'

'No, no, it's not *your* problem, Brian! I can take care of myself. I've had to for most of my life.'

'I'm so sorry, Vivy,' he says gently. 'It's not you who should feel humiliated. What a bastard.'

I smile a little. 'Exactly what Lucien said. And worse.'

'Look, I have money if you need it —'

'Thank you, but he gave some of it back and I have enough for a time.' I sit up. 'Please, just let me forget it for now. All I need is fresh air and sunlight and safety in my own small place. I'd rather not think or speak of him again.'

Brian nods. 'Whatever you want.'

'Well, what I *really* want right now is a fresh ham baguette and a madeleine from Madame Cloutier's. My stomach and I appear to have reached a truce, and I feel like living dangerously.'

Brian stands and offers his hand to help me up.

'No thanks, I'm fine,' I say. I rise, busily brushing sand off my legs and shaking out my towel.

∽

After a quiet chat with the librarian Madame Desvignes, she suggests I start seeing one of the more progressive doctors in the town, le docteur Allard. 'Progressive' may be too generous: Docteur Allard stares at me over his glasses with the air of a stern Victorian papa. Luckily his English is good as I'm already feeling too dazed to think in French. We establish I am newly resident in town and a married woman.

'Your husband's profession, Madame?' he says, busily writing notes.

'My husband is in the Netherlands, so it's not important.'

'Of course it is important. He is your next-of-kin.'

'No. We're separated and will be getting divorced.'

'You cannot raise a child without its father, Madame.'

'My husband is not the child's father. Perhaps I can give you my parents' details instead, although they live in Vietnam.'

'Ah. I see from your address you live at Mi-Côte with le professeur Appleby, do you not?'

(Villers-sur-Mer is too bloody small, I think.)

'No. The house belongs to my family. I live in one part. Le professeur rents the other.'

Dr Allard sighs. 'Since he, at least, is resident in this country, I will list him as your next-of-kin. Now, please undress behind the screen and put on the examination gown.'

I do so, and Dr Allard examines me smoothly and with surprisingly gentle hands. When I'm dressed again and sitting in front of his desk, he says, 'You are indeed pregnant, at around fourteen weeks. The nurse will take a blood sample and a clinic will check for irregularities. I will also prescribe you an iron supplement. Do you have any questions?'

'Um, actually, I was wondering, I had a small — accident. I ran into something, and it left a large bruise on my belly. You don't think it could have, well, hurt the baby?'

He glances at his notes, where he's written *séparée de son mari*. After a moment he says, 'Madame, even now your womb lies deep within your pelvis. It is safe from any ... accidents. Do not fear.'

He smiles gently, no longer a Victorian papa, and I'm stupidly relieved. Truth is, I'd been feeling a little anxious. Unsettled, too. Not sad (as long as I don't think about my shattered life in Amsterdam), but without a routine I usually get edgy.

I decide I *must* start practising my scales and exercises again. After I begin I suddenly realise I'm no longer singing for audiences who demand a popular repertoire. For the first time I'm free to explore some new songs I've always wanted to try — more experimental, abstract music. It's not easy, but as my skill develops it's certainly fun.

Although we keep to ourselves for breakfast and lunch, Brian and I have got into the habit of sharing the evening meal, taking turns at preparation. My rebellious gut has indeed called a truce, and if I'm careful I can eat almost normally now.

At dinner a few weeks later Brian says, 'I heard you singing rather a nice tune as I was getting dressed this morning, and couldn't stop humming it all day.'

'That's just something I'm playing around with. I'm glad it didn't bother you.'

'Bother? Not at all. In fact I meant to tell you there's an ad in the paper for a jazz concert in Trouville-sur-Mer on Saturday night. If you like, we could go.'

'Oh, *yes*. That'd be wonderful. I've been missing live music.'

In bed that night I try not to think about the fact that Brian's bedroom is just above mine, which is why he heard me practising as he was dressing. And the thought of him in a partly-clad state, listening to me, aware of me, makes me flush slowly and pleasurably from my toes to my scalp.

Bloody hormones.

⤫

On Saturday evening we set off for the jazz concert in the Hillman Minx. I've been back in Normandy for four weeks now and my body is expanding. My old clothes don't fit, so I had a look around town yesterday and found an embroidered Indian top in pale green cotton, which is rather nice over my blue jeans (waist button undone, of course).

It's only a fifteen-minute drive to Trouville-sur-Mer and we easily find a park near the club. As we walk to the door I see the name 'Jardin de Lune', Moongarden.

'I know this place,' I say, pleased. 'Great acoustics.'

'Have you sung here?'

'At a jazz festival, maybe six years ago.'

We get drinks at the bar (mine sadly alcohol-free), and sit at one of the few empty tables.

'It's packed,' I say. 'The band must be good.'

'What's their name again?'

I check the program. 'Mmm, le Quintette Bleu, Blue Quintet. Oh! It's *Edgar's* group!'

'Edgar?'

'Edgar Jefferson. A fantastic drummer I knew in Paris. Lovely man.'

The lights dim and the quintet plays. Their set sparks off flights of fancy about my own musical possibilities, and when interval comes I'm dazed.

'Wow,' I say, shaking my head. 'Just — wow.'

'Liked it then?'

I laugh. 'They're different to anything I do, but at the same time … still connected. I'm so glad we came, Brian. Thanks for suggesting it.'

'Hey, *Vivy*? That *you*?' Beaming down at me is Edgar, beer in his hand.

'Edgar!' I jump up and hug him. 'You were sensational! My God. How are you? It's been so long! What are you doing here?'

'Lot of questions, girl,' he says, grinning. 'Playing for my supper as usual. But what the hell *you* doing here?'

'I live nearby now. Edgar, this is my friend Brian. Brian, the amazing Edgar Jefferson.'

They shake hands, and Brian says, 'That was a wonderful session. Please join us.'

'Glad to.' Edgar sits and drinks his beer. 'Amazing, Vivy. Haven't seen you since, oh, the Cannes festival, sixty-three?'

'My God, I think it was! Such a good time.'

'But where you singing now, babe?'

'I'm not. Taking a bit of time off.'

'You?' Edgar laughs. 'Honey, hard to believe. Got sick of Amsterdam?'

'Could say that.'

Edgar gazes at me, then says, 'Join us for a song, Vivy. I know all your standards.'

'Mmm, I'm a bit sick of standards as well.'

Edgar laughs. 'Aren't we all? You been hearing what Miles is doing lately? Weird, and so cool.'

'I've been working on a few new songs, but not at that level.'

'So what's your latest stuff?'

'Um — do you know *Beyond the Shadows*? Or *Just a Moment*?'

'Well, *yeah*. But man, not your style at all.' He grins. 'I want to hear. Come on, sing with us.'

'No, I'm not prepared — and not dressed for it —'

Brian says, 'She's prepared. Trust me.'

'Hey, look at this crowd, honey. Not a sequin in sight. You're dressed just right. Come on. Interval's almost over.' Edgar finishes the last of his drink.

'Oh,' I say. '*Oh*. Well, all right. But just one song.'

'For sure. Reckon I'll let you grab the spotlight? Come on, babe.'

I follow Edgar backstage and he introduces me. I've met the bass player before, a quiet guy; and the trumpet dude, who's not. I know the saxophonist by reputation — he winks and I'm embarrassingly star-struck — but I haven't met the pianist before. He's from Stockholm and says shyly he's just sitting in for their regular guy. (He was amazing so he's not 'just' anything.)

'*Beyond the Shadows*, babe?' says Edgar. 'Guys, okay with that?'

Everyone murmurs agreement.

'E-flat?' I say.

'Cool,' says Edgar. A man draws the curtain back and Edgar sits down at his drums and speaks into the microphone.

'We're honoured tonight to have one of the first ladies of jazz joining us for a song. Please put your hands together for Miss Vivy McKee!'

I'm amazed at the applause, but take a breath and step forward, and it's surprisingly easy from there. 'One, two, three ...'

They're such a good band. The saxophonist's reputation is deserved, Edgar plays in his usual wild, sensitive style, the trumpet and bass players are brilliant and the pianist is simply a dream. When I finish *Beyond the Shadows* there's a few seconds of hush, then a roar of appreciation.

Edgar laughs and says, 'Ah, you're not getting away yet, Miss Vivy. What do you say, folks? I believe she's been working on *Just a Moment*. Want to hear it?'

The crowd applauds, so I laugh and step back to the microphone. Somehow the song goes beautifully, and again everyone loves it.

'But that's enough of me now,' I say. 'Let's hear it for the brilliant Quintette Bleu! Go, *Edgar*!'

I step away and the band takes over. I seem to float back to our table, where Brian is grinning. 'Pretty wild stuff, Miss Vivy McKee.'

It's such a great evening, and at the end Edgar comes over. 'Hey, babe, the guys want to know how you did that transition in *Moment* — the sax player's sobbing with envy. Want to grab a bite?'

We do, and end up in a back room in some dive (Trouville is more low-rent than posh Deauville across the river). The food is great, something Moroccan, and nicely digestible.

Turns out the band is based twenty kilometres away in Le Havre, but they play fairly often in Trouville, so Brian and I promise to come and see them again.

'Are you living here now, Edgar?' I say.

'Right on, Vivy. I'll never go back to the States. Treated like a human being here.' He smiles. 'Married a beautiful Frenchwoman, Lisette. Even have a kid now.'

His face grows hard. 'Reckon I'd get lynched back home.'

'Have you got a photo?'

He takes a small picture out of his wallet: a pretty brunette with a dark-eyed child.

'Oh my God, Edgar. *Beautiful.*'

'Yeah,' he says quietly. 'Lot easier living in Europe, I tell you that.'

The trumpet player nods. 'True, man. If I was still over there I'd be on a one-way ticket to Vietnam. Already lost a cousin to that meat-grinder.'

During the meal Edgar lights one of the biggest joints I've ever seen, and passes it around. Brian's eyebrows rise, but he takes it and draws deeply, then coughs and passes it on. When it gets to me I shrug and say, 'Sorry, can't. I'm pregnant.'

'Vivy, *honey,*' says Edgar. He turns to Brian. 'This guy looking after you? Dead if he isn't.'

Brian seems stunned and doesn't say anything.

I laugh. 'It's okay. Yes, he's fine, but he's not the father, just a friend. It's my baby, mine alone.'

'Ever need *anything*, Vivy,' says the bass player, 'come to us. We're here for you.'

The others nod, and I feel tearful. 'Thanks, guys. *Thanks.* But I'm fine.'

Afterwards they all hug me, and how good it is to feel their touch, their sheer solidity. How I miss simple human contact.

We bid farewell, then Brian and I walk to the car and start back to Villers-sur-Mer. After a few streets I realise Brian is driving very, very slowly.

'Are you okay?' I say.

'Actually ... I'm stoned out of my brain. Can you drive?'

'Not very well. And I don't have a French licence.'

'All right.' He takes a deep breath. 'I'll get us home.'

'By tomorrow?'

'Am I that slow?'

'I could walk there faster.'

'Sorry. The dope. Everything's so connected. Wow, it's, it's beyond ....'

'Brian, you had *one* drag and now you're seeing the mysteries of the universe?'

'It was rather ... a long drag.'

Finally we arrive at home and he carefully parks the car.

'Come on, you,' I say as we get out. 'Seriously, you go hanging around with jazz musicians you're going to have to cope better than this.'

Brian leans against the side of the car, his eyes closed. 'Vivy, you have no idea how strong that joint was. I'm going to be out of it for a week.'

I go around to him, laughing. 'Come on, pothead. Follow me.' I take his hand and draw him towards his part of the house and, once inside, sit him on the couch.

'Cup of tea'll fix you,' I say. When I bring the tea back from the kitchen Brian takes the cup with a murmur of relief.

I sit down and sip my tea. 'What a lovely night.'

Brian says, with all the earnestness of the very stoned, 'You were ... amazing, Vivy. You must sing more ... sing *lots* more.'

'We'll see,' I say. 'I'm not sure — *oh*.'

Brian puts his cup down. 'Are you all right?'

'Uh, yes. Just felt the strangest thing.' I laugh a little. 'As if a cat was kneading me with its paws, a gentle push. But it was from ... inside.' I stare at Brian. 'Could it be —?'

'Probably ... you're um, sixteen, seventeen weeks along? About when babies start kicking.'

I put down my tea, astonished. 'Really? But I didn't even *know* that!'

Those foolish tears start flowing again. Brian puts his arm around my shoulder and draws my head to his shoulder. 'Hey, Vivy, don't worry.'

I lean into his warmth and comfort, and simply rest. Dear man. Our breathing becomes slow and regular. A little later I think, no, no, must stop, this is far too nice.

I look up. His eyes are closed.

'Brian?'

'Mmm?'

'Are you asleep?'

'Mm-hum.'

'Go upstairs to bed. Now.'

He slowly stands and holds out his hands. I take them and rise. Resisting the desire to fling myself into his arms I say, 'See you tomorrow,' and head for my flat.

∞

After I've finished breakfast next day there's a knock on the door between my flat and the house.

'Vivy, can we have a quick chat?'

'I'll be there in a minute.'

Brian is seated at the dining table and lifts the teapot. 'Cuppa? I hear it'll fix anything.'

'Yes, please. So you do remember last night?'

'Every moment.'

'Not hung over?'

'No, I feel marvellous,' he says. 'But I had a thought. I saw a book about pregnancy in the secondhand bookshop the other day and wondered if you might find it useful. You know, for when the baby *really* starts kicking.'

'Will it kick harder than that?'

'Oh, yes. Boots and all, I believe.'

I shake my head. 'I don't have the foggiest idea about what's happening. What's the book?'

'*A Child is Born.*'

'Ah. Perhaps I should have read that one properly, not opened it and closed it again in horror.'

'I'll get it for you. My sisters swear by Dr Spock, but that's for after the birth.' He smiles. 'Did you see in the paper that right-wing Americans blame the doctor's kindly advice for all the kids protesting about Vietnam? I'm pretty sure that's not the reason.'

'Vietnam?' I laugh ruefully. 'Yet *another* damned thing I haven't got the foggiest about.'

'I thought your parents had been living there for years.'

'Yes, but it's only recently we've started talking to each other again.' I shrug. 'Look, it's not really their fault. They divorced when I was young, and Charlie — my mother — married the General. Then after Louis died in the Indochina War, Charlie and Dad remarried. They went back to Vietnam assuming I didn't need them any more at eighteen. But I *did*.'

'That's why you said you've taken care of yourself for most of your life?'

I nod. 'Still, lately, I'm starting to see the separation was also self-inflicted. I sulked for years and refused to visit them. Or learn anything about Vietnam, either.'

'Well, it might be worth finding out a bit more. Who knows how long your parents will stay if the Americans withdraw?'

'Are they likely to?'

'Well, yes. The US is pretty desperate to get out. If so, the North will probably win, and your parents will have to find a new home. Perhaps even here at Mi-Côte.'

'*Here*? No! Looks like I need to learn more about babies *and* Vietnam. Ah, what fun.'

'And keep singing. Your new songs did very well last night.'

'Funny, I always thought I had to stick to standards to make a living,' I say. 'Yet perhaps not.'

Brian smiles. 'There's that *perrrhaps* again. I've been meaning to ask about your accent, it's a real mix of Brit and Australian, with a trace of Hampshire too. But weren't you born in London?'

'I was, but grew up in Southampton.' I laugh. 'Funny, I hear it in your voice too.'

'I didn't always have this posh Oxford veneer, you know. Just a vicarage lad from Woolston.'

'Woolston! Dad managed the Spitfire factory there before it was bombed out. And I grew up at a farm on the South Downs.'

'My aunt was housekeeper at a farm over that way. Doris Spencer after she married.'

'Spencie? She was your *aunt*?'

'You knew her?'

'She practically raised me, that's all! Charlie was always away, and Spencie was ... *so* kind.' I sigh. 'She died when I was thirteen. It was an awful time.'

'Well, what a very strange coincidence.'

'Isn't it just! Meeting here, yet having that bond from the past as well.' I grin. 'Guess it means we're practically brother and sister.'

Brian is startled. 'God, I hope not.'

'Why?'

He gazes at me. 'Oh, just because. Anyway, I've got to go and buy some books —'

'I'll pay you back, of course.'

'You can get the tickets next time Quintette Bleu is playing.'

So at last I begin to learn something of what's happening to me. For a start my little interloper not only has feet to kick me with, but thumbs to suck: almost too weird to comprehend.

I also read about Vietnam, and can only shake my head at the bizarre unfairness of it all. And I find out, with librarian Julie Desvignes' help, something about divorce law in the Netherlands.

∽

This is rather a lovely summer. The days are sunny and long, the evenings mild and hazy. By August I've become undeniably stout but, luckily, loose cotton kaftans are all the rage. I've recovered from my early-pregnancy queasiness and feel surprisingly full of energy.

Although I don't have much money I decide we should repair one of the upstairs rooms. We ask M. Guillot, the locksmith, about fixing the roof and he suggests we hire nice young Michel who, for a small sum, is willing to clamber about at dizzy heights replacing slates.

After the roof is watertight we buy some second-hand timber and, with Michel's assistance, patch the damaged floor. Then Brian and Michel bring an old bed, chest of drawers and rug out of storage. Bedclothes from the linen press, and a vase of flowers bring the room to life.

That was the least damaged part of upstairs, and gloomily I recognise the money left in my account won't stretch to fixing up the rest.

In fact it won't stretch very far into the future at all, and even more gloomily I decide I'll have to contact Henk to see when (or if) he'll repay the rest of the money he stole from me.

The thought of speaking to him is sickening, and I ask Lucien if he'll be an intermediary.

'Of course, chérie,' he says when I ring him. 'And I will tell le cochon what I think of him.'

'No, Lucien, don't! Not till he's given back some of the money, at least. He owes me about 10,000 guilders, nearly 3,000 dollars, and I need every cent.'

'I will see what I can do, Vivy. And you are well?'

'Very well. In fact I feel wonderful lately.'

Lucien laughs. 'Ah, Manon would always say that too in the middle, then at the end she would curse me. And that professeur is treating you as he should?'

'He's being very helpful, but we're just friends, Lucien. By the way, have you heard anything from Mr Adler about tracking down the estate agent?'

'Sadly, no. But I believe he is still doing his best. Now, I will talk to Henk. I know of some little schemes he might prefer to keep quiet, which may be useful. Au'voir, Vivy.'

The phone is in the hall and as I hang up there's a knock at the front door — the postman with a telegram for Brian. I take it upstairs to his study, where he's peering into a microscope and jotting down notes. He reads the telegram aloud: WEEK FREE BEFORE TOUR STOP ARRIVING WED WITH MINKY STOP.'

'Minky?' I say.

'I have no idea who or what a minky might be. But it seems Annabelle has a week off and will be visiting us.'

'Lovely,' I say. 'And if this minky turns out to need a bed then at least we have a beautiful new room for her/him/it. Do you think Annabelle means *this* Wednesday?'

'Oh dear, I'd better find out. You won't mind the disruption?'

'Heavens, no. The house is yours, Brian. I'm looking forward to it, I'm sure she's a lot of fun.'

He smiles. 'She is.'

'We can chat about music, too.'

He pauses and says, 'Come to think of it, I haven't actually mentioned you. Our calls are always about the blessed wedding.'

'Your fiancee doesn't know I've been living in the flat for the last two months? Oh well. I doubt she'll be too concerned you've got an old pregnant lady next door.'

'Old pregnant lady?' He smiles. 'I think most women would still see you as a threat, Vivy. Still, Annabelle shouldn't — after all we're getting married in two months.'

'But perhaps she needs the groom to help her out rather than look at *Kosmoceratinae* in a microscope,' I say. 'Weddings are hard work.'

'Are they? A quick trip to the Registry Office would have suited me.' He grins. 'And don't think I didn't notice how easily *Kosmoceratinae* tripped off your tongue there. Have you been practising?'

'It's amazing what silly things you can pick up around here. Weren't you humming *Too Soon to Go* yesterday?'

'It worked its way into my brain and I couldn't forget it.' He gazes at me. 'You do have an extraordinary gift, Vivy.'

I look at him for a few moments then smile ruefully. 'Thanks. Look, you'd better go and find out what a minky is and if it's arriving this Wednesday. We'll need to get in some provisions.'

∽

We're sitting in the garden at dusk after a meal. Annabelle is as pretty as her publicity photos, prettier in fact: white-gold hair, sea-blue eyes and dimples in rose-petal cheeks, with the pleasing contrast of a deep, earthy laugh. Minky turns out to be the bass player for Electric Cloud, lanky and quiet, with clever dark eyes.

'Minky's just joined us,' says Annabelle. 'The manager was worried a girl playing bass would upset the fans, but she's *so* good, how could they resist?' She squeezes Minky's hand. '*And* she's my best friend already, so of course I thought if you met her you'd see how lovely she is, darling, and when we're married —'

Brian says, 'Well, it's a great pleasure to meet you too, Minky,' as he tops up their glasses (I'm drinking watered wine).

'And I can't *believe* you didn't tell me Vivy McKee was living next door.' Annabelle gazes at me solemnly. 'You've been my inspiration since I was a *child*, Vivy.'

'Thank you,' I say, feeling very old.

'And how sweet that you're having a *baby*!' she says. 'But where's your husband?'

'Oh ... busy working in the Netherlands,' I say. 'I just needed some sunshine.'

'Well, I'm *so* glad we've met. And now Minky and I are going to have a relaxing week at the beach, then we're on tour for five weeks, and as soon as I'm back everyone — except *Brian*, of course — is going to go bonkers about the wedding. Honestly,' she says confidingly, 'I don't understand why men don't get more excited about these things.'

'*Absolutely*,' I say. 'In fact I was telling him he really needs to give you more of a hand.'

'How kind of you, but I'm *so* lucky to have Minky to help. She's just been through a very painful breakup — she doesn't mind me talking about it — and she says *I'm* really helping *her*.'

Quiet Minky looks suitably haunted for a few moments, then returns Annabelle's glowing smile.

Annabelle yawns extravagantly. 'Golly, I'm so *tired*. That ferry trip took forever. But thank you, Brian darling for coming to collect us.' She turns to me. 'He said you and he have been busy lately, fixing up a beautiful country bedroom for us. I can hardly *wait*.'

I open my mouth to say something like *But aren't you going to sleep with your fiancé?* then shut it again as Brian says calmly, 'You'll love it. And tomorrow we can go to the beach.'

'I'm rather tired too,' I say. 'Wonderful to meet you both and hope you have a good holiday.'

'But you've got to be part of it as well, Vivy!' says Annabelle. 'So many things I'm *dying* to ask about your songs and the people you've worked with.'

'I'd like to know more about your music too,' I say honestly. 'I thought *Leave Me Tomorrow* had an amazing structure.'

Annabelle beams. 'What a lovely holiday we're going to have!'

∽

Next day we go to the beach, where I sit on my towel wearing a swimsuit deemed suitable for a pregnant woman. It's black, with a thigh-length skirt flaring from under the (ample) bustline.

Annabelle and Minky squeal and run in and out of the waves and splash each other, wearing little cotton bikinis in bright happy colours. I remember swimsuits like that in my past, when I was young and un-pregnant, and sigh.

'What?' says Brian.

'When *I* could wear things like that, I never once gave a thought to how other women might feel.'

'Children don't have to think about the feelings of adults.'

'The girls aren't children.'

He shrugs. 'Their generation is post-war. That makes a difference.'

After a pause I say, 'Did they sleep well in the new room?'

Brian laughs. 'Apparently, from all the contented murmuring. Do you mean did I sleep well with my fiancée in bed with someone else just along the corridor?'

'Not precisely —'

'Annabelle's never kept it a secret she likes both women and men, nor that she spends time with other people. She always comes back to me and swears our relationship is what she truly wants.'

Of course the world of music is full of people with complicated bonds that bear no similarity to the generally accepted pattern. Henk and me, for instance.

'Is it ... what *you* want, Brian?' I ask.

'I must admit feeling a little less certain right now. Still, I promised her marriage when we were both younger and more innocent, but by now the whole affair has become a steamroller.'

'Why does she want to marry you when she's not in love with you?'

'Why did you marry Henk? I have the feeling it may have been similar.'

We gaze at one another, then I nod. 'Yes, that was a pragmatic, unromantic choice.'

'Well, then,' says Brian. 'Romance isn't everything. You and I are both old enough to know that.'

The week passes easily. I share Annabelle and Minky's love of music, which makes us comfortable companions. They're nice people and seem very fond of each other, although Annabelle spends one night in Brian's bed (dear God, his room is above mine and I do *not* want to hear those bedsprings). On the following morning Minky is a little sad, but Annabelle whispers to her and hugs her, and things seem fine with them again.

We go to the club in Trouville when Quintette Bleu is playing and have a wonderful time. I sing two new songs and Annabelle does a jazz version of *Leave Me Tomorrow* that everyone loves.

Edgar pulls me aside in the interval and says, 'That girl going to *marry* your buddy Brian?'

'Seems so,' I say.

Edgar whispers, 'Does he realise she bats for the other side?'

I laugh. 'Yes, they've got it figured out. You know.'

Edgar nods sagely, then frowns. 'But what about *you*, honey?'

'He's my buddy, Edgar. Not my boyfriend.'

At the end of the week we drive Annabelle and Minky to the ferry terminal at Ouistreham, and bid farewell with extravagant hugs and kisses.

Driving home again I say, 'What a week! Annabelle swears they'll come back for the baby's birth, but it'll be just before Christmas so that's got to be pretty unlikely. You two'll be married by then and I can't even imagine where you'll be.'

'Probably here,' says Brian. 'So long as your parents don't throw me out.'

'Hell, I keep forgetting about that. Bloody *money*. Haven't heard a word about the absconding estate agent, and it looks like Lucien hasn't made any leeway with Henk either.'

∞

Mid-September, and I'm six months pregnant. A letter arrives from my parents. Last month, shockingly, their orphanage was hit by a rocket. One of their nuns was killed and part of the building badly damaged. Can I help?

I write sadly back. I have very little money now and cannot. My hopeful leads have come to nothing.

In an earlier letter I'd told them I had come to live in Villers-sur-Mer, but not why, although I expect it's obvious I'm separated from Henk. I say now that Brian and I have repaired one of the rooms of the villa, but still don't mention my pregnancy.

I'm furious with myself, but simply can't write the words. Is it because my baby will make them grandparents? And *then* what of our own complicated relationship? Too hard to even think about. I seal the letter and drop it in the mailbox.

After dinner that evening the phone in the hall rings. Brian answers it, then hands me the receiver, his face serious. 'I'll be in here if you need me,' he says, and goes back to the salon.

'Hello?'

'Ah, Vivy. It is lovely to hear your voice again.'

'*Henk*?' I sit down, my knees suddenly weak. 'What do you want?'

'I am being harassed by Lucien. He insists I pay you money I do not have.'

'Maybe stop subsidising your girlfriend's flat, Henk. Might free up a bit of cash.'

He laughs. 'I have missed you so, Vivy.'

I say nothing.

'Are you well?' he says. 'Six months pregnant, I believe.' You must take care of our child, Vivy.'

The hair lifts on my scalp. '*Our* child?'

'Of course. You do realise you can never divorce me?'

'Of course I can! You beat and imprisoned me. Those are grounds for divorce in the Netherlands.'

'But did you know that if you sue me for divorce, you must *prove* such ill-treatment? Ah, Vivy, that will be very hard. Everyone acknowledges how devoted I am to you.'

'But this isn't *your* child, Henk. Everyone also knows you've had a vasectomy.'

'Mere gossip. And of course, as the baby's father, it will be even harder for you to divorce me.'

'You just don't want to give me half of the proceeds from our flat, do you?'

Henk laughs. 'What is yours is mine, dear wife.'

'For God's sake. Just repay what you stole from me, at least!'

'But without money you must come back, Vivy. Why should I help you to stay away?'

After a long pause I say, 'Let me go, Henk.'

'No,' he says, and hangs up.

15. LEO: FULL MOON FESTIVAL (SEP 1968-JAN 1969)

We're gathered at the evening debrief, back at camp after a long day of work. The Commanding Officer looks around the table and says firmly, 'Mooncakes.'

'Mooncakes, sir?' says one of the engineers.

'Absolutely. The mid-autumn Tet festival will soon be upon us. A full-moon occasion — unlike the unfortunate events of February — and according to intelligence reports, likely to pass peacefully.'

'And what exactly —?' says one of the agriculture staff faintly, who'd recently brought a hundred chickens back from Saigon in a truck and still hadn't recovered.

'The harvest is complete,' says Lofty, the interpreter from Liaison. 'People relax, celebrate their lives. And eat mooncakes.'

'So we're going to supply the families of the local militias, ARVN, Regional and Popular Forces, with those mooncakes,' says the CO. 'On behalf of their benign and generous government.'

'And mooncakes would be —?' says a high-yield rice agronomist.

'Christ knows,' says the CO. 'I'm told the savoury sort have things like dried sausage, egg, bean paste, while the sweet sort have sugared lard and lotus seeds. They're covered in pastry and the Vietnamese love them. So. We need one thousand mooncakes.'

'Uh, where will we get them sir?' says the agronomist.

'Saigon. Obviously.'

The CO looks around the table. 'Lieutenant Bell,' he says ominously. He hasn't forgiven me for Claire coming on the Vung Tau outing.

'Yes, sir?'

'Go to Saigon and bring back one thousand mooncakes.'

'Of course, sir. When?'

'Festival starts on the 6th of October. Different date every year, God knows why.'

'It's always held on the fifteenth day of the eighth month of the lunar calendar near the autumn equinox,' Lofty says helpfully.

'Is it indeed?' says the CO thoughtfully, gazing at him. Lofty looks down and takes great interest in some pages in front of him. The CO turns to me. 'So you'll need to get a move on, Bell.'

'Absolutely, sir.'

Lofty agrees to come with me, and we find two Vietnamese officials who know the best bakeries in Saigon. We set off in a Landrover early one morning. I'm pretty anxious, because Highway 15 is always busy with Americans driving back and forth, and the NLF love to set ambushes.

Also I've been given the equivalent of one thousand US dollars to buy the mooncakes, which is terrifying. Just about anyone in the province would slit my throat for that, so I hide it in my socks. Yes, driving is uncomfortable.

The plan is to go up in the morning, buy cakes, return in the afternoon. We get to Saigon without problem then go to Cholon, the market district. I navigate between bicycles, motorbikes, cyclos, donkey-carts and jeeps, swamped by the reek of diesel fumes, rotting fruit and sewage.

At the first two bakeries we visit, the bakers say the order is too big for such short notice. Clearly we can't get it filled today so ask how long it would take. After discussion one baker agrees to work overnight and have the mooncakes ready for tomorrow morning. Much relief all round.

The two officials leave, happy to have a free night out in Saigon. We go to an army billet, contact Nui Dat and explain what's happened. Lofty has his own plans for the evening, so I leave him and ring Tu Do Street. My aunt Charlotte is delighted to have me over for dinner.

∽

Sadly our commo friend André is there at the dinner-table in the ornate salon. I haven't seen him for eight months, not since the dramatic events of Tet. He's as handsome as ever, dark hair, soulful eyes, European nose: a hybrid, a half-caste. Bastard.

What does Claire feel ...? Fuck knows. They're both across the table from me but I can't sense anything between them.

Perhaps it's as she's always maintained: he's a helper, a friend. Okay, give the prick the benefit of the doubt.

The old servant Vinh puts down a plate of something that smells wonderful, and Pete passes it to me, saying, 'Did we tell you we finally heard from our daughter Vivy in France?'

'That's good,' I say, helping myself. 'Has she sorted out your villa?' I pass the plate to Charlotte, beside me. 'Partly,' she says. 'Turns out our agent was stealing all the rent, but Vivy thinks she might be able to get some of it back. Here's hoping.'

Pete smiles. 'Odd thing is, we had another letter from her recently. No progress on the money, but it looks like she's gone to live in the flat at the Normandy house. Must be trouble on the marital front. We've never met the famous Henk but he always sounded a bit slimy to me. What do you think, darling?'

Charlotte nods. 'A bit too good to be true. I suppose we'll see. But, Christ, I wish something would happen soon.' She turns to me. 'We're done, Leo. Barely a dollar left.' She takes a drink.

'We're in talks with some American charities who may be able to support it,' says Pete. 'But nothing so far. Now all we have here is this house. And without this we may as well leave Vietnam.'

'Where would you go?' I ask.

'Our plan was to sell the villa in France, but it might be better to keep it as a last resort,' says Charlotte.

'Australia perhaps,' says Pete. 'Your mother and I were both born in Broome, Leo, and spent a lot of our childhood in Perth.'

'Broome?' I say. 'Wasn't that some wild pearling port?'

'In some ways, but a little country town as well. We'd go to Perth in the summers, but stay in Broome the rest of the year.' Pete shakes his head. 'Christ, it's beautiful.'

'How does that sound to you, Charlotte?' I say.

'Pete followed me to this crazy place fourteen years ago and coped, so I'll try to do the same wherever we end up.' She reaches out and squeezes Pete's hand.

Claire and I glance at each other and smile. Candlelight glows on her skin, her pale hair glints with gold, and she's wearing the jade bracelet I bought her. Pleased, I say, 'How's life with a laminated card, then?'

'Pretty good,' she says. 'But I found out something funny. Turns out the MACV card is a bit of a paper tiger. In other wars the US could legally exclude reporters from bad-news battlefields. Here they pretend they can too, but they simply can't — because they never officially declared war.'

'So what the hell do they call *this* mess, then?' I say.

'A temporary police action,' André says drily. 'Sadly for the Americans they did not realise they had stumbled into the tail end of a very long — and very real — war.'

The woman servant, Thu, brings a bowl of noodles, and André passes them to me, saying, 'How are things going for you, Leo?'

'Ah, okay. We've almost finished stocking the high school library and science block we built. Apparently it'll be officially opened in a couple of months.'

'Everything back to normal now after Tet?' says Pete.

I laugh in disbelief. 'Almost, then the government decided to draft all the male teachers for three months of military training. We don't have enough staff now to run exams or classes.'

André nods. 'Short-sighted. My department protested, but was, as usual, overruled. President Thieu is panicking, especially about the Alliance of National, Democratic, and Peace Forces.'

'Who?'

Claire says, 'The US likes to call the Alliance the "urban front of the communists," but they're doctors, businessmen, professionals, religious leaders. They say they represent the majority of South Vietnamese.'

'And do they?' I say.

André nods. 'They certainly represent the many who wish to find a path between the extremes of dictator Thieu or the communist North. They are also willing to work constructively with the NLF.'

'Come on, how can anyone trust the NLF?'

'Has Thieu — or puppet Diem before him — ever been worthy of trust?' says André.

I laugh. 'True.'

Claire says, 'The Americans don't really care because they're tippy-toeing away from this quagmire as fast as they can. They'd like this to be Thieu's war as soon as possible anyway.'

'The noble art of *jaunissement*,' says André, pouring wine for everyone.

'Yellowing?' I say, puzzled.

'The French pioneered it. Making sure all the new corpses are yellow, not white.' He shrugs. 'The Americans will implement it too now, hoping the protests will end. And of course they will.'

'Pretty bleak view.'

'But is it incorrect, Leo?'

'Mmm. Probably not.' I'm starting to find I don't dislike André as much as before. In fact he seems more-or-less okay, which is annoying.

I glance at him. Okay, he's unfairly good-looking, but (maybe I've drunk too much) his eyes are oddly bleak. Claire once mentioned he was an orphan, abandoned by his French father. Suppose he's made a good hash of things really, surviving and learning enough to become a government translator.

By now I've got to know quite a few Vietnamese — school staff, Ba Ria locals and soldiers, likeable and clever people. But their attitude to mixed-race Vietnamese is almost uniformly cold, so that probably makes André's life pretty difficult.

I almost feel sorry for him, then remember he's living here near Claire. So maybe not.

A light, sweet dessert is served, sort of a lemony rice, and I say, 'Ah, reminds me. I didn't explain why I've got a free night in Saigon. I'm on a mission to acquire a thousand mooncakes for the families of the local army forces.'

'A thousand?' laughs Charlotte. 'Good God.'

'I'm not even sure what a mooncake is,' I say.

Pete says, 'Acquired taste. Loved for their connection to festivals.'

'But also nourishing,' says André. 'Important for those living on the edge of starvation.'

'True,' I say. 'I've actually been shocked at how skeletal some of the kids of the RF militia are.'

'You mean the children of the country's military forces are starving?' says Claire. '*Christ.*'

'We've come full circle once again to our glorious government's neglect,' says Charlotte. She lights a cigarette, then coughs.

'Darling,' says Pete significantly.

'I *know*,' says Charlotte, turning to me. 'Leo, the doctors keep telling me to stop smoking, especially after that little episode the night the orphanage was hit.'

'Charlotte,' says Claire. 'You were unconscious with asthma. You *must* listen to them.'

'I will. But until we can at least get some sort of repairs going I'm feeling such stress.'

'What needs doing?' I say.

'One corner of the building was hit,' says Pete. 'Not a massive amount in itself, but if the structure isn't stabilised soon then the rest of the building will be compromised.'

'Aha,' I say slowly. 'I've just had an idea.'

'If it includes another day at the beach, I'm in,' says Claire.

'Sadly, not *that* good an idea.'

'Well?' she says, smiling.

'Well, our unit does quite a lot of construction work, and we recently repaired an orphanage in Ba Ria. Obviously Saigon isn't within our remit, but Civil Affairs does have a presence here. I can't promise anything, but I'll see if there's some way we can slip your Maison Lien into the list of proposed repairs.'

'My God, Leo,' says Charlotte. '*Could* you? That would make such a difference to us!'

'But you realise it wouldn't be free? You'd have to express your gratitude — loudly — to the South Vietnamese government, for its kindness and altruism. Could be painful.'

'We'll do anything,' says Pete. 'Since that night we've hardly had a moment's peace.'

'And the women at the orphanage are still shattered,' says Claire with a sigh. 'They lost lovely Sister Agnes. She was so young, and we had to dig her body out of the rubble.'

She glances at André, who returns her look with a surprising intensity. Is it shared sorrow or condolence or ...?

Pete says something about who'd like brandies, but I can't move or speak. Claire and André gaze at each other for just a few seconds — *microseconds* — too long.

Of course.

Suddenly I realise how carefully they've been avoiding each other's eyes tonight. I understand what they've been hiding, what awareness has flowed between them while we've chatted over this lavish dinner, across this civilised table, in this sickening ornate salon.

My chest thuds and my throat clenches with humiliation and loss.

∽

Claire's steady gaze tells me she understands what I've realised, but I turn away and leave for the billet as soon as I can. Next morning I collect the others, find the bakery again in the maze of damaged Cholon streets, and load up a thousand bloody mooncakes packed in about eight cartons. Once they're stuffed into the Landrover there's not much room, but we manage.

We drive back to Ba Ria and I don't give a fuck who may or may not be planning to ambush us on Highway 15. I shove the pedal to the metal — the approved technique in any case — and go. Lofty gets a bit white-knuckled but the officials love it.

We leave the mooncakes at the Ba Ria government offices, thank our companions and return to Nui Dat. Before lunch.

Then I throw myself into work as never before, doing anything possible to avoid thinking. I'm still the acting Youth and Sports Adviser — the real one never came back — so Phuoc Tuy province gets a program of upgraded stadiums and sports fields, and enough volleyball, badminton, soccer and basketball equipment to last for a decade.

October sixth arrives, the mid-autumn Tet festival. In the towns there are red lanterns and dragon dances, and the locals devour my mooncakes with apparent joy. I try one, a sweetish thing with flower-patterned pastry on top. It's not too bad but I seem to have lost my appetite.

That night the harvest moon rises fat and golden. I swat away the odd mosquito and think about the guerillas in the Long Hais, nibbling my mooncakes (of course they'd have been slipped a few). Are they looking up too, and wondering when they can go home and live in peace?

I start counting. Most of the guys keep a calendar, but I've never bothered before. I arrived here on the twenty-ninth of January, so now it's the sixth of October, with a bit over sixteen weeks to go till my allotted year is done. One hundred and fourteen days — or one hundred and thirteen and a wakey, the glorious day of departure.

Christ. Why can't I get some sort of *perspective*? The entirety of my relationship with Claire is some childhood memories, two kisses and holding hands (once). But how I miss her clarity and passion and courage. How I miss her blue eyes and our prickly friendship. How I miss her.

Simmo gives me some numbers for Claire, more mine casualties. In July, two of our men were killed, nine wounded. In August, twelve ARVN soldiers were blown up, and fifteen ARVN and five civilians maimed.

So there we are, André, all the latest casualties are Vietnamese people, jaunissment at work. Spot on, you bastard. I write Claire a brief letter with the data, and she replies:

Leo, it was true at the time I told you there was nothing between me and André. After the orphanage was shelled in August it was no longer true, but there was no chance to tell you: or in fact, no reason. You and I are no more committed to each other now than we were when you and Shazza were together. I have no plans or certainty for the future. You are my dear friend and I'm sorry to have hurt you. With love, Claire.

She's right. I shrug. One hundred and five days and a wakey to go.

∽

Still, I've got to fill the time somehow. More stadiums? We need to find a site for a new one at Dat Do, the large village at the head of the notorious minefield that runs to the coast, so I'm meeting officials to check out a couple of locations. Lofty the interpreter comes with me.

'First time you've been to Dat Do?' Lofty says, as I drive the Landrover.

'How can you tell?'

'You're not nervous, Dingdong,' he says. 'It's a very pro-NLF place, where all the mine-raisers are. You'll see a lot of missing limbs in the crowd.'

He's right. I've become almost indifferent to the sight of maimed people in this miserable country, but there certainly seem to be more than usual in the cluster of curious locals that gather around as the officials show us several possible sites for a stadium.

We agree on one nice flat area close to a large school, shake hands with the officials, and start walking back to the Landrover beneath a shady green tunnel of trees.

The air is damp and smells as usual of rotting vegetation. Suddenly I realise how eerily quiet everything is. The officials have disappeared along with most of the crowd, except for an old woman trying to round up a few laughing kids.

'Let's get moving,' says Lofty, his voice tight. We're just at the Landrover when there's a crackling noise from nearby trees. We fling ourselves to the ground behind the car, pull out our sidearms and fire back. I don't feel afraid, just astonished. This can't be happening.

Then the shooting stops. I grab the two-way radio and report to base. They say they'll send a helicopter gunship to cover us on the way back to Nui Dat. We look around.

The old woman is lying face-down in the green shadows, and a kid is writhing on the ground. The others have disappeared. Lofty crawls over to the old woman to see if she's alive, but glances back at me and shakes his head.

I kneel beside the boy as he slowly stops moving. His chest is open and all I can see is pink, frothy tissue that makes me think stupidly of the ruffled heads of roses.

I press my floppy bush hat over the gaping wound but it doesn't help: of course it doesn't.

The air, the trees, the ground itself seem to be surreally silent, then the birds start calling again, dogs howl in the distance, and a woman runs screaming towards us.

She cradles the child in her arms, sobbing and rocking him back and forth. Other villagers arrive. They stare at us with loathing, then take the dead away.

With the chopper thudding ahead of us, Lofty and I silently drive back to base. We report what happened and it's logged. We take showers and our uniforms are packaged up with the rest of the laundry to go to Ba Ria for cleaning: they're pretty good there at getting blood out.

I go back to work as usual. If I try to think about Dat Do, it's as if some blankness, like white noise, fills my head. I know what happened but just can't feel it. Probably for the best.

I take on classes helping older Vietnamese with English, and devise programs to teach new skills to refugees who only know how to plant rice and drive water buffalo. Mind you, they'd be perfectly happy to keep on doing that, except their paddies are bomb craters and their animals are dead.

And the poor bastards are stuck in a 'population resettlement' compound built by Civil Affairs, a wasteland dubbed Suoi Nghe. The agriculture guys teach them how to plant high-yield rice and sorghum and they're not doing too badly, but I doubt it compensates for losing centuries of connection to their ancestors' graves. Over one thousand refugees from three villages have ended up here, the detritus from 'cordon and search' operations.

Cordon and search ops take place when a village is quietly surrounded, everyone screened for their identity cards and huts searched for weapons or incriminating material. It's useful for picking up the poor sods who've deserted from Thieu's malfunctioning army, but not very good at finding real guerillas.

The sweetener is free medical and dental treatment while people are waiting, but a day lost in the life of a working village is costly: sometimes in more ways than one.

When the Americans do a cordon and search op it often ends in the village being torched and all the residents turned into refugees (that good old *clearing by fire* attitude).

Simmo says there are now one and a half million 'internally displaced' people in the south, twice as many as a year ago.

Christ, I'm sick of this place.

∞

I'm long overdue to take my official five days of 'out of country' Rest and Recreation, so put in an application which gets quickly approved. If I go back to Australia everyone will ask me how Claire is, so I choose Hong Kong.

A few days later I'm on a Caribou to Tan Son Nhut, then a Hercules to Hong Kong with a lot of noisy American servicemen. I take refuge with a couple of other Australians, Daz and Phil, and when we land we go together to our allotted hotel. After a lie down and a long shower, it feels like the height of luxury.

My two new mates and I get a taxi to where we've been told is the place to be: Wan Chai on Victoria Harbour.

The taxi driver says Wan Chai's night life is now supporting the entire Hong Kong economy, and once we're there it's easy to believe. We stagger from bars to night clubs to strip joints. The grog is good, the lights are dazzling, and the women are gorgeous.

My head is floating a foot above my actual skull, and in what may be a piece of luck I don't deserve, I meet a girl, Mei. She tells me firmly she's an escort, not a bar whore. If I book her for my stay she'll show me Hong Kong, not just a bedroom. She makes me smile, so I do, and she does.

We eat some great meals and see vistas of islands, long beautiful beaches, and twinkling lights from mountain-tops. And we have a lot of amazing sex. After a few nights I break down and tell sharp, sensible Mei my woes, and she says, 'You'll get over it, Aussie.' Which is nice to hear. And what she does after that is nice as well.

Too soon my leave ends. I say, 'I reckon you've got a heart of gold after all,' and Mei laughs and tucks a lot of my money in her purse.

I join Daz and Phil at the airport for the trip back. Daz thinks he's got the clap and Phil has forgotten everything that's happened since Wednesday. As we come into Ton San Nhut I wish I could forget everything that's happened for the last ten months, but no such luck.

Suddenly it's all heat and humidity again, the mouldy reek of tent, the sweat-stained clothes, the shadeless trees, the red dust and mud. The thwack of rotors, the scream of engines, the distant thud of artillery, the ground-shudder of bombs. Welcome back, Leo.

∽

At the end of October, President Johnson announces that the years-long campaign of bombing North Vietnam has come to an end. The air force boasts — boasts! — they've dropped nearly twice the tonnage of the entire WWII Pacific campaign on that one small sliver of land.

In November, President Thieu flatly refuses to attend the Paris peace talks, but the Yanks gently encourage him to rethink his approach by saying they'll start without him.

Slimeball Nixon is elected president and suddenly all the talk is about passing on the hot potato of war and getting the hell out. The Americans claim it's not 'de-escalation' as long as the South Vietnamese army replaces them. Ah, Claire, semantics again.

Lofty and I go back to Dat Do to check on progress on the new stadium. We don't talk much and the officials seem abashed, the crowd quieter. A woman comes over, bows and says something, hands me a small parcel and slips away.

Lofty takes a breath. 'She said — Australian soldier, you bring us too much pain, but you tried to help my son. Thank you.'

Back in my tent I open the parcel. It's my old bush hat, carefully washed and ironed. Feeling stabbed in the throat I shove it at the bottom of my bag. End of November now, so only sixty days to go. Fifty-nine and a wakey.

Despite everything, last month I put in a submission for work to be carried out on a prominent Saigon orphanage, one supported for many years by friends of the illustrious Madame Thieu and random MACV bigwigs and their wives. Probably since it's a quiet week it gets approved.

On 7th December the CO writes in the activity log: *Engineer inspection and works assessment of orphanage repairs SAIGON area.*

I'm glad. It should all proceed pretty smoothly from here. I won't be around to check though, of course. Fifty-three days and a wakey.

The local schools are still limping along. The headmaster, deputy head and male teachers will return from military training in January 1969. Education can resume then if, of course, Thieu resists the urge to send middle-aged teachers to the front line. And if he or anyone else can find it.

∽

While the schools are short-staffed they've partly closed down, so there's not a lot for me to do on the education front for a few weeks. One night in our tent Simmo says, 'We've got another cordon and search tomorrow. Want to give me a hand? Doctor's son and all that.'

'That was a point of information, mate, not a job application. What do you need me for?'

'Two of my assistants are off with malaria. I just need someone who can cope with blood.'

'Definitely not me, but I'll come. I'm bored.'

Most of the other blokes get pretty cautious as their last few weeks are counting down, but after the mooncakes expedition — and the ambush at Dat Do — I don't much care about anything (though that doesn't seem to affect the automatic edginess now built into my nervous system).

We leave early in the morning, mid-December, and proceed to An Nhut, about a forty-minute drive. The convoy has a Liaison officer and two interpreters, a DENTCAP dentist and two assistants, a MEDCAP team with two doctors, two interpreters, four assistants. And me.

The Ninth Battalion, 9RAR, is the muscle. They've carefully moved into place overnight, and surprise, next morning, the good folk of An Nhut discover they're surrounded and some grumpy ARVN lads are beadily eyeing their identity cards.

Before that, our people erect shade tents, dig and screen latrines for men and women, and prepare the MEDCAP and DENTCAP areas. The good folk are kept amused (or not) by Cultural Drama Teams and films in which the South Vietnamese guy battles the North Vietnamese guy and *always* wins the girl, the sterling products of the Psychological Operations team.

I help out with changes of dressings and dispense creams for horrible skin conditions, and herd clusters of village urchins through their medical inspections and treatments. They'd test the patience of a saint but they don't bother Simmo.

He ignores the giggling and bouncing around, and gives each one a sweet when their treatment is over.

At lunch (rations) Simmo points at the villagers waiting patiently in the screening area: more livewire kids, mothers with fractious babies, old men with bowed shoulders, old women who look like they've endured horrors I don't want to think about.

'Know what this op is called?' says Simmo. 'KING HIT.'

'You're kidding. How embarrassing.'

'You know, when I think of them, the fuckers who dream this stuff up, I wonder about the thing, the one thing, our masters have never taken into account.'

'Yeah?'

'Reincarnation,' says Simmo firmly. 'The vast majority of people here are Buddhists who believe in reincarnation. When they die they're sad to leave their families behind, but they know they'll be reborn and meet again.'

'Okay ...'

'So you put them up against your average Yank. When they die they *die*, and they're going to Hell because they've had sex or smoked a joint. One lot is terrified of annihilation, the other sees it as an inconvenient transition. And as long as the NLF cannon fodder don't care what happens to their current bodies, they're unbeatable.'

I stare at him. 'Simmo, that's — weird.'

He shrugs. 'Argue, then.' But I can't.

The day proceeds smoothly. DENTCAP treats fifty-two people and MEDCAP over two hundred, and they all probably go to bed that night in a lot less pain than when they woke up. Unlike me.

∽

Christmas 1968 comes. We give gifts of toys and sweets to village children and, now the wet is over, we take several lots of kids on beach outings, some from orphanages. The Unit has been doing a fair bit of work for orphanages lately — of course there are a lot more orphans than there ever used to be.

Thirty-six wounded kids in a US hospital — wounded by the US — get toys too. I won't even suggest what they'd prefer but I expect it's not Christmas in hospital. We get the day itself off. My parents have sent me a box of packages, all thoughtful, useful, or delicious.

My sister Jen sends me a tape of the *White Album* by the Beatles, while Simmo's sister, who obviously has more taste, sends him the Rolling Stones' *Beggars Banquet*.

The Stones suit my mood better and Simmo loves the Beatles, so we swap tapes and listen to them via headphones on our new tape decks, courtesy of the American PX store.

I also get a care package with a very nice bottle of brandy from Charlotte and Pete as thanks for getting work started on their orphanage. The card is also signed 'love, Claire,' but the sight of that hurts too much so I throw it away. Still, I've got to be grateful good old André didn't sign it.

Thirty-five days and a wakey.

Just before the start of the new year Simmo says, 'Hey, will you give me a hand again with a MEDCAP? Three of my assistants are out for the count now, only one's still upright.'

'If I must,' I say gloomily.

'You must, or I'll take back the Stones tape.'

'Bastard. I'll check with the CO, but should be okay. Still waiting on teachers to get out of the army, so things are quiet. What's the operation?'

'Oh, mate, MANLY FERRY. How do they dream up this shit? An Nhut, another cordon and search.'

'Busy little place.'

'On the road from Dat Do to the Long Hais, so fairly NLF friendly. Famous too.'

'Yeah?'

'Operation BEAUMARIS, two years ago. Search and cordon, three officers chatting together, one stepped on a mine, all three died. Sadly, the mine was from a barrier laid years ago by our good friends ARVN. Supposedly decommissioned.'

'Yeah? Not too well, it seems.'

He nods. 'Funny, you'd think that *should* have suggested the mine barrier concept was fucked. But dear old Brigadier Graham saw it as validation of his mad scheme, and off he galloped.'

'Hey, Simmo, why didn't you tell me any of this stuff before?'

'You mightn't have come.'

'Too right. Not sure I should this time either.'

'But the Stones tape ...?'

I groan. 'Ruthless fucker. Definitely the last time.'

He grins. 'Not to worry. The village is pretty clean now, sappers have done a good job.'

'Yeah, but we all know that shrapnel confuses metal detectors, so not a hundred percent, eh?'

Simmo shakes his head. 'Nothing's that.'

We're off to An Nhut before dawn and I find myself shivering. Christ it's cold for this time of year. Back to the same place, same setup — erect shade tents, dig and screen latrines, prepare the medical areas — but this time I see it all with new eyes.

'Hey, Simmo? That row of barbed wire over there, was that part of the old barrier?'

'Probably. But the mine explosion was on the other side of the village. Stop worrying, Leo.'

'Oh hell, here come the kids.'

The kids are big-eyed, cheeky and energetic. There are infected eyes and ears, hacking coughs, fevers, broken toes and suppurating splinters. Simmo calms them down, fixes them up, and sends them on their way with a sweet. I'm happy to help, any distraction is fine.

The air heats up and we stop briefly to drink water. I glance over at the barbed wire.

'Simmo, I reckon that bush wasn't here a month ago.'

'Yeah. Ever notice how fast things grow in this climate?'

'All right, I'm too suspicious.' I stop. 'But this is the same spot we did the clinic a month ago. What if someone left a little present for us in case we came back?'

'Actually, the whole place was swept first thing this morning,' Simmo says, grinning a little.

'Ah. Now why didn't you *tell* me that before, you bastard?'

'Just like to see you sweat. Come on, back to work.'

Another lot of kids comes through. One has a broken arm so that takes some concentration to get right — on Simmo's behalf, of course. I only hand him bandages soaked in plaster-of-paris.

Two of the kid's mates who already have their sweets are mucking around and one tosses the other's precious lolly into the air. It falls near the barbed wire.

He rushes over to get it and without thinking I yell, 'Hey, not over *there*!' Of course this means nothing to the kid. He grabs his sweet and returns, grinning. I shake my head. Fuck, I'm getting jumpy. It's such a hot day. I wipe my forehead.

'You all right?' says Simmo.

'Just overworked by some doctor prick.'

He smiles. 'Lunchtime soon.'

'And that's supposed to make me feel better?'

Lunch is delayed because a woman in the waiting area goes into labour. Simmo doesn't like how the birth is proceeding so we organise a chopper to take her to hospital. Later we grab something to eat but I'm not hungry. Thirsty, though. And so fucking hot.

But Simmo does all the work. He's a medical machine — I just hand him things when he asks for them. I'm almost feeling dizzy as the patients come and go, as wounds and ulcers and horrible ailments are calmly and trustingly presented to us for treatment: as Simmo somehow finds the energy to keep going while my legs are starting to wobble.

'Got to sit down, mate,' I finally say. 'Sorry.'

'Yeah. Have some more water,' Simmo says, busy wrapping someone's hand.

I nod and shuffle over to a stump and sit, drinking lukewarm water from my flask. My head hurts. It it heat-stroke? Unlikely, I've kept up my salt tablets.

But I feel sombre and uneasy. I glance at the leafy green bush near the barbed wire. It looks sinister, its branches weirdly like tentacles. The soil in the shadows beneath is smooth, as if it's been carefully swept, swept perhaps to hide ... what?

I stare at the bush and the smooth ground, wavering in the heat-shimmer. Sweat drips down my face, while the whole world around me seems to be slowly expanding and contracting with every throb of my pulse.

I blink and wipe my eyes and stare. Is there something in that smoothness projecting from the unsettling soil? Something like ... tiny, tiny prongs?

I leap up to yell, '*Mine* —' but can't because I'm falling as everything goes red and black.

∽

Nearly two weeks pass while I'm semi-conscious in hospital at Vung Tau. I vaguely recall being freezing cold and stinking hot and having amazing hallucinations, but at least my body is in one piece. There was no explosion: I've got malaria.

'Reckon you should go into the clairvoyant business,' says Simmo. He's sitting down for a chat now I can string a few words together.

'Come on, Simmo, I was out of it. Didn't mean to go troppo.'

'No, really. Just to be sure, the sappers did a careful sweep of that area. Near the bush that had you so spooked was an old ARVN mine. It went bang in a big way when they destroyed it.'

I stare, then laugh weakly. 'Only time ever. Otherwise not too good at reading the tea-leaves.'

'Bit of happy news, though — you're getting your discharge four weeks early. Tomorrow you'll go back to Nui Dat, then the day after you'll be winging your way home.'

'Not in four weeks? I'll be home in two *days*?'

'Nah, mate. Just one and a wakey.'

16. VIVY: AN INCANDESCENT SMILE (SEP 1968-JAN 1969)

We get happy, silly postcards from Annabelle and Minky on their world tour and, as Annabelle predicted, when she's home again everyone goes bonkers about her approaching wedding.

But as the tabloids circle they smell blood, and over the next few weeks, with mounting horror, Brian and I scan the headlines of the English papers in the local supermarché:

Annabelle and Boffin Brian to Marry at Oxford
Annabelle Yearns For Long-Distance Lover Brian
'Bass Player Minky's My Best Friend' says Annabelle
Worried Brian Waits Alone in Normandy
Minky and Annabelle Sizzle on Tour — Photos!
Who is Hunky Brian's Mystery Neighbour?
Annabelle's Night of Passion with Pouting Minky
Caddish Brian Flirts With Pregnant Songstress Vivy
Jazz Diva Vivy Always at Lonely Brian's Side
Annabelle and Minky's Secret Tryst
Sizzling Boffin Brian Strips Off at the Beach
Who is the Father of Sexy Vivy's Baby?
Annabelle's Mum Punches Our Reporter
Annabelle's Dad says Wedding is Happily on Track
Wedding of the Year Called Off
Sad Brian Abandoned at the Altar
Will Jazz Diva Vivy Ever Work Again?

After the last few headlines I hide away in my flat and refuse to go to the supermarché. Obviously Annabelle has had to cope with this as her fame grew, but until now the tabloids have mostly ignored her academic fiancé.

But how the hell did *I* get pulled into the circus? I rarely curse, but what the actual *fuck*?

'You okay?' says Brian, outside my door.

I yell, 'Are you stoned again? No, I'm not bloody okay.'

'Can I come in?'

'Go away, sizzling boffin.'

Brian laughs. 'Come on, Vivy.'

'That's Jazz Diva Vivy to you, thanks very much.'

'I'm certain you'll work again. I'll hire you myself if necessary.'

'To do what?'

'Mmm,' he says. 'To be by my side?'

'Not much of a job. Years of work and I'm just *songstress* Vivy?'

'Can I come in? I *have* been abandoned at the altar, after all.'

I sigh loudly, get up and open the door.

'Make me a cup of tea then,' I say ungraciously, and return to the couch.

'Just like old times,' Brian says, bringing it over and sitting.

'Yes, except I'm a laughing-stock and you photograph *very* handsomely at the beach. Have you heard from the girls?'

'Ecstatically happy in the Barbados, according to the latest postcard.'

'They're lucky to be out of it. What's today's headline, then?'

'I believe it's *Is Annabelle Corrupting Our Impressionable Youth*?'

I start laughing. 'Dear God. I thought my reputation couldn't get any worse when I came to live here, but little did I know. So how are you today, then? Hunky or Sad?'

'Caddish mostly — I'm just relieved that ghastly wedding's no longer hanging over my head.'

'Don't you regret losing Annabelle? You've been together for a long time.'

'Together was a relative term, don't forget. No, she's a darling, but I'm glad it's over. Marriage would have been a disaster.' He glances at me. 'Still, I'm truly sorry you got dragged into it.'

I shrug. 'I got called "sexy Vivy" once. I'll have to comfort myself with that.'

'Luckily Annabelle's mum punched somebody before they tracked down your husband.'

I laugh. 'Good on her. I'm just looking forward to next week's headlines: *Sizzling Brian Tells Boffins All About His Big Fossil*.'

'Unlikely, I'd never boast. But surely there won't be reporters at the British Palaeontology Conference.' He stops. 'You don't think ...?'

'You'll be fine.'

'But what about you here, all by yourself?'

'It's only three days. Still got a whole ten weeks to go, and I can always talk to lovely Julie Desvignes if I'm worried. Are you packed?'

Brian nods. 'Evening ferry to Portsmouth, conference in London, back home Saturday morning.'

∽

Late October now. The weeks of scandal have died down, and it's nice to know I won't be on the covers of the tabloids in the supermarché. Thankfully the news has moved on: apparently Jackie Kennedy is marrying Aristotle Onassis. Bless you, Jackie.

I climb steep Rue de Verdun with my groceries then stop for a breather. Glancing ahead I see a strange car outside Mi-Côte, a large, shiny car.

Good God, is that a Rolls Royce? As I draw level, the door opens and an elegant woman in the height of fashion steps out.

'Frederika?' I say. She looks displeased. 'How are you, Countess? Do come in.'

I open the door to my flat and lead her into the tiny living area.

'Please, have a seat. May I offer you tea?' I say.

'I think perhaps not,' she says, carefully lowering herself to the edge of the couch.

'Why are you here?' I say, my throat tightening a little.

She pats her hair. 'I was spending the week at Deauville, the Casino there is very good. Henk asked me to visit you and make you see sense.'

'Sense?' I say, turning my back and putting my groceries away.

She laughs shortly. 'Vivy, you *cannot* be serious. Living in this slum. Mocked by the hyenas of the press. Henk begs you to come home, to have the baby in the security of your own family.'

'He's not my family.'

'He is the baby's father, Vivy.'

'He's not, and you *know* he's not. This is absurd.'

'You must understand, you will not be allowed to divorce him.'

'Tough. I plan to anyway.'

Frederika shrugs. 'I will testify, the Commissioner will testify, even the doctor who performed Henk's vasectomy — a most discreet man — will testify, all of us, that he is the father of your baby, and you have no reason to divorce him.'

'He *hit* me, Frederika. Or rather, he punched me in the belly and locked me up in my own home. And stole my savings! Those are *very* good reasons and I think a court will agree.'

'And you have the proof of such charges, Vivy?'

'The manager at our bank knows he siphoned everything out of my account.'

'You mean Mijnheer Van Buskirk? I know his mother very well, and he never defies her.'

'Are you crazy? You'd get a *bank* manager to lie to stop me divorcing Henk?'

'I promise you, Vivy, a woman seeking a divorce from the blameless father of her child will find very little sympathy in a Dutch court.'

'*Blameless*? I can't —' I turn. 'Get out of here, out of my house.'

'Do you think the court will listen to a hysterical woman? One publicly shamed by vile newspapers? A sleazy *singer*?' She laughs. 'How naive you are.'

I advance towards her. 'You, Frederika — you who *bought* your cardboard title and your pretentious country manor — *you* threaten me? Get out, you loathsome bitch!'

She stands and sniffs. 'How you have fallen, Vivy. I shall show myself out.'

She leaves my flat with such exaggerated dignity I almost laugh. But then I sit down in despair.

∽

That night, shocked and anxious by the fire, I suddenly hear mysterious noises and jump up, my heart thumping. Brian isn't back until tomorrow and I'm all alone. What if it's another of Henk's nasty friends come to threaten me? Or even malevolent Henk himself?

There's a rap on the door and I start shaking as it slowly opens.

'Vivy?' says Brian quietly, then stares. 'What's wrong?' He steps forward and takes my hands and pulls me close. 'My God, what's *happened*, Vivy?'

I press my face into his shoulder. 'I didn't know it was *you*!'

'I managed to get home early. Sorry to give you a surprise.'

'It's not your fault, it's not. But I've had such a *shock* —'

'Tell me.' He draws me to sit on the couch. I'm still trembling and he holds my hands.

'Take your time, Vivy. Are you in pain? Let's go to the hospital.'

'No, the baby's fine. But someone came today, a fake Countess, a friend of Henk's. She said she'd lie, the Police Commissioner would lie, the bank manager, even the doctor who did Henk's *vasectomy* would lie, and tell the court that this is *his* child.'

I'm gasping. 'Brian, they'll swear he didn't hit me, that I'm hysterical, sleazy, shameful. And I'll *never* get away from him!'

'Come here.' He puts his arm around me and rubs my back. 'They can't, Vivy. I won't let them, I promise. You'll be all right, please don't worry.'

Brian feels wonderful, and at last I'm *safe*. Oh, how I wish I could stay here forever, in the comfort of his arms, breathing his heady scent of fresh air and warm, healthy male.

Time passes peacefully, then I murmur, 'Did your conference go well, then?'

'Very well. No reporters, thank God.'

'So Brian's Big Fossil won't be making the front page news?'

'Actually it will, but in the next Journal of Palaeontology. Though by then it may have a slightly less salacious title.'

I look up at him, both of us quietly laughing.

We gaze at each other, becoming silent, then Brian bends down and kisses me. I hold his head and kiss him back. A long, pleasing, dizzying time passes in which we slowly become horizontally entwined on the couch.

I murmur, 'Would you like something to eat?'

'No.'

'What about a glass of wine?'

'No.'

I glance at Brian's hand, caressing my breast. I say, 'Bed, then?'

'Yes.'

'But I'm enormously pregnant. Will it be all right?'

'For you, me or the baby?'

'I'm not sure.'

'The baby and I will be fine. I'll make certain it's pretty good for you too.'

∽

Ah, the luxury of connection after so long. My body has brought me more than a few surprises these last few months, but none so surprising as how intensely, how delightfully, I respond to Brian.

'I didn't even *know*,' I say. '*A Child is Born* is so coy. It says women lose desire, but sex can continue as long as women desire it. Seems a bit roundabout, and not in accord with what's happening here. Do your sisters have any words of wisdom?'

'Can you doubt it? Susan swears that sex induced her son's birth when she feared she'd be pregnant forever, and Felicity just gazes into the distance and says she gets as randy as a rabbit.'

I laugh and nuzzle Brian's delicious neck. 'But why did it take us so long? Why didn't we jump into bed the moment we met?'

'Well, with your sprained leg you weren't jumping anywhere. And me? I was so astonished you'd walked into my life — or rather fallen into a puddle — I was simply incapacitated with lust. And, let's face it, at the time you were a jazz diva with a bad cold and a husband in Amsterdam.'

'Details, details. I got myself back here pretty quickly.' I kiss him, and we lie peacefully for a time, then I have a sudden unwelcome realisation.

'Brian, have you *really* thought all this through?'

'I haven't been doing a lot of thinking, I must admit.'

'Seriously.' I lean up on my elbow, and gaze at his (beautiful) grey eyes. 'I'm pregnant with another man's child. We haven't really considered that before.'

'So?'

'But won't you feel ... I don't know ... whatever primal thing it is that men are supposed to feel in such situations?'

'When I find out, I'll tell you. But really, I just want to take care of you and your baby.' Brian smiles. 'Does this mean you felt *primal* when Annabelle was in my bed?'

'Your bedsprings are so noisy I wanted to throw a can of oil at your head.' I sigh. 'But of course you had every right to sleep with your fiancée.'

'And you had every right to sleep with someone you cared about, and keep the pregnancy as well. It's okay, Vivy. We're grownups, we've both seen a bit of life.'

'True. I seem to recall you saying pragmatically, *Romance isn't everything.*'

He laughs. 'My God, I was a fool. You're the most romantic thing that's ever happened to me.'

∽

My belly expands relentlessly. Brian and I find delightful ways to accommodate it in bed, but I'm slowing down. I get puffed more easily, so we drive to get groceries rather than plod back up the hill. My legs swell a little but long, slow massages help, and by the time they reach the tops of my thighs it doesn't matter.

Librarian Julie Desvignes, who's become a good friend, puts me in touch with a midwife, Ginette Noyer, a small, clever woman. Ginette gets me doing various breathing exercises, so when I reach some ghastly crux of childbirth that I can't even imagine right now, I'll be able to keep myself calm and the baby well-oxygenated.

Dr Allard says I'm *une primigeste âgée*, an elderly primigravida — which stings a little — and he's calm about midwife Ginette's involvement. He will supervise, but Ginette will otherwise handle the birth. I'm booked into a nursing home for the big event, to occur in mid-December.

There are a range of anaesthetics available, which I plan to use without a qualm, but after talking to optimistic Ginette and some of the other women she's assisting, I'll try to see how far I can get with natural childbirth before I start begging for oblivion. Despite these sensible steps, the pregnancy still seems remote and unreal, and I remain strangely unperturbed.

I get occasional contractions, but it's only my womb getting into practice, Ginette says. The baby has started kicking like a small horse but it doesn't bother me, and the ripples simply enchant Brian.

And when my belly seems to lie lower one day Dr Allard says it's called the 'lightening.' Apparently the baby's head has engaged with my pelvis, which means it will be born within four weeks. I'm glad (because my breathing is easier) but I still don't believe childbirth will ever happen.

Julie Desvignes and Madame Cloutier give me gifts of knitted caps and socks, but I cannot picture them in use by a real baby. Brian brings home a pram one day, an old-fashioned wicker thing, and again I find the idea of a future occupant incomprehensible.

On one hand I'd love to be back to my normal self, for this small creature to get the hell out of my personal primeval sea, but on the other hand ... what happens when it's out? What happens when it's not some ammonite bouncing on my poor bladder, but a real baby?

∞

It's the start of December. Two weeks to go now, but the days drag by like years. Brian and I enjoy lovemaking as much as ever, but I *really* hope Susan was right and sex induces birth, because I've had about as much of this as I can stand.

I get a letter from Dad. A copy of some British scandal sheet has turned up in Saigon, with a breathless account of Brian and Annabelle's non-marriage and the apparent culprit: pregnant jazz diva Vivy McKee.

Darling girl, we're so happy for you, although Charlotte — at almost sixty — maintains she's far too young to become a grandmother. In fact she's secretly ecstatic. I assume you haven't mentioned it so far because of complications in your life, but please feel free to tell us more when the time is right. And when IS the big day? We'll have our fingers crossed for you.

I hadn't even thought about those rotten papers appearing overseas. And in Australia too, of course.

So my friends will know I'm pregnant, but don't know where I am or why I've left Amsterdam — I've been too fuzzy-headed to write and bloody Henk hasn't forwarded any of my mail. Still, I'm glad my parents know at last what's happening.

When Brian and I go to buy groceries that afternoon, Madame Cloutier rushes out from behind the counter at the bakery and hugs me. 'It is a *miracle*, Vivy,' she says. 'Ce salaud has returned our money!'

It takes me a moment to focus. 'Oh, Baudet?' (The estate agent who'd run off with everyone's rents is generally known as 'ce salaud'.)

'Oui. His office has opened again. He is not there, a young woman of most serious demeanour is in charge. She said it is all a terrible mistake, the money was placed in the wrong account and M. Baudet was too ashamed to admit it and ran away.'

'Do you believe that?'

'Of course not. But I have my money back, *and* some interest! Mon Dieu, what a fine day. Go too, Vivy, and claim your money.'

Intrigued, Brian and I make our way to Rue Boulard. The old office is looking new and tidy, and a young woman behind the desk is shaking the hand of M. Guillot, the locksmith. He nods at us, grinning happily as he leaves. The woman's nameplate reads Mlle Sophie Soulier, and she is indeed of serious demeanour.

I introduce myself and she nods gravely. 'Ah, the McKee property?' She opens a file. 'I see no rents were forwarded for six months, and a large sum sent from Vietnam also ... went astray.' She points at a page. 'Is this the account number for the owners of the property?'

I check, and sign to confirm it is correct.

'I shall deposit those sums this afternoon, Madame. This agency is now owned by l'Entreprise Aigle, who offer their apologies for the distress caused by the previous owner. Should you wish to engage us for future transactions we would be most happy to help.'

Amazed, I thank Mlle Soulier, and she says politely, 'I have a letter here for you also.' I open the envelope and laugh. Aigle Enterprise is owned by Mr Adler, of course.

Dear Vivy,

I must apologise for the time it has taken to persuade M. Baudet's patron to untangle this matter. It became clear to me that real estate in coastal Normandy has great potential, so I assisted the decision by taking the business off the patron's hands. The foolish M. Baudet has returned the purloined funds and is now operating a small franchise not far from the Arctic Circle.

I believe you are anticipating a happy event, so I offer you my congratulations. However I hope this does not mean you depart from the world of music — that would indeed be a tragedy. Please give your parents my warmest greetings, and tell them I am glad to have helped resolve this small affair.

With my warmest regards,
Moshe Adler

How wonderful! As Brian drives us home I can't stop smiling. I'll write to my parents tomorrow with all the good news about Mr Adler and their money.

Once they've organised their own finances they should still have enough to repair Mi-Côte, so it must be safe at last from being sold. And of course, I need to tell my parents the baby is due in just a fortnight.

But as we get out of the car I feel an odd sensation, a squeezing in my lower back and pelvis. I realise it's been coming and going faintly all day but I could ignore it. Suddenly I can ignore it no longer and have to lean against the car, breathing heavily.

It occurs to me that writing letters may be the last thing I'm capable of tomorrow.

∽

It starts out innocuously enough. Pressure, tightening, relaxation. I can do this, all the books say so. I pace around at home, trying to breathe as I was taught, Brian pacing beside me until I order him to sit down.

We eat lunch — goat's cheese and tomatoes on fresh baguettes, sunshine from the pale winter sky slanting across the table.

Then the squeezy bits start coming faster, working themselves into something surprisingly uncomfortable. I lie down for a while, then pace some more.

Brian talks to midwife Ginette on the phone, who says she'll drop by and see me, but it's far too early to go to hospital. I was hoping she'd say I must leave this instant and it'd all be over by dinner, but no such luck.

Ginette arrives mid-afternoon, tells Brian to make tea, and insists she shave (shave!) me, and even more mortifying, inserts an enema suppository, which I've never experienced before. The subsequent process *hurts*. I am disliking this 'happy event' more and more.

My contractions are now coming every four minutes, but Ginette seems to think this is all perfectly normal. I am starting to wonder if she's insane.

She leaves, then comes back at six in the evening and says everything is progressing well. *Well*?

The worst bit is the sheer relentlessness of it all. I just begin to relax after a contraction that should qualify me for general anaesthesia, when it starts all over again. Everything takes on an air of unreality and I yearn desperately for a pause.

'Ginette, can we stop now?' I say hazily. 'We can start again tomorrow, but I just need a *rest*.'

She laughs and calls me chérie, and pats my cheek. I'd kill her if these bloody contractions would stop for long enough.

She checks me again and says, 'You are now six centimetres dilated, Vivy. Perhaps it is time to go to the nursing home. I will meet you there.'

'Yes, yes, let's go,' I say, my mind running over all my options for anaesthesia. Brian drives slowly, but the road seems to have become very bumpy since yesterday. A nurse meets us at the nursing home, puts me in a wheelchair and takes me to a room.

'Shouldn't there be, well, devices and drugs here to ease my pain?' I ask. The nurse helps me onto the bed. 'Non, ce n'est pas une salle d'accouchement, c'est une salle d'attente.' She leaves.

Brian says gently, 'Just a waiting room.'

'But ...' I say weakly, then try to breathe my way through another contraction.

What madman — or madwoman — came up with the notion that *breathing* would help when you're climbing yet another mountain of pain? Aeons pass, oceans rise and fall, ammonites live, die and become fossils, and *still* this continues.

Brian gives me his hand to hold and my nails draw blood. 'Ouch.'

'Wimp,' I say with contempt.

Ginette arrives. 'Do you wish to wait outside, Professeur?'

'No, I'd prefer to remain — if it's all right with you, Vivy.'

'Only if you stay here by the top of the bed.'

Ginette examines me and says, 'You are doing well but I think I will rupture the membrane. Things will go faster.'

I'm not sure if that's a good thing, but soon I'm back in the wheelchair and being whizzed off to a room with lots of chrome and enamel. Modern science at last!

Ginette inserts a sort of crochet hook (so much for modern science) which leads to a gush of warm fluid, but then the contractions get worse. I suck on a tube of some sort of gas supposed to help ease pain. It doesn't.

'Won't be long now,' says Ginette cheerfully.

'Please, *please*, can I have an epidural?' I whisper.

'Oh no, it is much too late for that. You are doing well, Vivy, everything is fine.'

I now loathe Ginette with every ounce of my being, or would if I weren't stifling moans instead.

Suddenly I feel an intense urge to push, but Ginette says firmly, 'Non! Stop, Vivy.'

'Stop?' I could weep. '*Stop*? Can't I push, just a little bit?'

'You must stop. You will tear your cervix. Wait.'

Why should I care? At this stage my damned cervix isn't doing anything on my behalf except hurting. But I obey and, apart from wrestling during contractions with that dementing urge, the pain seems to ease off a little. Further aeons pass.

Ginette examines me. 'Ah, good, now ten centimetres. Vivy — at last you may push.'

Like a wave the next contraction comes towards me, and I do. It feels amazing and *nothing* hurts. What bliss!

'Breathe now, Vivy, *breathe*.'

I pause to take a breath and the urge fades away. What? *No* ... Okay, here comes another wave, go with it!

Ginette stops me again in the middle. 'I *can't*,' I say frustrated. 'Just let me push.'

'You must breathe, too.'

We go through numerous cycles of this and I start getting tired.

Ginette says, 'You are not progressing, Vivy. I am concerned. I will ring Docteur Allard.'

She leaves but a junior nurse stays with us.

Brian, whose hand is scored with red lines but is wise enough not to mention it, says quietly, 'Why not take a *very* deep breath, and then don't stop?'

I nod in desperation, empty my lungs, then fill them till my head is buzzing with oxygen. A wave rolls towards me, and I push and push and *push*.

'C'est la tête!' squeals the junior nurse and runs to the door. 'Madame Noyer, la *tête*!'

I take a deep breath. '*Is* it the head?' I ask Brian.

'You insisted I stay at the top of the bed, love, so I've no idea.'

'Oh, for God's sake. Modesty is beyond me now. Just have a bloody look.'

Brian goes to the business end of proceedings. Astonishment comes over his face and he says, 'It's the head.'

'I'm getting sick of hearing that.'

'But ... it's got *hair*.'

A wave rolls towards me again and I breathe deeply and push desperately, as Ginette bustles back into the delivery room. 'Slowly, Vivy,' she says. 'I'll turn the shoulder —'

She does, but I don't care because I'm riding the wave and not stopping for anyone, and suddenly the wave gushes into the most glorious hot, wet, slithery, real *thing*.

Ginette says, 'Vivy, une belle fille!'

She lifts up a blueish object which mewls and wriggles, then places it on my bare breasts (see comment on modesty above). I hold it, this warm naked *baby*, which snuffles and blinks and appears to be radiating violet light. This, by now, seems perfectly normal.

'We must cut the cord and weigh her,' Ginette says, and does so.

When the baby comes back to me she's wrapped in a soft cotton blanket and I just want to hold her and look at her small surprised face and whisper foolish, comforting things as I kiss her head.

Brian sits beside us and says, 'My God, she's beautiful. Oh Vivy, how hard you worked! She's wonderful, you're *both* wonderful.'

I feel another wave of contraction, and after a bit of fussing Ginette says, 'Ah, the afterbirth, and it is complete. It appears you will not need stitches, either.'

'This is really such a *complicated* business,' I murmur to Brian.

Ginette comes to my side. 'You did very well, Vivy. Do you still want to kill me?'

'Did I actually say that? I do apologise.'

She smiles. 'Now, I must attend another confinement, so I will see you tomorrow.'

∽

Lying in a fresh nightgown after a sponge bath, the baby asleep in a cot beside me, it's hard to relax. I'm so excited, recalling over and over the triumph of that explosion of life: the delight, the relief, the genuine *miracle* of it.

Finally I doze. After a welcome breakfast next morning, the nurse helps me put the baby to the breast. I won't have milk for a few days but apparently I still produce something useful.

It's not uncomfortable and I'm pleased that what I'd thought of as merely pleasurable objects to fill out a glittering gown suddenly have a new and important task.

Brian comes to visit and brings me a large bouquet of flowers. The baby is asleep again, and he leans over her cot, murmuring besottedly.

'Well there we are,' I say. 'My duty to the human race is done.'

'You're stopping at *one*?'

'Of course I am. I'm not greedy.'

He laughs. 'How are you feeling?'

'My arms and legs hurt, which is odd as I was lying down.'

'You were working with every muscle in your body, love. I'm not surprised.'

'The obvious parts ache a bit of course, and my breasts are tender. But so far, so good. I'm tired, but apparently in a few years' time I'll be allowed to get some sleep.'

Brian kisses my hand. 'I'll help you as much as I can.'

'I know.' I suddenly feel an odd lump in my throat.

'And what are you going to call her?'

I stare at him and swallow. 'Funny, I didn't even think about names. Everything just seemed so hard to contemplate, and I didn't really *believe* the birth would ever happen ...'

I start crying helplessly.

Brian hugs me. 'Dear Vivy. Plenty of time to find a name.'

'But I didn't *believe* in her and now she's *here* and I'm going to be a *terrible* mother!'

'Whoa, hold on. How did you get from point A to point Z so quickly?'

'Don't know. For some reason I've started to feel terribly, terribly ... sad.'

'But remember what the books say? Hormones! All those helpful hormones that made the baby are fading away and leaving you depressed. This is supposed to happen.'

'So I not only have to give birth but then have to feel miserable about it? Bloody unfair.'

Brian kisses me. 'It'll pass in a few days. Don't worry.'

Tears gather again in my eyes. 'But the poor little mite hasn't even got a *name*.'

'Well, are there any you like? What about some version of Charlotte? Charline, perhaps?'

I gaze, appalled. 'Never.'

'Your father, Peter? Petula.'

'Are you serious? Brian, have you ever actually named anything?'

'Certainly. A very handsome ammonite, a *Peltoceratoides* —'

'No.'

'I had a turtle once. Does that count?'

'What did you call it?'

'Speedy.'

I stare at him, open-mouthed. 'Is that true?'

'Sadly, yes. I was an optimistic child.'

I laugh and he kisses my head. 'I know,' he says. 'What about your stepfather Louis, who first brought you to Villers-sur-Mer? Louise, perhaps?'

I think for a moment. 'Louise? That's rather pretty. Does she *look* like a Louise?'

We lean over the cot. Her hair is dark fluff, her skin fair, her features neat and small.

'I'm not sure what a Louise looks like,' Brian says. 'But I think it might suit her.'

'Hello, Louise,' I say softly, and she snuffles in her sleep. 'Well, that settles it. Louise. Oh, Brian, perhaps I won't be a terrible mother after all.'

'You're doing all right, love,' he says gently.

∽

The pregnancy books need revision. Yes, they say new mothers will feel emotionally up and down. But do they say a new mother will look in the mirror one dark night and see the face of a crone? A crone who hasn't slept for a decade? I don't think so, and it's a serious omission.

There's all this glossing over the matter of babies and breasts too. It starts off easily enough, but Day Four of furious nipple-gumming is getting pretty ghastly. Day Five at last brings, to both of us, the great relief of milk. Seriously, Mother Nature, why take so long?

My emotions slowly stabilise, Louise and I get to know each other, and after six days I go home. Not to have the profound, limitless sleep every cell in my body screams for (hollow laughter), but an hour or two, now and then, on Louise's schedule.

Somehow I manage. My routine becomes hers, my life becomes hers. I sleep, eat, feed the baby, change her nappies, wash and dress her. Brian helps with all the care that doesn't require the intervention of breasts, and in my weepy moments that truly makes me weep.

But I'm starting to see that for most of the pregnancy I was, basically, as stoned out of my brains as if I'd smoked one of Edgar's joints all by myself.

Apart from refusing to (a) believe I'd ever give birth, (b) tell my parents I was pregnant, or (c) think about a name for the child, there are so many other things I didn't come to grips with.

Henk of course is the obvious omission, as well as the friends in Australia I simply stopped writing to, but as my mind slowly focuses I realise there's one issue I didn't consider at all once I'd discovered my refuge at Mi-Côte.

Stav. I can't call him Louise's father: he's not. Every day Brian's devotion to the baby grows more profound, a connection that has nothing to do with biology.

But at some time I'll have to tell Stav I didn't get rid of the 'problem' as he demanded, and one day I'll have to tell Louise who Stav is and what was once between us. And *very* soon I need to tell Brian more than 'I became pregnant to my now ex-lover.'

Six weeks pass. Life with Louise becomes almost routine, but perhaps that's the slave getting used to the shackles. Of course I'd do anything for her, but at the same time I'm driven by a sense of duty. The baby cries, the baby gets colic (don't ask), the baby sleeps. She wakes, she eats, she has nappy changes, she sleeps.

And then one day Louise focuses her slate-blue eyes on me with a slightly puzzled look, and a smile lights up her face, a smile of such recognition, of such incandescent *ecstasy* at the sight of me, that I go weak at the knees. All I can do is grin foolishly back, flooded head to toe by the kind of bliss that saints are supposed to experience.

After that we know each other, Louise and I, and it's such a calm, sweet connection. Sometimes I wonder if Charlie and I ever felt a similar bond? I don't think so, which makes me feel sorry for her. Fancy going through such emotional and physical labour, and never knowing *this*.

At last I understand what the books try to explain but simply can't. I think of the passionate mountain-climbers, the earnest enlightenment-seekers, the wild-eyed mystics, and laugh.

You poor yearning fools: it's here, it's all here in a baby's thousand-watt smile.

Everything that matters is *here*.

PART III. IMPERIAL GREEN

17. JEN: LONG BAY (OCT 1968-AUG 1969)

They put Ash into Long Bay gaol. It's supposed to be the worst prison in the country, and looks like some brutal medieval castle. Long Bay is less than ten miles from Tina's place in Kings Cross, but Dad says firmly, 'Don't even suggest going near the place, Jenny,' so I don't.

In any case within days I'm whisked back to Newcastle, with no chance of returning to Sydney until Christmas, months away: and in between looms the Higher School Certificate. At least those few days of Ash's help have somehow unblocked my progress in maths, and I also start liking biology lots as well.

One night over dinner Dad mentions something connected to a unit I'm doing. Apparently an old colleague has just won a scientific prize for work on malaria, and Dad says wistfully, 'It's one of the final links in the puzzle. But he deserves it.'

Mum says, 'Do you regret leaving all that behind, Harry?'

'I suit being a general practitioner more, love.' Dad smiles. 'But ah, research, the sheer joy of it.'

'Joy?' I say, finishing off the last of my apple pie.

'Joy,' he says firmly. 'To have the time and focus to push the boundaries of knowledge on a single topic, Jenny? Joy is the only word to describe it.'

'Then why ...?' I stop. I know he was a researcher before the war, then was in a prison camp, and afterwards went into general practice. Maybe this is a touchy subject.

'Why?' he says. 'Ah, sweetheart.' (That's a change — he hasn't called me sweetheart since I got arrested.) 'In Singapore — in the camp — I understood how much more important general medicine was. That's all. But that doesn't mean I didn't love what I did before.'

'But what *did* you do?'

'Tried my best to untangle the malaria puzzle, and along the way contributed a small step towards the real solution.' He smiles wryly. 'Still satisfying.'

'Dad,' I say hesitantly, 'We're doing a unit on blood-born disease and I'm having a bit of trouble with it. Do you think you could give me a hand?'

He's surprised. 'If you like. My knowledge is probably out-of-date, but I can suggest some possible directions.' For a moment he looks happy and young, not grumpy and tired, and I'm glad I mentioned it (and also glad because I'd love a bit of help).

Mum glances at me with thanks in her eyes, and I realise she worries about Dad more than I ever noticed. They must have problems they keep to themselves, while all the time I'm wallowing, confused. Do the *grown-ups* never figure some things out either?

I write to Ash, with his prisoner number on the envelope, care of Long Bay Correctional Facility, and he replies. He says he's okay, his cell-mate's okay, prison life's okay. So I guess it's not. I write again and ask him to help me with some maths problems. That seems to please him and his letter in return is less reserved.

I also get to hear how the redhead and a couple of other friends have visited. Of course it's great that people have gone to see him, but it makes me feel grumpy. Apparently the redhead's name, pretentiously, is 'Genevieve' which makes me even more grumpy.

Oh God. Am I falling for *another* of the Adler brothers?

Absolutely not. My broken heart over Tibor still aches, and it *does* feel as if it's broken. I can't even imagine liking someone that much ever again, and I simply don't want to.

⸎

Some of my classes are going reasonably well. I love art without wanting to go to art school, apparently the ambition of the rest of the class. I just enjoy the work and immerse myself in the practice, so it all ticks along.

French is okay too. I like the texts, the dreamy *Le Grand Meulnes*, and Voltaire's *Candide*, with the enigma of that final declaration: Il faut cultiver notre jardin. Obviously, 'we must cultivate our garden.' But what *is* that garden? Our aspirations? Our lives? Our withdrawal from the world's hurley-burly? Our genuine hands-in-the-soil harvest?

What do gardens *mean* anyway! Of course the Biblical Garden, but then I remember Kate Webb's astonishing line about the attack in Vietnam: *It looked like a butcher's shop in Eden, beautiful but ghastly.* That makes me shiver, but I love considering these possibilities, and write what the teacher says is a good essay on the topic.

A-Level English is still the hard one, but I try. And when all the marks are totalled, despite my teacher's constant carping, somehow I've come top in the class. I can't believe it!

At the end-of-year ceremonies, I'll get an award, usually a book, for coming first in English. I'm ecstatic, I've never won anything academic before!

Then the teacher announces that this year, unlike previously, the English award will go to whoever is top in Latin and English combined. This doesn't make any sense: until it does. The teacher's favourite is a fop who's first in Latin and second to me in English.

At home I can't hide my pain. I know it's only a book, but it's an acknowledgement too, an acknowledgement of *me*. I tell Mum what's happened, and she becomes thoughtful.

A few days later she comes home and says, 'Jen, I had a word with your English teacher. He agrees with me that the English award has nothing to do with Latin. Don't worry, darling.'

I hug her. I always knew, without being told, she did something during the war that needed power and confidence, and I can feel that within her now; my small, quiet mother.

November approaches. Despite his awful circumstances, dear Ash still writes to me with encouragement, insights and tips on playing with mathematics, and it helps me so much.

The ordeal ahead makes my gut tighten in terror, but still, still: I have the tools to deal with it. So the turmoil arrives. I don't remember anything, it's like an avalanche, a slow, two-week avalanche.

My classmates gather in the quadrangle, terrified. We sit at widely separated desks in the gym, fill in our student numbers (I know mine off by heart for two weeks then forget it forever), work on our papers, and depart, shaken.

And then it's over.

The end-of-year ceremonies are held in the school hall. I'm awarded *Fowler's English Usage*, which is surprisingly interesting. The English teacher won't meet my eyes, but what do I care now about that mean little man?

My friend Linda's father belongs to a union with holiday cabins for their members beside a beach, forty miles north of Newcastle, so five of us girls go to stay at small, quiet Fingal Bay. After the slog of the exams, what a holiday!

Fingal Bay is a cluster of cabins a few steps away from a long, curved beach. We lie in the sun, splash in the water, try to learn how to ride a surfboard and fall off, squealing, a lot. On a couple of nights we put on trendy clothes and take the bus the few miles away to Nelsons Bay, and meet boys in discos. It's silly and nice.

But Linda has decided she's not interested in British pop music now, just soppy things by people like Johnny Farnham. She's getting married in a year, so she's not even going to study to be an accountant. Instead she's got a job lined up at David Jones — in the shoe department, which is somehow a bit sad.

The holiday ends, and at home I wait and wait in the summer heat. And then, mid-December, the results appear in the newspaper.

I've done well, so well I'm offered a Commonwealth Scholarship, a scholarship to study whatever I want at any university I choose.

Mum and Dad are stunned. So am I.

I read various university handbooks and course outlines, and think and think, then finally tell them: 'I'm going to do biology at Sydney University.'

'Biology, love? Good choice.' Dad says smiling, then stops. 'Sydney? Where will you live?'

'With Tina at Kings Cross, if she'll have me. It's less than half-an-hour from there to the uni.'

∞

Christmas this year is very different from before. I find myself wondering — is that sweet time of family celebration now over? Was an entire chunk of my life that mattered so much, was it only *temporary*?

I had somehow assumed *I* would grow up, *I* would change, but everything else would remain the same. But of course, after what's happened this year with Ash and Tibor, and Leo away in Vietnam, I should have known everything else could change as well.

Still, the party at Billie and Nikos's place is comforting, with music and drinks and family friends, although Ash's parents look older and his absence feels enormous. In the kitchen I find Rob and Dev pouring themselves soft drinks.

'Are Tibor and Ursula coming along later?' I ask.

'No, they're too busy. They got *engaged*,' Dev says. 'She's such a cow. And she's not even Jewish, so Mum's really upset.'

That's another thing to puzzle over. In all my fantasies about Tibor, religion never came into the equation. I'm technically a Protestant, but my parents dislike churches (we believe in science, says Dad).

As far as I know the Adlers are more observant but, other than celebrating the Sabbath, religion doesn't seem an enormous part of their lives.

Dev and Rob, as usual, are gently bickering. Rob continues, '*Anyway*, Dev, if László Richter's my father then technically I'm Jewish. So *I* should have gotten a bar mitzvah party this year when I turned thirteen. It's not fair.'

'Silly,' says Devorah, putting the bottle back in the fridge. 'Being Jewish comes from your *mother*, not your father. Anyway, a mitzvah happens whether or not you have a party.'

'No *party*? What's the point of it then?'

'If you were Jewish it would mean you're an adult, but since you're not, you're not.'

'Totally unjust,' says Rob. 'And I can't believe anyone'd think *you're* an adult either.'

Dev smiles with wise eyes.

I pour a beer. 'Rob, have you asked Tina about László yet?'

'Are you *crazy*? I prefer to go on living, thanks very much.'

'You'll have to ask her sometime or other.'

'Guess so. But not yet.'

Billie comes into the kitchen. 'Got everything you need, kids?'

'Yes, thanks,' says Rob.'Come and play records, Dev.'

Billie pours herself some white wine from the fridge. 'That's a great tan, Jen.'

'Spent a week lying on the beach,' I say.

Billie looks at her freckled arm ruefully. 'Never much good at tanning, but always loved swimming.' She smiles. 'There's a beautiful spot, Wind Rose Cove, where Nikos and I often take the yacht.'

'Hey, is it true, Billie? Mum said you were thinking of giving up flying your seaplane.'

She sits on the edge of the kitchen table and shrugs. 'Looks like it. Reflexes are getting a bit slow. Probably safer for everyone if I stay on the ground.'

'Won't you miss flying?'

'Biggest part of my life. But everything changes, doesn't it?'

'Funny, I'm only just starting to realise that myself. It's a bit — I don't know — scary.'

Billie nods. 'Never stops being scary, either. Heard anything from your mate Ash?'

'A letter last week, but he doesn't say much. I wish I could see him, but Dad says I'm not allowed near the gaol.'

'You're moving to Sydney in January though, aren't you?' She smiles. 'Maybe with a sensible adult to escort you it'd be okay.'

'*You*? Billie, thank you! That'd be great. Though don't say anything to Dad, all right?'

'Okay. Just noticed the footwear — no Mary Quant tonight?'

After a moment I say, 'Nah, I'm a bit over Quant. These are from David Jones, nothing special.'

Billie glances at me. 'Okay. Better pass around some food. Give me a hand?'

The big news at the party that night is that Vivy McKee, my cousin and a famous jazz singer in Europe, has had a baby. Everyone seems very intrigued, mostly because she's not living with her husband in Amsterdam any more, but with a scientist somewhere in France.

Next day Dev brings over a copy of a magazine she'd kept because of a story on Electric Cloud (she adores Annabelle), although she hadn't realised the notorious pregnant singer in the story was *our* Vivy.

Rob and I lean over her shoulder to read it. Even though they took a photo of her in an ugly black swimsuit she's still really pretty, and the scientist is handsome too.

Rob nods firmly and says, 'She looks nice. I bet she'll help me find my real father.'

∽

January 1969, and I pack to go to live at Tina's, mostly summer clothes. When the weather gets cooler I'll come home and pick up some winter things. Still, I squeeze Ash's duffel-coat into the suitcase — I wouldn't leave that behind.

Mum and Dad are driving me to Sydney, not only to install me at Tina's, but to go to the airport to pick up Leo from Vietnam! It turns out he's been a bit unwell so he's being released from the army early. He's had malaria, which I thought wasn't a serious disease nowadays, but anyway, I'm glad he's back home at last.

I'm also glad he's home from Vietnam, because in Sydney I plan to go to every anti-war demo I can find and it might be a bit awkward otherwise.

Ash's imprisonment seems to have horrified a lot of people, and at night protesters climb up railway embankments or hang over bridges, and paint 'FREE ADLER.' Radio disk jockeys snicker and ask when will they get *their* free adler, and seem to imagine they're being funny.

Mum, Dad and I arrive at Tina's, then next afternoon we drive to Kingsford Smith Airport. We watch the silvery speck coming closer and closer to the ground, touching with puffs of dust, then slowing and taxiing around to the gate.

Ground staff push staircases out to the front and rear doors of the plane, and soldiers come down with backpacks and boxes under their arms.

I can't tell which one's Leo, they all look the same from here. The soldiers come into the waiting area and families gather around them, exclaiming and hugging. But after a time everything goes quiet. No one else is coming through, although three or four other families are still waiting.

I look out to the tarmac, where medical staff are carefully helping men down the steps and into the backs of ambulances. An attendant speaks to a couple of the other groups then comes over to us. 'Bell?' he asks. 'Lieutenant Bell is going to Royal Prince Alfred Hospital, Camperdown. You'll be able to visit him once he's admitted.'

Hospital? We drive there, only a few miles from Tina's place. We sit in the waiting-room, my parents checking every fifteen minutes or so to see if Leo's ready for visitors yet. Then we're told it's dinner-time and we have to leave, and the next visiting hours aren't till seven tonight.

We go to Tina's and eat sandwiches. Dad doesn't say anything much, just taps his fingers with a far-away look, stopping every now and then to read a medical journal. At half-past six we drive back to Camperdown.

The ward has eight beds in it. I glance at the patients but they don't look at us. Some are bandaged or have drips and tubes attaching them to machines.

One is asleep but thrashing about and whimpering, another appears fine, until I notice the bed is flat where his legs should be, and the last two are really old men. And that's everyone. Where's my brother?

'Mum?' whispers one of the old men. '*Leo*,' says my mother, her voice choking. She rushes to the bedside and they hug. 'Oh my *darling*.' Dad joins her, everyone half laughing, half-crying.

'Jen?' says Leo. I sit on the side of the bed, stunned, and take his hand. He's so thin his face is just lines and hollows. His skin is yellowish, his shoulders are bony, his wrists skeletal, and a drip is running into his arm.

'Thank goodness ...' I say. How is he so terribly *sick*?

Dad quietly gets the clipboard from the end of Leo's bed and flips through the pages.

'Hmm,' he says. 'You've been doing it rough, old mate.'

Leo nods. 'Not a picnic, Dad, that's for sure.' He takes a deep breath. 'But at least I'm out of there. It's over.' He closes his eyes. 'Oh, Christ, I'm home.'

My brother developed cerebral malaria in Vietnam and could easily have died, which seems so unfair. He managed to avoid guns and ambushes for a whole year, yet in the end was almost killed by a tiny parasite carried by a hungry mosquito.

'*Plasmodium falciparum*,' Dad says grimly. 'During the merozoite phase the parasites invade blood cells and multiply till they burst. Then the dead erythrocytes clog capillaries in the brain. Ghastly stuff.'

I nod because I studied this for the exams and actually know what he's talking about. Or I know it as a rare complication in a disease that's easily treated in western countries: I just hadn't imagined it'd be my brother who'd bring my textbook to life.

Leo stays a few days longer in the ward, then my parents take him to Newcastle, to a rehabilitation hospital. Dad says it could take him a long time to recover.

After they go I settle into life at Tina and Rob's place. It's pretty easy and I know how my aunt likes to run her household. She's not enormously demanding but the house has to be kept tidy, the washing-up done.

On the weekends we usually have a roast dinner. 'This is kind of old-fashioned,' I tease her one day, as she's carving the chicken.

Tina smiles. 'Jen, do you remember your grandmother Jessie?'

'A bit. She died when I was nine.'

'Mum was straight-laced and Scottish, and as far as she was concerned she might be bringing us up in this heathen country, but by God, your dad and I were still going to sit down to a roast dinner every Sunday, and that was that.'

'Was she nice, your mum?'

'Lovely. Our own dad died when I was only little so she brought us up by herself. She was smart and kind, and had the softest, prettiest accent.'

'I wish she was still around.'

'Don't we all?'

Rob says coolly, 'So what did my grandmother look like, Mum?'

'Oh, Jessie was short like me, and had wavy red-gold hair when young.' She laughs. 'Like me too I suppose, but my hairdresser's now the one responsible for that.'

I laugh too. You'd never know Tina wasn't young, she's so pretty and has a nice sort of shape.

I pass a plate of vegetables to Rob, who seems unusually grumpy. 'And do *I* look like my grandmother, Mum?' he says, frowning.

Tina shrugs a little. 'More like, oh, I don't know, my father?'

'But from the portrait in the hall he was fair-haired, and I'm dark and brown-eyed.'

'True. But you can't tell where your colouring has come from, darling.'

'Am I like Jimmy Kelso, then?' says Rob.

'Who knows? Genetics is hardly a precise science.' Tina looks down at her plate and starts eating again.

'Or what about László Richter?'

Tina drops her fork, then carefully places it on her plate. She looks up and says, 'Róbert?'

'I said — do my looks come from László Richter?'

Tina stares at him. 'László?'

'Is László Richter my father? My *real* father?'

Tina's hands are flat on the table. 'Why would you —'

'I put all the clues together, Mum. Tell me the *truth* now.'

Tina takes a slow breath. 'It was all a long time ago, darling.'

'So?'

After a time she nods. 'I suppose you should know. I'd hoped not yet, but ... well. Jimmy? It's no secret he was a thug. I was desperately unhappy. László was too, and for reasons far worse than mine. He was my dear friend and one afternoon, just briefly, we comforted each other, and ... I became pregnant. That's all.'

'But then he left.'

'Jimmy said he'd made László leave. Knowing Jimmy, I thought — he wanted me to think — he'd murdered him.' Tina bites her lip. 'Then he threatened *you* and attacked Moshe's brother.' She stops. 'But it was an accident. Jimmy drove off a road in the rain. No more.'

Rob nods. 'I don't care about him. What happened to *László*?'

'A few months later Harry ran into him in Melbourne. László had escaped, but to protect us he was about to leave for Europe.' She sighs. 'So László went away, and even after Jimmy died he didn't want to come back. Róbert, we'll never see him again.'

'But he's my *dad*,' says Rob. 'I look like him and probably act like him and if nothing changes I'll never *know*.'

'If nothing changes?'

'As soon as I'm old enough I'm going to Europe, Mum. I'm going to *find* him.'

'But Moshe's been looking for him for years. László doesn't want to be found. Not by me, or by Moshe, or by you. My darling, he's gone.'

∞

'The bus takes half-an-hour or so,' says Billie. 'Easy. Here it comes.'

'But why aren't we driving there?'

Billie looks at me. 'Jeez, kid. You want me along with you every time?'

'Oh. Maybe not.'

We board the bus, buy tickets from the conductor, then settle back. Far too soon we're getting off outside Long Bay Gaol.

'Billie, it's *scary*.'

'That's the idea of prisons. Come on.'

Billie is good-looking, straight-backed and terrifying, and the warders are almost deferential. We put our bags inside lockers, and with empty pockets are herded towards the meeting-room.

'I can't —' I say.

'Don't be a silly cow,' says Billie. 'Of course you can.'

We sit on one side of a small table and other visitors sit at their tables. After a time (I'm almost dizzy with suspense) the door opens and men are ushered inside by warders. One of them is Ash. He sits at our table and smiles a little. I stand up, wanting to hug him.

'No contact,' says a bored warder.

I sit. Ash is pale and thin, his beautiful dark curls shorn to a crew-cut.

'How are you?' I say, then wince at my inadequacy.

'Hi Jen, Billie,' says Ash. 'Thanks for coming all this way.'

'No probs,' says Billie. 'Good to see you. I'm just going to pop out for a minute, okay?'

Billie leaves (the warders practically bow).

'Ash,' I say. 'Oh ...'

'Jen. Yeah. What do you think of my salubrious surroundings?'

'I don't even know what salubrious *means*, Ash.'

'Me neither. Sorta good, maybe?'

'No. This is *awful*.' I take a breath. 'How are you? You're so pale.'

'Solitary will do that to you.'

'Ash! Don't be like that. It's *me*, not some stranger.'

He stares at me. 'Sorry. Sorry, Jen.' He slowly slides his hand until our fingertips are discreetly touching. 'There. Can you feel me?'

Though the tips of my fingers there's his warmth, his constancy.

'I've missed you so much, Ash.'

'You too, Jen. But *hey*, a Commonwealth Scholarship? Won by someone who didn't even know how to handle basic equations?'

I laugh. 'Yes, won by someone with a *fantastic* mathematician to teach her. Thank you so much.'

He shakes his head. 'You did the work, don't forget. So what's next?'

'Living at Tina's. Biology at Sydney uni.'

Ash grins. 'What? Wow. Hope you have a great time.'

'Think I will. But what about *you*?'

'I hear there are a few protests.'

'*Lots* of protests. Perhaps they'll apply enough pressure —'

'Perhaps. But I've got to assume I'll be here for two years, Jen. I have to just cope, keep a low profile.' He smiles briefly. 'Some of the other prisoners are okay.'

'But some aren't?'

Ash nods. 'How are things at Tina's?'

'Fine. Rob finally broached the László question. Tina handled it, told him the truth. It was one afternoon of passion when they were both really sad, she said, and then he went away.'

'Good thing that Rob knows now, at least. And how's old Leo going?'

'He's at home in Newcastle, and slowly getting better. But it's been scary —'

Just then Ash's mother, Ilona, arrives. 'Oh, *drágám*, I am late, the traffic was blocked. But at least you have had Jenny for company.' She smiles at me.

I say, 'I'll just go now so you've got time with your mum, Ash. I'll come back next month, I promise.'

'Jen.' Ash closes his eyes for a moment. 'Please. Please do.'

I make my way outside, where Billie is waiting. 'Had enough of prison life?' she says.

'Ash's mum is here, so I let them be. So little time — only twenty *minutes* every four weeks!'

Visitors start emerging, and Billie says, 'And it's over already. Pretty cruel.'

Ilona comes up to us, her eyes damp. 'Ah, Billie. How kind of you to bring Jenny.'

'Hi there, Ilona. Good to see you.'

'Did you drive here?' Ilona asks. 'If not, I would be happy to offer you a lift home.'

A light rain has begun so it's a welcome offer. The Adlers live in Rose Bay, not far from Billie's place, and it's easy to drop me off along the way.

When we pull up outside Tina's house, Ilona says, ' If you'd like, Jenny, I can take you in the car for the next visitor session. I think it makes Asher happy to see you.'

'That'd be great, thanks.'

∽

Because uni doesn't start till the end of February, I'm still enjoying an extended, lazy summer holiday. One day after browsing the department stores in central Sydney, I arrive home to find Moshe Adler sitting in Tina's lounge-room, solid and formal.

'Ah, Miss Bell,' he says.

'Jen, please.'

'Jen. Thank you for taking the time to visit Asher. Ilona and I are very grateful.'

'Ash is my friend! Of course I want to visit him. Do you think the protests will help?'

Mr Adler shakes his head. 'I don't know. I hope so.'

Tina says, 'Moshe was just updating me on Vivy's progress. She's well, and the baby is eight weeks old already.'

Mr Adler nods. 'Her ex-manager in Paris is a friend, and keeps me informed.'

'Do you know her address?' says Tina. 'I'd love to send some presents over for the baby.'

'Oh!' I say. 'And Rob will want her address too. He says when he's eighteen he'll go to Europe and ask Vivy to help him find László.'

Mr Adler says slowly, '*Find* László?'

'Ah, yes,' says Tina. 'I was just about to tell you, Moshe. Róbert has realised László is his father. He worked it out by himself.'

'Devorah has been asking pointed questions of us as well, so I wondered.' Mr Adler leans forward. 'Tina, it *is* the right time for him to know.'

Tina shrugs helplessly. 'Of course, and I should have told him before this. I just wanted to preserve his innocence a little longer.'

'He's not *that* innocent,' I say. 'He's three-quarters of the way through the Encyclopaedia Britannica by now and knows all sorts of strange things.'

'So young Róbert knows about László?' Mr Adler smiles. 'A new era, Tina, but I am glad for you both.'

∽

Before uni starts I pop up to Newcastle to see how Leo's going and to grab some more clothes. I take the train of course: I love it. Dad loves it too, but always says it's changed a lot since his day. (Of course it has, that was yonks ago.)

The trip takes about two and half hours. The locomotive steams slowly out of Sydney Central, chuffs through the inner-city slums, then the pretty suburbs, and into the wild bushland.

Then the roaring tunnels close in without warning. I gaze at my reflection in the darkened window. My face, dramatically reduced to shadowy cheekbones and pointy chin, is nothing like real life.

But then, how *do* I appear to the world? Am I plain or pretty? How can I even tell?

The Hawkesbury River emerges, the dark hills around it folded and plunging to dirty green water. Then we clatter across the big bridge — always a thrill with the steel columns flashing by.

Below, the remnants of the old sandstone bridge still stand in the water, like castle turrets with seaweed skirts.

More tunnels, grey-green bush everywhere, expansive river bays, mysterious little houses dotting the shoreline far away. Who lives there? Would *I* like to live there? It might be thrilling. Or magical. Or terrifying. On second thoughts, perhaps such solitude isn't for me.

Gosford, half-way now. More bushland follows, but it's less interesting without a swirling great river through it, just little towns with little stations. Closer now.

Fassifern, Booragul, Teralba, Cockle Creek. Then Cardiff, Kotara, Adamstown — all the lovely familiar names that are *home* to me — Broadmeadow, Hamilton, Wickham, Civic, then nice old Newcastle station. And darling Mum to pick me up.

It's only a few blocks to our house, an old terrace near the ocean. I've only been away for a matter of weeks, but I feel a silly ache of nostalgia seeing it again. My room is as it always was, untidy but nice. It's upstairs at the back of the house, and when I was young I'd often sit by the window and shiver, watching the black clouds and flickering lightning of the southerly busters storming up the coast in summer.

Leo is slowly getting better. He stayed three weeks in rehabilitation hospital but is now at home. At dinner he's clearly gained some weight, though his face still has grooves down his cheeks.

'Went for a surf today at Nobbys,' he says. 'Third time this week. Getting back into condition.'

'You're looking better,' I say. 'Brown instead of yellow, for starters.'

Leo grins. 'Sydney uni, eh? Guess that's why you're so cocky.'

'I'm not cocky. *Jeez*, Leo, I'm terrified. Anyway, what do you think you'll do when you're better? Go back to teaching?'

Leo flinches a little. 'Unlikely. No idea really.' He clears his throat. 'Actually, I saw my old mate Bazza today. He came home — when was it? Last May? Ah, eight months ago?'

'Nine, darling,' says Mum.

Leo shakes his head. 'Still having a bit of trouble remembering and numbers. It'll come back.'

'It will, son,' says Dad. 'Don't push yourself.'

'Yeah. Anyway, saw Bazza.' Leo looks puzzled. 'Not doing well, pissed off at some drongo who said he wasn't a returned soldier because Vietnam wasn't a real war.'

'How can anyone claim that?' I ask.

Leo laughs shortly. 'Because it's true. War was never officially declared, so it's just a *temporary police action*. Semantics.' His mouth twists. 'Anyway, poor old Bazza says he can't settle. Nightmares, depression. So guess there are guys worse off than me.'

Mum touches his hand for a moment, then goes to get dessert. When she's back, she says, 'Now, Jen, we've got some news. Since you're about to launch into your great university adventure, your Dad and I have decided it's time for a change for us too.'

'I'm retiring, sweetheart,' says Dad. 'And your mother and I — and Leo too if he wants — are going away for six months.'

'Six *months*? Where?'

'Broome,' says Mum. 'I was born there and haven't been back since I was a teenager. I'd love to see it again. We'll stay over autumn and winter — it's mild and lovely — and just so *different* from everywhere else.'

'I don't even know where Broome *is*,' I say. This is perturbing. Adventures are supposed to happen to me, not my parents.

Mum smiles. 'North-west Australia, as far from anywhere else as possible. Golden beaches, red earth, emerald mangroves, turquoise water.' She closes her eyes. 'Silence, only birdsong and human voices. Amiability between exiles, and almost everyone's an exile. Such extremes, too — heat and mildness, storms and peace.'

I sit, my mouth agape.

'I've never been there, Jenny,' says Dad. 'But I'd rather like a change. Don't look so shocked. It's just for six months.'

'Okay,' I say uncertainly. 'And Leo too ...?'

'Good surfing, I hear,' he says. 'Why not?'

'I think you said that about Vietnam,' I say coolly. 'Let's hope it works out better this time.'

I feel so hurt. The people I love most in the world won't be here for *me*!

∽

'They're going in a *fortnight*, Ash. Up and leaving, just three weeks after I start uni. I won't have time to tell them anything about it. They'll too busy packing.'

'But it'll be good for Leo, especially, won't it?'

'Yes,' I say grudgingly. 'He's still so thin, and really needs to be somewhere warmer.'

'And when they get older, people really start to miss where they came from. At least your mum can go back to her childhood home. My parents can never do that.'

'Is their house gone?'

'Well, if it wasn't bombed, someone's probably stolen it. I really meant their circle of friends and family. Wiped out.'

'*All* of them, Ash? I can't imagine ...'

'Nor me. I was born here, remember, though Tibor lived through it as a kid. I sometimes think it's why he needs to charm everyone. To protect himself.'

'But how did he survive at all?'

'He and Mum were hidden on a farm by friends. Dad — well, you know — Auschwitz. It's a miracle he lived.'

'Does he ever talk about it?'

'Never. Not even on days of remembrance. But occasionally, late at night, I hear him weeping. And my mother trying to console him. Then next day he's perfectly normal.'

'Oh. Your *poor* dad.' I nod. 'So you reckon I should just stop being a sook and be glad my mum is able to go back to her childhood home?'

Ash smiles. 'Did I say that? But at least you can tell *me* about uni.'

I laugh. 'I was going to, anyway. Ash, it's *fantastic*! We had Orientation Week, and there were students dressed up in silly clothes, and stalls with barbecues and handouts about all the student societies, and really nice people to chat to.'

'What did you join?'

'The Science Society, and I was talked into the Bridge Club. I don't know how to play Bridge!'

'Guess you will soon enough.'

'And the Union is brilliant, with a great cafeteria. We've started lectures too, in big auditoriums — auditoria? — anyway, they're all old wooden things with tiers of seating. I really like the lectures, and we've already been given assignments!' I sigh happily. 'It's all just amazing. I'm so lucky.'

Ash nods. 'You are.'

'But I shouldn't be glad — you're still stuck in here.'

'I am. But it's okay to enjoy it all.'

'Thanks, Ash. But look, I'd better get your mum. It's nice of her to let us chat by ourselves.'

'She wants to comfort me but doesn't know what to say, so ... it helps her to have you here, Jen.'

'Poor her, too. Why is everything so *hard* for people, Ash?'

He smiles. 'Sounds like you need a unit of Philosophy in your degree too.'

∾

Driving home from the prison with Ilona, there's nothing much new to say about Ash's regimented life, so I ask, 'When are Tibor and Ursula getting married?'

As we pull up at a red light, Ilona says crisply, 'Never, if I had any say in the matter.'

'Oh. Um, is that because she's not Jewish?'

'Yes, that's important.'

'But why? If they love each other and are happy —'

Ilona looks at me, her plump, kind face serious. 'You do understand recent history, Jenny?'

'Of course, but ...'

'Two out of every three Jews in Europe were slaughtered in the war. For survivors to marry outside our religion weakens us even more.'

'I'm sorry, Mrs Adler. Of course, that makes sense.'

Ilona puts the car into gear and we start again. At the next red light she says, 'But worse, I cannot get Tibor to see that Ursula is unkind and stupid.' She smiles at me. 'Perhaps, Jenny, that's what worries me most.'

I laugh. 'Makes even more sense.' I hesitate. 'I hope ... I don't want you to think ... there's anything like that between Ash and me, you know. We're just friends.'

We drive again. Ilona says, her eyes on the road, 'I understand, and I don't worry for you or Asher. His future will be complex and intellectually challenging, and I doubt domesticity will ever matter very much to him.' She smiles. 'Nor to you either, I imagine.'

'Me?'

'Do you see yourself as a quiet little housewife, Jenny?'

'Not really, but I expect *sometime* in the future —'

Ilona shrugs. 'You have a very good mind and a thirst for knowledge. You're stubborn too.'

'*Me*?'

Ilona pulls over to the side of the road, parks the car, lights a cigarette and gazes at me.

'I seem to have surprised you, Jenny. But of course I've given thought, not only to your relationship with Ash, but also to you as a person.'

'Have you?' I laugh a little helplessly. 'No one else ever has, or at least they haven't told me about it. Stubborn *and* a good mind?'

'Your abilities are obviously excellent. Asher was astonished at the scholastic progress you were able to make, given a little encouragement. Encouragement clearly lacking at your school.'

'I suppose everyone just assumed ...'

'Assumed?'

'Well, I'm a girl, so not much was expected. And one of my teachers always called me lazy and immature, and it's true, I was too preoccupied with — shoes and clothes and —' I stop before I let slip Tibor's name.

Ilona smiles. 'Of course you're a girl but, Jenny, you're also very smart. Your mind will drive you, more than you can understand right now. Your life will not be straightforward, and perhaps it won't be easy.'

I stare. 'But I want a nice life, Mrs Adler. I want a home and love.'

'And you also want science and mathematics, and ideas and inspiration, yes?'

I don't know what to say.

Ilona stubs out her cigarette. 'Do you know, my dear, what I did before the war?'

I shake my head. I'm ashamed to realise I've never once thought about Ilona as anything more than Ash's mother.

'I was a physicist. I worked at an institute, doing fascinating research. I married Moshe, a brilliant young lawyer, and we were so very happy.' She takes a breath. 'Then the nightmare began. I lived in terror, working on a farm, protecting my child, aware that any day I might be betrayed. Aware too that Moshe was almost certainly doomed.'

'I'm so sorry,' I whisper.

She shakes her head. 'No need. Baruch Hashem, we were spared. We came here as *displaced persons*.' She smiles drily. 'Displaced, indeed. European qualifications were scorned by our hosts, along with our troubling European ways. Moshe survived by his wits and built a new life for us. It was, of course, outside the law — but then, what did the law ever do to save two out of three of us?'

'And you?'

'A housewife.' She sighs. 'I supported Moshe gladly, but all I had learnt, all I had achieved, all I *might* have achieved? Nothing. Of course I took joy in my family, but to lose that life of curiosity?' Ilona clears her throat. 'If you are lucky enough to find it, Jenny, never let it go. *Never.*'

∽

I'm astonished to hear that Ash thinks so highly of my abilities, and Ilona too. I don't, but then I think about how much I love uni.

Physics, chemistry and maths are all fun, but most of all I'm fascinated by the new fields of biology opening up before me. I groan along with everyone else when we get a new assignment, but I'm usually secretly pleased.

I like living at Tina's house too and, now the grand secret of László has been revealed, Rob and his mum get on much better than before. It's great to hear Tina talk about the old days, when she and László set up her club Tempo and young jazz musicians would play, people who are now famous that even I've heard of.

We also hear about Jimmy Kelso's glamorous nightclub, the Starlight Lounge, once *the* place to go in Sydney but now just an empty shop-front. And she talks wistfully about Rob's father László, who educated her and protected her, and loved the music as much as she did.

One day at a bus-stop, as my legs are freezing in the wind, it suddenly occurs to me I can wear *jeans* for the rest of my life and never need wear a silly dress again. Jeans make me feel so confident and independent, and of course, with Ash's duffel-coat on top, I become invincible.

This comes in handy at demonstrations. I go to as many as possible and am arrested once more. I feel like an old hand in the cell and before the magistrate. He doesn't even bother with a pretence of a misdeed, but simply fines me. I glare at him and think rude words. Ash would approve.

Ilona and I visit him every month. We take him textbooks he asks for, but they're sometimes confiscated then randomly returned. The warders threaten to send him to another prison far out in the country too, but in the end they leave him be.

Protests over his sentence keep growing and finally questions are asked in Parliament. The government wriggles and fibs, but the sheer unfairness of Ash's plight — especially as other objectors are free and unbothered by the law — is obvious.

The government is desperate to find an excuse, any excuse to defuse the situation, and one day in August 1969, out of the blue, there's an announcement.

The Attorney-General has submitted to the Governor-General that 'clemency should now be exercised on compassionate grounds, due to the poor health of Adler's parents'.

After only half of his two-year sentence, Ash is to be released as soon as possible.

'Poor *health*?' says Ilona, driving to the prison. 'Any excuse, eh, Jenny?' She grins.

'You must be so happy! But where's Mr Adler today?'

'Ah,' she says, looking into the distance. 'He is not able to go where there is imprisonment of any kind. He breaks down. I thought you knew this.'

Once again I'm mortified at my carelessness. 'I'm so *sorry*, Mrs Adler. I hadn't realised. He's such a strong, capable man.'

'He is, but some things no strength can overcome. Do not worry. He is overjoyed.'

At the prison there are reporters and photographers clustered outside the main gate, but Ilona and I are quietly ushered into a side room.

My heart is beating wildly as the door opens and Ash is escorted out by a warder and I'm swamped with such *tenderness* at the sight of him. His old clothes sag on his now-thin body, and he's clutching an armful of textbooks.

Ilona hugs him, murmuring in Hungarian. Ash says, 'Hey Mum, it's okay, it's *okay*.' He grins at me over her shoulder. 'Hiya Jen. Take these, will you?'

I grab the textbooks before he drops them. 'Hey, Ash. Wow, fantastic to see you!'

'Wow, absolutely. Come on, Mum, it's okay.'

Ilona wipes her eyes. 'Drágám.' (I know now that means *darling*.)

Ash says intently, 'Listen, Mum. If I go home the press will follow and make your lives hell. I'm going to stay with some friends in Glebe till things quieten down.'

'Are you *sure*?' says Ilona.

'Don't worry, I'll see you soon. My love to Dad.' He looks at the warder. 'Okay.'

The warder opens the outside door and Ash goes ahead, facing the yelled questions and startling flashlights of the photographers.

Ilona and I follow. I don't quite understand what's happening. Outside a car has pulled up. I recognise the two boys in front as protesters. In the back seat is the redhead, Genevieve.

Ash turns to me and takes the stack of texts, saying, 'Thanks, Jen. See you.'

He gets into the back seat beside Genevieve — who kisses him — and the car drives off.

I can hardly breathe. *Ash?*

18. LEO: COMBAT FATIGUE (MAR-JULY 1969)

'Okay, I'll come with you to Broome,' I'd said, but it's harder than I imagine. Of course, all that packing nonsense — what will we need for six months? For me not much, though Mum insists on helping with my stuff and fussing till I want to scream. But keep calm, Leo. Keep calm.

So. Train to Sydney in late March. By now I've been out of Vietnam for nearly three months. We have dinner with Tina, Rob and my sister, who's sulking because she's started uni and what matters terribly to her doesn't to the rest of us. Bridge Society? Sorry, Jen.

Then a flight, Sydney to Perth, and a round of reunions with relatives I've never given a thought to, like grandmother Rosa, who's been absent from our lives forever.

And Rosa's sister, Mum's beloved aunt Lucy, who apparently gave Mum all the warmth Rosa couldn't, and her husband Danny. Turns out one of their kids, Liam, lives in Broome, so at least we'll know someone there when we arrive.

We board a plane and after four or five bumpy hours finally arrive at Broome. The airport terminal is a tin shed which reminds me of Vietnam, and it's almost as hot and humid.

My parents have rented a small house in the old section of town, facing onto deep green mangroves and aqua water. The soil and sand of the bay are an orange that dazzles my eyes, and in the first few days the brilliant colours of the whole place almost overwhelm me.

I buy an ancient car with roof-racks, and get a surfboard from Castaway's second-hand shop, and find my way over to the ocean-front side of Broome, where there's a sprawling old caravan park. The surf at Cable Beach is fantastic and I soon get on nodding terms with a few of the locals.

Sometimes I go drinking at the Roebuck Hotel, the Roey, in Broome's Chinatown. It can apparently get pretty wild, but tonight's fairly peaceful.

Everyone in the pub is tanned and long-haired, and the only way you can tell the hippies from the surfies or labourers is that the hippies have beads, the surfies have sun-bleached locks, and the labourers have muscles.

While I'm waiting for my schooner at the bar, a girl gives me the eye. I smile back and soon we're chatting like old mates. She's got long brown hair parted in the middle and a weird ring in one nostril like an Indian woman.

She's wearing a short silky top without a bra, and keeps lifting her arms to run her fingers through her hair. She's also wearing a long skirt with little mirrors on it, but I think I like the top better.

Her name is Michelle, for the Beatles song, though it's really Debbie, she says. I don't care what she wants to call herself as long as she keeps fussing with her hair.

She's got a room in a hippie house a block or two away, so we go and share a joint with a couple of her friends who are listening dreamily to Pink Floyd on the record player.

I used to smoke dope now and then with surfing mates in Newcastle, but was too nervous to try it in Vietnam (though plenty of other guys did). Now I love the way I don't have to care what malaria has done to my mind and body, I can just ... relax.

One thing leads to another, and the night is amazing. At dawn I kiss Michelle and leave. The sun is coming up and the air smells of mud and salt and tropical flowers, and I feel better than I have for a long, long time.

∽

Back at home I crash out. Mum lets me sleep till the afternoon then taps on the door. 'Leo, my cousin Liam is coming over for dinner. Reckon you'll be up by then?'

'For sure. Just convalescing as my doctor recommends. Dad, that is.'

She laughs and leaves. I get up and have a lazy shower, and it's evening by the time I emerge. The old house has a wide, open veranda where we usually eat or sit in armchairs watching the sky, and tonight someone new is there, sipping a glass of beer.

'Leo, this is Liam Whalen, my cousin,' Mum says. 'Liam, Leo.'

We shake hands then I get myself a beer and sit down. Liam is a few years younger than Mum, so he's in his late fifties. He reminds me of his father Danny, but he's also dark-eyed and tanned, with streaks of grey in his hair.

After we've chatted for a bit I start to notice he also has a slightly exotic look, as if he's got some Asian or Aboriginal blood. Hmm. Of course, around Broome there are so many people of mixed heritage it's almost unremarkable, but I guess I should have paid a bit more attention when Mum was trying to explain her tangled family tree to me.

Apparently he's a painter, like Eliza's mum Rosa, but different too. He's brought my parents a gift of one of his paintings — just sea and land and sky, but the colours are amazing and it seems to suggest ... *something* I can't quite grasp, though I want to. I start to get an idea of why people are always going on about art.

We eat the nice meal Mum's prepared, and to be fair, Dad has helped her in the kitchen too for the first time in his life. (I told him he'll be thrown out of the Dinosaurs' Guild, but he just laughed. Looks like Broome is affecting him as well.)

'When did we last meet, Lizzy?' says Liam to Mum. 'Must have been just before you hopped on that big sailing ship.'

Mum laughs. She's looking really pretty tonight. 'Don't you remember, Lee? You told me — and I never forgot — I'd have a wonderful time brace-hauling and keel-hauling and over-hauling and whatever else it is I'd have to haul. And I *did*.'

'That's where you two met, wasn't it?' asks Liam.

Dad nods. ' I thought she was a silly young flibbertigibbet and she thought I was a dour old salt.'

'And you *were*,' says Mum. 'It took you until we crossed the Equator to unbend.'

'So it was love at first sight, then?' I say.

'Hardly,' says Dad, smiling. 'We had a few complications to untangle in our lives.'

'And I was a slow learner,' says Mum. She gazes teasingly at Dad. Wow, I've never before thought about my parents meeting and getting involved with each other. And becoming *lovers*.

Unimaginable.

'Anyone else want a top-up?' I say, and go around refreshing the wine and beer. 'So did you always live in Broome?' I ask Liam.

'I was born here, but spent time in Perth studying art, then driving an ambulance during the war. But I came back in the mid-fifties and found my people.'

I'm puzzled. Liam looks at Mum. 'Haven't you explained it?'

She laughs. 'To Leo, family history is the proverbial water off a duck's back.'

'All right,' I say. 'I'm listening now.'

Liam leans forward. 'My mum Cristina had an Aboriginal grandmother, so because of the racial laws she and my dad Danny couldn't marry. Cristina died and Lucy raised me as her own. That's all. Trivial situation now, but in the old days it made life difficult.'

'And ... your people?' I say.

'Indigenous artists. They've taught me what I'd been looking for all my life.'

Mum says, 'Leo, you should be aware Liam is not just my cousin, he's a famous painter too.'

Liam laughs. 'Now if only fame meant a decent living, Lizzy, not having to nurse at the medical centre. Hey, Leo, if you like I'll take you out to Reedy Creek station one day to meet my mob.'

'Okay. Some time.' (Think I'd rather go to the beach.)

∞

I settle into a great routine. Surfing, drinking, Michelle. She's pretty good for my ego after everything that went wrong with Claire, so I feel like a lucky bastard.

Slowly I recover physically from the malaria, and my mind seems to follow. The kaleidoscope colours around me, the delights of the body, the sheer enjoyment of life, all help heal my shattered nerves and foggy memory.

And Claire? I try never to think of her. If I do it breaks my heart, so I have to drink more, surf more, fuck more, forget more. I can barely remember Vietnam, I tell myself. Often.

But it's there in my dreams, of course.

The lucid blue of Claire's eyes (her eyes turned towards someone else). The jasmine-covered rooftop terrace. The flares exploding like fireworks. The thudding of choppers. The shadowy green tunnel where a child died. The branches writhing above a hidden mine. The stink, the ugliness, the cruelty, the waste, the death.

Of course I can barely remember it! Who'd *want* to remember it?

Then one day in May I round a corner in Chinatown, and run into my old tent-mate, Simmo.

'*What*?' I say, and we hug. 'What the ever-flying fuck, Simmo?'

He laughs. 'Good to see you too, mate. Hey, if I'd known *you* were here I'd have rescheduled.'

'But why Broome?'

'Oh, after discharge I went back to Singapore to see someone. Didn't work out and couldn't face going home, so a place I'd never been before sounded good.'

'Ah, it's *great* to see you, man! Come and have a drink.'

At the Roey bar we clink glasses and Simmo says, 'Hardly recognised you, Leo. What's all this hair? You a hippie now?'

'Too right. Got to fit in, you know.'

'They like it short in Singapore. Guess I'd better get started growing it long.' Simmo is a nice-looking guy but his short, dark hair is really out of place here.

'Reckon you'll stay around?'

Simmo nods. 'Like the town already. And you seem a lot better than last time I saw you.'

I laugh. 'Sex, beer, surfing. I'm set for life.'

'Sex?'

'Ah, you'll meet her sometime. Lovely chick, Michelle.'

'Good on you.'

'Where are you staying, Simmo?'

'Some crappy motel.'

'Well, Michelle said there was a room free at her hippie haven. If you can stand the smell of dope you might like it.'

Simmo settles easily into Michelle's house, and it's good to have him around. Of course by now I've got a few mates, but having someone here who *knows* what's in my bones and my dreams and my terrors? I need him, and I think he needs me just as much.

Simmo was always pretty reserved, and now he's even more so. Vietnam of course, but maybe his failed romance as well. Still, he refuses to talk about that, so we usually just drink and joke around and go to the beach.

As a Melbourne kid he didn't get to do much swimming before, but here he's learning to surf and getting good at it. Girls at the pub try to pick him up, but though he's friendly enough he doesn't crack onto them.

One night at the Roey I tease him about it but he says, 'No *way*, man, still getting over that Singapore crash and burn.' Then he grins wickedly. 'But speaking of love-life disasters — meant to tell you, I ran into your Vung Tau reporter girl, Claire.'

I can't speak for a moment, then say, 'Yeah? Where?'

'At the official bash to celebrate the repairs to that Saigon orphanage. Just before I was leaving the country, so I went to grab some nibbles and warm beer on the way out. Had a good chat, and I told her that once I was gone I'd get someone else to send her the mine casualty stats.'

'She'd appreciate that. Ah — so the repairs got done? Great. And was she ...?' (Was Claire content? Safe? Missing me?)

'Seemed happy enough. I met your aunt and uncle too. Got the impression they're pretty fed up. Now the orphanage is fixed up they might be handing it over to some Yank God-botherers.'

'Probably a good thing,' I say. If Pete and Charlotte leave the country, what will Claire do? What will André do? Would she stay there for *him*?

'Actually, we're not here tonight to talk about what interests you,' says Simmo. 'We're here to talk about what interests me.'

'And what would that be?'

Simmo smiles a little. 'Got a job.'

'I thought you couldn't have enough of the beach.'

'Need some dosh as well. We can't all live with our parents at what — twenty-three?'

'Don't rub it in. But got to admit, good food and undemanding oldies is nice. So what's the job?'

'Medical clinic in Broome, where Liam works. And visiting the settlements and stations.'

'They'll be lucky to have you,' I say, thinking of Simmo's easy expertise in Vietnam.

He clears his throat. 'No dustoff choppers, at any rate.'

'Yeah.'

We're silent.

∽

I keep an eye on the news from Vietnam. Not too closely of course, but I get the gist of what's happening. The morale of the US forces is worse than ever. Discrimination towards Black troops is vicious and 'fragging' enters the conversation: the killing of abusive officers with anonymous grenades. Sounds fair enough to me.

In April 1969, that shyster Nixon says (and Simmo nearly dies laughing) "prospects for peace have improved due to political stability in Saigon."

Nixon says he's going to gradually withdraw US forces in a new policy of *Vietnamization*: guess that's American for *Jaunissement*. Given there are over half a million troops in the country, it could take a while.

In May it turns out that the American plans for *enhancing political stability* includes secretly carpet-bombing Cambodia. Secretly, of course, because it's completely illegal. They've been at it for months now and call it Operation MENU, because the areas attacked are code-named Breakfast, Lunch, Dinner, Snack, Dessert, and Supper. What laugh-a-minute guys.

Apparently the Yanks are trying to obliterate what they call COSVN, the Central Office for South Vietnam, which is in hiding near the Cambodian border and coordinating enemy forces — kind of like a barefoot jungle Pentagon.

The Prime Minister of neighbouring Laos bitterly announces that US planes have been regularly bombing the shit out of his country too, so somehow it's difficult to see how this is going to improve the prospects for peace either.

In June, Life magazine prints '*The Faces of the American Dead*'. It's eleven pages of the photos and names of all the American troops killed in just one single week in Vietnam.

There are two hundred and forty-two men, brass and grunts, pictured smiling at graduation, confident at work, serious in new uniforms, exhausted in fatigues. Some have the remote eyes of those who expect they'll soon be dead. And now they are.

∽

Simmo keeps reading the newspapers even when I don't, and one evening in the mild, perfect Broome winter, when I'm sitting on the veranda looking at the stars and thinking about getting a new surfboard, he drops by.

'Got something for you,' he says. 'But get me a beer first.'

Settled in the armchair beside me with a drink, he produces a newspaper clipping. 'Article by Claire in the national broadsheet, no less. She's really made the big time.'

'Yeah?' I say and take the clipping. It's bylined Claire Fenn, AAP, Saigon, 9 June 1969.

On 8 June, the Provisional Revolutionary Government of the Republic of South Vietnam (PRG) announced it has been created as an underground government-in-exile, in opposition to President Thieu's Republic of Vietnam.

The PRG reflects a range of nationalist, anti-imperialist and communist political viewpoints, but all are seeking a negotiated settlement to the war and the reunification of Vietnam.

The new party has been soundly rejected by the Thieu and US governments. Due to President Thieu's repressive tactics against political rivals, the PRG has no offices or overt presence. It is believed to have a headquarters camp in jungle near the Cambodian border, where the new ministries of the government-in-exile are being organised.

The PRG was formed from a coalition of the Alliance of National, Democratic, and Peace Forces, the National Liberation Front, the People's Revolutionary Party, and several smaller ethnic, regional and religious groups. It has announced it expects to take up a seat to represent all Vietnamese at the Paris peace talks.

As I read 'Alliance of National, Democratic, and Peace Forces,' I seem to hear André's voice saying that phrase, and my head becomes full of noise and feels as if it's being squeezed.

I'm suddenly back at the dinner party with Claire and André in Charlotte and Pete's lavish salon. But I'm not simply remembering it, I'm *there*.

We're chatting easily about politics and mooncakes, eating good food and drinking fine wine, and I have no idea, not in the slightest, what's about to hit me. To carpet-bomb me.

'Leo?' says Simmo. 'You okay?'

I manage to reach the veranda railing before vomiting into the garden below.

∽

Michelle believes in some guru in India. Over the grapevine she hears she needs to go and sit at his feet, so that's it. I drive her to the airport.

She's wearing the long skirt covered with little mirrors, but her top is some boring t-shirt. She doesn't fuss with her hair, either, but gives me a bunch of flowers before she enters the tin-shed terminal.

'Remember me as a rose in your heart, Leo,' she says solemnly.

'Mmm, okay. Well. Have a good trip then.'

We kiss and she gets on the plane and leaves. In the car I throw the flowers on the seat, and go looking for Simmo. It's late afternoon so he's almost finished at the clinic. A few people leave, then Simmo comes out.

'Wanna drink?' I say.

'Too right, long day,' Simmo says and hops in. He grins, holding up the flowers. 'Hey Leo, you courting me?'

'In your dreams. From Michelle — she's on the plane now.'

'Nice of her. They smell great too.'

Simmo holds them out and I focus on the ruffled pink roses. Suddenly I'm not in Broome any more, I'm in Vietnam staring at the fragile, gasping lung tissue of the small boy who was shot at Dat Do.

Everything around me shudders and I gag. I grab the door handle and leap out of the car, and vomit in the gutter.

When I'm finished Simmo says, 'Ah. Come on Leo, think we need a chat.'

We go to his place. Fortunately the dopeheads are out, so we sit at the kitchen table with coffees.

'What the fuck is *wrong* with me, Simmo?'

'Combat fatigue, mate.'

'Bullshit. I was barely in combat. Got a few bullets thrown my way, but nothing serious.'

'Doesn't matter. Look — you, all of us, spent a year in suspense, waiting for *something* to happen. The pressure, the constant pressure, was there all the time. You heard about the ops, you heard about the casualties, you *knew* what was happening out there. It screwed with your mind just as much as if you'd gone on patrol.'

I shake my head. 'Jeez, that's hard to believe. I had it easy, nothing like the infantry guys.'

'Well, tell me this. Did you remember something, or did it feel like you were actually there?'

I stare at him. 'I was *there*, Simmo, fucking there at Dat Do, when the kid ... his wounded lung was like ... those petals.'

I put my hands over my eyes. Crying over some *flowers*?

Simmo pats my shoulder. 'We all suffer from it. Different triggers, that's all.'

'Yeah? And what about *you*? What's your trigger?'

Simmo laughs shortly. 'Haven't run across it yet. But I expect it'll hit me the same way.'

∽

Another night I go out to the Roey with Simmo and Mum's cousin Liam. We get a few odd looks when we go in, and after we find a table Liam says, 'It's okay, Leo. Laws against Aboriginal people drinking have just been lifted, so these dozy buggers aren't used to the sight of one in a pub.'

'For you, isn't that —?'

'Awkward, painful, ugly?' says Liam. 'Yeah. I don't care.'

'Ah, well, okay. So talking of dozy buggers, how's Simmo getting on at the medical centre?'

Simmo laughs. 'They don't know how they managed before without me. Right, Liam?'

Liam nods. 'Actually his *best* quality is he's willing to go on long outback trips to do clinics. He reckons it's a luxury after Vietnam.'

'Hey, I'll take *anywhere* they don't want to shoot at me, mate,' says Simmo, drinking.

'Do you go outback very often?' I ask.

'Once a month,' says Liam. 'But everything's a bit up in the air right now, for the worse too.'

'Yeah?'

'New laws have just come in saying Aboriginal workers have to get paid for their jobs.'

'They didn't before?'

'Hey, I'm from Melbourne and even *I* knew that,' says Simmo.

'What do they live on then?'

'They used to get food, tobacco and clothes at the whim of the station boss, sorta like slaves,' says Liam. 'Then the best stockmen started getting paid about six dollars a week, which appalled the St Georges Terrace cockies —'

'Who?' I say, laughing.

'Like Pitt Street farmers, but for Western Australia,' says Simmo. 'Rich, absentee pastoralists who wear an Akubra hat every now and again.'

'They've paid bugger-all for the land for decades, but don't bother improving it as they're supposed to, so the government's raised the rent,' says Liam. 'Now the cockies are flogging off their stations to overseas companies, and *those* bastards are ruthless.'

Simmo nods. 'A few months ago, some station managers were told to load up all the old people, the dependants of their stockmen, and just dump them at camps outside Derby. No facilities, not even running water.'

'*What*? Why can't the stockmen work at better stations?'

'Few stations are any better, but that's not the point, Leo,' says Liam. 'You see, Aboriginal mobs can't just leave where they are, they're tied to their land. They've got responsibilities for particular parts of country, and they'd be breaking their own laws if they went somewhere else.'

'Laws? But isn't it all just *bush*?' I say, puzzled.

'Only to whitefellas,' says Liam, sounding tired.

'Sorry, Liam.' I feel like a clumsy fool. 'Maybe I've got a bit to learn.'

'A bit?' says Simmo. 'But hey, mate, aren't you the clairvoyant?'

'Ah, ya bastard,' I say without heat. My mad moment of perception — or malarial delusion — regarding the hidden landmine is already legend, and I don't mind the teasing. After all, apart from a stadium or two, it was the most useful thing I ever did in Vietnam.

'One place isn't too bad,' says Liam. 'Reedy Creek. The manager's okay, mob have a good camp by the creek and the old people get most of their pensions. A lot of places the pensions go straight into the bosses' pockets, and social services don't do anything about it.'

'Wow,' I say, shaking my head. 'This region's amazing, but there's so much crap goes on in the background too.'

'Maybe you should come and see Reedy Creek sometime, Leo,' says Liam, smiling a little.

'Dunno about that. Don't like to get too far away from the sea.'

∞

Claire writes another good article for the big newspapers. After I finish it I sit on the veranda in the twilight, thinking about her memorable final line: *Everyone else is there for a year, the Vietnamese are there forever.*

I'm glad she's doing well. She's built up her reputation through her own efforts, on her own terms.

Christ, I was a fool not to show her more support when I had the chance! She went through such a hard, lonely time at the start, with no backing, no agency and precious few friends. Except André, of course. I swallow. Will the thought of him make me heave? Okay, that's good, dinner stays down.

Fact is, I was like a sulky kid where that bastard was concerned. But it wasn't *me* who guided her through dodgy situations and the surreal politics of Saigon. Compared to André I did fuck-all for Claire, yet somehow I assumed my sheer existence was compelling enough for her to put me above anyone else.

Of *course* we care for each other in some deep, fundamental way: that's been a foundation of my whole life. But Claire doesn't love me — and why should she? Even Michelle finds some old Indian guy with a wispy beard and a fat, bare belly more fascinating.

That makes me laugh aloud. What a self-pitying fuckwit I am. Come on, get up. Gotta sort out a few things to take tomorrow.

I've eventually yielded to all the not-so-subtle nudges, so I'm going to Reedy Creek station with Simmo. Liam's already out there, visiting some artists. I imagine the place is, well — dry and grim, with miserable, shuffling natives and sad, flyblown kids. And no peaceful blue *ocean*, the constant of my existence.

My old backpack is in the cupboard, unopened since we got here. Mum got it ready for me when I was still pretty sick, so it's probably full of city clothes I'll never need. I yank it out, and start throwing things on the bed.

Spot on. Shirts and ties? No, Mum. Two pairs of long trousers? Come on. Woollen socks — are you nuts? Ah, some clean undies. They'll be useful. I scratch around a bit at the bottom and pull out something that feels familiar.

I stand there, the room buzzing around me, then suddenly I'm on my knees in a tunnel of green shadows. A tiny old woman is lying face down. A child is drifting away from life.

I'm trying to seal his ruffled wound with this useless thing in my hand. This canvas hat, neatly washed and ironed by a woman who's lost *everything*, yet she still takes the time to thank me.

Funny, I don't vomit this time. I'm just frozen, a million miles away. Dad says something to Mum in the lounge-room. She replies. A car drives by. A dog barks. Time passes, and finally I can move again.

Then Lieutenant Leo Bell, graduate of Scheyville, officer in the Civil Affairs Unit, and veteran of two years' service to his country, sits down and sobs out his heart.

19. CLAIRE: THE FISHHOOK (FEB-NOV 1969)

The Tet New Year holiday is a movable feast, and this year, 1969, it starts on 17 February. Small-scale NLF attacks take place at dozens of sites, but are easily beaten off: more of a pointed reminder than a serious effort.

March brings something more sobering. Large communal graves are discovered at Hue, the scene of vicious fighting between North Vietnamese and US forces for a month in last year's Tet offensive. Nearly three thousand bodies are eventually unearthed. The Americans immediately proclaim them all victims of the North, but that doesn't make any sense.

There's certainly proof that hundreds of people associated with Thieu's government were deliberately murdered, but I also hear from reliable sources that when Hue was retaken, ARVN soldiers killed hundreds of others they deemed 'leftists'.

The city itself was almost obliterated by American bombs, and it's known that thousands of civilians disappeared in the onslaught. So what's happened to all their bodies?

'Lovely Claire, you cannot apply logic to a propaganda coup,' says André. He kisses my forehead, and I nestle against his shoulder. 'A chance to lay every death at the enemy's door? Perfect. Still, it is cruel that only the victims of the North seem to matter. Those who died at ARVN hands or beneath US bombs are merely the collateral damage.'

'How I loathe those words,' I say. 'And I'll never comprehend why the Americans don't even *count* civilian casualties. It's insane.'

'No, it's clever. Selective ignorance.'

We're quiet for a time and I drift, gazing at the long translucent curtains moving in the twilight. Finally I say, 'We'd better get ready for dinner. Pete and Charlotte said they might have news.'

I go back to my room for a quick shower and we meet again at the table, where Pete has already opened a bottle of champagne.

'Something to celebrate?' I say.

'Potentially. An American charity, the usual puritans, are on a mission to save Vietnamese kids from Buddhism and make them good little Christians.' He shrugs. 'I shouldn't carp. At least they'll get families. '

'Yes you should, darling,' says Charlotte. 'Those grey men give me the shivers. But they're the only ones who care nowadays, and they have the money to save the orphanage, so ...'

'In any case it's not a done deal,' says Pete. 'But hopefully.' He hands glasses of champagne around and says, 'Cheers, everyone.'

I take a sip. 'And if you do sell?'

'We're not sure yet, but it seems our time here is coming to an end,' Pete says regretfully.

Charlotte glances around the ornate salon and sighs. 'I know it's absurd, but I *will* miss this place. And this maddening, self-destructive country as well. It was paradise once, and now? Damn that crook Thieu and the stupid Americans.'

It's rare to hear her express a political opinion and I smile. 'Careful, Charlotte. Thieu may hear and you'll end up in gaol with the Alliance leadership.'

'Has he finally moved against them?' says Pete.

'He held back for a time, but he has now arrested some prominent men,' says André. 'Fortunately their families have escaped to an Alliance camp in the Fishhook.'

'Isn't that near the Cambodian border and the NLF and COSVN camps?' I say.

'I believe there are multiple bases, many kilometres apart. It would be too tempting a target if they were close together,' André says. I glance at him thoughtfully. I didn't know that.

Thu and Vinh bring in the dishes, and we eat and drink, perhaps a little too much (Pete is determined not to leave too many good bottles of wine in the cellar for the next owner of the house).

Later, feeling tipsy, I think of the first time I saw the salon, dazed after my long flight from Australia. Flowers, palm trees, ornate plaster, soft rugs, and those hallucinatory curtains rolling against the charcoal sky.

And since then, of course, all the happy meals I've shared here with Charlotte and Pete and André.

And occasionally with Leo.

Irresistibly (yes, I *am* drunk), I remember that time of Tet when we slept beside each other. Without even touching I knew Leo was there, as I knew every shift of his thoughts the day we went to Vung Tau, the evening he gave me the jade bangle, the night he realised André and I had become lovers.

Yet it's strange. For all my happiness with André, I'm still not sure I understand a single shift of his thoughts.

∽

In bed a week later, André says, 'I am going away for a few days. I have heard I may have an uncle, a brother to my dead mother, in Tay Ninh. I wish to go and meet him.'

'Uncle?' I say. 'Not Uncle Ho, I hope.'

André laughs. 'I doubt I would be here with you, Claire, if my uncle was Bac Ho.'

'Why not? Oblivious Australian journo? Perfect cover.' I turn towards him and touch his face. 'André? Come on. We both know you're not just an interpreter. You doubt too much. You understand too much.'

'Ah,' he says lightly. 'But, Claire, surely you underestimate the breadth of interests of employees of the Ministry of Culture and Education.'

I'm silent for a moment. 'If you say so. Tay Ninh? That's over towards the Cambodian border, isn't it? Close to the Fishhook?'

'Vietnam is a small country. Almost everywhere is close to everywhere else.'

After a long silence I stroke his soft dark hair. 'Well, you be careful, eh?'

It's not as if André is always here. He has to travel for his job, coming and going, but still the next four days pass slowly. Then he returns one morning when I'm in my office, working on a story.

I jump up and hug him when he opens the door. 'You're back,' I say stupidly.

'Yes. It was a long trip.' He's unkempt and dusty, and as I hold his hands I realise they're covered in scratches and small cuts.

'Why are your hands so damaged, André? '

He laughs shortly. 'My uncle wished to take a walk in the country. My ankles are in worse condition.'

Given the unlikelihood of anyone strolling for fun in the Vietnamese countryside, pretty much solid jungle over near Tay Ninh, it's clear he didn't stay peacefully in a town.

'And your ... uncle?'

'He is well, and I am glad we met. But I am very tired, and need to sleep now.'

'I thought the road to Tay Ninh was a fast, easy one.'

'No road here is fast or easy, Claire. I will see you later.'

After a shower and a sleep he looks better. In the evening light we take coffee up to the roof terrace and sit on the wicker armchairs, while the traffic below distantly honks and hums.

'Are you going to tell me now?' I say.

'There is nothing much to tell. As a young man my uncle disowned my mother when she married a French man, so he did not know she had died, or that I existed. But now we have found each other and I like him.'

'How did you get in touch again?'

'Friends brought us together.'

He pauses, gets up and goes to the small frangipani tree in its pot. He lifts a cluster of creamy flowers and slowly breathes their perfume, gazing into the distance.

After a time he sits down again. 'Beyond that, Claire, there is something I would like to talk about.' He hesitates. 'I feel I must talk about. I can hardly believe it myself, but then,' he shrugs. 'Why not? It is simply one step further.'

'André? I've never seen you like —'

'Indeed. I have been told of ... of a massacre, one year ago at a village, My Lai. Not a battle, not a military operation. A *massacre*. Of women and babies and helpless old people, hundreds and *hundreds* of people. And not simple death. Pack rape, torture, burning, mutilation ...'

He clears his throat. 'On and on, from morning until night. And the killers —' his voice breaks. 'The killers stopped for an hour to eat their pre-packaged lunches. Then they began again.'

I can hardly breath. 'Who?'

André shakes his head in disbelief. 'The defenders of the Free World, of course.'

'The *Americans*? But how do you know this?'

'From those who are helping the few survivors.'

'But that's *appalling*. Why isn't this publicised?'

'It has been suppressed by the US.' He laughs bitterly. 'The Americans imagine themselves so virtuous, so blameless! They had a *photographer* there, the survivors said, one who took pictures all day long. Pictures of rapes, of torture, of corpses. Of terrified, breathing people in the instant before they too became nothing but corpses.'

'But isn't there, oh my *God*, can I —?'

He shakes his head. 'Claire, you can reveal nothing. This is known only to those who are protecting the survivors. And of course, it is known to the monsters who did it. But it will not remain a secret forever.'

∞

Two months later, in May, André goes to visit his uncle in Tay Ninh again. He's away for a fortnight. I'm in a state of anxiety until one day I think, What's *happened* to me? The year is rushing past and all I can think about is horror and death.

But there are joys as well. Pete and Charlotte's daughter Vivy had a baby last December, Louise, a small prune-like thing that everyone thinks is utterly beautiful. Well, she *has* got pretty eyes. Dear Vivy looks marvellous in the photos, and so does her new man. Why can't I focus on happy things like that?

Guess I decided I simply *had* to be a journalist, à la Lois Lane, I think bitterly, and insert myself into one of the most tragic conflicts of the century, and for some reason imagined it would be a fulfilling career, for God's sake.

Sadly too, Pete and Charlotte have managed to sell the orphanage to the American charity, and this house — my home, my refuge, for almost two years — will soon be up for sale. And when it's sold? When Pete and Charlotte leave Vietnam? What then for me?

André comes home scratched and exhausted.

That night, when he's relaxed with satisfied pleasure, I say, 'Okay, you certainly haven't been visiting Tay Ninh. Tell me the truth.'

He sighs. 'The truth? It was a hard journey.'

'André. No more.'

'You know I can't tell you everything.'

'You can't tell a journalist. But love — I'm not sure that's what I am any more.'

We rarely use terms of affection, and it disarms him.

He gazes at me. 'Claire?'

'Everything's *changing*, André. Please be honest with me.'

'But it would put you in danger.'

'Ignorance can be far more dangerous.'

There's a long pause.

André sits up on the side of the bed and rubs his face. I stroke the length of his lithe, beautiful back.

He takes a breath and says hesitantly, 'There, they are trying to bring together, to create, an alternative to the government.'

'At the Fishhook?'

'In that region.'

'*Who*?'

After a long pause, he says, 'The Alliance and the NLF.'

I gasp. 'Will they succeed?'

He smiles a little. 'They are already doing well, organising ministries, drafting laws — Claire, *humanitarian* laws never seen before in Vietnam, to be implemented when ... if ...'

'Oh my God, an *alternative* government for the South?'

He nods.

'And *you*?'

'They need people who can translate the subtleties of Vietnamese into brute English.'

'You.'

'Me. And many others.'

'*Is* there an uncle in Tay Ninh?'

'Indeed there is. In the old days he was fighting with the Viet Minh. Now he is alone, so it has been good for us to meet. But he lives in the Fishhook, of course, not Tay Ninh.'

'I can hardly comprehend this. Oh, my *love*.'

'Claire, we've been careful never before to speak of ...'

'I know. But now — does it matter?'

'No. My love.' He leans down and kisses me.

∽

When it's official, when the announcements are ready to be made, André gives me the heads-up, and my scoop in June 1969 — on the groups that have come together to form the new Provisional Revolutionary Government — is my biggest story yet.

Amusingly, the PRG time their announcement to overshadow a meeting on Midway Island between Presidents Nixon and Thieu, and it certainly does.

Until now the Alliance, the major partner in the PRG, was easy to dismiss, but as the coalition unashamedly includes the National Liberation Front it's quickly recognised as the Vietnamese government-in-exile by the non-aligned states around the world.

The Americans like to call such states 'commos,' but nowadays many more than communists want to keep their distance from the flailing, heartless behemoth the US has become.

The PRG are asking for a negotiated settlement and the reunification of Vietnam: more than enough to send the American and Thieu governments into ritual dances of rage.

But behind the scenes? The Paris peace talks are at stalemate. The Americans insist Hanoi must recognise the continued sovereignty of South Vietnam.

Hanoi demands the withdrawal of US troops, dissolution of Thieu's government and a return to the Geneva Accord, and no one will give ground.

But suddenly the PRG provides everyone with a face-saving alternative. It brings together the hopes of North and South, and offers the allies a plausible escape route.

And the PRG want a seat at the peace talks.

∽

Late at night there's an urgent tapping at my bedroom door.

'André? My *God*.'

He staggers in and sits down heavily on my bed.

'I am sorry. I will make a mess ...' he says faintly.

'*Sit*. I'll get the medicine chest.'

I dash to the hall cupboard to get it and return.

'Now, water, hot water.' I grab a small basin and fill it in my ensuite. 'Cotton wool, antiseptic, okay.' I pull up a chair and start dabbing at the blood on André's face. He winces as the bruised flesh below appears.

'Your poor hand! André, what's *happened*?'

'Ah, the wrong place at the wrong time.'

'That says nothing.'

'I was in the street, not far from the Rex Hotel. I passed a group of Americans.'

'Soldiers?'

'Three. With a journalist we see sometimes at the five o'clock follies, the little man with the hat.'

'Oh, *him*. And?'

'The journalist said something. The soldiers looked at me and did not like what they saw. So.'

'What did that bastard *say*?' André is silent.

'Was it about you and me?'

He nods, and winces as I apply a plaster to a cut on his cheek.

'*Merde*,' I say viciously. 'Okay, your hand now. Oh Christ, I think the finger's broken. I can bandage it for now, but you'd better see the doctor tomorrow.'

He nods again.

'André?'

He gazes at me. His eyes are sadder than I've ever seen. 'I am surprised it has taken so long. People know, Claire, and they hate me for daring to be with you.'

'Not everyone, just this bunch of bloody psychos.'

He shakes his head, smiling tiredly. 'The same thing almost happened last week, with a group of Vietnamese soldiers. If I had not been with Minh ... he is a good friend. A good talker.'

'But does it *matter* if we're exposed?'

'Yes, Claire. Saigon is a very small and very spiteful city.'

'We can ride it out, André.'

He shakes his head. 'No. You see, now ... even before this happened, there is something I have been planning to tell you.'

'Let me just —' I finish bandaging his hand. 'Okay. What?'

He takes a deep breath. 'Love, I am going away.'

'Tay Ninh again?'

He smiles briefly. 'It is on my path. But this time I shall not be returning to Saigon.'

'Not for a while?'

'Not at all.'

I sit back, staring at him. After a while I say shakily, 'You'll *stay* there? Stay with the PRG? You won't be here with me any more?'

He slowly shakes his head.

I gaze at my hands. After a time I say bitterly, 'Well, that's certainly revolutionary zeal in action.'

'Claire, it is time for me to go.'

I look up. 'But think of *tonight*, think about the way most Vietnamese treat people like you —'

'A child of the dust?'

'*Yes*. How can you be so sure they'll welcome you, André, accept you as one of them? You're useful now, but if the North prevails —'

'Then I will have no place here, Claire, I know that. I know I can never be fully Vietnamese. But until that time I will do anything I can to help reunify this country.'

'But ... what then?'

'Perhaps I will go to France.' André smiles mirthlessly. 'Track down my father's family and see how much I can horrify them. Who knows?'

'You'd give your life to help defeat the South, then step *away*?'

'Yes, of course.'

I take the bowl of blood-stained water into the ensuite and wash it. When I return I sit down and say, 'But your new-found uncle? You'd leave him alone too?'

'He was once with the Viet Minh. Now he is with the NLF. He does not expect to survive.'

I feel a punch of realisation. 'You don't expect to either, do you?'

André smiles gently. 'Of course I will, Claire. I am a simple interpreter, not a soldier.'

I take a deep breath. 'When do you go?'

'In two days. My love, I am so sorry.'

∞

We tell Charlotte and Pete that André is going to live with his elderly uncle in Tay Ninh for a time. They're sorry he's leaving, but throw him a fine dinner with affectionate farewells. Now and then Pete glances at me with curious eyes, but I pretend equanimity.

Later, lying in bed, I say, 'But what will I do without you?'

André strokes my face. 'Do you remember what you once made me promise?'

I gaze at his beautiful eyes. 'I said never tell me to go home.'

He nods. 'But now I must say it. My love, go home.'

I'm incredulous. '*Why*?'

'As a reporter you are now part of a monstrous machine to explain, to *justify*, this war to the world. But there *is* no justification. There never was, there never can be. However well-meaning, your words will not help resolve this tragedy. Only the Vietnamese themselves can do that.'

'But I just want to bear *witness*, to convey the truth to a greater audience,' I say helplessly.

'There are many audiences, Claire, and even those in small, peaceful towns still need their journalists. But Vietnam does not need you, my love, and you do not need it.'

'But I don't know *what* I need, André. Oh Christ, I'm going to miss you.'

'And I you. But you must understand, we will not meet again.'

'Don't *say* that!'

'It is true.' After a long time he says, 'I also think, one day, you should let yourself be with Leo.'

I shake my head. 'No. I want to be with *you*.'

'My dear,' André says gently. 'I must leave, and it will — truly — be forever. But Leo has been waiting for you his whole life.'

∽

André goes away in July, his few belongings taken or discarded.

I don't cry. I rarely do, in any case. Here in Vietnam my emotional response to tragedy is usually dry horror, followed by a rage to find the words to pin it down and tell the world.

I've only wept twice: once for a small girl who stepped on a mine, and once for a puppy, horribly mistreated, clinging to life. André ended the pup's suffering, and held me as I sobbed.

Still, it's stupidly hard to deal with the loss.

At the same time the house on Tu Do Street goes up for sale, and soon it's sold. The ornate, beautiful white house belongs to someone else, its contents stored, the rest left behind. Only the jasmine-covered rooftop terrace, and all my memories, remain.

I rent a small flat in an ugly cement building nearby, then in August drive Charlotte and Pete to the airport: they're off to see Vivy in France and I can't even imagine how that's going to go.

How I miss them. How I miss André.

Sometimes I go out to cafes with other reporters and drink too much. Or go to depressing, dope-foggy parties and drink too much. Or stay in my room and drink too much.

Despite André's words, I tell myself that explaining Vietnam is not *justifying* it. But in the grey hours before dawn I sometimes wonder.

By reporting this war as a serious, urgent crusade, rather than the lazy, corrupt quagmire it's always been, did we journalists offer it respectability? Normality? Business as usual? Why didn't we scream from the rooftops how mad, how unfair, how pointless it all was? Well, that's obvious. We needed the work.

What was Eisenhower's phrase? Yes: the military-industrial complex. Is *that* the monstrous machinery I'm now part of? It certainly seems to be the only entity profiting from this nightmare. America the Beautiful has discarded all sanity, failed its youth, squandered its wealth and made itself into a global pariah.

But I keep working. What else can I do? I can't *stop* being a reporter.

∞

An interesting story comes my way. I hear on the quiet from worried soldiers about a US operation, going since the early sixties, dubbed Ranch Hand, and still in full flow.

Ludicrous amounts of herbicide are being sprayed onto Vietnamese jungles, forests, paddies and crops, to starve the NLF and force villagers into the pro-government cities.

The main concoction in this saga is called Agent Orange, but there's also a grotesque rainbow of other Agents — Pink, Purple, Blue, Green, and White — that destroy not only plants, but poison people and animals too.

The exposed US soldiers tell me anxiously they're getting sick with skin cysts, tingling, limbs swelling, difficulties breathing. The ARVN men speak furtively about villages they know with deformed babies and terrible illnesses; places where animals abort or die, places where the harvest never returns.

Over the last few years, the United Nations has charged America several times with violating the Geneva Protocol on chemical and biological weapons, but the US simply blusters, defeats all the resolutions, and keeps going. So I write a story about Ranch Hand, but (surprise!) no one wants to print it.

Then on 2 September comes the extraordinary news of the felling of a giant. Ho Chi Minh, the man who helped Vietnam resist the Japanese, resist the French, resist the Americans, dies at 79 from heart failure.

What a heart, I think, and what a life. I recall one of his gentle, pointed statements that always makes me smile.

In 1966 he said, '*Everything depends upon the Americans. If they want to make war for twenty years then we shall make war for twenty years. If they want to make peace, we shall make peace and invite them to tea afterwards.*'

If only the Americans had listened. If only they'd recognised for a moment the juggernaut of sheer commitment they were facing!

Still, Jaunissement — sorry, Vietnamisation — continues apace. Nixon announces withdrawal plans for 35,000 US troops, blathering, unconvincingly, about ending the American involvement in the war.

Then a few days after the death of Ho Chi Minh, I'm astonished to read that one Lieutenant William Calley has been charged with six counts of premeditated murder at My Lai in March 1968.

The US Army is actually prosecuting one of its minions for a war crime? But only six counts? I recall André's horrified words: *hundreds* of people died in torment.

Then, on 13 November 1969, the full story of My Lai finally appears, courtesy of reporter Seymour Hersh. Apparently the US forces were ordered to destroy everything in the village that was 'walking, crawling or growling.' So they did.

And Ronald Haeberle's photographs of the atrocity — of the day-long, excruciating, multiple atrocities — are published. I try to imagine who in this world could take such images and still remain sane, but fail.

20. VIVY: FRANZ NAGY (FEB-SEP 1969)

One mid-winter evening, after Louise is asleep, Brian and I are sitting by the fire. 'Something I wanted to talk to you about,' I say.

Brian looks up from his book. 'Sorry, love. I really *did* mean to move that *Hecticoceras* upstairs.'

I shake my head. 'Oh no, it makes an excellent door-stop. Actually, it's Henk. I'm going to have to take him to court to get a divorce, and he's already sworn he'll claim Louise as his. That terrifies me—what if he wins?'

'He may need more than some good mates who are pretending he's fertile,' says Brian. 'At least, in some cases, blood tests can show who *isn't* the father.'

'Really? There was certainly a lot of fuss in the hospital about our blood types.'

'Do you recall what the two of you were?'

'I'm type A and Louise is AB. Is that of any use?'

'I'll just check, but it might.'

He goes upstairs quietly — we do everything quietly when Louise is sleeping — and comes back flipping through a textbook.

'As I thought. If the mother is type A and the child AB, then the child *cannot* be fathered by someone of type A or O blood. Do you have any idea what Henk is?'

I think. 'He once cut himself badly at Frederika's estate. She made ghoulish jokes about transfusions and Henk boasted he'd be fine because fifty percent of people had his blood type. Does that help?'

Brian smiles. 'It does indeed. O is the only one common in half the population. He'd have to be formally tested of course, but if it's true, there is no possible way he could have fathered Louise.'

'How *marvellous* science is! I'm so glad I met you.'

'I hope you're glad for more than that, but I'll humbly accept whatever's going.'

I sigh, relieved, then hesitantly say, 'Brian, something else.'

'I do hope I've got a textbook to cover it.'

'Probably not. Something I should have told you about ages ago, but in the fuzziness of pregnancy I kept procrastinating. Louise's biological father.'

'Ah.'

'He's, well, he's Stav Loukas, a composer who lives in Berlin. We grew up in the same circles in Sydney, and when I started singing, Stav and his friends became my band. We fell in love and were together for three years. Then he left me to study music in Greece. Soon afterwards I came to London.'

Brian nods, gazing at me.

I take a breath. 'Well, fast forward a decade, and Stav turned up in Amsterdam. His girlfriend Nina caught Henk's eye, so we couldn't avoid each other. We got together again and it lasted long enough for me to get pregnant, Stav to insist I have an abortion before dashing off to Berlin, and Nina to take my place in my bed and my job. So that's about it.'

'Okay. Do you think Stav will want to claim Louise as his?'

'I doubt it. He's very trendy — and kids are not. But at some time I'll have to tell him.'

'Only when you feel like it, love.'

I nod and put my head on Brian's shoulder.

He kisses me. 'Now, there's something I wanted to talk to you about, too. Once you've freed yourself of the obnoxious Henk, I'd quite like us to, well ... get married. If you want to as well, of course.'

I can only say, '*Oh,*' but feel the kind of head-to-toe wave of bliss that Louise usually triggers.

'Oh?' says Brian.

'Yes, I mean,' I say. 'Rather a good idea.'

'It is, isn't it? I can see the headline now,' he says. '*Hunky Brian tamed by sultry songbird Vivy and adorable waif Louise.*'

'Appropriate. But let's just do it in secret? When we can.'

∾

My parents and I write, and I send them photos of Louise and, hesitantly, one of Brian. My mother replies, 'He's as nice-looking as the scandal sheets said,' which makes Brian laugh.

I explain a little about Henk's abuse of me — and abuse of my finances — and they're pleasingly outraged on my behalf. I wonder if I'd never before quite accepted how appalling Henk's behaviour was? It's satisfying to have it recognised.

Still, that doesn't help with *money*, and I'm determined to both divorce Henk and get back the funds from my share of the flat, more than half — I had three popular albums and put extra money into our mortgage. But how on earth do I prove the bastard sold *our* property and pocketed the proceeds?

I ring Lucien and ask if he's had any success at retrieving my money from Henk. He's embarrassed. 'I'm sorry, Vivy, he has covered his very tracks well. But I wonder, did you ever see anything that might be a point of vulnerability? Taxes, perhaps?'

'No, Lucien. I trusted him and never paid attention to important things like that.'

He laughs, a gravelly chuckle. 'Chérie, the *only* important thing now is your baby. Henk will make a mistake: we must be ready to recognise it. But now, Manon would like to send you a box of tiny pink objects she has been knitting. Are you prepared?'

'Tell Manon I am eternally grateful, and give her my love.'

∽

Feeling brave, a few weeks later I sit down at the phone and ring Henk. Nina answers.

'Ah, you,' she says, bored. 'I will get Henk.'

He says, 'Lieveling, I can almost *feel* how motherhood suits you. How is our little one?'

'She's wonderful, Henk, and if only your blood type was B, she'd be *ours*. But you must understand, no matter how much your friends lie in court, they cannot deny your blood type is O — and hers is AB. Louise is not your child, and can never be.'

'Ah. You are not as stupid as I'd always assumed, Vivy.'

'I'm going to divorce you.'

'You can't.'

'I can. And by the way, where are my *royalties*? I haven't seen a cent for months.'

Henk chuckles. 'I have directed those funds to Straat Records, of course.'

'You can't, you bastard.'

'Yes I can.' He puts down the phone.

A few days later I'm playing around with a tape recorder Brian bought to encourage me to keep singing. Louise is asleep so I'm at the table and have managed one phrase that sounds good. I tell myself a single phrase does not a repertoire make, and press 'record' to try again.

At my elbow the phone rings. We got sick of it being out in the cold hall so Brian got an extension and it's now here in the cosy living room.

I answer and to my surprise it's Nina. 'Are you ringing for Henk?' I ask.

'No. For me.'

'What do you want?'

'I want you to divorce Henk.'

'Well so do I. Any tips?' I think for a moment. 'Why?'

'He has promised to marry me when you are divorced.'

'And you *want* that? Seriously?'

'Of course. We are useful to each other. We will be happy.'

'You must be mad, but look, Nina, I'll do everything I can to help. I just want a divorce myself. Why won't he let me go?'

'Money, of course. But *I* am doing so well he soon will not need your little royalties.'

Bitch, I think, and say, 'Perhaps you should be more careful with your own money, Nina. You do realise Henk has sold our flat and stolen my half-share of the proceeds?'

'Sold?'

'Yes, he sold it to his parents' trust behind my back. Did you not know this?'

'But, no, I am *helping* him pay off that mortgage —'

'*Are* you now, Nina?' I laugh unkindly. 'Oh, dear.'

She hangs up.

The tape recorder was running all this time so I play it back. That's interesting. Henk is not only exploiting Nina, but I wonder what he really thinks about the prospect of marrying her?

So I ring him one evening, very carefully press Record on the machine, and put the phone close to the microphone. We spar as usual, then I say, 'Henk, is Nina there?'

'No, she is out. What do you want?'

'I'm curious. I spoke to her the other day. She thinks you want to marry her if we divorce.'

'Marry her? My *God*, Vivy, she has bats in her belfry. I do not want to marry her. All the time it is me, me, me. Her silly clothes, her spotty face, her awful *bottom*. I cannot bear it.'

'What's wrong with her bottom?'

'I explained to her it was not quite perfect, and now she is obsessed. My God, I yearn for you. So sensible, so understanding. Nina is charming, you understand, but *marriage*? I could not cope. Vivy, come back to me.'

'Never.' I hang up and press the Stop button.

∽

'Nina, How are you?'

'All right,' she says suspiciously. 'He is not here, you know.'

'That's okay. There's something I'd like to share with you.'

'*Share*? What do you want, Vivy?'

'Just this. Listen to this.'

Over the phone I play the recording of my conversation with Henk, then click Stop.

Silence. 'Are you there, Nina?'

'Yes.' A pause. 'Interesting.'

'Perhaps it's time to rethink your involvement with Henk. Financially, at least.'

More silence, then she takes a breath. 'Indeed. Since we last spoke I have investigated carefully, and I am most unhappy to discover I am paying off a mortgage that does not actually exist.'

'I can imagine that.'

'I want my money back.'

'And so do I. Nina, there's a filing cabinet in his office —'

'Indeed, I have discovered it. I have been going through it and carefully reconciling the accounts.'

'Reconciling?'

'Vivy, are you aware of my profession before I became famous?'

Not *that* famous, honey, I think. 'Well, what did you do before, Nina?'

'I was an accountant. A very good accountant.'

I can't speak for a moment then slowly smile. 'So you know all about financial matters?'

She says coldly, 'Oh, I *know*. And Henk does not realise how much.' She hesitates. 'It did not occur to me to even question him, you see, before. I trusted him.'

'So did I. He's extremely plausible. Is there anything I can do to help you?'

'I am fine, Vivy. You and I both shall have a financial resolution, very, *very* soon.'

'Wonderful. And Nina?'

'What?'

'Your bottom is *fantastic*. Seriously. I'd kill to have one like it.'

She sighs. 'It is only Henk who is critical. I have never had a complaint otherwise.'

'Remember that, then — only Henk.'

She's silent, then says, 'Yes. Thank you, Vivy.'

∞

In a miraculously short time Nina sorts everything out and we don't even have to go to court. A large sum of money appears in my account one day, and a letter arrives that sets out exactly what Henk has stolen from me over the years.

It's signed by Nina, her name followed by an impressive list of qualifications. She also sends all my legal papers and royalty agreements, as well as a recent letter from a big company wanting me to do a new record for them — Henk, the bastard, had never even mentioned it!

Then, to a fanfare of publicity Nina joins a new record company. The cover of her latest LP shows her from behind, gazing sexily over her shoulder, her bottom very prettily outlined in a silky slip.

Good *on* you, I think.

Henk rings me one night, sobbing, saying Straat Records is almost bankrupt and Nina's left him and it's all my fault. 'I will not divorce you! You will *never* be free.'

'We'll see about that, Henk. I've got the money now to fight you, and I doubt your fairweather friends will want to perjure themselves for a bankrupt.'

He abruptly hangs up.

Next step, I tackle the task I'd avoided for so long: ringing Stav in Berlin.

'Ah, Vivy,' he says coldly. 'I was wondering when you might contact me.'

'Hello, Stav. I suppose you've heard —'

'I've heard you blithely went ahead and produced an illegitimate baby. I hope you don't think I'm going to support you. Or it.'

'*It* is a beautiful four-month-old girl called Louise. But no, your support is not required. I didn't put your name on the birth certificate, so you're safe.'

His voice a little relieved, he says, 'I'm sure that's best for us all. Are you — well?'

'Better than ever in my life, thank you. And by the way, your old girlfriend Nina has been an absolute gem. You never mentioned she had such amazing qualifications.'

'*Does* she? No idea.'

'I suppose it wouldn't interest you much.'

'You're sounding a little bitter there, Vivy. You're not turning into one of those mad women's libbers, are you?'

'They actually seem rather sensible to me.'

He snorts in contempt. 'Look, another thing. It was Dad and Billie who told me you'd had a baby, but they don't know ...'

'You're the father?'

'And I don't want them to know,' he says stiffly.

'But Nikos would be delighted to find out he's a grandfather.'

'It's nobody else's business. Vivy, don't tell *anyone*.'

'Well, good luck with that. Henk is very keen to blacken my reputation, so half of Amsterdam already knows. I haven't told anyone in Sydney, but it's only a matter of time before the word gets around.'

'Shit.'

'Oh grow up, Stav! It's hardly the end of the world. I'm not going to pursue you for child support, so what's your problem?'

He says pompously, 'I happen to believe it's *irresponsible* to bring children into this uncertain world.'

I laugh. 'Come off it. It's because fatherhood isn't young and cool, isn't it? Bad for the image.'

'Well, unlike *you*, some of us take our careers seriously.'

I'm stung. 'I've always been damned serious and you know it.'

'And you're going to keep working with a baby at home that needs its *mother*?' he says sneeringly. 'Face it, Vivy, this child will be a millstone around your neck. Your career is over.'

'Go to hell.'

I hang up, then sit staring at nothing.

Stav's words have touched on my deepest fears. Darling Brian encourages me to keep singing, but when do I get the time to practise?

If and when Louise sleeps I have to grab those few moments to rest, I'm so tired, so incredibly tired. Dear God, I love her so much, but how I want just *one* night's unbroken sleep.

Then Louise cries out from her cot.

I trudge upstairs to sooth her, and feed her, and change her. Sultry songbird Vivy's real career.

⁓

Louise is six months old. I have a little more time to myself, but haven't practised my singing for ages. I let Brian think I'm still working at it when he's at the Black Cow cliffs, or away at occasional meetings or conferences, but I'm not.

If I open my mouth now the sounds that emerge are so unconvincing they horrify me. I see Docteur Allard and mention it casually, and he says, 'Madame, your body has undergone profound changes at the level of muscles and ligaments. You may recover la tonicité, your muscle tone, but it will take much effort and time.'

Later I try a run of scales, once as easy as breathing: it's humiliating.

Sadly I recall all the musicians I've worked with over the years. I desperately need someone to practice with, but here in provincial Villers-sur-Mer I'm completely isolated. Although Edgar's band sometimes plays in nearby Trouville, they live in Le Havre, which is hours away.

My career is indeed over.

Occasionally Brian mentions going to see some music but I usually plead tiredness. One day, looking up from the newspaper, he says, 'Hey, Edgar's group is on at Trouville this weekend. Come on, surely you want to see *them* again?'

'Well ... yes. But — what about Louise?'

When I have appointments and Brian isn't around, Louise sometimes stays with my librarian friend Julie Desvignes (her own kids have left home), so Brian says, 'She'll be fine with Julie. Express some milk into a bottle and Louise won't even know the difference.'

'That's a depressing thought. Well, I suppose going out would be rather nice.'

That night I'm anxious. What if, what if? How can I leave my baby for so long? Oh God, perhaps Edgar will expect me to *sing*! But Julie reassures me — about Louise at least — so I get myself dressed in something ordinary and off we go.

The nightclub, Jardin de Lune, is as it was before: it's only me who's completely different. But we find a table on one side (Quintette Bleu is getting too damned popular, we can't even see the whole stage).

At least I have the consolation of being able to drink wine, and Edgar's band is, as usual, wonderful. At the interval Brian and I go backstage.

'Oh, *babe*,' says Edgar, 'you look so *fine*!' I tell him all about Louise and he laughs in delight.

'Ah, Vivy, freaking good. Now, will you do a tune with us?'

'No, honestly, *no*, Edgar. I'm totally unprepared. Come on — remember how your wife was when the baby was six months old? Please. Be kind.'

'Honey,' he says gently. 'I can see things are pretty hard. Maybe next time, right?'

'Of course, next time,' I say, lying. I can't look at Brian.

'But, hey, you must meet our new guys at least. Well, the sax player's new, but our old piano player's come back to us at last.'

He introduces me to the sax player then, as I turn, Edgar says, 'And here's our fabulous ivory tickler, Franz Nagy.'

Everything goes quiet.

The man says, 'Vivy.'

'László?' I can hardly breathe.

He's older of course, greyer, solid, lined, but here he is, the man who supported me and protected me and taught me almost everything I know about jazz.

'*László?*' says Edgar, laughing. 'No, babe, this is Franz.'

I shake my head and say, disbelieving, 'You? It's really *you*?'

He nods as gravely as ever, and takes my hands. 'Vivy, it is me.'

∽

We sit together at a table: Brian and Edgar have diplomatically left us alone to talk.

'But how could you *disappear*, László?' I say. 'Moshe searched and searched. And Rob's almost fourteen and asking Tina about his father, his *real* father, because he's the smartest kid under the sun and he's figured out for himself that Jimmy Kelso had nothing to do with him.'

'How much does the boy know?'

'Last I heard from Tina he's figured out it was *you*, and he's planning to come to Europe and find you when he's older.'

László sits back. '*What*? I cannot … that is impossible.'

'He's your son, László, and everything's different now. Tina's alone. She's seen a few men, but nothing's lasted. I don't think anyone has ever mattered to her since you.'

'It was just a moment,' says László quietly.

'For *years* you were her closest friend, helping with the club, the music, the people. That wasn't just a bloody moment, László.'

He winces slightly. 'And what do you suggest I do?'

'I'm not saying you've got to rush back to Sydney. But you should contact Tina, tell her the truth about what you've been doing, what you've been feeling. And see what she says.'

László says carefully, 'Perhaps.'

'But why disappear like that?'

He lights a cigarillo and breathes deeply. 'I left Australia with false papers as Franz Nagy. Auschwitz had been a decade before, so I believed it was behind me. But once here, simply the sound of my real name would throw me back to … then. I found I could only feel safe as non-existent Franz Nagy. So that is who I became.'

I slowly nod. 'Would you like me to call you Franz from now on?'

He shakes his head. 'Time has passed. From you, Vivy, I can bear to hear my true name.'

I touch his hand, hardly believing even now he's real.

László gazes sternly at me. 'But, now, what is all that nonsense you told Edgar? You, *unprepared*?'

'Since the baby, my voice doesn't work the way it used to. László, I've lost it all.'

'If anyone in this world has lost it all, it is me. And yet, here I am, playing tonight —'

'Like an angel.'

László smiles. 'Playing, that is all. So Vivy, you too must sing. And that is all.'

At home I tell Brian about talking to László and, at last, reveal my fears about my voice and my lost career. He promises to do whatever he can to help, but still, I can't expect him to understand how isolated I feel.

∽

In August, out of the blue, we receive a telegram from Charlie and Pete to say they're coming to France, to stay with us, arriving in *two* day's time. Louise and I have long since moved into the main part of the house, so Brian and I hurriedly prepare the flat for my parents, with fresh bedding and provisions.

When it's all done, we sit and stare at each other.

'Oh God,' I say. 'Are they coming here for *good*? It's their house, after all.'

'But I'm their tenant,' says Brian. 'They can't eject me.'

'How long does your lease run?'

'Actually, it expired shortly after I met you. Unfortunate. Are you anxious about meeting them, love?'

'Yes. We haven't met since, my God, September 1954. I was eighteen, and my freshly-widowed mother had come to Sydney, supposedly to see me sing. Turned out it was actually to seduce — or re-seduce — my Dad, and whisk him away to Vietnam. Without me.'

'Ah. You've only ever mentioned before they'd remarried, not these juicy details.'

'It was such a turning point in my life. Left me pretty bitter.'

'So, almost fifteen years later, how do you think things will go?'

I bite my lip. 'No idea.'

In the summer dusk two days later, we wait at the station, Brian holding an adorably sleepy Louise. Finally we see the smoke of the train, then it chuffs alongside and halts with a gush of steam.

A few people disembark, mostly locals we nod to, then I see a man and woman at the end of the platform who come towards us with their bags. They seem smaller than I remember.

'Dad, Charlie?' I step forward.

'*Darling*,' says Dad, and hugs me. I turn to Charlie. 'Vivy?' she says, and hugs me lightly too. She's both familiar and unfamiliar, and I laugh shyly and step back.

'This is Brian, and of course, Louise.'

'Sweetie, she's *beautiful*,' says Charlie.

'Let me take your bag,' I say. 'The car's just out here.'

Charlie sits in the front seat, and I'm in the back with the baby and Dad. He strokes Louise's cheek and glances at me, and we smile. He's tanned and older than I expected.

'*Oh*,' breathes Charlie as we pull up at Mi-Côte. 'I've so terribly wanted to be here again.'

We get everyone inside, and show my parents the flat, which they insist is just perfect, and agree to meet for dinner in an hour.

I feed Louise — who, thank the Lord, is now taking bottles of formula as we wean her off my battle-weary breasts — while Brian finishes cooking. Louise goes to sleep in her cot, and we sit with my parents to eat. It's good, we agree. We ask them about their travels (delays in the flight, luggage apparently lost at Orly but found again, train trip fine).

We discuss Louise's milestones: not many, but then she's only nine months old, and Brian's work. With great restraint he barely mentions the *Oppelia*, a tiny thing he found last week, on which he's already written half a paper; and we touch upon my career — on hold, naturally, for the moment.

But I can't stop glancing at Charlie. No longer the invincible blonde goddess of memory, the glorious being who swooped in one glittering night and stole my father away from Billie: and from me. She's thin now, and she smokes and coughs.

And then there's the question, the giant hovering question ... are my parents simply visiting or have they left Vietnam for good and plan to live here? And no one is brave enough to broach it.

∾

Next day Brian takes Dad to see the Vache Noir cliffs, but Charlie just wants to sit in a deckchair in the back garden and relax. I don't blame her, it's a perfect day. I make us tea as Louise burbles contentedly in her pram.

'Thank you, sweetie,' says Charlie, as I hand her the tea and sit in the other chair.

'Beautiful morning,' I say.

'Mmm,' says my mother. 'The bougainvillea is looking wonderful.'

'The what? That giant thing with all the swaying pink flowers? Brian tried to cut it back but it's covered in thorns.'

'I remember when Louis planted that, just a seedling. He knew the plant from Vietnam and was hoping it would flourish here. It clearly has.' She turns to me. 'Do you remember much about Louis?'

'I only saw him on holidays here with you, but I liked him. He did seem old and serious, though.'

She smiles. 'Not that old. We were very happy together.'

'Didn't stop you hanging about too long before remarrying Dad,' I say shortly.

She shrugs. 'I enjoy company.'

I take a breath. 'So what are your plans? Is this a holiday and you're returning to Saigon or ...?'

'No. We've sold the orphanage to a charity and left completely.

We've done what we could, found homes for thousands of kids with no hope of a reasonable life. Gave them that, if nothing else.'

'Nothing else?'

'Well, they usually ended up far from their homelands, their language, their culture. The cruel equation: survival or heritage?' Charlie sighs. 'Pete and I chose survival, and we had to give up caring otherwise a long time ago. But we can't do it any more. We loved our life there, our house, our friends, but in the end, Vietnam defeated us.'

I say quietly, 'And now you're here.'

'For the first time in years we have no plans. It's rather nice.' She turns to me. 'And you, Vivy? I'm amazed to see how well you've adjusted to motherhood.'

'Adjusted?' I laugh. 'Not much choice about it. It just *happened*.'

'Do you think? It seems to me you're coping very well.'

'In some aspects.'

She says lightly, 'I never adjusted. I adored you, but simply couldn't do motherhood.'

'I do understand. The *Kindertransport*, the refugee kids, the essential war work. Anyway, I had Dad and Spencie and Billie, so what need did I have of a mother?'

Charlie pauses for a moment then tries to smile. 'I'd have been a lousy mother, truly.'

'Odd. I've found I can rise to the occasion, no matter what.'

There's a long silence.

Charlie gazes at sleeping Louise. After a time she says hesitantly, 'As it happens, Vivy, my own mother was quite mad ... physically violent towards me. When I had you I thought I'd escaped her. But then I became deeply depressed. I was terrified I'd do to you what Ilse did to me.' She swallows. 'That's it. That's really why I left.'

'But ... but why on earth, why didn't you ever tell me this *before*?'

'Too ashamed, I suppose. I'm sorry, Vivy.'

I can't speak for a moment. 'Well, I survived. More tea?'

I bring us fresh cups and settle down again in the sunlight.

'You do realise,' says Charlie, sipping, 'you're carrying on a family tradition?'

'In what way?'

'Illegitimacy, sweetie. I had you before I married your father.'

'*Did* you? Goodness, I never knew.'

'Of course, in those days such things were glossed over. But I needed to get out of an earlier marriage, so you were eight months old when Pete and I were finally able to wed.'

'First time round,' I say drily.

Charlie laughs. 'Will you ever forgive me for that *bloody* night?'

'Probably not. Poor Billie —'

Charlie leans forward. 'Vivy darling, please *think*. Billie and Pete could have worked out their differences and married long before then, but in truth he never got over me. From all I hear, Billie has been very happy with Nikos for years. She simply wasn't right for Pete. And I was.'

And suddenly I see that is perfectly true.

∽

Dad has always had wide-ranging interests, and after a day with Brian looking for fossils, he's clearly found a new one.

Over dinner he says, 'What an extraordinary place this is. At the cliffs I found a small, complete *Hecticoceras* — is that right? — for Brian's collection.' He peers at me. 'And, darling, that tiny golden specimen around your neck is delightful.'

'It's from Vietnam, Dad,' I say. 'Brian gave it to me.'

'Very nice,' says Dad. 'Now, Charlotte and I have had a chat.'

I feel tense. Are they going to move into this house? Do they want us to go somewhere else? (Brian should *not* have got Dad so enthused about ammonites. And good luck with getting all those tons of fossils downstairs.)

'As you know, we've been scraping by these last few years,' says Dad. 'Not much fun. But then you got Moshe onto the case and a nice chunk of money landed back in the old account.'

Charlie smiles. 'We got a good payment for the orphanage too. And our house in Saigon — oh, Vivy, I *wish* you could have seen it. So beautiful.' She sighs. 'Ah well. Some puffed-up little American general paid too much for it, so we have more money than we know what to do with.'

'And,' says Dad, 'we do *not* want to maintain some eccentric old villa in Normandy.'

'I feel a thump of distress. 'Do you plan to sell Mi-Côte then?'

'No, darling. We plan to make it over to you,' he says. 'And whether or not you tie the knot with this fossil-hunting madman, it's yours. But of course, if and when you do tie the knot, we expect to be accommodated in utter luxury for the wedding.'

I laugh. 'Really? Mi-Côte is going to be *mine*?'

'And Louise's after you,' says Charlie, a catch in her voice.

Brian says, overcome, 'But what are *you* planning to do?'

'Australia,' says Dad. 'My God, how I've yearned to go home. Perth in summer, Broome in winter: perfection. And darling Charlotte to set the cat among the pigeons wherever we go.'

∞

Two weeks later my parents catch a flight to Perth, two weeks of laughter and confidences that make up in surprising ways for the long years of separation. And when they leave, we share a wealth of promises to meet again, in France or in Australia.

But before they go we take them to see Edgar's Quintette Bleu in Trouville. Dad knew László well in the old days, and they're both delighted to see each other.

Later, in a quiet moment, László and I find a table by ourselves.

'Here you are,' I say, passing him a photo.

László takes it and gazes for a long time. 'The boy —'

'*Róbert*,' I say.

'Róbert. He looks like my father.'

'He looks like you.'

László smiles. 'Poor child. But Tina has not aged a day.'

'She'd disagree, but yes, she still looks wonderful.'

He goes to return the photo to me, but I shake my head.

'It's for you. Tina's address is on the back.'

László takes a deep breath, then carefully tucks the photo inside his jacket. He gazes at me. 'These last few years I have been writing songs. One of them, I could only imagine you singing.'

'Me?'

'Where I was in the camp ... there were no gardens. But how I dreamt of them.' He sighs. 'Lately I cannot stop thinking about loss. About beauty, about Asia, about destruction, about Vietnam.' He shrugs. 'Why a Hungarian would care for Vietnam, such a place, but ... the song is called *Lament for a Garden*.'

'Lament? What a beautiful word, László.'

He hums a few bars that make the hairs prickle on my neck.

'That's amazing. But why me?'

'You have the depth for it now. You'll understand.'

'Yes, please. I'd love to work on it.'

He smiles and sips his drink. 'I will write to Tina, but on one condition only.'

'Yes?'

'I've discussed this with Brian. A piano will shortly be arriving at your house.'

'A *piano*? My goodness, just what the living room needs.'

'No. Just what you need.'

'I don't play the piano, László.'

'But I do.' He smiles gently. 'Vivy, will you sing with me?'

21. LEO: RUSTY (JUL 1969-DEC 1969)

'Happened again, Simmo,' I say, as we bump along a red dirt road. The first hundred miles were on tarmac, but this is just balls-achingly bad. 'My bush hat. Reminded me of Dat Do —'

'Vomiting?'

'No, thank Christ. Just ... coldness. Frozen.'

'Tears?'

'Yeah.'

'Good.'

'*Good*?'

Simmo nods. 'Could be for the better. Who knows?'

'Your diagnostic skills need a bit of work there, mate.'

'Probably. Been doing some reading, though. At first your body couldn't cope, hence the emesis.'

'The what?'

'Vomiting. Can't imagine why I ever imagined you'd be helpful as a medical assistant.'

'You may recall I actually went along under protest.'

'Still got my Stones tape?'

'Yeah. And you can't have it back.'

Simmo smiles. 'But no emesis, simply stasis then lacrimation.'

'Couldn't have put it better myself.'

'No, really. A sort of a progress.'

'What about this weird feeling of *being* there — not remembering, but actually *being*?'

Simmo nods. 'Some scientists think part of your brain, the hippocampus, is what connects up your memories, so you know where and *when* they belong. But under stress it zones out, so some new memories stay sort of — I don't know — untethered. When you hit one, your body responds as if it's happening for real, right here and now.'

I sit stunned, then say, 'Wow, Simmo. That actually makes sense.'

'Course it does. But look, we're here.'

We park the Landrover beside a cluster of rough buildings, tin sheds, and a paddock with a few horses and some gum trees. Maybe fifty yards away is a wide, green creek flowing towards low orange hills. It looks nice.

'Bit different from what I expected,' I say.

'Yeah, not bad. There's Liam.'

We get out of the Landrover, stretching, then shake hands with Liam and an older Aboriginal man he introduces as Tender Jack. My eyebrows must rise, because Liam laughs and says, 'The tender is the most vital job on a pearling lugger, and Jack was one of the best.'

Liam leads us to benches in the shade of a shed, and pours us cups of tea. A couple of kids peep glumly around the corner at us.

'Good you're here, Simmo,' he says. 'We've got a stockman with a broken arm, those kids have ear infections, and Evie Richardson is about to give birth. She lost a baby two years ago, so ... everyone's hoping.'

Simmo nods and drains his teacup. 'Okay. Let's sort them out.'

Liam leads him away and I'm left with Tender Jack, who looks anything but tender. He's brown-skinned, wiry, grey-haired.

'Pearling luggers?' I say.

'Darwin and Broome, after the war. Japs couldn't work here then, so we come in handy.' He smiles drily. 'Back from Vietnam, eh?'

'Yeah. About six months now.'

'Still half-there, but?'

'Well, hard to forget ...'

After a pause he says, 'I was a soldier myself.'

'Pacific War?'

'Yeah. You calling Vietnam a *war*?'

'Nah. Apparently it's a temporary police action. Who'd have thought?'

Tender Jack laughs, all white teeth and crinkled eyes. 'Back in those days they weren't supposed to enlist us, but then they got a bit desperate.'

'Where did you serve?'

'Northern Territory, Torres Strait, New Guinea. Government needed pearlshell to pay the Papuans to build airfields, so we went diving for it. Raised shell worth thousands. Didn't do us much good.

They still don't pay us for the work, not to this day.'

'And after the war, did you, well, keep remembering ...?' I'm suddenly embarrassed.

'Remembering bad things?'

I nod. I can't look at him.

Tender Jack sighs. 'Yeah. For a while, too much. Like not here and not there.'

I glance at him. 'I don't know how to make it stay in the *past*.'

'Country might help.'

Country — the *bush*? I suddenly feel defeated. Why did I imagine he'd understand? 'Sorry, haven't the faintest ...'

Tender Jack nods. 'Okay, young fella.' He stands up. 'Go get your swag and some water.'

It's evening and I was looking forward to a promised barbecue, but for no obvious reason I go to the Landrover and get my sleeping-bag, canteen, and a couple of sandwiches Mum packed for me that I'd earlier scorned.

'Follow me.' Tender Jack starts walking away from the settlement with an air of authority, and after a moment of puzzled indecision I follow him.

Anyway, I tell myself it's good to stretch my legs after the long drive, and fall into an easy rhythm beside the older man. A small reddish dog comes with us, a young kelpie female who darts ahead and runs back, tail wagging.

I'm not much used to dogs. We didn't have one when I was a kid because Mum and Dad worked full-time, and in Vietnam they were poor, vicious, diseased things you wouldn't dare go near. But this one is healthy, with pricked ears and light gold patches above her eyes that make her look amused.

'What's your dog's name?' I say.

'Doesn't have one. Runt of the litter, useless as a working dog. I'll have to get rid of her.'

I don't want to ask what will happen to the happy little bitch, here in the outback where animals are mere commodities, but I can imagine. As the light fades we finally arrive at a bend of the creek, with a low red cliff rising behind a pebbled strand.

Jack says, 'Let's make a fire,' so we gather twigs and branches. He lights a small fire near the base of the cliff, then stands and says, 'See you back at camp tomorrow.'

'What — you want me to stay *here* tonight?'

'Got your swag and water, what else do you need?'

'Oh, some company, maybe?'

'The dog seems to like you. You'll be fine.'

I can't answer that. Jack turns and leaves, and I realise how dark it is around me.

I say, 'But ...'

But nothing. He's gone.

Everything is silent and I couldn't find my way back to Reedy Creek by myself if I tried. What's Jack playing at? Leaving me out here where there could be snakes or scorpions or fuck knows what? Okay, I tell myself. Make the best of it. Settle down and return when it's light.

I put my legs inside the swag, lean against a boulder, and open Mum's ham and cheese sandwiches, which now seem a great idea. The dog sits calmly to one side, so I give it the crusts.

I have some water from my canteen, then pour a bit into my palm and offer it to the dog, who licks it up then pads in the dark over to the creek. I hear her having a long drink.

I spread bushy branches beneath my swag, put some wood on the fire so it'll last for a while, and snuggle down to watch the flames.

The dog returns and settles into the curve of my back. She wriggles and goes quiet, softly breathing. She's warm and the evening's cold, so if she's got a few fleas it's probably worth it.

As the fire burns down, the night sky emerges, a river of stars streaming from horizon to horizon. I turn on my back and stare. I'm a city boy and haven't seen anything like it before.

After a while I sigh.

This might be amazing, but do Liam and Tender Jack *really* think a night out in the bush, here in their precious country, is going to solve all my problems? Not fucking likely.

'What do they expect of me, dog?' I say. She thumps her tail. 'Look,' I tell her. 'I didn't *want* to go. Or at least I didn't resist. Guess I quite liked all that shit about being an officer and a tough guy. Didn't know it would all get so ugly and sad. But it's the past and I *really* don't want my fucking memories popping up all the time now. They're *over*.'

The dog snuggles closer and yawns. The creek gurgles softly, nightbirds call, and twigs crackle as (no doubt) man-eating creatures shuffle past, wondering if I'm edible.

I haven't been alone like this for years, and certainly never in such a place. After a time of watching the flames my mind drifts, and of course it drifts to that day at Dat Do.

Careful, Leo, careful.

I look at the trees first, the green shadows along the road, and then slowly, the poor old woman lying face down. I didn't give her a thought at the time, but now I see her arm is flung out and blood seeping through her embroidered blouse.

How brave she was. She knew we were walking into an ambush but still she tried to save the children. And the boy, the little boy who haunts me? Christ, there's nothing I can do to help you, kid.

I'm sorry, it's so *unfair*. You deserved a long, full life, not that grotesque, cruel ending, your poor mother bent over you in agony, wailing. I take a shuddering breath.

Okay, start again, Leo. In my mind I slowly re-enter the scene, carefully registering details I didn't notice before. This time seems a little easier than before.

I take some more deep breaths and watch the stars for a while, then try again. Yes, it is a little easier. At the end, does it — perhaps — feel less like *now*? In this place of solitude, is this awful scene turning into *then*? I shake my fuzzy head.

Oh kid, you poor little bugger, I won't forget you, I promise. But now I'm somewhere new and I need to be somewhere new and I *have* to let you fade away into the past.

I gaze at the last of the embers and take a deep breath. That feels almost okay. At least I'm not heaving, so maybe we're on a roll here. I laugh mirthlessly.

Somehow the dog has crept around and is now snuggled against my belly, so I caress her silky head. What do you reckon, little red girl? Will I check out the other memory, the one I *really* can't stomach?

I close my eyes. Come on then, Leo. Slowly, slowly.

And there we are. The hot night, the ornate salon, the good food and wine, Claire across from me, her face luminous in the candlelight, my green bangle on her arm. And a man beside her, a man she gazes at with desire.

My throat tightens and I gasp. Keep calm, Leo. Just feel it, feel that godawful moment I realise Claire wants someone else, someone who's not me. My throat clenches.

Okay, leave it, leave it. I take a drink of water from the canteen and lie back again. The stars are still there, as amazing as ever. I stroke the dog's warm neck. Try it again.

So I do. After a few goes, trying, failing, trying again: slowly, at last, I can feel it was *then*, not now. And *now* I've got to grow up and accept it. Okay. Claire wants someone else.

Simple enough, you fucking fool. My heart wrenches and the red dog briefly licks my hand. Then I think of Claire's eyes and forget myself as I'm flooded with anxiety, anxiety for *her*.

My love, care for any bastard you like, sleep with anyone you want, but just come home, come home *safely* from that insane, violent country. And I weep a little. Sorry, Simmo, do I undergo lacrimation? Whatever, it's okay.

Again I gaze at the swathe of stars above till my eyes start to close. The dog snuggles into me and I'm not sure anything in my life has ever felt so comforting.

I take a deep breath and fall asleep.

Next morning I get up, walk over to the creek and have a drink. It tastes stupidly good. I shake out the swag and roll it up. No snakes, no scorpions, and a calm, peaceful night.

Is *this* what 'country' is? Is this the place Jack has his responsibility for? I gaze at the garnet cliff, the shimmering water, the gemstone pebbles, the reeds like emerald brushstrokes.

Christ, it's perfect.

'Okay, dog,' I say. 'Show us the way back to camp.'

She gazes at me with her alert amber eyes. I say, 'What's your name then?' and she sits back on her trim haunches, ears pricked, her red coat lit up by her golden brows and muzzle.

For no reason I say, 'Maybe your name's Rusty, do you like that?' She comes over and rubs her head against my hand, then turns and starts to leave.

'Hey, Rusty, wait for me!' I say.

She looks back and wags her tail, and for the first time in years I feel as if I've done something right.

∽

Back at Reedy Creek all is good in the world: the stockman's arm is in plaster, the kids with ear-aches are looking a lot happier, and Evie Richardson is delivered of a crumple-faced baby she's nursing in the shade of the shed.

Simmo, Liam and Jack are sitting around a small campfire.

'Had a busy night, then, Simmo?' I say.

'Too right. Heard you were having a picnic out in the country.'

'Not quite a picnic. In fact I'm starving.'

'Here,' says Tender Jack, handing me a frying pan. 'Eggs.'

The eggs taste wonderful, and I slip Rusty a mouthful or two as well. 'That was a great place to spend the night, Jack. Thanks for taking me there.'

Jack nods. 'King Browns didn't bother you, then?'

'Ah, King Brown *snakes*?'

'They love the creek,' he says, nodding, then looks up and burst out laughing. 'Jeez, your face.'

'So, ah, there weren't any snakes, you're just joking?'

'Nah, young fella. Plenty. But the dog would have told you if any come near.'

'Glad she was there.' I clear my throat. 'Actually ... I was wondering if you'd sell her to me?'

Jack looks at me from under his eyebrows. 'What're you offering?'

I pull out my wallet, which has a lone twenty-dollar note. 'I've only got twenty on me, but can send you some more —'

'Nah, that's enough. You'll take care of her?'

'I will, I promise.' I pass the cash to Jack and rub Rusty's ears. 'Wanna come to Broome, girl?' She thumps her tail.

We make our way home in the Landrover with Rusty in the footwell, her head on my knee.

Simmo says, 'You got a hell of a bargain there — Liam said he was stunned Jack let her go. He can get fifty dollars easily for any of his bitch's pups, they're legendary working dogs.'

'But he said she was useless, he'd have to get rid of her. I thought she was going to be put down.'

Simmo smiles. 'Gullible bastard. You rocked up there looking so pathetic I reckon he thought you needed a friend.'

I laugh and stroke Rusty's head.

∽

Of course that's not the end of it, but it's the beginning of the end, the start of a slow healing. I have flashbacks and occasional nightmares, but now recover faster from them.

My concentration's not great, but Simmo is pushing me to get a part-time teaching job that's advertised at the local high school, and I'm starting to think it's within the bounds of possibility.

He and I are still what he calls hyper-vigilant. We discover this at the Roey one night when some fuckwit lets off a penny bunger. Simmo and I end up flat on the floor, protecting our heads, before the echoes have even stopped.

Rusty comes everywhere with me. She chases seabirds while I go surfing, then afterwards we run along the beach and I throw things for her to catch. She's got a lot of energy but sometimes I wonder if she really has that obsessive herding instinct a cattle dog needs: it's not very obvious.

That makes me smile. Was Jack more canny — to both our benefits — than I imagined?

But weirdly, as I slowly find myself on more stable ground, I become less sure how Simmo's going. He's doing long hours at the clinic and outback, and hasn't been surfing much lately. I go to his place one evening and insist he comes to the pub.

'You're looking like something the cat dragged in,' I say, plonking down a couple of schooners. He seems thinner, and pale under his Broome tan. 'Working too hard?'

He shrugs. 'Nah, all good.'

There's a silence.

'Simmo? Hey. You okay?'

He shakes his head and looks away, then says, 'Remember we talked about triggers? Reckon mine's found me.'

'Have you been ...?'

'Yeah, same crap.' He takes a drink. 'I told you about it once. The boot with a foot inside it? Keep seeing fucking boots.'

'Council workers got to have *something* on their feet, mate.'

Simmo laughs a little. 'Bastard.'

'So, we got emesis, stasis and lacrimation?'

'Christ, you telling me you actually *learnt* something, Leo?'

'Don't change the subject.'

After a time he says, 'Yeah. All that. Anger too, irritated about everything. Hey, how come it never hit you like that?'

'Think I was a bit flattened with the malaria. Of course I got cranky, but not over the top.'

Simmo takes a long drink of his beer and empties the glass. 'Okay, enough of that. Let's talk about something more interesting. The beer tastes pretty good tonight. I'll get another round.'

When he comes back with the drinks he says, 'Was out at Reedy Creek last weekend. Tender Jack sends his regards, and says he'll have your guts for garters if you're not looking after Rusty.'

I laugh and Rusty, at my feet, thumps her tail. 'She's good. Look at that glossy coat.'

Simmo leans down and strokes her, then straightens up and takes a long drink. 'Hear anything much from Michelle?'

'Nah. One postcard, that was it. Guess the guy with the fat tummy won her heart. You still happy living in the hippie house?'

'Yeah,' he says, after another long drink. 'People come and go. Lots of good music on the record player. Hey, you slacker, it's your round now.'

'Already? Jeez, let me just finish this one.' I get us more beers. Funny, Simmo doesn't usually drink this much, or this fast. Still, if he's feeling low it makes sense.

Back at our table a couple of hippies from Simmo's place are standing there, one I haven't seen before, so I say hello. The new guy, Roy, is good-looking in a thuggish sort of way, blond curls to his shoulders, lot of beads.

I offer to get them drinks but Roy says, 'Nah, man, we're just here to score.' They wander over to one of the town dealers in the corner, chat for a bit, make a transaction, then go. Simmo is staring at his drink, and I realise he didn't seem very friendly to the new guy.

'Not your best mate, then, that Roy?'

'We had an argument earlier.' He drains his glass and takes a deep breath. 'Hey, Leo, my car's stuffed. Drive me over to Cable Beach, will you? Feel like a swim.'

'Surf was pretty high today, bad weather off the coast. Let's go for a drive, but better not go in the water.'

'Okay.'

At the long wide beach the surf is loud and fierce, and broken clouds are flying across the bright moon. The beach is pale, then suddenly dark, then light again in patches.

'What a night,' says Simmo, getting out. 'Come on, let's have a paddle, if nothing else.' He starts down to the beach below before I can even get Rusty out and go after him.

'Wait *on*, Simmo,' I say, but he's ahead of me and almost at the waterline. The waves are crashing and they're a lot higher than they were this morning.

'Simmo, you stupid *bastard*!'

He turns back to me. 'I'm just paddling, Leo, for fuck's sake.'

He holds out his arms and takes long, exaggerated steps in the shallows, as breakers thunder and collapse behind him. The idiot's totally pissed. Rusty starts barking, nipping at his heels, and for the first time she's become all working dog, trying to get him to move away from the water.

The light from the moon is coming and going and suddenly Simmo's not there. I stare and then, heart pounding, I see him further out.

He yells, 'Going for a swim now. Bye, Leo.'

I splash into the water and reach him and grab his arm. 'Come on, this is no place —'

Then the sandbank collapses beneath us and we're both neck-deep in a swirling rip that's dragging us away from the beach. And Rusty is yelping in terror.

'Swim *across* the rip!' I yell, pulling Simmo's arm.

He struggles and gets away. 'Just let me *go*!'

I grab him and clout him across the ear. 'You *fucker*,' I scream. 'Rusty's *drowning!*'

I drag him again and he follows me as we try to swim across the wavefront, to find where the undertow eases off and we can get ashore. A horrible, choking, exhausting time later we collapse on the sand. Simmo lies there, gasping.

Rusty's yelps have stopped.

I get up and stumble and call her but she doesn't come. I start sobbing her name, then fall on my knees and howl in agony because all I can hear are the breakers, crashing over and over.

Time stops.

I'm cold and wet and can't move because I've never been in so much pain in my life. I hear Simmo calling, 'Leo?' against the roaring of the sea. Fucking, *fucking* Simmo. I hate him so much I can't even lift my head.

Then someone whimpers against my ear. And licks it.

I sit up, staring, and throw my arms around a sodden, ecstatic dog, and cry like a baby.

∼

I drive us to my parents' house. They're asleep but they're used to me coming back late and won't wake up. I throw some dry trackies at Simmo, rub Rusty with a towel, and get into some fresh clothes. I put the kettle on and make coffee, and give Rusty a nice bone.

I sit across the table from Simmo under the harsh kitchen light, holding my coffee-cup for warmth. My teeth are clenched with fury and anguish.

'I'm sorry, man,' whispers Simmo. 'I'd never want to hurt you or Rusty.'

'Funny way to show it, you prick.' I put down my coffee cup.

'Just wanted to die, Leo. That's all.'

'Well, maybe next time go slash your bloody wrists in privacy.'

There's a silence. Rusty nudges my leg and leans her head on my thigh. I stroke the velvet fur beneath her jaw and take a deep, shuddering breath.

'She's all I've got, Simmo. How could you be so *stupid*?'

He shakes his head in misery. 'Just wanted to die.'

'You spend a year dodging death some place *everyone* is trying to kill you, and *now* you want to die?' I laugh harshly and cover my face with my hands.

More silence. Simmo clears his throat. 'Leo ... look, mate, there's something I never told you. Couldn't tell you. But ... I'm queer. Don't fit in anywhere.'

'Yeah. You're certainly one of a kind, Simmo.'

'I'm a *poof*, you fucking drongo!'

I look up. 'Jeez, of course I bloody knew that. The Singapore disaster, the pretty thug Roy. Must have been quite some argument you guys had. Afterwards, at least.'

Simmo says sadly, 'He wanted money for dope and hit me till he got it. But I can't *cope* any more. Pretending at school, hiding away in the army, always despised, rejected, beaten up. What chance at a real life do I have?'

I gaze at him, exasperated. 'Well if Claire's mothers had said that, you fucking idiot, she'd never even *be* here. So I reckon there are possibilities you mightn't have yet considered.'

There's a stunned silence.

'What, Claire's got *two* mothers?'

'Yeah. And her father was a flaming queen. So Simmo, you need to find out a bit more about the world before you try to top yourself *and* take my amazing dog along with you.'

Simmo blinks and sips his coffee. 'Really? Wow.'

'Yup. Wow.'

After a while he says, 'You know — your Rusty was after me like a top working bitch. If I was a cow she'd have had me out of that water in two seconds flat.'

'If you were a cow, mate, you'd have had enough bloody brains to not go in.'

After a time he sighs. 'What'll I do, Leo?'

'Dunno. But you could try asking Tender Jack. And pack a couple of sandwiches.'

I apply for that part-time job teaching English at the local high school and get it. I'm scared going into the first class I'm taking, but then I gaze around at the room of twelve-year-old kids.

Half of them seem to be part-Asian or Aboriginal and I'm reminded of the beautiful eyes and mischievous grins of the kids I taught in Vietnam and the small differences I made in their lives, and after that I'm not scared.

In September Mum passes on the news that Pete and Charlotte have left Vietnam and are now living in Perth. I hope Claire is okay in Saigon, but then she's got handsome Uncle Ho by her side, so I suppose she'll be fine.

I apply for a full-time opening at the school and get it. I like the other teachers, a different bunch from my surfie mates, and start to feel more and more anchored in Broome.

Simmo is fed up with the hippie den and comes to live at the house I'm sharing with my parents, which is pretty useful because they're talking now about going back to Newcastle next March — and I've decided I want to stay here.

At Christmas I send Claire a card, saying:

If you ever feel like visiting the Garden of Eden, you'd be welcome to drop into Broome. I've taken a job teaching English at the local high school and the kids are great. I'm a lot better than I used to be — got a dog called Rusty now and she's had a lot to do with that. But I'd like to have a chance to apologise to you for being such a self-centred fool in Vietnam. I didn't appreciate for a moment how everything was going for you, Claire, and I'm sorry. I wish I'd done better. Leo.

She doesn't reply.

22. JEN: BACK TO THE GARDEN (OCTOBER 1969-JULY 1970)

I've loved Tibor Adler since I was six years old. But at eighteen I stop. The occasion is his wedding to Ursula in October 1969. In his morning suit Tibor is as handsome as ever, although his smile may be a little desperate. His best man is a complete stranger to me, and so are the three bridesmaids, who are wearing an unflattering shade of pink.

Still, Ursula's dark hair is dotted with flowers and her long-sleeved empire-line dress is a haze of creamy lace. Billie, beside me, nods with respect. (I don't look at the bride's shoes: who needs that kind of grief?)

Ash sits on my other side, and beyond him are his parents and Devorah. They are all carefully expressionless, but Ash's hands are tense. Ursula had insisted the marriage take place in a Catholic church and spineless Tibor acquiesced. Yet despite this concession, the bride's parents and relatives still look pretty miserable.

At the reception I sit with Dev, Rob and Ash. 'What would a Jewish wedding be like, then?' I say. 'I've never been to one.'

'Well, it's *happy*, for a start,' says Dev, biting viciously into a bread roll. 'And the food is a million times better.'

'Dev took me to one,' says Rob. 'It was great. There were candles, and a sort of a tent, and the groom broke a *glass* with his foot.'

'And thus are centuries of spiritual tradition rendered into the Bugs Bunny version,' says Ash, as he eats. 'This food is truly disgusting.'

I glance at his head. 'You're wearing a kippah today,' I say. 'I've never seen you in one before.'

'Solidarity with my parents,' he says. 'This is really hard for them.'

Moshe and Ilona are at a nearby table, gazing stony-faced at nothing. Billie, Nikos and Tina are with them too, but no one's saying anything much. (My parents and Leo are still away in Broome of course, when they *promised* me they'd come home in six months).

'Mum was crying this morning,' says Dev quietly. 'It was awful.'

'Tibor didn't have to do it like this, the bastard,' says Ash. 'There could have been a compromise, maybe a secular ceremony, but Ursula insisted it be held in a church. She's not even Catholic, she just fancies the stained glass.'

Dev says thoughtfully, 'What *is* it with that guy being tortured to death, anyway?'

'What?' I say.

'You know, on a cross. What a weird symbol for something supposed to be hopeful.'

I laugh. 'No one ever thinks about it much, they just follow it.'

'Good old Christianity in a nutshell,' says Ash. 'Hey, Jen. We're painting placards this week for next Saturday's demo. Want to come over and help?'

'Not sure. Got an essay to write and exams are coming up.'

'We're a bit short-handed. Genevieve's away and so is Paul.'

'Where've they gone?'

'Some music festival up north.' For a moment he's as stony-faced as his father, and I wonder what's happened now with the fickle Genevieve.

'Okay, maybe.'

There's a ding-ding-ding to attract everyone's attention. The best man gets up and says something, chortling, but we're too far away to hear properly. Tibor says something, abashed. Ursula's father says something, grumpily.

Wow, Tibor, I think. You're not going to be made very welcome in *that* clan, yet look at the damage you've left behind in your wake.

Can you stop loving someone forever because they've chosen to hurt their own family?

Because I did.

⁓

'Hey, they look *great*!' I say, as we prop the placards against a wall and stand back to admire them.

Ash nods. 'Thanks, Jen. But I'm pissed off no one else helped.'

'Losing interest?'

'Probably same as you, exams coming up. Anyway, in the US they haven't lost interest. Did you hear about the Moratorium?'

'Sounds a bit creepy. Is that like a crematorium?'

Ash laughs. 'I think it's some legal term for not doing stuff for a while. Anyway, more than a half a million people turned up last week to protest beneath that banner. Nixon claims it didn't bother him, but he's probably lying.'

'Were his lips moving?' I say. 'Okay, he's lying.'

'Come on, let's eat, I owe you. Chinese?'

'My hero.'

We cross Glebe Point Road and share chicken with cashews and black-bean beef. It's fantastic. As we eat I say, 'We just heard the most amazing thing in a lecture. Remember when Leo thought he was going to be based in the jungle in Vietnam?'

'Yeah. Did all those training courses.'

'Well, he wrote to me at the time, all surprised because the countryside was so open, with bamboos and lines of trees and green fields, and pink and purple flowers around the towns. It sounded lovely.'

Ash laughs. 'Poetry from Leo? Wow. So?'

'Well, thank *heavens* he wasn't in the jungle! Turns out the Americans have been dropping herbicide on it for years. Not just the jungle either — mangroves, forests, fields, *everything.* They've poisoned thousands of square miles, and even worse, at *twenty* times the proper concentration.'

'Mmm. It's the Yanks, what do you expect?'

'But this stuff doesn't just kill plants, it hurts people and animals, and hangs around forever. Anyway, our lecturer said a new international crime has been proposed, *ecocide*, the murder of ecosystems. But he wasn't very hopeful it'd be taken seriously.'

'Good thing old Leo managed to avoid it, then.'

'But it's wrong, Ash! It's all just so *wrong*!'

I'm surprised he isn't as indignant as me but then, I guess he isn't much into nature.

He pours us more jasmine tea and says, 'Did I tell you about Dave?'

'Um, baked that yummy bread one day?'

'Yeah. Well, he's decided to join a Buddhist monastery.'

'Seriously? A monastery?'

'Apparently.'

'So you'll need someone to take his room?'

Ash nods. 'Hard at this time of year too. After the exams a lot of students go back to their parents' places till March.'

'Ha! I *wish*. My parents are still on the other side of the country.'

'Aren't you happy living at Tina's?'

'Love it. But something weird has happened. You know how Vivy discovered your Dad's friend László a few months ago?'

'Yeah. Gave Dad a new lease on life, at least until the wedding. *Bloody* Tibor.'

I say primly, 'Ash, I believe the correct term is *fucking* Tibor.'

He grins. 'I see I've taught you well. Anyway, Dad was so happy for a time, letters back and forth, but after the wedding things are a bit sad again. What's that got to do with Tina?'

'László wrote to her too. She cried and said it was an apology, as well as a greeting to Róbert. She wrote back, then got *another* letter, and she's been in a bit of a daze ever since.'

'So?'

'So now she's collecting travel brochures. *Europe in Winter, Enjoy France, Visit the Normandy Coast*. The school holidays will be on soon, December and January, and that's winter in Europe. I reckon she's planning to take Rob to meet László.'

Ash sits back. 'Wow.'

'Do you think it'll be all right? I mean, László left her all those years ago. Maybe he won't really want to see her now.'

Ash shakes his head slowly. 'Sounds like the second letter could have been an invitation. But what *I* don't understand is why he didn't come back here once Jimmy Kelso was dead.'

'László lost his family in the war, and Tina told me he couldn't face caring for anyone again, especially not a child. But time has passed and I suppose he feels brave enough now. And perhaps he and Tina will fall in *love* —'

Ash rolls his eyes. 'Perhaps they'd only want to be friends.'

'You total bore. How unromantic of you.'

'You say that as if you're surprised, Jen.'

'Oh, all right, Mr Sensible. So how's dear Genevieve going?'

He shrugs. 'Got a postcard from some place called Nimbin. She plans to stay. Apparently the Tarot cards said she should.'

I laugh. '*Honestly*?'

'Honestly.'

'Are you — I don't know — okay?'

'Yeah. It's cool.'

I glance at Ash. Everything about him is cool. His prison-short hair is grown out, curling around his ears. His glasses are surprisingly trendy and his hippie clothes are fashionable now. Don't suppose he'll have any problem replacing Genevieve.

∽

November comes, and — story of my life — I have to sit bloody *exams*. But at least this year I've enjoyed most of my courses. So study is more a process of reducing what I know to lists and summaries, then summarising the summaries, then learning the final few pages off by heart.

It works, and I do well. I write to Mum and Dad and get lots of congratulations in return, though I still wish they were here. Christmas is coming up and for the first time ever they won't be at Billie and Nikos's house for the annual party.

They said they were going away for six months, and now it's been nine, and Mum writes they'll probably be home next March. A whole *year*? Apparently Leo is fine and has even got a dog now. Good for him. What about me?

Then I feel ashamed. Poor old Leo nearly died and now he's better. And I've had a lot more independence at eighteen than if Dad was still around. So good for Broome too, I guess.

The Christmas party is great and the Adlers are happy. I think they've decided having László emerge from his self-imposed exile and Asher out of gaol is enough to offset Tibor's unkindness (he and Ursula were invited but don't appear).

We catch up with everyone's news. In January Billie and Nikos are sailing their yacht to Queensland. I can't understand their obsession with the wild ocean waves, but I expect they'll have a good time.

Klara and Yvonne are unusually sombre. They're worried because my Uncle Pete and Aunt Charlotte have left Vietnam, and Claire is alone in Saigon. But after two years over there you'd have to expect capable Claire can look after herself.

The big news, of course, is that Tina and Rob are off to France — and László — in a few days. Tina is in a complete tizzy and quite unable to come to grips with anything.

'We'll only be away for four weeks,' she says. 'You'll be fine here. Won't you? Or what about staying with the Adlers?'

'Tina, it's all *right*. I'm going to live in Glebe at Ash's house. I'm there half the time anyway, and they need someone to make up the rent because Dave's gone to a monastery.'

'Oh,' she says in relief. '*Wonderful*. Now where have I put my winter coat?'

◦◦◦

Tina and Rob leave, and I move to Ash's place on New Year's Day. Luckily I've got the money to pay the rent, from my scholarship and a small bequest from my grandmother Jessie, so I don't even have to mention it to my parents.

I love the old house on Glebe Point Road. It's a terrace with a small grassy yard, neglected for years. The woodwork is peeling, the plaster crumbling and the iron lace rusting.

The big front room has a bay window, and opens to a second large room. Behind that, a bedroom, kitchen, bathroom, and tiny paved yard. Half-way up the stairs, another bathroom (civilisation!), then at the top a small room that was once Dave's and is now mine.

At the front are two larger rooms, one belonging to a pair of friendly women with short hair, the other Ash's. His looks out onto Glebe Point Road and has an old fireplace and a pretty iron-lace balcony.

There's almost always music on the record player, echoing down the hall. Jimi Hendrix, Cat Stevens, Bob Dylan, Joan Baez, Santana, Rolling Stones, Beatles, Procol Harum, Joni Mitchell, the Moody Blues. Nobody cares what's playing, it's just mesmerising, amazing music.

I adore the Moody Blues song, *Nights in White Satin*, and Ash gets plenty of teasing (and not just from me) when he buys some sheets from a charity shop: a pristine set in purple satin.

'They'll be comfortable,' he says defensively.

'*Nights in purple satin*,' I hum. 'Doesn't *quite* have that vibe —'

Ash laughs and throws them at me.

People come by, nice people, who sit around and cook food and smoke dope, and crash in the front room, which has a couch, a mattress, and a couple of sleeping bags. There are always cool ideas and conversation and unexpected things happening all around us. How I love the house on Glebe Point Road.

∽

Since he left gaol, Ash has been doing some tutoring at the uni, though he didn't enrol in a higher degree course. One muggy summer evening not long after I move in, we sit on a rug in the front yard eating slices of orange.

'So what are you going to *do* this year, Ash?' I say, putting a chunk of skin on the plate and taking another sweet segment.

'Mmm,' says Ash. 'Good.'

I wait. After a time he says, 'There's a possibility ...'

'Uh-huh?'

'A possibility of a maths post-grad in a field I really want to study.'

'Fantastic. Will you start this year?'

'Hope to. Problem is, the position isn't here in Sydney.'

'So where?'

'Um. Amsterdam.'

'Amsterdam? But isn't that in ...?'

'Holland. Yes.'

'*This* year?'

'Yes.'

'But — when would you start?'

'March.'

The traffic on Glebe Point Road passes by with the usual hum, and the street lights still shine above us, but the world has, impossibly, changed.

'Less than *two months*?'

'Yes.'

'You didn't tell me before.'

'I didn't have confirmation before.'

'You should have *told* me.'

'We're not —'

'No, we're not. Not like you and Genevieve. But we're *still* —'

'I know. We're still — something. I'm sorry, Jen.'

The window to the big front room is open and someone in the house puts *Nights in White Satin* on the record player. The first few chords — hovering, promising, crystalline — stab my heart and I put my hand over my eyes.

'*Jen*. Come on, we were never more than friends.'

'That's bullshit, Ash. We were *always* more than friends.'

‿

Late that night, when the house is sleeping, I go to Ash's room. I don't knock, but quietly enter.

The light from the streetlamps shows me he's asleep, breathing softly, his dark hair against the pillow, his bare shoulders above the sheet. I take off my nightie and get into bed beside him.

He murmurs in pleasure as I press myself against his back, and turns towards me, stroking my hair and pulling me close. We breathe together for a time, then I whisper, 'Ash?'

He comes slowly awake. '*Jen* ...?'

'Me.'

'Uh ... why?'

'It's the right time, Ash, and you're the right person.'

'But I'm leaving.'

'I don't care. I want this now. I know you'll soon be far away, but it doesn't matter. This is *now*.'

He gazes at me in consternation, but as heat flows between us his face softens. 'Jen. Really?'

'Really.' I stroke his cheek. 'A night in purple satin is just what I need.'

He smiles and presses closer to me. 'Um, Jen?'

'Yes, you idiot. I'm on the pill. *Yes.*'

He laughs softly and kisses me, which I like a lot. And what follows is interesting and not unexpected and rather pleasant, if a little sweaty and noisy (not on my behalf) towards the end.

So that's the big moment, then.

Ash seems more overcome than me: in fact he's practically unconscious afterwards. I snuggle against him and when he recovers he moulds himself around me, falls asleep, and the rest of the night passes peacefully.

He's a bit of a bore next morning, all anxiety and self-recrimination, but I do what I did with my hands last night, and he quickly shuts up. I can't say I encounter the ecstasy that's supposed to overtake a woman during the grand event, but it's still pretty nice. I'm sure I'll get there in the end.

After a while Ash stops the self-recrimination and we spend a fair bit of time in bed. I'm getting better at sex, but sometimes I wonder if, I don't know … if I could go on top it might feel nicer?

When I was younger I experimented a little (and no, I'm not providing any details) and discovered I could bring about a burst of nice sensations, which I assume is the big deal with sex.

But somehow it's hard to find the same delight with someone squishing me flat. I mention it once to Ash, but he's puzzled and can't see the point of a different position. So that's that.

∽

At the end of January Tina and Rob come home. I go to their house to welcome them back, and I've never seen Tina like this before. I realise what people mean when they say someone is glowing.

'Well, what happened?' I ask Rob while Tina's in the kitchen.

'It was crazy nice,' he says. 'France is great, can't even explain how good the *cakes* are—'

'Not the cakes. Your Mum? László?'

'They went out a lot.' He grins. 'And sometimes didn't come back till next day. I just stayed with Vivy and Brian, who are fantastic and live by the sea, though it was too cold to go swimming. And their baby's only a year old and said my *name*. Or maybe she burped.'

'Did you like him — László?'

Rob nods. 'He's nice, Jen, really nice. And you know something? He smokes these little dark cigarillos, and I seem to almost remember the smell.'

'But how old were you when he left?'

'A few months, Mum says. But I *do* remember, I'm sure I do.'

'Rob, how fantastic. And now what's going to happen?'

'Dunno. Maybe he's going to come over here for a holiday. Mum keeps saying, we'll see, which can mean *anything* as far as she's concerned.'

Tina comes in and I say, 'Sounds like it was a pretty good holiday.' She smiles. 'Yes.'

'And is László coming out here?'

'We'll see,' she says. 'Now, have you packed your things at Glebe, Jen? I can come and pick you up so you don't have to carry them on the bus.'

'Well, I've kind of settled in there, and if I go now they'll be stuck for rent. So I'm thinking I'll stay there till uni starts again in March.' I hesitate. 'And Ash is going away to study then, so maybe that's the best time ...'

'Where's Ash going?' says Rob.

'Amsterdam. Holland.'

'The real name for that country is the Netherlands, Jen,' says Rob.

Tina gazes at me. 'You *have* asked your parents about this?'

'Actually, no.' I meet her eyes. 'Tina, I'll be nineteen in a month. Probably it's time I start making decisions like this for myself now.'

'Nineteen? Heavens, seems just like yesterday you were born.' She smiles. 'Well, you can be the one to tell Harry, not sure I'm up to it.' She leans forward. 'But Jen, if you need something or anything goes wrong, just call me. Promise?'

'Thanks, Tina. Promise.'

∞

The guy who lives in the downstairs bedroom is Russ, long-haired and moustached. He's nice but a bit weird. His room is dark, with velvet curtains, and he's into meditation, the I Ching and the Tarot.

A couple of months ago Russ had a Grand Idea. Among the multitude of classified ads in the newspaper he noticed a snippet offering fifty acres for sale near Wollombi, in the bush about forty miles west of Newcastle. The price is low, $5,000. What about getting together a group of people to buy it?

Go back to the land, build a mud-brick house, commune with nature? It's a seriously Interesting Idea, and a few of the people who live or crash at Glebe Point Road are seriously interested.

Parents are consulted, some of whom are lawyers. Between say, six people, the cost wouldn't be onerous. The lawyers nod and the deeds are signed.

I'm just an onlooker, but I go with Russ and the others in his Kombi van to see the property. It's some farmer's failed dream: hilly bushland, ragged pasture rising to a flat section with the foundations of a long-gone cottage, the perfect site for the proposed mud-brick house. There's a creek lined with casuarina trees — sheoaks — so the place has been called Sheoaks since it was settled.

Ash hates it. 'Total, self-indulgent wankery,' is the most polite of his opinions. 'Back to the *land*? The bloody land that some poor farmer, with a lot more experience than any of you dreamers, couldn't work? Sheer fantasy.'

'It's not me, Ash. I'm not an owner. But I think it's a nice idea. And they're not trying to run cattle. Maybe build a house, plant some trees, grow vegetables.'

'Fucking madness, if you ask me.'

'I'm not sure anyone is.' I turn over in bed, away from him. 'How's the packing going?'

'I'm not leaving for weeks yet. Not much to do anyway.'

'How's your mum coping?'

'She's fine. She and Dad'll visit me. They've got friends there.'

There's a silence.

'Jen? I've scored some LSD. You want to take it with me this weekend?'

I turn back to him. '*LSD*? Really?'

'Yeah. I've tripped a couple of times before. It's amazing.'

'With Genevieve?'

'Um, yeah. And with Dave too.'

'Probably why he fled to a monastery.'

'He didn't *flee*. Seriously, it's an incredible experience. Builds bonds between people too, unbreakable bonds.'

'Bonds stretching all the way from Sydney to Amsterdam?'

He laughs. 'Maybe.' After a time he says, 'What do you think?'

∽

I'm not a fool. I've read what the naysayers claim and the enthusiasts proclaim. It's pretty clear LSD isn't the gateway to Hell nor the gateway to Heaven. It's just something that sparks a chemical cascade in the brain and causes euphoria and beautiful hallucinations.

Sounds good to me. And perhaps, perhaps, a lasting bond with elusive Ash?

Next Saturday we go over to Balmain, to Elkington Park. The land slopes down to the water, with massive old trees, a rotunda in the middle, and the blue harbour beyond.

Russ has kindly come along as a psychedelic guide. Ash and I each chew a tiny piece of blotting paper, and lie back on the grass and wait beneath the trees. It's a beautiful day. Warm, a little cloudy, a little sunny. Kids are playing on the monkey-bars further down the park. Time passes and nothing happens.

'Are you sure this is the real thing?' I ask Ash.

'Supposed to be.'

Russ says, 'It takes about three-quarters of an hour to kick in. Relax, guys. Everything's cool.' He crosses his legs, closes his eyes, and murmurs 'Om' to himself. Funny, though, after a while it's not to himself. The sound seems to ripple out and through the park. The leaves in the trees above seem to echo it as well.

'That's nice,' I say to Ash.

'The seagulls? Yeah, they're amazing.'

A croaking sound mingles with the Om, and I notice we've got a couple of seagulls edging speculatively around us. 'Hi,' I say. One flutters her wings. Her eyes are piercing, magnificent.

'I haven't got any food for you,' I say, desolate. The seagull leaves.

Ash sits up. 'Come for a walk, Jen? I want to see the rotunda.'

I get up and follow him along the path, then stop. 'Ash? *Look.* Every square of concrete. The patterns. Like Turkish tiles. I've never seen such *patterns.* And they're there, all this time, and I've never even seen them before.'

Ash stares at the path. 'Mm. There's a face in that one. Let's keep going.'

'A *face?*'

He nods. 'A sort of cranky face.'

'Oh, okay.'

The rotunda is nice. Brick columns, a sturdy roof above. The bricks are amazingly red and gold and orange and brown, and they *ripple.* And now, wherever we look, everything we see and touch and hear, layer upon layer, is mesmerising.

The trees are especially beautiful. Russ says the big ones are called Moreton Bay figs. They have roots buttressed like small mountains, and their canopies glitter like crystals of sage and olive.

Near the water are the sheoaks, their elegant needles fluttering in the breeze. Palms are dotted like exclamation points along the pathways, and best of all, if you look *very* closely at the grass, every sweet-scented blade seems to radiate courage and hope.

At one stage, Russ says, 'So are you guys in love, then?'

I say, 'No,' and, lying beside me, Ash says, 'Just friends.'

After that I move between parts of myself, one absorbed in the light and colours, another intrigued by that absorption, another contemplating my words and Ash's.

I walk around again and see the face in the concrete path too, and it *is* cranky, so I ignore it. When I lie down on the grass, there's a great onion dome above of pale lines criss-crossing in the sky.

After a while my mind empties and I feel nothing but contentment, then I seem to become that contentment. I don't recall much beyond that.

The lovely day eases into a soft evening and the shadows deepen beneath the trees. Russ says, 'Guys, think I'll drive you home now. Things to do. You'll be fine.'

He drops us at Glebe Point Road and he's correct. We're fine. We go into the kitchen and, although we're not very hungry, everything we eat is divine.

And upstairs in bed we gaze into each other's lucent eyes, and graze skin upon skin, and taste each other's hair and inhale scents that put perfumes to shame and intermingle our limbs like dancing, laughing gods.

Slowly, we come to rest. Above us the ceiling displays its ancient, intricate patterns, the archetypes of beauty that have been here with us forever, and all we had to do was look.

And when we close our eyes in the dark the patterns are still there, lining our eyelids with glory.

∽

The day arrives. Ash has left most of his things at his parents' place, and only has a suitcase and backpack to take on the plane. I sit on the side of the bed, my throat spiky with pain.

'Well,' he says. 'Better get moving, Jen. The cab'll be here in five minutes. And I'll pay for the return trip from the airport ...'

'No need. I'm not coming to the airport.'

'What? But my family'll be there.'

His puzzled eyes are like brown velvet beneath the charcoal sweep of his brows.

'Then that's all you need. Not me, Ash.'

He sits and takes my hand. 'I wish ... I'm sorry, Jen. Look, remember that day in the park? Of course we're much more than friends.'

'I know.' I hug him and his hair smells like everything I've ever wanted in my whole life.

'Hey, it's only three years. I'll be back before you know it.'

I laugh quietly. 'I won't be here.'

'Where will you be?'

'Don't know. London? Amsterdam? Glebe?'

A car horn toots outside and he stands up.

'That'll be the taxi. See you later, Jen.' He kisses me briefly and leaves.

It's as if some great circuit that connects me to the world has suddenly gone dark.

∽

After Ash leaves for Amsterdam I don't return to Tina's, but stay on at the Glebe house. I still like living there and in any case it's convenient to uni and my second year has begun. Mum and Dad return (at long bloody last) from Broome, although Leo is staying behind because of his dog or his job. Or something.

I go to see my parents in early April, during the Easter break. I don't feel my usual pleasure at the train trip and I'm also not looking forward to telling Dad I've moved out of Tina's. It's not as if he's got to pay the rent! Still, he can be unreasonably difficult sometimes.

During the latter part of the trip, as the long blue Watagan range lines the western horizon, I think about Sheoaks lying just beyond the mountains. The six purchasers of the land are already arguing about their future direction.

Russ and his new girlfriend (Karen) want to immediately start a mud-brick production line. The two women in the upstairs bedroom (Janice and Vicki) prefer to wait for guidance from the spirit of the land, and the couple who took over Ash's room (Mick and Marilyn) think a small for-profit camping site could pay off the loan faster.

Meals at the house are becoming increasingly fractious, although still I love it: the music at all hours, the occasional dope, the hippie friends who use the front bay window as a doorway and are always welcome to crash overnight. It's cool, man, everyone says, and it really is.

At Newcastle station I see the small, trim figure of Mum waiting for me. Suddenly I'm so overwhelmingly *glad* to see her, my long sooky sulk at her absence just evaporates.

'You're so brown,' I squeal, hugging her. 'Oh, *Mum*! Did you have a good time?'

She laughs and leads me out to the car. 'Amazing, love. I'll show you the photos. But it was time to come back. The summers are brutal, almost more than Dad could take.'

As we drive to our house she glances at me. 'But how are *you*, darling girl? You're a bit pale.'

I shrug. 'Hey, everyone's going to look pale to someone with such a great tan.'

We pull up and get inside and I can't believe the change in Dad either. He's brown too, and the worry lines on his face are almost gone. He gives me a big hug and dances me around the room.

'Daa-ad!' I wail. 'You're so *embarrassing.*' We laugh and sit down to drink tea and catch up. Finally we get to the bit I've been dreading.

Dad says, 'How did you go, Jenny, living by yourself while Tina and Rob were away?'

'Um, well, I stayed somewhere else. You know that house in Glebe, the one Ash was sharing with some friends?'

'Glebe?' says Dad, frowning a little.

'I had a little room at the back of the house. Very nice people. Responsible too. Some of them have just bought a farm near Wollombi.' (I have no idea why I think this is somehow reassuring.) 'And, actually — I decided to stay there, even after Tina came back.'

'In Glebe, you say?' says Dad.

I nod, and get a piece of paper out of my pocket. 'This is the address. They don't have a telephone installed but I still see Tina pretty often, so ...'

Dad says, 'Isn't that just near the university?'

'Only five minutes on the bus. I walk too, when the weather's ...' I trail off, bracing myself.

'Well, Glebe sounds extremely convenient,' Dad says. 'And, love, if you need help with the rent, just say. Next time we're in Sydney we can drop by and meet your friends. Farmers, eh?'

'*Wonderful.* Yes.'

(I hope they tell me before they turn up: the dope paraphernalia and some *very* weird posters will need to go in a cupboard.)

∽

Later, just as I'm about to turn off my bedside light and go to sleep, Mum taps on the door, comes in and sits on my bed.

'Are you all right, really, Jen?'

I nod without looking at her. 'Mmm.'

'What about Ash going away so suddenly? I expect that was a bit of a shock.'

I nod. My throat hurts.

'Three years isn't that long,' she says gently.

Suddenly I can't stop myself. 'Yes it *is*. But anyway, we're just friends. Ash has *lots* of friends.'

'None are like you, love.'

'No. Whoever they are, they're prettier than me, and sexier than me, and *way* more interesting than me. And they might be with him in Amsterdam, and I'll be *here* ...'

Misery overwhelms me and I start sobbing. Mum puts her arms around me and murmurs. Eventually I recover enough to grab a tissue and mop my face, and sit back with a deep sigh.

'And don't tell me we're both young. I *know* we are. And maybe I won't even care about him one day and I'll meet someone else and it won't matter. But it matters now. Everything's gone dark and nothing makes me happy any more.'

Mum nods.

I look at her in despair. 'Isn't there anything you can say that makes me feel better?'

She smiles and slowly shakes her head. 'No. It's awful, that's all. I'm sorry, love.'

'Really?'

'You already know what you need, Jen. Of course you're heartbroken, and of course, one day, you'll get over it. But for now you've got to enjoy what you can, and wait for the dark to lift. And it *will*, I promise.'

I hug her again and she's so lovely, with her familiar scent and gentle voice and comforting arms. 'Oh, Mum, I'm so *glad* you're home.'

⌑

I try to enjoy what I can. The house is a constant pleasure of course, and the bickering among the 'farmers' of Sheoaks becomes almost amusing. I tease them by drawling, 'Hey, peace and love, man, peace and love,' whenever they start arguing. Slowly cooperation grows.

Once Janice and Vicki feel they've consulted the spirit of the land enough, Russ's mud-brick production line, the winning idea, begins.

Most weekends they take friends to Sheoaks and start the slow process of creating enough bricks to build the house whose plans they draw and re-draw at the kitchen table. It's a creative time.

Still, none of us turn away from what's happening in the world, and suddenly an awful lot is.

For someone who spends so much time meditating Russ is deeply interested in politics, and has been arrested at demos nearly as often as Ash. In late April, Russ marches into the kitchen and throws the paper onto the table in front of me.

'Hey, fucking *Nixon* says he's withdrawing 150,000 troops from Vietnam over the next year. I'll believe it when I see it.'

I say, 'I just heard some politician on the radio announce the same thing. Australia won't send any more new troops over there when the previous ones come home.'

'Craven lapdog government,' says Russ.

I nod. 'Finally seeing sense? Amazing.'

And of course it's too good to be true.

Barely a week later Russ comes home again, almost speechless in horror. 'Look!' he says, pushing the paper towards me. 'I can't, just fucking *can't* ...'

'The Cambodian *Incursion*?' I read. 'What? Why?'

'Bastard Nixon's desperate for a victory before getting out of Vietnam, so he's going to fuck the Cambodians over now.'

'I heard they're all pretty casual about wandering in and out of Cambodia — Yanks, North *and* South Vietnam — but that's *crazy*.'

Russ nods. 'Looks like that coup to install a pro-US leader lit the fuse. The Yanks keep bombing the border, so all the insurgents — COSVN, the NLF and the PRG — are retreating to Cambodia. *And* the North Vietnamese have invaded to protect their bases too.'

'What's the plan?' I say, scanning the paper. 'Christ. Nixon's sending 50,000 US and 60,000 South Vietnamese troops across the border? But it's raw jungle. That won't be easy.'

Massive protests at the escalation break out across America. Universities go on strike and hundreds of thousands of protesters march. Then on 4 May 1970, students at Kent State University gather to protest. The National Guard is called out and starts firing at them.

In full view of the world, four kids are killed and nine wounded.

So then millions of people start protesting what happened at Kent State. But that's soon followed by the bayoneting (*bayoneting*!) of eleven students at the University of New Mexico and, at Jackson State, the murder of two teenagers and injuring of twelve.

Every day we read the paper, more astonished and outraged. Finally we dust off our placards, and on 8 May 1970, join two hundred thousand people across the country, protesting in the first Australian Moratorium.

In June, the Americans meekly withdraw from Cambodia, trumpeting victory because they've captured some easily replaced weaponry. But they've brutally destabilised the country; while neighbouring Laos, already bleeding from a US-fostered civil war, is being increasingly and viciously bombed. Illegally, of course, under every international law.

As was so often predicted by pundits over the years, societies across Asia are toppling like dominos. But it's not the communists doing the toppling.

∽

At uni I really like my second-year courses, Ecology especially. We get an assignment to measure plant populations at a site and relate them to the local geology, so one weekend I go to Sheoaks with the others, sleep in a tent, and measure, count, record, take samples and write up the results.

'Can't believe you call that fun,' says Russ.

'It is, truly. And you know, if and when you get your vegetable garden going, I've got some good tips for enriching the soil.'

I run across an intriguing area of bushland that appears almost untouched, with plants and old trees I don't see in the other areas of the farm. A remnant perhaps of the time before foreign species invaded their niches?

And the older gums show the blackened touch of fire as well. When did bushfires sweep through here? How often? Did they change the biology? Will they come again if ... or when ... the heat of summer dries up the creek?

My assignment gets an A+, and the lecturer says after class, 'Jen, there were a couple of species you mentioned on that land that are pretty rare nowadays. Keep an eye on them, I'll be interested to know how they get on.'

He gives me a few references that make me realise how special some parts of Sheoaks might be. After that I sometimes go with the others to help out there, loving the drive through the aromatic bush and the nights sitting lazily around a fire, and even the slow labour of creating building blocks for the dream house.

One Saturday morning we're on the three-hour trip to Sheoaks, and I'm watching the trees flickering past hypnotically. They're lush — this region is on the slopes of the Watagans and gets a lot of rain. Even the gums, usually drab like Lec's army uniform, have shimmery bursts of emerald and fern, while the open paddocks glow apple-green in the sun.

Russ's pride and joy is a tape deck he's had installed in the old car's dashboard, and music begins that sounds like some experimental thing, a choir singing wordlessly with an orchestra, rising and falling with the waves of the treetops outside.

It's wonderful, and I love how it seems to echo from the landscape deep into my mind.

When it ends I say, '*Wow*. What was that tape? Amazing.'

Russ shakes his head. 'Nah, the bloody deck's broken, no music this trip.'

'But I ...' Oh.

Acid flashback? I'm not sure that one pleasant trip taken months ago qualifies, and in any case flashbacks are usually visual: certainly not twenty minutes or so of heavenly choir.

'*Really*? No tape on the deck just now?' I say.

'Bummer,' says Russ. His girlfriend Karen sighs. 'Jeez this takes forever,' and sighs again. Finally we get to Laguna, stock up with munchies at the tiny petrol station, then drive a few winding miles west to reach the land.

I jump out at the gate and open it. The word 'Sheoaks' is barely legible on a piece of silvery timber. Russ drives the Kombi through then I close it and get back in. A dusty narrow road leads to the old foundations and the new stack of mud bricks.

Not a very large stack, it's true. It's going to take a lot of labour to make enough for the dream home. Maybe they should revise their ambitions down a little?

But I say nothing, and after we have some soft drinks and nibbles, work happily enough beside the others. We pour water into wheelbarrows full of dirt, squish it into smooth mud, add chopped-up straw, and empty it into moulds. Luckily there's a giant peppercorn tree beside us for shade.

It must have been planted by the farmer who was once here, and is probably over a century old: it certainly outlived his little cottage. (Oh, peppercorn tree, I love you, but this isn't really your land.)

Mid-afternoon we drive the Kombi the half-mile to the creek to fill our now-empty stack of plastic containers. A levee here on the creek turns it into a jade-dappled pool, deep in one place, reedy at the edges and shaded by slender, weeping sheoaks.

'Swim, anyone?' says Russ.

After our labours that's a great idea, so we strip off and jump in. Well, mostly strip off. Vicki and I are 'uncool' and keep some underwear on, but the others are less inhibited. It doesn't matter. The water is wonderful, and I float on my back as the breeze ruffles the drooping casuarinas.

Finally we stop enjoying ourselves, fill the containers and get back to work. After two more hours we stop. It's winter now and, although the sunny day and our labours have kept us warm, as soon as evening comes it feels cold.

At the camp we pull on jumpers and track pants and sheepskin boots, set up tents, build a small fire, and cook some food — potatoes and veggies in the embers, sausages in a pan — and nothing could possibly taste better. Then there are mugs of tea, a couple of shared joints, the crackling fire, and the glimmer of stars above in the inky-black sky.

Later, snuggled in a sleeping-bag in my small tent, I try to recall the music I heard as we were driving here, the swelling choir, the rising and falling harmonies. Not melodies, just sound, beautiful sound. As if the trees *themselves* ...

I laugh. Honestly, that's ridiculous. I'll be consulting the spirit of the land next, like Janice and Vicki.

Ash would think ... well, what *would* he think?

He's been gone for four months now. He writes fairly often in his neat, clear hand, and says he likes his studies, and sends me postcards of canals and bridges and houseboats. Amsterdam is pretty, I suppose.

He recently sent a photo of himself standing in front of a medieval tower. I wonder who took it? That spiky feeling in my throat starts again and it takes a while to get to sleep.

Next morning it's cold and we're all achy from the day before, so we sit around the smoky fire and drink tea. Then we work for an hour, but soon it's time to pack up and go back to Sydney.

ㄥ◯⌒

Russ's girlfriend Karen decides she hates mud, and mud-bricks, and Russ most of all, so she splits. One night as I'm studying in my room, he knocks and comes in.

'Hey, Jen,' he says. 'How's it going?'

'Okay. You know you need lots more phosphorus at Sheoaks?'

'What's that? Hope it's organic, can't have that synthetic shit.'

'Well, synthetic fertilisers have their uses, but organically, just lots of pee and shit. But you've got to understand, Russ, the land itself is really depleted, not just the phosphorus, and it's overrun with some super-bad weeds. No wonder it was abandoned.'

'Okay.' He sits down awkwardly on my bed. 'Actually, despite that phosphorus problem, we were wondering if you'd like to buy into Sheoaks. Karen's share. She really wants to get rid of it.' (And of me is his unspoken lament.)

'Buy into it? I've never thought ...'

'Well, think about it. Um, $100 for Karen's share of the deposit and $13 a month repayments.'

'Oh. The deposit's a fair bit. But thanks, Russ. Let me see.'

He leaves and I feel restless. I grab a blanket and wander out to the front yard and sit cross-legged, snuggled in the blanket, and ponder. I've still got my grandmother's bequest so I wouldn't have to ask anyone for the money.

But do I *really* want to get myself involved in this project?

I already know it's pie-in-the-sky, and the ecology is a disaster. As for the other shareholders? Mad as cut snakes. I shake my head. Not bloody likely. I've got a degree to finish.

The traffic hums, the streetlights gleam, and after a time I take a deep breath and can taste a hint of fragrance on the night air. Winter is almost over and spring will soon be here.

I love spring in Sydney, when the jacarandas go mad and cover the ground in blue-violet swathes and the jonquils nod in creamy clusters (I know they're introduced species, but *still*).

And there's a native tree too, sweet pittosporum, that has the most magical drifting scent in the evenings. Perhaps that's the elusive perfume I can sense in the air.

I wonder what spring would be like at Sheoaks? A lot more subtle, but probably still fragrant. Or summer, when every drop of rain is precious, or autumn, when the campfire smoke draws a straight line up to the still blue sky?

It'd be fascinating to see what unfurls in that untouched area of bush too. Perhaps an analysis would make a good assignment, or even a thesis?

Stop it. Don't be silly.

After all, I don't have to buy land to enjoy it, or study it. I can always visit the farm with the others. And what about my dreams of going to London (or Amsterdam) when my degree is over?

But then, do I still *want* to go to London? I stretch my legs and wiggle my sneakers, and recall my absolute conviction of a few years ago that one day I'd find myself in a sports car wearing a Pucci shift, silk headscarf and Mary Quant shoes.

Now I'm in flares and t-shirts, without a maroon patent-leather shoe in sight: and couldn't care less. Does this just mean fashion has moved on, from mod Carnaby Street to hippie Haight-Ashbury?

Perhaps not. My urge to go *away*, to somewhere more than boring old home, certainly remains. Yes, I'd still like to see London. And Amsterdam? Ah. We'll see, as Tina would say.

From Mary Quant to sneakers: does this mean *I've* changed? Suppose so: fifteen to nineteen is a big jump. From a kid whose brother had just been drafted, to someone who knows too many horrible things about the place that nearly killed him.

I lie back on the ground, wrapping myself in the blanket, and think of the tormented jungles of Asia. How lucky I am to live in this quiet country, with its everyday options of friends and study and farmland, and all the time I can be fairly certain no war criminal is planning to obliterate everything I love.

The window to the front room is open, and inside the house someone puts the latest Joni Mitchell on the record player.

We are stardust, we are golden.
And we've got to get ourselves back to the garden.

Back to the garden? Two centuries ago, wise Voltaire said we must cultivate our garden, and he was right. All our gardens, our grasslands, bushlands, jungles, forests, mangroves, keep us alive in ways we can't see, connected in ways we can barely comprehend.

And *cultivate*? We graze them without mercy, strip them of life, flatten them for pulp, cover them in concrete, reduce them to ash, poison them forever.

I groan and rub my face. Don't despair, Jen, I tell myself. Perhaps one day there'll be movements to protect the Earth as great as the anti-war protests — dear God, something must bring this insanity to an end. For now, all I can do is study and learn, and be ready to help however I can.

But that doesn't mean buying into some crazy, worn-out bit of bushland! I can't waste my time making mud bricks, or planning a house that'll never be built, or arguing whether science might have something useful to offer beyond an assembly-line of destruction.

Of *course* I love floating in a pool beneath casuarinas, and lying beside glowing embers, and watching ancient stars drifting in a sea of night. Who on earth wouldn't!

Yet that's hardly a sensible basis for decisions about my future. Ash would think I'm every kind of idiot.

But then ... who cares what bloody Ash would think?

I breathe, and taste that sweet fragrance again on the cool air.

What *would* spring be like at Sheoaks?

23. CLAIRE: INTREPID GIRL REPORTER (DEC 1969-SEP 1970)

Life continues in dreary Saigon. I attend meaningless briefings, file meaningless copy, go to meaningless parties. One night after drinking too much I awake at dawn with a vivid memory.

I was fifteen. Klara, Yvonne and I had gone to Newcastle for a week in winter to stay with Eliza and Harry. Their house is near the beach in Newcastle East, a comfortable two-storey terrace. My parents were in the downstairs guest room and I had the spare bed in Jenny's room.

We didn't see much of Leo as he was always out with his mate Bazza. The rest of us ate at cafes, or went shopping, or took walks along the beach.

That day we'd taken a drive through the bush to blue, symmetric Mount Sugarloaf, famous for its views and its new aerials, like small Eiffel towers, that relayed the TV signals from Sydney.

It was a long day, so we went to bed early. Jenny chatted in the dark about her current preoccupations: dogs and high-jumping. When she fell asleep mid-word, I was still wakeful.

After half an hour I decided to get up and have some hot milk to make me drowsy. The fire in the lounge-room grate was still burning, so I sat on the couch with my milk, watching the flames, wondering why I felt so terribly ... *sad*.

It had started this morning on our drive. I'd been watching the trees flickering past, all sage-green and silver, thinking about what job I'd have one day. Most girls I knew wanted to be nurses, waitresses, secretaries or teachers, and most planned to resign (or would be forced to) when they got married.

I already knew how different I was from my schoolmates, and this was further proof: a job like that — a *life* like that — would only make me feel trapped.

Then a thought hit me so hard that tears came to my eyes. What a fool, I was *already* trapped. I'd never fit in. I'd always be the outsider, the Brit who spoke poshly and read books all the time.

I was merely a *girl* and I'd never meet interesting people, or write interesting things, or go to all the interesting places I yearned to see. I was trying to swallow my tears when Leo came in the front door, followed by a gust of cold air.

He stood in front of the fire warming his hands, then said 'Shove over, Claire,' so I did and he sat down, slouching, on the couch.

Leo had grown and filled out in the two years since the night we'd watched Sputnik. I found him disturbing—loud, tawny, smelling mysteriously of *boy*, and taking up far too much room.

To fill the silence I said, 'So where have you been?'

'Bazza's. Reading comics.' He pulled a folded magazine out of his pocket. 'Brought one home for you. *Superman's Girl Friend, Lois Lane.* Bazza reckons you'd make an intrepid girl reporter, especially if you had red hair like Brenda Starr.'

'Well I don't. Have red hair, I mean. And that's only in *comics*, Leo. Girls can't become reporters, everyone knows that.'

'Course they can.' He turned to me. 'Why are you crying?'

'I'm not.'

'Can I have a sip of your milk?'

I handed over the half empty mug and he drained it.

'Mmm, vanilla, thanks.'

'There's more in the saucepan.'

Leo took my mug to the kitchen, brought it back full, and sat down again to drink with a grunt of satisfaction.

After a time he said, 'Honestly, Claire. What's wrong?'

'Oh, well.' I took a breath. 'Just thinking — you know. I don't sort of fit in anywhere. I want to do something *real* with my life, to travel and do amazing things, not be a waitress. Or whatever.'

'You won't be a *waitress*. You've got the best chance out of all of us kids to do something special with your life.'

I stared at him. 'Why on earth would you say that?'

'Remember that night we watched Sputnik?'

'Yes.'

'And I said you always looked at things as if you could see right through them? Well there you are. You've got the brains, the sharp tongue, and definitely the sharp eye.' He laughed. 'You'd be a great reporter, Claire.'

'But ... I never said I wanted to do that.'

'Come on. Your face just gave you away *big* time. You do, don't you?'

I nodded, my throat tight.

'Look, I bet by the time we're grown-up things'll be different and then you *will* be able to,' said Leo, putting his empty mug down on the coffee table. 'And you know, I reckon you'll be a pretty intrepid one too.'

After a day of unhappiness I sighed with gratitude. '*Really*? You think so? Thanks so much, slippery eyes.'

I bent forward to fondly thump his shoulder (teenage etiquette 101), but as Leo turned towards me our faces came close and almost brushed and, after a moment of breathlessness, stillness, suspense, I pressed my mouth against his.

I was shocked at the sense of his lips. And of mine. How could something be so familiar yet so unknown? All that softness, all that heat, all that boy-scent that so disturbed me suddenly disturbed me in a very different way.

After a few moments Leo took my arms and kissed me back, deeply. The warmth of his tongue was another revelation, but suddenly it was simply too overwhelming. I gasped and wriggled away, and flung his hands off my shoulders.

We stared in amazement at each other.

'How — Leo? How *could* you?'

His face was as astonished as mine. He said faintly, 'But Claire ... you kissed *me* ...'

'I didn't mean to, not like *that*! I was just saying thank you.'

Leo tried to keep his mouth straight but his eyes crinkled with delight, and like some movie gunslinger he drawled, 'Well, thank you *too*, ma'am.'

I jumped up and hissed, 'Don't you *dare* make jokes! And don't you dare tell anyone this happened! Or ever, *ever* mention it again. *Do you hear me*?'

Leo suddenly looked young and uncertain, and nodded. 'Okay. Sorry, Claire.' He shrugged. 'Already forgotten.'

But Leo never forgot, although I buried the memory and kept my distance from him for years.

Until one night beside the whispering Moreton Bay figs, he suggested a pathway to my dreams, and in drunken delight I kissed him again. Then treated him coldly. *Again.*

I groan. Even worse, here in Vietnam I let him believe I was slowly dismantling my defences — and really, who knows what might have happened between us?

But the shock of destruction and death shattered my reserve and André helped me find my way to pleasure. And poor Leo discovered, as brutally as possible, that he'd lost me.

I gaze at his beautiful jade bangle, cool and soothing on my wrist. Leo, you've always believed in me and I've been so *unkind* to you. I'm sorry. And my lonely misery coalesces into heartbreak.

∽

After My Lai is revealed, many reporters leave the country and are glad to go. They're replaced by the latest clutch who still go all shiny-eyed at the tired old clichés: kill ratios, friendly fire, tunnel rats, hueys, body bags, on and on. And, oh, how the newcomers love all those spiteful slurs for the people their country has mortgaged its future to 'protect'.

Outside my apartment block one day, someone says softly, 'Miss Claire?' It's old Vinh, one of Charlotte and Pete's servants.

The American general who bought their house promised solemnly that Vinh and Thu would keep their jobs, but Vinh and I manage to establish, via pantomime, English and Vietnamese, that the general had molested Thu, and when Vinh tried to protect her he fired them both.

Vinh has no idea what's happened to Thu, and I can only hope she's safe somewhere in the chaos of Saigon. It turns out Vinh has come to live with a nephew on the first floor of my block, so now we sometimes see and greet each other on the stairs.

A card arrives unexpectedly from Leo, telling me about his beloved dog and contented life in Broome. I'm glad for him, but it's obvious there's no place — there could be no possible place — for me in Leo's new-found Garden of Eden, no matter what my insurgent ex-lover happens to think.

I don't know what to write in reply, so eventually don't.

At Christmas I go to Mass at Notre Dame Cathedral as I once did with Pete, Charlotte and André. This time I'm alone. The candles still flicker dreamily and the windows still glow like jewels, but I feel only despair.

∾

The rain stops, the heat takes over, and the new year of 1970 begins. In February Tet comes and goes, and is unusually peaceful. You could almost imagine ordinary life has returned to Saigon, although small-scale actions still pop up now and then. By now no one pays much attention.

One day in March a few bursts of gunfire come from somewhere in the city, followed by sirens and a boom or two. I think, wearily, hope nothing's going on nearby.

 Not today, thanks very much, NLF.

Gloomy and perturbed, I look around my small grey room with dislike. I must tidy up a bit. It's not as if I've got much anyway. A few books, a few clothes.

I move some papers and something falls to the floor: a diary I kept for a while with copies of the photos Pete liked to take. I sit down and open it.

There we all are, happy at dinner. And on the next page, me, tousled pale hair, looking up from a newspaper, Charlotte smoking moodily in an armchair, and an off-centre snap I took of Pete and Charlotte toasting each other.

Then one of Pete's beautiful images: André drinking coffee in the salon, smiling a little, morning light on his face. I stare at the photo of the dark-eyed, handsome man.

Who *were* you, André? Where are you now? Were we ever more than passing comfort to each other?

I turn the page.

Ah. Leo with me on the beach at Vung Tau, the day of the picnic. I look pretty good, and Leo does too — tanned, broad-shouldered, high cheekbones, laughing eyes. And you, Leo? What are we now to each other?

Yells start echoing in the street and I hear scattered gunshots few blocks away, coming closer. Shit. Suddenly there's a thudding of footsteps on the stairs outside and a pounding at my door.

I look up, startled. The door splinters open with a crash. A beefy American officer fills the entry, omincus, ugly, and smirking. 'Waaall, if it isn't the little Aussie gook-lover. Heard you were here.'

'What do you want?' I try to sound calm although I'm terrified.

'We're on a security sweep, honey, and you look fucking *dangerous* to me.' He kicks the door shut, sniggering, and starts unbuckling his belt.

I'm only wearing a silk kimono and feel terrifyingly vulnerable. My head buzzes with shock and I can't move. I hear rapid shooting in the street below and soldiers yelling out.

The man comes towards me, rips the silk of my kimono, and tries to push me backwards onto the bed. The diary falls, a glass breaks, and the sudden noise shatters my paralysis. I try to ward him off but he lifts his arm and clouts me hard over the ear.

It feels as if a bomb has exploded. I shake my head, my ears ringing, my eyes filling with tears. I try to wriggle away and fall onto the floor. '*Slut*,' the man says, breathing heavily. He stamps on my wrist and kicks me in the side, and I scream.

Someone yells from outside, 'Sir, sir — NLF, too many, gotta *go*!'

'*Fuck!*' the major yells. 'You fucking, *fucking* ...' With each word he kicks me, then snarls, 'I'm coming back to *get* you, *bitch!*'

Heavy footsteps clatter down the stairs. Guns fire, men scream, noises move away. After a time there's almost silence except for the ringing in my ears. I lie there, whimpering, then slowly try to get up, grunting in pain. Finally I'm on the bed, gasping, holding my left side. Is my rib broken? Is my entire *ribcage* broken?

Slowly the immediate agony ebbs, and I work my way across the room, reach the door and push a chair under the door-knob. Then I stare around wildly. No more, no more! I've got to get away. Not from this room, this building, this street, this city, but from this mad, violent *country*!

Think, Claire, *think*. Right. There's a flight every evening from Ton San Nhut to Australia. Oh Christ I could go *home*, to Sydney, to my mothers, my gentle mothers who'd stop this terrible pain.

I sob and fumble my way to the wardrobe, to the medicine box, and find a bandage — never know when you'll need a *fucking* bandage in this *fucking* country — and grunting, wrap my ribs.

Okay. Painkillers. I take four tablets, and stare in the mirror. Thank God, no blood, but my cheek is red and my head is on fire. A sudden rush of rain begins and it sounds like the silk of my kimono ripping.

Slowly I dress. With every noise I jump. Is he coming back? I throw things into a suitcase. I'll have to leave most of my books, just take what can't be replaced.

Notepads, diary, small mementos into a backpack. Passport, bankbook, purse, in my shoulder-bag. Okay, almost everything —

There's a knock at the door.

'Who is it?' I say, my throat dry.

'Vinh.'

I hobble to the door. The old man is there, his face anxious. 'Miss Claire, okay?'

I shake my head. 'No. Please help me?'

I indicate the suitcase and backpack, which I've just realised I can't possibly get down the stairs by myself. 'Taxi, Tan Son Nhut?'

'You *go*?'

I nod. 'Must go.'

He nods regretfully. I look around. Have I got everything?

My beloved jade bangle lies on the floor, snapped in two. My wrist hurts, but not too badly: the bangle must have deflected the sledgehammer boot that might have smashed every bone in my hand. I shudder, pick up the green pieces and put them in my shoulder-bag.

Vinh helps me latch the suitcase and calls out to someone in the hall. His nephew comes in and, after some rapid-fire Vietnamese that includes the airport name, takes the suitcase. Vinh lifts the backpack and looks at me with sad eyes.

'I'm sorry, Vinh. I *must* go.'

Somehow I get down the two flights of stairs. The nephew has hailed a taxi, and my suitcase is already in the open boot. I fumble in my purse and find the little bit of Vietnamese currency I keep for emergencies, and push it into Vinh's hand.

He shakes his head and says, 'No, no,' but I say, 'Yes, yes. Thank you so much.'

There are tears in his eyes and I hug him. 'I will tell Charlotte and Pete how you helped me,' I say, my own eyes stinging. 'Goodbye, Vinh.'

∽

I fall into the back seat of the taxi, wincing, and manage to wave as we leave. Then I put my head in my hands until we arrive at the airport. I pay the driver in the usual military certificates and he puts my suitcase and backpack on the pavement and drives away.

I stand there, feeling like a broken fool. What do I do now? People are passing me busily but I can't leave my things to go and get one of the trolleys I can see inside the entrance.

'Want a hand?' says a man in uniform and I almost jump in terror. But it's an Australian soldier, one with kind eyes, so I say shakily, 'A trolley would help.'

He wheels one to me, easily lifting the heavy suitcase onto it.

'Going home?'

I nod. 'If I can get a seat.' I realise I'm holding my ribs protectively but can't let them go or I might collapse.

He glances at my clutching hands and says, 'Look, I'll just push this thing, will I, over to the ticket office? Let's see if we can get you a seat. The afternoon flight, Perth?'

'Perth? Not Sydney?'

'No, Perth today. The Sydney flight's tomorrow.'

'Okay, fine.' I can figure it out when I get there. Charlotte and Pete are living in Perth now, so it'll be all right, they'll help me get home.

'Come on then,' the man says. 'Slowly, though, got a gimpy leg.'

The pace is easy as we move through the crowd. I have no problems buying a ticket. I almost say — but this is Vietnam, *surely* there's a problem — but decide not to tempt fate.

My new friend's name is Bongo and he's from Nui Dat. He helps me to the check-in area, where my luggage is taken away to be loaded onto the plane, and to Customs, where my Australian passport is deemed acceptable and firmly stamped.

I turn, exhausted. 'You've been amazing, Bongo. Can't imagine what I'd have done ...'

He nods shyly. 'You wouldn't remember, Claire, but I was on security that day you came to Nui Dat. Couldn't believe bloody Bell had the cheek to bring in a girl reporter. The CO never forgave him. But your story about Vung Tau was a good read.'

'Thank you. And thanks for remembering me too.'

He grins. 'Come on, who'd ever forget you? Now, just go through there and find somewhere to rest till your flight is called.'

He pauses and says carefully, 'And I hope you got the number-plate of whatever truck it was that hit you.'

I laugh shortly. 'Think I'll have to rely upon karma for that. Or maybe the NLF.'

'Jesus, not one of *ours*?'

'No, some bastard Yank. Probably thought he was back at My Lai.' I glance at him. 'Just an attempt. Didn't succeed.'

'Bloody sorry, anyway.'

I clear my throat. 'What about your flight?'

'Military,' he says. 'Wounded personnel.'

'Your leg?'

He nods and sighs. 'At least I'm going home.'

'Not happy about it?'

'Too unreal, to be honest. Don't know how I'm going to fit in after all this.'

'Yes. Same for me.'

'Better go and rest now, Claire. And will you say hello to old Dingdong for me?'

'Oh, I won't be seeing ...'

But Bongo has gone.

I shuffle through to the waiting area. The pain under my ribs is almost bearable (if I don't breathe) but my left shoulder now aches.

Finally the flight is called, the plane takes off. The stewardesses are nice and a cup of tea is ambrosia. And best of all, bloody, bloody Vietnam is receding behind me.

After a few hours we stop at Singapore. I cope, barely. Then the long leg to Perth begins and I eat a little food, but feel more and more nauseous. I'm lightheaded and my eyes seem fuzzy.

I take more painkillers and manage to sleep for a few hours, but when I wake up I'm scared and confused, and it takes a few moments to recall where I am and what's happened.

I get up and go to the toilet, and in the mirror my eye-socket is red and my face white. When I come out, one of the stewardesses glances at me, then says urgently, 'Madam, are you all right?'

I turn to her, trying to focus, and she takes my hand, which is a good thing because the plane seems to be rotating around me. I try to say something but don't know what, and that's all I remember for an indeterminate time.

I become slowly aware I'm lying on something, being wheeled somewhere. A man is with me, a dark-haired man who looks vaguely familiar. 'Simmo?' I whisper, confused. Oh no, am I back in *Vietnam*?

'Claire, what happened to you?' he says urgently.

'Someone kicked me ...'

'Where?'

'Here ... my ribs.'

'Does your shoulder hurt?'

'Yes, but he didn't kick me there ...'

'*Shit.*'

I don't remember anything else.

∞

As I come awake and try to focus, I think, *Am* I back in Vietnam? Am I gazing at a photo of a high-cheeked, laughing man in the moments before the world splintered into horror?

But the photo moves and his eyes are not laughing. 'Claire?'

'*Leo*?' I croak.

'Don't try to sit up. Here, have a sip of water.' It tastes wonderful.

I whisper, 'Where are we? Not Vietnam, *please* ...'

'No, no, of course not. It's all right, Claire, you're in Broome, at the hospital.'

'How? Why?'

'They diverted the plane, medical emergency. An army nurse on board realised you had a ruptured spleen.' He pauses. 'You were ... in real danger.'

I take a breath, then wince a little.

'Careful, you've had an operation. I'll just get the nurse, now you're awake. Back in a minute.'

I close my eyes, confused.

The nurse comes and takes my blood pressure. 'Ah,' she says. 'Better now. The doctor'll do his rounds soon. He'll talk to you then.'

After she leaves Leo sits down again beside my bed.

'Better *now*?' I say. 'How was it before?'

'Rock-bottom.' He smiles a little. 'You're pretty pale at the best of times, but ...' He shakes his head. 'You'd bled into your abdomen and were blue-white. I've never been so scared.'

The doctor arrives, checks my chart, and nods. 'Excellent, Miss Fenn. You were very lucky. Usually a ruptured spleen needs removal but we were able to repair it. Hopefully you'll recover completely.'

He leaves. Leo stands and goes to the window, then after a few moments turns.

'How did it happen, Claire?' he says evenly. 'Simmo tells me —'

'Ah, it *was* Simmo.'

'He was meeting a friend when your plane arrived, so helped out. Now, Simmo tells me that ruptured spleens are common from motor-bike accidents or violence in the home.' Leo's eyes are hard. 'Don't think you've taken up Harleys, so ... was it *him*?'

'Him? André? Of course not! He's — oh look, Leo, I'll tell you later, too tired. I was attacked. By a bastard Yank.' I laugh weakly. 'And saved by the NLF.'

'The *NLF*?'

'Later,' I say. 'Must sleep.' And I do.

∞

It turns out Eliza and Harry left Broome just a week ago and went back to Newcastle. I still have plenty of visitors, though. There's Simmo, and a nice family relative called Liam, and then, wonderfully, Pete and Charlotte, who fly here from Perth.

Everyone seems happy I'm alive, but it's all a little overwhelming. Leo doesn't say much, but after a day or so turns up with a red dog.

'Are animals allowed in here?' I say.

'I know the nurse. She's cool. Anyway, this is Rusty.'

The dog wags her tail and nudges at my hand, so I stroke her warm head.

'Hello, Rusty. Goodness, has she just had pups?'

'Yeah. I feel like a proud papa, but it was probably the blue heeler up the road, the handsome devil. The runt has his speckled coat too.'

'Her first litter?'

'And her last. I'll get her spayed soon. Don't want her to end up like those poor mutts in Saigon.'

I nod. 'Good. Many pups?'

'Five, but most have gone to new homes now. Rusty's mum is a famous working dog, so they were in hot demand. I sent the smartest one to Tender Jack at Reedy Creek. He gave me Rusty in the first place, so I owed him a favour.'

'Who, what, where?' I say laughing.

'When you're better I'll take you out there. Amazing place, amazing people.'

I stop stroking Rusty, and say, 'Don't think I'll be here that long.'

'Where are you going?'

'Sydney. Home.'

Leo nods. 'Of course. Okay.' His voice is resigned. 'Well, we'd better go. Pebble needs a feed.'

'Pebble?'

'The runt. Still pretty tiny but doing all right. See you later.'

Yet it's not so easy to leave Broome. The doctor says I mustn't fly for at least four months, some sort of potential blood issue, so it's going to be ages before I can see my mothers. But then, to my joy, on the fifth day in hospital I look up and they're at the door.

'You're *here!*'

'Of course we are here, Claire,' says Klara, elfin and precise. 'Although it was certainly a long trip. I am glad the doctor forbids you from travelling, it would be too stressful.'

'We decided to come for a while, darling,' says tall, untidy Yvonne. She strokes my face. 'It's wonderful to see you.'

'Indeed,' says Klara. 'You have been gone for two years, dear child, and for a writer you are not a very good correspondent.'

I laugh and hug them both.

After a week Charlotte and Pete go home to Perth. It's summer in Broome and Charlotte says, 'I've done my time in the tropics, sweetie, and much prefer the south. But on your way home the planes stop in Perth, so do come and see us for a few days.'

Pete says, off-hand, 'Heard from André? Tay Ninh, was it?'

'Well, somewhere near there,' I say. 'No, we don't write.'

'Guess the postal service is rather poor,' says Charlotte drily, 'given the Americans are bombing the shit out of the PRG bases.'

I stare at them. 'You knew?'

'Of course,' says Pete. 'I think we always did. But good luck to him. He's a dear boy, and by God, he's got the courage of his convictions.'

∽

Leo's house is large and comfortable, and he kindly offers Klara and Yvonne a room. I go to stay there too once I leave hospital. The house has a serene view over the jade-green waters of Roebuck Bay, and it's a good, peaceful place to recuperate.

Simmo lives at Leo's as well. He's a doctor at the medical centre now, clearly lonely and with his own personal stresses, but he sometimes chats quietly with Yvonne, and seems happier afterwards (she has that effect on people).

I recover quickly, and a fortnight later hug my mothers goodbye as they board a flight home, saying I'll follow them to Sydney when I'm allowed to fly.

As Leo and I drive back from the airport he says hesitantly, 'You didn't mention your plans for the immediate future, Claire.'

'Haven't thought that far. I've heard a lot about the town motel's two-inch cockroaches, though.'

'Nah, three inches at least. Look, you're welcome to stay on with Simmo and me. I'm not around much, so won't be a hassle.'

'You're never a hassle, Leo. Thanks — I'd really like to stay, but you've got to let me pay some rent.'

Leo grins. 'Cool.'

'But I'm *not* doing the cooking, at least not on a regular basis.'

'Still cool. Simmo and I are masters of the barbecue.'

'And the house-keeping tasks must be equally shared out.'

'Hey, I'm a graduate of Scheyville. I can clean and mend with the best of them. Still got my little army sewing kit, as it happens.'

'Excellent. I actually need some repairs to my shirt. My only shirt. Left everything behind in Saigon, so now I'm feeling better I need to buy some new clothes.'

'Yeah. Actually ... you did say you'd tell me what happened over there, but so far —'

I shake my head. 'Look, I'd rather not right now. Another time?'

He nods. 'Okay. Whenever you feel like it.'

I settle into life at the house but, as Leo said, he's not around much. He's busy teaching at the local high school, and spends the rest of his time at the beach, or sometimes out at the bush station with Liam and Simmo.

My operation scar wouldn't cope with a long bumpy drive in the outback, so I'm happy to stay at home. I sit on the breezy veranda and gaze at the emerald mangroves and scarlet earth and turquoise water, or go shopping in sleepy Chinatown.

When the boys are here we cook and chat, although none of us talk about Vietnam or what happened to us there. Some evenings we drive over to Cable Beach and eat fish and chips on the sand.

Leo and Simmo go surfing, swooping down, up, around and over the waves in displays of careless skill. Rusty waits on the beach, staring fiercely out at Leo in the surf, while puppy Pebble leaps joyfully as I throw little sticks for him.

∽

When I've been in Broome about two months a storm builds up at sea and becomes a small, late-season cyclone. That evening Leo and Simmo fit shutters to the windows, and move mattresses and blankets to the central lounge. 'Just in case,' Leo says.

The horizon fills with green-black thunderheads, and then the darkness descends. We sit in the lounge trying to chat or read as the rain clatters, the wind screams, and the house shakes. The temperature drops and I'm suddenly colder than I've been for years, then the electricity goes out.

We lights candles and, if you ignore the dreadful crashing outside, the room looks almost romantic. I try to relax, but everything sounds like a door splintering open and it's hard to control my trembling.

I tell myself I'm just cold, I'm not back *there* ...

After what seems like an eternity the racket slowly fades. 'Is it over?' I whisper.

Leo shakes his head. 'This is just the centre of the storm, the eye. It'll start up again pretty soon.'

'Oh. Doesn't seem to bother the dogs.' Rusty and Pebble are with us, curled up on a blanket. Rusty thumps her tail and Leo smiles.

The pandemonium re-commences. Simmo yawns and lies down on one of the mattresses. He become quiet and starts snoring.

'Is he *asleep*?' I ask, astonished.

'Even at Nui Dat he could sleep through anything, so I guess so. You should rest too.'

'I can't.' I shake my head. 'Ever since ... then, any sudden noises freak me out.' I'm still shivering.

Leo gazes at me. 'Claire, don't be afraid. I can hold you.' He hesitates. 'If you want.'

He's expecting my usual rebuff, and my heart twists in remorse.

But beyond that I'm freezing, so I say lightly, 'Look, let's pretend it's Tet all over again. I never told you, but I was so happy to have your company that night.'

I lie down. Leo pulls a blanket over us. 'Last chance, mate,' he says. 'Rusty's a champion cuddler. You could have her instead.'

'She's got Pebble. *Please*, Leo, I'm so cold.'

He puts his arms around me and I feel his warmth. Suddenly there's a very loud crash, and I jump.

'Roofing iron, probably,' Leo says. 'Don't worry.' His breath is soft on my neck.

We're silent for a time, the cacophony continuing.

The raging rain sometimes sounds like bursts of bullets. Or the ripping of silk fabric. Although I'm slowly getting warmer I keep shuddering in sudden bursts.

Leo says quietly, 'Seriously, isn't it time you talked about what happened, Claire? It might help.'

'Doubt it.' After a time I take a breath. 'Look, there *was* something I meant to tell you. When I was fleeing from Saigon I met a lovely man from Nui Dat called Bongo. He helped me at the airport, remembered me from Vung Tau, and sent you his regards.'

'Bongo? Great bloke. Good on him.'

'He called you Dingdong.'

'Sadly some people imagined that suited me.' Leo pauses, then says, 'Claire, it's all right. Truly. Please tell me who hurt you so badly you had to flee from Saigon?'

Suddenly I'm swamped with rage and bitterness and can't stop. 'Some Yank broke into my room, convinced that rape was his birthright. National characteristic apparently, especially where women and small Asian countries are concerned. Didn't succeed though. As I said, the NLF saved me.'

'But *how*?'

'Attacked the bastard's squad down in the street, so he had to run for his life. After he'd kicked the shit out of me.'

'*Jesus.*' Leo breathes out. 'So where was bloody André, then? Why wasn't *he* there to protect you?'

'He'd left Saigon, left me, months before.'

'Left you?'

'You were right all along, Leo, he *was* a sympathiser. He truly cared for me, but in the end he had to go. He was working with the PRG, trying to help them set up an alternative government.'

'What a fool to leave you for anything.' Leo shrugs. 'Well, good luck to the PRG. And to him.'

'I suppose some causes are more important than personal lives. A few generations of Vietnamese would say so, anyway.'

We're silent. The wind howls and the rain clatters outside.

Leo says quietly, 'Ah, see you got rid of my jade bangle.'

'No, not by choice. It stopped my hand being crushed when that bastard attacked me, but got snapped in the process. I'm getting it repaired, though.'

'Yeah?' His voice eases. 'Didn't I say it'd always protect you? Premonition, obviously. Which reminds me, I've never told you the story about my stint as a clairvoyant. Now *that* was the best thing I ever did over there.'

He tells me the tale and tells it so amusingly I can't help but laugh, although it could have ended very differently. So many things could have ended differently for us both: we were skating on the edge of disaster for so long.

More sudden loud noises, and at the sound of some glass shattering I start shaking again uncontrollably. Leo pulls me closer. 'It's all right, Claire.'

'Um ... weren't you going to tell me a bit more about Trader Joe, or somebody?'

Leo laughs. 'Tender Jack from Reedy Creek, who gave me Rusty and a night out in country, the start of my healing. Not the end of it though. Not sure there'll ever be an ending. Nor for you, I expect.'

I nod. 'Christ, we're barely in our mid-twenties, yet we've already lived lifetimes. How do we cope?' More crashing, and I shiver. 'Leo ... look, I wanted to tell you how *sorry* I was, how sorry I *am*, for hurting you when you did so much to help me.'

'Wasn't that much, really.'

'Vung Tau? You got me the job, the start of my career.'

I feel him shake his head. 'I didn't give you any true, practical support. It's me should apologise, Claire. I was stupidly selfish and didn't see how hard everything was for you.'

'No, lately I've come to realise you've given me support my whole *life*, Leo. You've always believed in me even when I didn't believe in myself. Thank you so much for that.'

'Ah,' he murmurs. 'I recall once saying at a delicate moment, *Well, thank you too, ma'am*, but it wasn't much appreciated then, so I won't respond in kind.'

I smile. 'Appreciated now.' By now Rusty has snuggled up to Leo's back, Pebble is curled against my belly, and my shivering has eased.

'Suppose you're looking forward to getting back to Sydney pretty soon,' Leo says.

'Don't know. At first I was desperate to get home, but now I'm not sure I could cope with a city again, not after all the peace here.'

There's a crashing outside and I gasp. 'Okay, the peace *sometimes*.'

We laugh, then Leo says hesitantly, 'Look, I just want you to get better, Claire. If you'd like to stay for a while, I'll keep out of your hair. I won't always be hanging around.'

'I don't mind if you're around, Leo, you mustn't think that!' I take a breath. 'Maybe I've just always felt wary cf getting close to you. All I've ever wanted is to learn and write and work. I can't become someone's wife with nothing in my life but kids and a husband.'

I hear his smile. 'Not certain I've ever exactly *proposed*, Claire.'

'Mm, guess not. But ... if we got too close, maybe I'm scared that *I'd* be the one proposing.'

He murmurs, his face warm on the back of my neck, 'Well, how about I always turn you down, no matter how hard you beg?'

'Ah. Now *that's* a tempting possibility.'

Relaxing in his arms, I realise the noise of the storm is slowly becoming distant and a little dawn light is gleaming through a shuttered window.

'Has it finally passed?' I ask.

'Think so. Let's have a look.'

Simmo is still asleep so we quietly go outside, the dogs padding after us. To the east, over Roebuck Bay, the receding dark clouds are pierced by rays of gold and pink.

'Beautiful,' I breathe, then look around. 'My God, what a mess!'

Leo laughs. Somehow, perfectly, he's still holding me.

'All that rain means the wildflowers will soon explode everywhere. Like a crazy garden with incredible colours and flowers you can't even imagine. Tender Jack always says, *After the cyclone everything blooms*. Mind you, there's a lot of damage to clean up before you get to enjoy the flowers.'

∽

I think I spot André once in a news photo, grave and handsome among a group of dark-clad Vietnamese at the Paris peace talks. Rumour has it that the PRG, with all their hopes for a unified, democratic country, are being sidelined, and Kissinger, Nixon's Machiavelli, is secretly meeting with the North Vietnamese.

By the time those cold-eyed gangsters have divided the spoils I doubt there'll be much left over for the middle-ground idealists and their humanitarian laws. Still, I hope André's uncle in the NLF survives.

I hope André does too, and finds a home somewhere he's seen as more than a child of dust. I remember telling him I wanted to bear witness, to convey the truth to a greater audience, and he said, 'There are many audiences, Claire, and even those in small, peaceful towns still need their journalists.'

One day in Chinatown I notice an ad on a card outside the local newspaper office. The paper needs a deputy editor with shorthand, typing and 'experience'. That'd be me, I think. Too much bloody experience. Still, the thought of city life still makes me dizzy, so I walk in and ask about the job. The nice Chinese lady on reception and the white-haired editor are equally startled at the sight of me, but they must be desperate because I get hired on the spot.

As I leave, feeling even dizzier, I think — well, some extra money and time here won't hurt. I don't have to stay forever, but it'd be nice to find out a bit more about this place, with its odd mix of European, Asian and Aboriginal people.

As I settle into the job (mostly school sports, council feuds and local festivals) I start to relish the doings of the little town, with its customs and scandals and long, hard history of pearlshell diving.

In the array of people and food, too, I'm reminded of what I liked best about life among the resourceful Vietnamese. But here, any flashes on the horizon are only lightning and the loudest racket is usually the Roey on a Saturday night.

Yet in my own way I still bear witness: I start writing a book about the tragic minefield of Dat Do. At first I'm afraid that revisiting my notes and talking it over with Leo and Simmo might be more than we can handle, but rage and indignation sustain us.

As I write I find I quite like the calm unfolding of a manuscript rather than the quick splash of tomorrow's chips wrapper. A small independent press in Melbourne wants to publish the book, but they warn it may be disparaged, denied, even blocked by political interests. Guess I'll find out.

My contentment grows. A jeweller repairs the broken jade bracelet so it has a delicate gold hinge on one side and an ornate latch on the other: the greens are deeper than ever. Of course, as if ordained by Tender Jack (who turns out to be an old charmer), Rusty's pup Pebble is now my small, warm shadow.

Still, like Leo and Simmo, any sudden loud noise usually finds us cowering on the floor: sometimes it's almost funny. Recently a few other veterans have drifted into town, and Simmo is becoming adept at treating war's invisible wounds. Although our scars may never fade, he helps us cope with the lingering terrors.

It's not easy, but it's a beginning.

There's no moment of dewy-eyed revelation on some moonlit night: Leo and I already know what we mean to each other. But now, for the first time, we simply let ourselves grow together in friendship and trust and sweet desire.

And the wildflowers are glorious.

Thank You, Readers

Thank you for reading *Shadows in Jade*. If you've enjoyed it, please recommend it to your friends and give it a review or rating on your favourite book site.

This is the fourth volume of the Tempo series, and follows *Harbour of Secrets* (1950s), *Embers at Midnight* (1940s), and *Testing the Limits* (1930s).

https://seabooks.net provides links to all my books, with reviews, extracts, images and background information.

About the Author

I grew up at Speers Point on Lake Macquarie, NSW. My background was in science (PhD in astronomy) and Internet technology (the wild 1990s-2000s), then I ran across the charmed life of an old Broome pearling lugger and fell into the joys of historical research and writing.

My first book, *Redbill: From Pearls to Peace*, won the Western Australian Premier's Book Award for Non-Fiction, and the second, *Alan Villiers: Voyager of the Winds*, won the Mountbatten Maritime Award.

Since then my novels include *The Turning Tide* and *Atomic Sea* (as CM Lance), and the Tempo Series: the foundation story *Silver Highways*, plus *Testing the Limits*, *Embers at Midnight*, *Harbour of Secrets*, and this book, *Shadows in Jade*.

I'm mother to two sons and live in green South Gippsland, Victoria, with a small and bossy poodle (alas, the literary whippets of earlier volumes are no more).

I post on Mastodon as **@katela@aus.social** and Bluesky as **@katelance.com**, and make no apologies for my passion for K-pop and Asian drama. [Image above by Alex Lance.]

Acknowledgements

When I went looking for a military environment as background for Leo's story I ran across the 1st Australian Civil Affairs Unit. In a world dominated by media focused on the self-obsessed American view of the Vietnam war, it was surprising to discover how different the Australian experience was, especially that of 1ACAU.

Although it was openly a vehicle to credit the corrupt South Vietnamese government with the civilian care it so rarely provided, 1ACAU was staffed by young soldiers who shared their professional expertise with Vietnamese people, often with a kindness and commitment that went beyond any official requirement.

With minimal resources and only 40 to 60 or so members at any one time, during 1ACAU's five years in Vietnam its personnel built schools, markets, roads, bridges, sportsfields, playgrounds, dispensaries, plumbing systems, windmills, houses, and an entire village.

The unit taught English to many hundreds of people, as well as provided medical care for thousands more, supplied new crop varieties and animals for farming projects, and distributed emergency supplies and materials in war-damaged areas.

In later years, some members of the unit have felt it was all in vain, yet I believe that would be far from the experience of anyone touched by their life-changing efforts in such painful times.

I'd like to particularly thank IACAU's unofficial historian Barry Smith, for his gallant attempts to educate me in military ways, and for reaching out to other unit members for their opinions and recollections. I have much benefited from his writings, careful proofreading and personal memories, especially the wonderful tale of the mooncakes.

I'd also like to thank Don Limn for kindly providing me with a copy of the 1ACAU memoirs, *Doves of War*, as well as its compiler Dr Doug MacLennan and all those who contributed, from which I have shamelessly lifted anecdotes and perceptions.

An invaluable resource has been the Australian War Memorial's orals histories, and the Australian army commanders' diaries and activity logs for 1ACAU, from which came the true entry of 7 December 1968, exactly when and where fiction demanded it.

Some of my other inspirations were reporter Kate Webb herself, as well as her humane, courageous book *On the Other Side*, Greg Lockhart's scathing dissection of deliberate ignorance, *The Minefield*, and Truong Nhu Tang's *A Viet Cong Memoir*, on his dual life as a Saigon businessman and NLF/PRG member.

While many books offered me valuable insights, particularly important were: *You Don't Belong Here* by Elizabeth Becker, *The Nashos' War* and *Australia's Vietnam* by Mark Dapin, *Ridding the Devils* by Frank Palmos, *Vietnam: A Reporter's War* by Hugh Lunn, and *War-Torn,* a compilation of female reporters' experiences in Vietnam.

I could not begin to list the online images and stories that have contributed to my understanding, but many thanks to Meredith Burgmann for her delightful account of being arrested at a Martin Place demo, https://www.labourhistory.org.au/hummer/hummer-vol-14-no-1-2020/1968-2/.

Special appreciation must go to Remi Bouchenez, for inspiring me with his Normandy recollections and a floor-plan of the real Mi-Côte in Rue de Verdun, Villers-sur-Mer; and Ian Bruce, who helped refresh my memories of Glebe Point Road, the land at Wollombi, and beautiful Elkington Park.

Good friends Gillian Clarke and Alison Shields provided their thoughtful editing, and Friday-night zoomers Jane Keany, Tony Hill, Donna Karp and Kevin Karp sustained me with their fine company.

My thanks as always to Joe Rowley, Remi Bouchenez, Alex Lance and Megan Dennis for enjoyable arguments and their constant support.

FICTION BY KATE LANCE

HARBOUR OF SECRETS (TEMPO 3) — KATE LANCE, SEABOOKS PRESS, 2022

"Kate Lance explores the wider view. Like an unfolding fractal, the more she delves the more there is to delve into."

The war is over. The reckoning is not.

It's the hip 1950s on Sydney's shimmering harbour, but how do you reconcile a past that gave — and stole — so much? Tina runs Tempo jazz club at shady Kings Cross, keeping secrets with, and from, her beguiling boss Jimmy: and from her lonely husband.

Ex-pilot Billie now works at the flying-boat base. When her old lover Pete turns up with a new wife there's a lot she prefers to conceal, especially from herself.

Harry yearns to forget his days in a Singapore prison camp, yet his friends won't let him. Nor will his conscience. And once Harry's wartime memoir is published, no one can postpone the reckoning.

EMBERS AT MIDNIGHT (TEMPO 2) — KATE LANCE, SEABOOKS PRESS, 2021

"The writing is beautiful and haunting. The characters are drawn with razor-sharp precision. It's compelling reading of the highest standard, full of evocative triumph and tragedy."

In the late 1930s, a group of old friends at a sunny wedding could not imagine what storms are about to engulf them.

Pilot Billie is glad she's got a job at last — only trouble is it's in some little dust-up in Spain. Secretive Toby has no wish to volunteer for anything: until he finds out for himself what *blitzkrieg* means.

Newlywed Eliza is posted to Intelligence at Singapore — safer than London, she thinks. But when fortress Singapore is reduced to embers, it is actress Izabel who is forced to play the role of her life.

TESTING THE LIMITS (TEMPO 1) — KATE LANCE, SEABOOKS PRESS, 2020

"I can't recommend this series highly enough: the writing is brilliant, the story wonderful, and you can't help but fall in love with the characters."

1930s England: will the sunny days of ships, flying and love ever end?

Eliza McKee sails away to a new life in London, where her glamorous aunt Izabel is a star with a secret to hide.

Her brother Pete yearns to fly, but has no idea how much he needs to learn from fierce pilot Billie Quinn. Eliza's friend Harry loves golden Charlotte, but Charlotte just loves gambling with flyboy Pete's heart.

And when a great white barque encounters the coast one foggy night, not only an era of sail finds itself tested to the limits.

SILVER HIGHWAYS — KATE LANCE, SEABOOKS PRESS, 2018

"A beautiful and poignant coming of age romantic tale that kept me reading from start to finish."

From pearling to war. Is there any way home?

In 1906, Lucy Fox is sailing to Melbourne with her sister Rosa, when a tragic landfall leaves her life entangled with three seamen: gentle Sam, cynical Danny and beautiful Gideon.

After Rosa's scandalous elopement, trader Min-lu draws Lucy into a new world of silks, spices and the silvery pearlshell of Broome: a place where breaking the rules is a way of life.

The Great War begins and Lucy's beloved must go to sea, where ruthless U-boats stalk the last of the old sailing ships. But with peace comes the influenza pandemic ... and Lucy discovers how cruelly she has been betrayed.

ATOMIC SEA — CM LANCE, SEABOOKS PRESS, 2016

"Brilliant! Every chapter holds a twist you can't see coming. Fast moving and worth the reading ride."

Chernobyl, the nuclear power station that contaminated Europe. Fukushima, smashed into radioactive rubble by a tsunami. And now ... Broome?

Worm Turning nuclear waste plant is fast-tracked on sacred ground near Broome. A certain Great Power says it'll take all responsibility. Sadly it's lying. Life ashore becomes surprisingly threatening for scientist Lena and hacker Jessie, and their only refuge is Simon's old lugger. Sadly he's lying too.

An eerie blue boat turns up with a glowing cargo, the grand opening of Worm Turning is just days away, and a cyclone called Cyril is on the move. And Lena discovers being stuck on a committee isn't her worst nightmare after all.

THE TURNING TIDE — CM Lance, Allen & Unwin, 2014

"It took me about two pages to fall in love with this beautiful Australian book."

Mike Whalen trained as a commando in 1942 at rugged Wilsons Prom and fought in East Timor. Now a widowed academic in his sixties, and more damaged than he realises, he meets Lena, the granddaughter of his glamorous old friends Helen and Johnny.

When Johnny died in the war he left Mike with a burden of secrets, and as Lena draws him back into her family he discovers more secrets existed than he ever imagined. From the Prom to devastated Hiroshima, this is a saga of adventure, hope and passion.

NON-FICTION BY KATE LANCE

ALAN VILLIERS: VOYAGER OF THE WINDS

2nd Edition, Seabooks Press, 2020. Fully revised, over 100 photos. **Mountbatten Maritime Award 2009.**

"A delightful warts-and-all biography of one of the world's most notable chroniclers of seafaring life."

When Australian journalist Alan Villiers sailed on the last of the giant merchant windjammers in the 1920s and '30s, his writings and photographs made him famous.

Villiers crewed on beautiful *Herzogin Cecilie* and tragic *Grace Harwar*, took tiny *Joseph Conrad* around the globe, sailed on Arabian dhows, led wartime landing craft, captained *Mayflower* II across the Atlantic, and inspired sail training and ship restoration projects.

Drawn from his personal diaries, this award-winning biography of the author-adventurer reveals both his mythmaking and his achievements. It is a tribute to the greatest sailing ships ever launched—and to the extraordinary man who loved them.

REDBILL: FROM PEARLS TO PEACE

Fremantle Press, 2004. 2nd Edition, Seabooks Press, 2025. **Western Australian Premier's Award 2004 for Non-Fiction.**

"Lance has presented the biography of Redbill with quiet passion and exquisite detail."

Redbill is the true story of a sailing boat's voyage through a century of history. She began life as a Broome pearlshell lugger owned by the buccaneering Captain Gregory, then became naval vessel HMAS *Redbill*, bombed in Darwin during WW2.

After the war *Redbill* went pearling in Papua, then worked for Greenpeace in Tahiti, and raised funds for refugees. *Redbill* also filmed a Bass Strait voyage, *If It Doesn't Kill You* and reunited a young Aboriginal man with his long-lost family.

Finally she took on an epic voyage around the coast of Australia, to return to the North-West to face her greatest challenge yet: Rosita, the most powerful tropical cyclone to strike Broome in ninety years.

www.ingramcontent.com/pod-product-compliance
Lightning Source LLC
Chambersburg PA
CBHW070618260626
47161CB00007B/2478